Dry Water

Other Avon Books by
Eric S. Nylund

A GAME OF UNIVERSE
PAWN'S DREAM

Dry Water

ERIC S. NYLUND

AVON BOOKS NEW YORK

AVON BOOKS
A division of
The Hearst Corporation
1350 Avenue of the Americas
New York, New York 10019

Cover illustration by Donato
Published by arrangement with the author
Library of Congress Catalog Card Number: 96-25670
ISBN: 0-380-78542-0

First Avon Books Trade Printing: February 1997
First Avon Books Hardcover Printing: February 1997

Printed in the U.S.A.

QPM 10 9 8 7 6 5 4 3 2 1

To the dead storytellers who have come to me, shared a campfire and a cup of coffee, under stars, in my dreams—echoes of their words in mine.

To Syne Mitchell, *who was with this story from its conception on the porch swing in the middle of a lightning storm, through famine and hurricane, through the spring orange blossoms and groves of basil, across the country three times, lost in* Texas, *with me every step of the way down our own* Dai Esthai *. . . my gratitude and love.*

SECTION ONE

s u m m e r

Chapter 1

LARRY DROVE FAST; HE HAD TO. HE WAS BEING CHASED BY LIGHTNING.

He saw a red crack in the sky and a flicker of iridescence in the earth—lightning before it struck. Larry saw the future. It was normal for him. What wasn't normal was lightning chasing him, personally.

A filament of blood twisted in the air. It danced in the middle of the road, directly in the path of Larry's van. Fear congealed in his stomach and he hugged the steering wheel tighter. He knew he had maybe six seconds to put distance between it and him.

First second: Larry spun the wheel clockwise. It slipped in his sweaty hands. He went onto the shoulder.

Next second: he floored the accelerator.

Third and fourth seconds: his '65 Econoline van fishtailed; it made an "S" in the sand, and sent a fountain of dust into the air.

Fifth second: back onto the road. The tires slipped, squealed, then grabbed.

Sixth second: Lightning. Brilliance fell from the sky, one hundred million volts, traveling fifty-five thousand miles per hour. When it was sixty feet above the road, another discharge erupted from the ground, a second fork of current that embraced the first. The air heated to fifty thousand degrees. It exploded.

Larry swerved on the asphalt. The light reflected in the rearview mirror. He closed his eyes, but it still dazzled him. His hair stood on end.

Anticipating it didn't help. It was gunfire, and cannons, and steel drums knocked over like bowling pins. And loud. So loud it tore through his skin. A wave of high pressure rolled through the van and wrinkled its metal shell. The back windows shattered; the front windshield and the side mirrors cracked. The engine stopped.

Larry stomped on the clutch, jammed the gearshift on the steering column into second, then popped the pedal. The motor coughed. The van lurched, and the engine turned over.

He knew you stayed in your car if power lines had blown down. You waited for help. The tires were excellent insulation. At least, that's what he remembered reading. He wasn't about to bet his life on it though.

The purple pinpricks in his eyes faded, and he spied in his future three more bolts of lightning, serpentine and scarlet in front of him. They were in the right, left, and right lanes of the road, equally spaced about as far as his van could swerve back and forth. And while Larry knew it was impossible, he got the feeling that someone up there was aiming at him.

His second sight usually didn't predict the weather. It was fickle when it came to rain and hail. He hoped it kept working. Sometimes he saw when people were about to die, from massive coronaries or a faulty navigational computer in an airplane, and he always knew when the milk had gone bad without looking at the date. That drove his ex-fiancée, Linda, nuts. Like most people, she never believed Larry; she had to smell the milk to make sure—and it was always sour, just like their relationship.

Larry spun the wheel left, right, and left. The van staggered, back and forth and back, teetered on two wheels, then slammed back onto all four. His possessions sloshed to the rear, boxes toppled over, papers scattered, and books spilled. He heard the clink of glass. Larry prayed it wasn't his computer monitor.

The lightning fell precisely where he wasn't, but it was close. Thunder ripped through him and left his ears ringing. Fear grabbed his mind. It cut straight to the animal part of his brain, making him want to hide in a cave. He peed his pants.

The van raced past a sign, "Dry Water 3 miles," then a billboard, "Silver Bullet Bed & Breakfast. Sleep in the same bed Matt Carlson was shot in!'' Larry saw the town on the horizon, eclipsed by a towering thunderhead of boiling black ink and veils of gray silk beneath. The clouds were solid, so dark they looked impenetrable, a place where the sky ended. But higher, over his head, it was cloudless and sunny, full of the crystalline luminosity that made the New Mexican sky famous. Crows circled there, black specks on turquoise.

Larry scowled at the shade of blue and wondered where the damn lightning was coming from. He should turn back; it was safer the farther away he was from the storm. Should he turn all the way back? Go back to Linda? His boss had offered him a raise if he stayed. The money would come in handy.

''I can't go back,'' he said.

When Larry spoke to himself, that drove Linda nuts too. She said it was neurotic.

''Linda can go to hell,'' he said. ''I'm not staying. I'm not selling my soul for a paycheck and an IRA. And I'm not getting trapped into marriage.''

Two bolts coming, farther up the road. They blocked both lanes, and it was too far to try and make a run through. Larry slammed on the brakes, downshifted, and screeched to a stop. His toolbox slid to the front along with a Styrofoam ice chest, and a crate of newspaper wrappings and china fragments. He jammed the van in reverse.

Lightning filled the road with white splinters of electricity. Thunder blew the windshield in. Pebbles of green safety glass sprayed into the cockpit and into his face. Larry smelled ozone and ammonia and urine.

He screamed out the shattered window, ''You're just a storm. You can't be after me.'' Lightning came from clouds, and there wasn't even a jet's vapor trail overhead. Lightning didn't *try* to hit you. It hit TV antennas. It hit golfers with their clubs raised high into the air on flat grassy fields. It hit electrical lines, but it didn't try to hit Econoline vans with rubber tires.

Larry set his hand on the passenger's seat where Linda's knee would have been. It was a silly habit. Linda wasn't there, only a road map of New Mexico folded incorrectly and a plastic commuter cup.

Linda panicked in storms. She kept an umbrella and coat in her trunk, and if a drop touched her, she'd go home and fill herself with chicken soup. She'd still get sick. Larry was always going out of his way to comfort her; he wanted to, and she, naturally, wanted that as well.

But he had seen what it would cost him. Like he knew when people would die, which cars were destined for head-on collisions, and who had lung cancer, Larry had seen his own death. Two months ago he looked in the mirror and saw it. It was a slow death. Forty years he figured. He'd marry Linda, get promoted to middle manager, and get stuck there until retirement. Slow death watching computer codes crawl by on his monitor. Slow death as Linda dragged him down with shopping lists, and stupid home improvements, and her cold feet, and lukewarm sex, and two children who would require braces because they'd inherit her teeth. He knew, gazing at himself, and gazing at his future self, that he would take it too. He'd take it all with a smile, happy to be there for her, happy to give up his writing, and happy to waste his life.

Motion on the side of the road: a man waved Larry down.

Larry scrutinized the sky. There were no red lances waiting to fill with a million volts. He slowed the van. He saw it wasn't a man, but a child, maybe eight years old, Hispanic or Indian, big smile, and wearing a shirt tie-dyed red and black.

Larry put on his right blinker and slowed to a crawl. He was a sitting duck if he stopped, but so was the kid. He had to stop.

The van overshot the kid, then halted. It did so because Larry became distracted when he saw that it wasn't a tie-dyed shirt the kid wore; it was pajamas. They were soaked with blood.

He was still standing, though, and smiling even. How hurt could he be? Larry reached over and threw open the passenger door. ''Come on, kid,'' he yelled. ''Get in. I'll get you to a hospital.'' Larry stayed inside. There was no need to get out. No need to forfeit the protection of those insulating rubber tires.

Larry glanced at his shattered side mirror and saw a hundred images of the kid reflected in a starburst pattern, motionless behind his van, his hair matted with blood, smiling at him like he was his long lost uncle.

He opened his door and stepped out onto shaking legs. As soon as he touched the pavement, Larry knew the lightning would be back. He couldn't see it, but he felt it, a static charge building, the wind dying, adrenaline in his stomach. He couldn't just leave the kid here, hurt, in the middle of nowhere.

The sky was clear, free of any angry red or blinding light, brilliantly blue, and deceptive as hell.

Larry ran to the back of his van. Chunks of blasted asphalt had peppered both back doors. And the kid wasn't there.

A giggle came from the front of the van. Larry wasn't in the mood for games. Maybe the kid had a concussion and didn't realize what kind of danger they were both in. He dashed to the front. No kid.

He dropped on all fours and looked under the van. Nothing. With his nose in the red soil, Larry saw the imprints of his sneakers . . . but only his.

Another laugh, this one from a cluster of creosote bushes along the road. Larry saw red. A blob, translucent and hardly noticeable, took shape directly overhead. Static itched his scalp. The lightning would be here soon.

He hesitated, then tore into the bushes, afraid that the kid might run away, deranged, or hallucinating from that knock on his head. Then they'd both be caught out in the open when the lightning came. They'd both be fried.

Resinous creosote leaves stuck to Larry and scented the air with their medicine odor. In the center of the clump, he heard a rustle, maybe the kid. He pulled himself through a tangle of branches, ripped his turtleneck, and stumbled into a clear patch. The kid wasn't there, but it wasn't empty either; there was a cross.

It was three feet tall, and stapled to the whitewashed wood were plastic daisies, fading roses, and ivy that twined halfway up, but had come loose and hung limply, pendulating in the wind. At the base was a tiny statue of the Virgin Mary, knocked over. And where the crosspiece met the four-by-four center post, a plastic frame had been nailed. Inside was a photograph of the kid, same smile on his face, and the words: Niyol Rodriguez. May God protect his soul.

Lightning could have struck Larry then and he wouldn't have noticed. His skin crawled and his hair stood on end. The wind picked up and he heard the kid's laughter on it. Then it was gone. And so was Larry.

He sprinted back to the van, and didn't even close the door before he sped off.

Larry resisted the urge to look in the rearview mirror for five seconds. He glanced and saw the lightning strike. He saw the child standing in the middle of it. He saw him cast a thousand shadows. Then he saw only the shadows. Then he saw only a blurry purple afterimage.

Knowing who's going to die, Larry could handle that. He willed his hands to stop shaking and failed. But playing tag with a dead kid . . .

The van rushed past the Dry Water city limits sign.

Overhead, the sky faded from turquoise to silver to onyx. Raindrops the size of half-dollars fell. Lightning lanced from cloud to cloud. It fell miles away. It struck the mountains. But it no longer was after him.

He turned on his windshield wipers. The blades flopped back and forth over glass that wasn't there. Larry watched the sky so closely, he didn't care.

Larry had begun his journey to Dry Water fifteen hours ago. From San Francisco, he took Highway 40 into New Mexico. He stopped in Grants to gas up, then doubled back and got on the 605, north into the Cibola National Forest. He turned right onto the 509, pointed himself straight toward Mount Taylor, went five miles, then got on Agua de Viva Road, and wound through aspen groves, into the honey mesquite and creosote covered hills of Seco County.

Of course, there was a thunderstorm that tried to murder him, and a ghost along the way, but that was nothing out of the ordinary for Seco County.

Most people don't bother with that part of New Mexico. The only certified tourist attraction is Chaco Canyon, and only by the wildest stretch of the imagination does the route curve through the town of Dry Water. Decades ago, there were hot springs said to heal the sick, but no one comes for the water anymore. There are plenty of hot springs with fancier accommodations north of Santa Fe in Ojo Caliente.

There are attractions in Dry Water however, for the brave, for the curious, and for the foolish. In 1964, Hoover James wrote his thesis, *The Natural and Recent History of Seco County*. He had it published by a small vanity press, paid for it himself, and sold only sixteen copies. His thesis told of canyons with wandering ghosts, unidentified flying objects in the desert, secret societies that practiced ritual sacrifice, and Spanish silver tucked away in hidden caverns. No one believed him. The University of Southern California politely asked him to leave.

Two authors read the thesis. Intrigued, or wondering if Hoover James was insane, they took a vacation to Seco County to see if there was enough material to write a short story. One wrote a horror novel, *The Cave Dweller*, the other a science fiction trilogy, *The Riemann Cycle*. Both were bestsellers. Both were set in Seco County. Both used sexual innuendo to prop up their cardboard characters. And both blatantly plagiarized Hoover James.

The New Yorker ran a two-part article about the authors and Seco County. They printed that D.H. Lawrence had passed though Dry Water during his travels, and called it a "writer's haven." Scores of artists and writers immediately moved to Dry Water, not liking the snow of Northern New Mexico, and not being able to afford the rising price of the land in Santa Fe or Taos.

So Dry Water has artists and authors. It has a reputation for being an oasis of haunted places, unusual occurrences, and inexplicable phenomena. Some of it is true. And it is getting truer every day.

The gas station sat on the unofficial edge of Dry Water. Its fluorescent lights cut through the sheets of rain. Aluminum awnings offered shelter and gave the storm a metal drumroll voice. There was a three-bay garage and an attached gift shop. The sign in the window read: *Spencer's Gas. Authentic Indian blankets, pottery, and dolls. Cheap smokes.* Larry pulled in.

From one side of town, Larry could see the other. Dry Water was a single thoroughfare, five blocks long, with a few side roads that ran up into hills and cottonwood groves, and others that snaked down into Lost Silver Canyon, full of spiny lechuguilla, prickly pears, and purple sage.

The stores along the main boulevard were blurred in the rain, but Larry could make out the glowing neon of a tavern, and an adobe church with a bell tower. Atop the church was a filigree cross of black iron. It reminded Larry of the little white cross in the creosote bushes. Goose bumps crept along his back. He wanted to forget Niyol Rodriguez and his bloody pajamas.

One thing was certain: Dry Water was not the sophisticated artists' colony he read of in *The New Yorker*. "This is what I left San Francisco for? What I left my job for? A town where the social high points are a visit to the saloon and a chat with the priest on Sunday?" No. There had to be more. There had to be writers and all-night coffeehouses. There had to be bookstores and art galleries and a theater. There had to be. Maybe the town would look better after he got some sleep. He'd just been driving too long, fifteen hours on the road, and before that up all night arguing with Linda.

Thinking of her and how he had left her crying made Larry forget the lightning, the ghosts, and the rustic charms of Dry Water. He indulged himself in an acid bath of self-loathing and guilt. Had he done the right thing?

There were two pumps, regular and supreme; Larry grabbed the regular.

Before he squeezed the handle, an old man in coveralls ran out of the gift shop. "Hang on there a second. I can't let you do that."

"I was just—"

The old man took the nozzle from Larry, set it back in the cradle, then took it out and pumped the gas for him. "No self-serve here. Never has been, and never will be." He smiled a set of yellow teeth at Larry. *Spencer* was stitched on his crisp blue coveralls. The fabric looked new, except for the worn patches around his pockets, which was more than Larry could say about Spencer himself. His tanned skin was wrinkled: smile lines, and laugh lines, and frown lines, and crow's feet, and an ancient road map of lines beneath those. He smelled of tobacco and grease, and his stomach bulged.

Larry knew Spencer was going to die.

It was his liver, bloated and ulcerated so badly that Larry felt a twinge inside his own abdominal cavity. Thirteen more drinks, he knew, thirteen more beers at the tavern down the street, thirteen more shots of the bourbon he had tucked away in the flask in his back pocket, and he'd drop. There wasn't a thing he could tell Spencer to make him stop. Larry knew that too.

"Thanks," Larry said.

"Rest rooms are through the gift shop," Spencer told Larry, and graciously did not stare at his torn sweater and soiled pants.

"Uh, thanks," Larry repeated. He opened his van, grabbed a pair of dry pants, and went inside the shop. Rows of kachina dolls danced and stared at Larry from the shelves, turquoise and silver jewelry glittered in a display case, and an antique soda machine held glass bottles in a refrigerated compartment. The bathroom was spotless. Larry washed the urine out of his old pants, then slipped into the dry ones. It took him a few minutes to stop shaking.

He returned to Spencer, tried to act casual, and remarked, "Strange storms you get around here. Lightning and . . ."

Spencer nodded, but his attention was focused on Larry's windshield. "I can fix that for you, if you want. The back windows too. I got an old Ford just like this sitting in my backyard. I'll throw in the mirrors too. Save you fourteen years bad luck. What do you say?"

Larry wanted to ask the old man if the lightning in Dry Water normally chased tourists, and if ghosts were a common occurrence on the Agua de Viva Road. But he couldn't think of a way to ask and not sound insane. "How much?"

"Them old windows ain't doing no good sitting around. I'll charge you for the labor—that's twenty an hour. So I figure forty, maybe fifty bucks tops . . . and you'd owe me a beer or two." He smiled his ivory teeth again. "Unless you're in a hurry. Going up to Chaco Canyon? Or you taking the long way to Santa Fe?"

Larry sighed. "I thought I might stay in town a few days. See what it's like."

Spencer's left eye narrowed. "You ain't no painter, or no New Age minister, are you? I had enough deadbeat artists come through here. And if you're a priest you can fix your own damn windows. I ain't working for anyone who tells me what I can and can't do. Telling me I'm going to hell." The nozzle shut off automatically. Spencer set it roughly back in the cradle.

"I'm a systems operator," Larry explained, "for a computer network."

Spencer shook his head. "Ain't no computer guy come up to Dry Water to 'see what it's like.' "

Larry didn't like to admit he was a writer. His friends gave him strange looks when he told them—not because he was a writer, that was fine, but because he was a writer of science fiction, which was an inexcusable lapse of sanity in their opinions.

"I . . . I'm a writer too."

Spencer nodded. "Writers are OK. At least you folks know you can't make a decent living, and get a good day job." He circled to the back of the van. "The seal on the front window looks fine. I won't have to replace it. These back ones though, they're kinda torn up. I'll have to order new ones. Takes three days to ship here. And it's gonna cost you an extra twenty bucks." He fished a screwdriver out of his coveralls and poked at the rubber around the safety glass. "You put a new window without good rubber to hold it in, and the first jolt the thing pops out. You gotta have . . ."

Spencer's screwdriver twisted in his hand. He looked at it and chewed his lower lip, then let the tip drop toward the rear bumper. He knelt down and let go of his screwdriver. It fell; twisted in midair, then stuck to the bumper.

"Magnetized," Spencer declared. "You got close to some lightning, didn't you?"

"When I came into town," Larry replied. "It was strange. There was no storm. There were clouds, but they weren't close. They—"

"Lightning does a lot of strange things in Dry Water, mister. We got lightning that strikes itself, and lightning that spins round and round into a tight ball, then disappears. We got lightning that leaves a green tail in the sky; we call that one 'The Devil's Tail.' We got sheet lighting, and bead lightning, and ribbon lightning." Spencer grabbed his screwdriver and stood. His knees cracked. "And we got lightning that falls from the top of thunderheads. That stuff can land miles from a storm. The old-timers called them 'bolts from the blue,' because there weren't a cloud in the sky. Still kill you though."

The rain slowed. The afternoon sun appeared. "Bolts out of the blue," Larry echoed, and he watched the sky. He saw no lightning. Maybe he had just been driving too long, gone too long without sleep. Maybe he had only imagined the lightning. Sleep deprivation. Hallucinations. But his shattered windows were no hallucination.

If the lightning was real, and if it did come after him, then why did it stop?

"Now," Spencer said, "if you're staying in Dry Water for a spell, go down the street two blocks, then head left one. That'll put you at the Silver Bullet Bed & Breakfast. You tell them Spencer is working on your van, and they'll give you a good deal. They got a triple-A discount too, if you're a member. But tell 'em that after you get the first discount." He winked at Larry.

Larry smiled back, then watched with dread as the old man pulled a silver flask from his coveralls. Bourbon. With a smooth motion he spun the cap off, took a slug, then back into his hip pocket it went. Larry felt the liquor going down Spencer's throat. It burned, then became a pleasant warmth in his chest—as it ate his liver. Make that an even dozen snorts left, Larry thought. Twelve more toasts and you're gone. Enjoy them, old man. I've got the feeling you've earned them.

He hoped he didn't have to see Spencer after he died.

Chapter 2

NICK WATCHED THE LIGHTNING, HIS LIGHTNING, FROM THE TOWER'S BALCONY. He inspected the thunderhead squatting over the town: a bouquet of iron gray, held tight at the bottom, overflowing at the top, and full of static. Shadows gathered underneath, unnaturally dense as if attracted to the gloom.

The storm waited for his enemy, a prophet.

He checked his pocket watch again: 4:35. He should be here by now. Nick had never known a prophet who wasn't punctual. And good timing always helped in a murder.

Nick ran his thumb over the gold watch cover, tracing the design: a fiddler and a cow jumping over a crescent moon. When the watch was flipped open it played a phrase from Beethoven's ''Moonlight'' Sonata. It was a century old, and one of the few antiques he indulged in. Old things reminded Nick of his past—and there were too many things in his past. It was a seduction; he could so easily lie with his memories and forget his purpose. Some days he felt like an arrow traveling through time, the seasons passing with a frightening velocity, mounting to the zenith of his trajectory, and falling to the earth.

He stroked the warm metal again, then stuffed it back in his jeans.

A chill gust of wind blew. Behind him, the doors to his study banged open and closed. His windbreaker fluttered against the body he had chosen for this task. The body was muscular, in its forties, Italian, and not, he believed, entirely unattractive.

This prophet would be different; Nick knew because his divination had been unusually vague. The materials he had gathered were of the highest quality—a saint's profanity, a pair of whispered "I love yous" torn from new lovers, a metacarpal from a six-fingered man, and a salamander's tear—all boiled together and frozen with a scream. Certainly *he* had made no mistake with the incantation, so it must be the prophet.

Nick's portent showed the man riding a white horse dappled with red blotches. He left a city by the sea and a woman in tears. He wore silver armor that was not metal, and mist clung to him and obscured his face. He sought a water that could not be drunk. And in his vision, Nick saw the city limits sign for Dry Water, New Mexico.

The sun hid behind a wall of nimbus. Gray light settled over the land. Nick saw every detail though. Three miles, past the slopes of cottonwood and creosote, ran a ribbon of asphalt, the Agua de Viva Road through Dry Water. There was the glare of Spencer's Gas fluorescent lights, an island of illumination in the rain, and the pink neon of the Three of Diamonds Bookstore and coffee shop. His gaze lingered on the adobe church with its cross and bell tower, admiring the fiery colors of the clay, warm even in the shadow of the storm.

There was lightning too—impossible to ignore—flashes inside the thunderhead, luminescence trapped in smoky quartz. A bolt flickered south of town, then another, then a third. Blurry afterimages peppered Nick's vision. The prophet had come at last. And he had certainly been struck.

No.

More lightning came, three in a row, silver cracks in the sky, then a pair—one on top of the other—close to the last. Sheet lightning flashed in the thunderhead, made it black on white, and white on black for a full minute. Then a single blast, the entire charge sent at once.

Something was wrong. Either the lightning failed to kill or it missed. Both options were equally improbable. Nick waited. No more discharges.

He whispered: "Dempsey, come to me."

A ripple in the storm and the clouds calmed. They remained murky, lightning still fell, but the thunderhead no longer seethed; it no longer cast abnormally dark shadows. The magic had vanished.

Inside the tempest a new light, like a candle just lit, appeared. It faltered, then flared solid and pale blue. It was not lightning, for it continued to shine rather than discharge. It was ball lightning, rare, and inexplicable. It fell from the sky, arced over Dry Water (avoiding the church by a wide stretch), then curved up Seven Horseshoe Ridge and paused. There it blurred, divided into three smaller orbs that circled about one another twice, then they rejoined and raced up to the tower.

The hair on Nick's arm bristled when the ball came close. It made the fillings in his molars buzz. His tower had been constructed from blocks of volcanic rock and reinforced with steel bars that ran deep into the earth. It was very well grounded. He took comfort in that. He touched the warm copper band on his pinky and took comfort in that as well.

"Speak, Dempsey," he commanded.

The globe of lightning opened: petals unfolded, two arms, one with clipboard in hand, legs, a head capped with hard hat, and a black beard shot with white sparks. "Great one," Dempsey's voice crackled with static, "I have failed."

Nick crossed his arms, and waited for his excuse.

"It was as you described," Dempsey said. "A man upon a white horse with red spots came. He drove a white van, rusted. I saw it."

"But you did not obey my wishes. You missed. You who were expert in all things electrical. You who installed the first wires in New York. Was not the taste of the hundred thousand volts that charred your body enough? Do you require more to become one with the lightning?"

Dempsey looked at his clipboard as if he would find something there to appease his master.

Nick exhaled through clenched teeth, then, "I am . . . disappointed."

"It was not my fault, Great One. I was blocked. There were fluctuations in the air, and a cascade in the dielectric breakdown—"

"Silence."

Dempsey dimmed.

"Your excuses mean nothing." He turned his back on the ball of light. "I gave you energy, *my* life energy, which you wasted. Thirteen days I must now rest. Meanwhile, our enemy is here, growing stronger." He added in a whisper, "There are many dead men who would serve me better. Fail me again, and I shall banish you to the Paradox Coil for a century."

Dempsey sank to the stone floor of the balcony. Sparks arced through the steel reinforcements. "I have more to tell you," he pleaded.

"Speak."

"Someone . . . something approaches from the hills. It has an aura of yellow and green, wild like grass aflame. I tried to get a better look, but it hid. I think it saw my true form."

A new threat? Nick wondered. One he had not foreseen? Or perhaps this prophet had more power than he suspected.

"I shall decide your fate later," he said, "after I discover if it was your negligence or another who prevented the lightning from finding its target. Go."

A flash; electricity writhed across the volcanic stones, and Dempsey vanished.

Nick shut the balcony doors. He wanted neither the light nor the warmth from the study to distract him. It would be easy to dismiss Dempsey's claim of a power in the hills as an excuse. It would be easy to go inside and sleep, replenish the energy he had wasted to control the ghost. He was exhausted. But the lightning had missed—something that had never happened. And there was too much at stake not to investigate why.

He sat upon the cold stone floor of the balcony, crossed his legs, and zipped his windbreaker all the way up. A chill crept into his chest as if he had guzzled liquid ice. It oozed into his arms and his abdomen. His heart stopped. His lungs collapsed. A last breath squeezed out.

He peeled himself away from the flesh he only temporarily inhabited. First came the hands, slipped off as if they were mittens. Then he squirmed out of the head and chest, wriggling free. Finally he pulled the last of his essence from the legs. He observed his Italian body from the outside. It was strong. It had served its original owner well, breaking legs and fingers for the Mafia. The face was a bit disappointing—narrow features and a Neanderthal brow—but after the hair had been bleached, the skin closely shaved, it was almost civilized.

Calling lightning was a tricky thing, but this, this he knew, this space in between realities, the netherealms. This was the power he trusted.

In the netherealms, life and death mingled. There were layers. On the surface both living and dead coexisted, spirits and mortals, ghosts and humans, but deeper there was only death, and beyond that, things even Nick dared not explore.

In this in-between state he could expand his consciousness across the hills and beyond. He perceived the spirits that wandered the world, no longer invisible, and they, in turn, saw him. He perceived his own aura, deep purple, near ultraviolet blackness.

He hunted ghosts here, binding them as his slaves, banishing the deranged ones or, occasionally, setting free those who had trapped themselves with rage, or self-pity, or those who were simply lost. It exhilarated him; yet, there was a danger. He could not linger. The tides of death that washed through the netherealms affected his soul as well. Already they tugged at him, trying to pull him deeper. If he let them, if he lost his concentration, he would be pulled away from the world of light. He would lose his way forever.

Off the tower he leapt, and soared over the hills. Below, a cluster of cottonwood trees shimmered. The faces of seven men twisted in their bark, men who had died there and had their essence absorbed by the plants. Nick heard the echoes of the echoes of their long-spent pistols.

There were animal spirits too. A coyote in Lost Silver Canyon barked questions to the moon, asking it what it saw so high up; a hummingbird, blur of electric blue, darted home, and left a trail of northern lights behind; wind devils soared through the thunderhead, poking it with sticks, trying to rouse it from its torpor; and a one-eyed crow crouched on a tangle of mesquite, watching him. It called, "Fall, fall, fall."

He made a note that Navajo shamans were active in this region.

South on Agua de Viva Road, he spotted an afterimage of lightning, but shattered as if viewed through a mirror of cracked glass. A small figure ran away, a boy, a shadow of a boy, then the shadow was gone too. While Nick's curiosity was piqued, this was not the ghost Dempsey had seen, the ghost with the aura of green and yellow.

He saw it ahead, the color of burning grass, green with fingers of orange and yellow. It was just the outline of a human body, but had no body to go with it. It sat on a flat rock, in the open, burning. It was not a complete aura either. It was translucent, barely visible to Nick. He risked descending a level into the netherealms. Perhaps there was more to it, deeper.

His own aura dimmed as he sank closer to death.

The animal spirits grew silent. In Lost Silver Canyon a ghost army of Spanish Conquistadors rode four hundred years ago. They charged fifty men on foot. Rifles discharged, horses trampled men, lances impaled, and blood clouded the stream. Screams of victory filled the canyon, followed by the wails of the dead.

The aura of green and fire had vanished, however. It was only on the surface, so it was not a true ghost. He left the lower region of the netherealms, and rose high above the hills. There was a second aura like the first by the setting sun, and there, north, was a third. They made a precise equilateral triangle about his tower.

It was too uniform. The beginnings of an incantation?

The auras undulated with identical patterns and rhythm. They vanished.

Uncertain what these triple auras were, and if they meant him harm or not, Nick flashed back into his body.

A quick inhalation of air; his heart beat again, eyes opened, and warmth spread back into his extremities. He felt clumsy and slow; he always did upon returning to flesh and blood. He flexed his hands and stretched.

Those auras were the same. They were not ghosts. They were reflections of something, three reflections in a mirror. They were auras, but more mirage than real power. They must have been—

The balcony doors were ajar. A woman stood there. She finished his thought, "Illusions? Shadows cast by me? Or am I a shadow too?"

She had long auburn hair, and eyes that were twin green mirrors, dark. Her skin was tanned and made sleek from the oil of palms gathered on the banks of the Nile. She wore a short jacket lined with crushed gold velvet. The outer shell was all leather leaves, blowing in the wind, frozen: amber, emerald, and olive sewn together. She wore faded jeans and suede boots, and she carried a stake of alder wood in her right hand. Its point was chiseled and on the shaft were etched seven runes. Nick did not have to be in the netherealms to see they bristled with magic.

He shifted uneasily, both from the malevolent witchcraft directed at him, and at seeing her unexpectedly after two hundred years. "Hello, Raja," he said. "It has been too long."

"Much too long, Judzyas."

"I no longer wear that name." The sound of his birth name gave life to dead memories . . . memories of the Aegean Sea, a rocky coast, the endless surf, and a cottage where they had lived together for three seasons, drank sweet plum wine, ate barrels of olives, and made love.

He remembered the odor of sea salt always in the air, and the smell of her musk always on his skin.

He had loved her then, but he never told her. He never got the chance. The Napoleonic wars came, and he left. He had to. Another prophet came. Another prophet had to be killed.

He held open his arms and stepped closer.

She raised the point of the stake, aimed for his chest. A calligraphy rune of *Confinement* flared opalescent and made the wood smoke. "You *are* Judzyas. I see your colors clearly enough. What name do you wear now?"

He took a step back. "Nikolos."

"A Greek name, at least," she said. "Nikolos . . . no, I think I like Nick better. I shall call you Nick."

"With that pointed at me, you may call me whatever you desire. And you? Are you still my Raja?"

"No." She lowered the stake. "I have not been anyone's Raja for two centuries. It took me decades and the broken hearts of six men to get over you." She tossed her head back, and gazed hard at the face he wore, past the flesh to see what was inside. Nick let her.

He remembered how he held her, how she felt beneath the weight of his body, and how they had watched the summer stars wheel over them.

She set the stake down on the floor, then turned her back to him and went inside. "You may call me Raja."

Inside, one wall held paperbacks and science textbooks on pine shelves. A large desk occupied the corner, atop which sat an Underwood typewriter, a mound of yellow paper, a cup of pens, and dust. Two logs blazed in a Franklin stove. And close to the fire was a couch and a La-Z-Boy covered with plaid fabric. A spiral staircase came up through the floor. Above, the ceiling crested to a point; stained-glass birds, stars, and bats flew there.

Nick followed, but he didn't touch the alder wood stake. It still fumed with enchantments. Her magic was unfathomable to him. She was a witch; she knew of life and cycles and growth. He was a necromancer; he knew of death and decay and endings. For a time he thought he had understood how both worked. When they lived together they were the Sun and his consort Moon, Osiris and Isis, the Corn King and the Goddess, Judzyas and Raja.

Now the only thing he knew, and trusted now, was death.

She studied the books on the shelf and pulled out a copy of Heinlein's *Time Enough for Love.* ''I haven't read this in years.''

''Had I known you would pay me a visit this evening, I would have procured your favorites. But you didn't come to borrow books.''

She nodded, but nevertheless secreted the volume inside her jacket. ''This tower belonged to a friend of mine, a writer. He wrote stories about ghosts and vampires, witches and warlocks. He died of a heart attack this spring.'' She sat on the couch and drew her legs close to her chest. ''You didn't have anything to do with it, did you, Nick?''

''I know of no such thing,'' he said. ''I arrived three days ago. This tower was on the market, overpriced, but it appealed to me. I bought it. Simple. Fair. And no murder.''

She narrowed her eyes. ''Not that you would have thought twice about it if you had to . . . or if it would have been more convenient.''

''Had I wanted the gentleman killed, he would be dead. But I did not.'' He sighed. ''Shall I conjure his spirit to tell you the truth? Show me which room he died in.''

She let her legs uncurl and set her feet firmly on the floor. ''No, let him rest in peace.''

He sat close to her on the arm of the La-Z-Boy. ''Is this why you came? To see if I killed your pet?''

''I saw power up here: lightning and ghosts. This is my territory, Nick, and I won't stand for you killing my people.'' She made a fist. ''They're not pets. They're friends.''

Her aura was muted in the mundane world, but he sensed her power simmering just below the surface. It made his skin flush, and it was not heat. She had cast three shadows of herself, and with no preparation. It was a mere five weeks past the summer solstice. Her magic was still potent. It would be foolish to fight her.

''What are you doing here?'' she demanded.

''This is not your land. You may not impose your will as law.''

She leaned forward. ''Seco County and the people here *are* mine . . . unless you want it for yourself. Then you may challenge me. I promise you a fair fight.'' She smiled—cold. ''Otherwise you may stay as my guest, my special guest. But I will not tolerate the murder of my friends, or raising the dead, or whatever it is you have planned.''

''And the stake? You brought that to expunge my presence?''

She shrugged. ''I did not know what I would find up here. If it was you . . . you could have been after me this time. It was a precaution.''

"I would never hurt you. I come for another, a man who must die. After, if you desire, I shall withdraw. Or, if you desire, I shall stay."

She edged closer to him, then caught herself and moved back. "Is it a debt of blood?"

"No. It is not what the man has done, it is what he shall do." Nick stood and warmed his hands over the stove. "I will not be stopped in this matter. Allow me to stay and take this one life from your domain. Please. Then we can decide what we shall do with one another."

"Kill who you have to then," she whispered, "but just one life. No more." She got up and came to him, close, and breathed, "As for the rest, let us begin where we left. Do you remember?" She touched his chest, ran her fingers up and across his cheek. "You wear a different face, but there is more to us than flesh, more to our love than bodies . . . although that too can be pleasant."

He forgot his weariness and took her hand. "I remember."

The jacket fell from her shoulders. Nick shouldn't trust her, but he drew her to him nonetheless, and kissed her. She entwined her body around his. He sensed her aura; it flared, brilliant and hot, and it also wrapped about him.

He lowered her to the hardwood floor. She moved beneath him exactly as he remembered. Her skin was warm against his cold flesh, hotter than the stove, full of life.

She undid his trousers, ripped his shirt apart, sucked his nipples, bit him. Nick let her rub over his body. He let his hands wander down her sides, stroking the curves of her scalding, sweaty skin. Her jeans and T-shirt were already off.

Strands of their spirits merged. Fingers of flame grappled with one another, his dark light, and her glowing jade.

He rolled over, and she straddled him, playfully pinning both arms over his head, letting her breasts dangle in his face. He caressed them.

They moved together, bodies sliding in unison—fast, animal motions. Nick forgot the prophet, the illusions, and the ghosts. He let passion flood his thoughts. The outer fringes of the light that surrounded them blurred, overlapped, and turned pure white.

Then they slowed their grinding, not wanting to exhaust each other, waiting to make it last, wanting to touch forever. She rocked slowly atop him. He wiped the drenched locks of her hair from her face.

"Why must this man die?" she asked, and traced the ridges on his stomach.

"You seduce me to pry my secrets loose . . ."

"Tell me anyway."

"Tell me why *you* are here? You prefer Paris for art, and Tibetan glaciers where the spirits are familiar to you. Why this desert?"

She bent closer to him, starting again, and whispered, "I too seek something. Now answer my question."

This they continued for a time, slow unified rocking, savoring the intimacy, bathing in each other's light. Then Nick replied, "The man I seek, I saw in a prophecy. He comes on a white horse spotted with red. He comes to find a water that cannot be drunk."

She paused. Her skin and aura grew slightly cool to Nick's touch.

Raja then rocked hard, reached back with her hands, and raked her nails along his thigh. He grabbed her waist, slid his fingers across the small of her back, and pushed her harder onto him. Nick touched her deeper, her essence: she was a torrent of verdant flame, passion and life; he was shadows and purple, cool whirlpools of silent power.

In his peripheral vision he noticed a glow under the desk. On the floor, her enchanted alder wood stake lay. It was a long way to roll from the balcony door, but he dismissed it. Nick had other things to occupy him.

His appetite swelled, peaked. Gold and shadow and lavender blended. Silver passion scorched the shadows; green fire did seethe and blister, grow, and bloom. Their colors bleached together, burned away—left only dazzling luminescence, a moment of pleasure that stretched forever . . . then faded, throbbing to their rhythmic pulses.

He lay exhausted beneath her. She quivered, arched her back, and collapsed backwards upon his legs.

Nick saw another alder wood stake, this one by the La-Z-Boy. He glanced at the balcony doors. A third stake lay there. He connected the lines between them: an equilateral triangle, him in the center. Three illusions like before. And the real one?

Raja sat up, and brought her knee down hard into his stomach. The real alder wood stake blazed in her right hand. She thrust it through his ribcage with all her weight upon it. The wood found his heart and pierced it.

Nick shuddered under her once and cried out. He lay rigid, pinned, his eyes open. Blood foamed on his lips. Where the wood touched his body, the flesh smoldered.

She removed herself from him. His blood smeared her torso, and trickled down her legs. "I seek the same water as your damn prophet. If he knows where it is, then I can't let you kill him, my sweet Nick, my Judzyas, my love."

She leaned over him, shoved the stake deeper. "The magic woven into the grain of the alder wood pins your soul to this body. You will not find another. No astral travel. And no ghosts will come to haunt me or my dreams."

Raja pulled on her jeans and donned her jacket with a flourish, then headed down the spiral stairs, and paused. "Death is the only thing you ever trusted, Nick. Maybe it's the only thing you ever loved. Now you can get as close as you want to death. You can finally die."

Chapter 3

NO GHOSTS CAME FOR LARRY THAT EVENING, NOT THE KID ON THE ROAD, not Spencer, not even Matt Carlson, whose bed he slept in.

He rolled over into horizontal lines of light. The slats on the shutters hadn't been closed last night, and the morning sun poured through. It was warm on his skin. That was good. He was still alive. No thunder. No lightning.

Still . . . he opened his eyes cautiously, afraid of what might be lying next to him. There was nothing but wrinkled sheets and the nightstand with a brass plaque. The sunlight made the burnished surface of the plaque hard to read, but Larry knew what was on it. He'd seen it last night. That's why he had slept with the lights on.

It read:

> In this bed, the infamous outlaw, Matt Carlson (1866–1887), met his demise. His band of cutthroats rode the Santa Fe Trail robbing, raping, and murdering settlers headed for California.
>
> On November 11, 1887, Texas Rangers found him here (then called the Silver Star Saloon). The lawmen waited until he was drunk, followed him upstairs, and shot him thirteen times while he slept.
>
> The upper portion of the bed frame was repaired by the owner

of the Silver Star in 1891; however, if you examine the underside, you can still see where those fatal bullets splintered the oak.

Larry rubbed his chest: heartburn. It was from his dream. There was a stake shoved into his heart, a stone tower, and lightning, all in black and white; there was a woman in his dream, too. Sex on a hardwood floor, he remembered that distinctly. Her skin was liquid fire in his hands. Larry rolled to the shady side of the bed, tried to go back to sleep and find this dream woman.

He couldn't.

Instead, his thoughts were filled with the ghost of that kid, and Spencer's liver, and another woman, Paloma.

He had met her when he checked in last night. She worked behind the front desk—twenty-two, he guessed. She had large brown eyes and a tall athletic figure.

She examined the registration card he had filled out, then remarked, "Your surname is unusual, Mister Ngitis. Asian, isn't it?"

Larry wanted to be charming. He wanted to say she might have seen his name on the cover of his books . . . then what? Invite her up for a drink? It would have been easier for him to dance on water.

"Chinese," he muttered. "I'm one-quarter Asian." He handed over his credit card and avoided her eyes. He didn't have the nerve to ask *her* name. The only way he knew was from the tag on her blouse.

After the drive out here—who could be charming? It was also too soon after leaving Linda. In a perfect fantasy world, if he had invited Paloma upstairs, and *if* she had come, then Linda would have driven to New Mexico that evening. She would have burst into his room and found them in a fleshy knot. She'd have shot him in the same bed Matt Carlson died in.

It wasn't his precognition that told him this; it was his guilt speaking.

He should give Linda a call to let her know he made it safely and see if she was OK. He reached for the black rotary phone. No. It was too soon. She'd be hysterical. She'd make him feel like a jerk. And he might be tempted to go back.

He forgot to ask for the discount last night too. His savings were low. This was the only unoccupied room, and it had cost a fortune. Aside from Matt Carlson's deathbed there was a white pine floor, thick Navajo rugs, and an adobe fireplace built into the corner of the room.

There was split oak and tinder stacked beside it. Smoke stains curled up the wall to the ceiling.

Larry got up, pulled his computer out of his overnight bag, and reviewed last night's journal entry to see if it made sense. All the details were there: his physical reactions, the smells, fragments of dialogue, how people moved. He compulsively jotted notes in his journal. It was how he wrote his novels.

He would change the names, alter Econoline vans and gas stations to galactic cruisers and exotic spaceports. His fictional people and places were almost real. That's why his first three books sold well. At least, that's what his editor told him.

But the ghost wouldn't fit. Not in a science fiction novel. The lightning? That could be weather control used as a weapon, or terraforming gone awry. And Spencer would make a great bartender in the pub on the space station in chapter four. But a ghost? That verged on horror, or worse, fantasy.

Larry wanted the ghost. He was certain he had seen it. There was too much detail for him to have made it up: the blood matted in the kid's hair, and his smile. It was all very fresh, all very creepy. The image of the kid waving good-bye wouldn't leave him. He reread the part when he stumbled upon the cross, and when he saw the kid's picture nailed on it.

Larry sensed someone reading along with him, peering over his shoulder.

He turned and saw only motes of dust in the slatted sunlight. But there were swirls and eddies, as if someone had passed through the space. The motes settled into random floating patterns.

The feeling vanished.

Larry returned to his journal. The ghost wouldn't fit. His publisher had been specific about what they wanted in this fourth book: the same thing as in the first three.

He hated his protagonist, Captain Kelvin, and he hated the Space Empire he worked for. His fans loved it. They had bought two hundred thousand books, and showed no signs of letting up. But the characters were unbelievably stereotyped. The setting had no technological authenticity. Larry wanted to write about real people with real problems: alcoholism, divorce, depression, maybe a few murders, and maybe a ghost.

Instead, he was stuck on chapter two with seventeen more to go, and only six months to deliver the manuscript. His agent thought he was halfway done. His editor thought he was three-quarters. Larry didn't need precognitive powers to know there were late nights and gallons of boiled coffee in his immediate future.

The low battery icon flashed. Larry rifled though the overnight bag for the AC adapter. It must be in the back of the van. He'd have to go get it if he wanted to work today.

He showered and dabbed on some cologne, Royale Knights, then recalled it was a Valentine's Day gift from Linda. He washed it off, but the odor lingered; it reminded him that she liked to stay up late and sleep till noon. He got up with the sun. They hardly ever saw each other.

"Breakfast first," he told his reflection in the mirror, "then you can indulge your self-pity." He stuffed his loneliness deep inside, and shoved his questions about the ghosts and lightning next to that, then marched down to the Silver Bullet's dining room.

Halfway down the stairs the smells of sautéing onions and garlic caught him. Five more steps and there was the odor of sweet peppers and sausage, and when he reached the main floor, the aromas of bacon and baking bread.

There were five tables in the Silver Bullet's dining room, two empty and three with tourist couples. They had brought their cameras to breakfast. One couple snapped pictures of the pine beams overhead and the Anasazi petroglyphs carved into them.

Paloma was there too. She flitted from table to table, asking the guests what their plans were. Her voice was the same smooth, friendly music Larry remembered from last night. To the older couple with Brooklyn accents, she suggested they tour the old Moon Lady mining museum in town, or visit the Chaco Canyon ruins for the afternoon. She wore a loose denim skirt, a white lace shirt, and a bead choker. Her nose was slightly crooked (he hadn't noticed that last night). To Larry she looked liked an Indian princess. She glowed with vitality.

He skulked to the empty table farthest from her and looked for a menu to bury his face in. If he could have been suave, he would have invited her to sit with him, and maybe share a cup of coffee. His stomach twisted into a knot just thinking about it. There was a vase of black-eyed Susans, a red cloth napkin folded in his water glass, but nothing to hide behind.

Paloma spotted him and came over. She moved so gracefully Larry imagined that she skated over the Spanish clay tiles. She smiled at him and said, ''Are you hungry this morning, Mister Ngitis?''

''Starved,'' Larry lied. His appetite had vanished. His pulse pounded in his throat. What if he said the wrong thing? What if he made a fool of himself? Better to say nothing at all.

''Then I'll load up a plate for you,'' she said. ''I'll be right back.'' A whirl of her skirt, and she ducked into the kitchen, singing to herself.

Larry wanted to leave. He wanted to stay. He couldn't stop thinking about Linda, but he couldn't stop thinking about Paloma either. This is stupid, he thought. He was thirty-five, slightly overweight, with a cheap haircut. He still got pimples when he ate chocolate. The girl wasn't flirting with him. It was her job to be friendly with the guests. That's all.

Paloma returned with a silver platter filled with biscuits and sausage gravy, lean bacon with ground pepper on its edges, crisp chili rellenos, an omelet stuffed with cheese and tomatoes, a bowl of plump strawberries, a glass of orange juice, and a pot of coffee. ''You're the last to eat this morning,'' she said, ''so you get leftovers. I hope you don't mind.''

She set three plates out for Larry, then sat down in the chair opposite him. She poured him a cup of coffee. ''Cream?'' Her smile was lovely.

''Please.'' Larry couldn't help smiling back, despite the lump in his throat. To be polite, he took a bite of chili relleno. Delicious. He sipped his juice, took a gulp of his coffee, and stared at her. It wasn't that she was beautiful (she was); it was her hair. There were red highlights in her black mane, highlights that rippled, tangles of light, barely visible, like the shadow of a flame on a sunny day. It had to be a trick of the light.

''I knew I had seen your name somewhere before.'' She looked down, embarrassed. Then, ''At the bookstore this morning, I found your trilogy. It's really quite good. At least, what I've read so far.''

The highlights in her hair glowed a rosy pink, and filled the air. To Larry it looked like a halo. Its heat warmed his skin. It was hypnotic to watch; it was fire; it was alive.

It was not a precognition.

Larry had gut feelings, empathetic burnings in his liver, flashes of insight, but never sustained hallucinations like this. Ghosts last night and auras this morning—had he lost his mind?

''Uh, thanks,'' he said.

He glanced at the other guests. The old man from Brooklyn

coughed. A violet cloud condensed over his head, then evaporated just as fast. Larry felt a twinge of pain in his rectum. Prostate cancer, he knew, seven months to live.

Larry then remembered how the lightning had appeared to him: red filaments that filled with electric white. Perhaps these hallucinations were part of his powers after all. It was distracting. He wished it would go away.

"Did you say 'bookstore'?"

"The Three of Diamonds Bookstore on Agua de Viva. If you'd like, I can show you it after breakfast."

Larry picked at his omelet. Half his thoughts were on him seeing things he'd never seen before, half were on Linda, and half were on Paloma and her hopeful smile, her burning hair. The melted cheese and grease suddenly didn't look so appetizing. "Maybe some other time. I probably won't be in town that long, so I . . ."

"Oh," she said softly. Her smile vanished. The flames about her head shrank and cooled to navy blue. "Well, I'll wish you a fine meal then, Mister Ngitis. I hope you enjoy the remainder of your stay in Dry Water. If I can be of any assistance, please let me know."

She got up.

Larry stood—a gentlemanly gesture he had never offered to Linda—and said, "Uh, thanks again for the food." But she had already turned her back to him and was marching out of the dining room.

It was sunny outside. The only clouds were high, innocent puffs of cotton, pure white and incapable of any electrical discharge. Larry breathed deep. The air was crisp and clean and cold.

He should have taken Paloma up on her offer. He hadn't intended to offend her. And as impossible as it seemed to Larry, she apparently *was* interested in him. She had even bought his novels. She had said she enjoyed them. But there were too many things on his mind: writing, ghosts, and guilt.

He walked by himself along the raised wooden sidewalk of Agua De Viva Road. From a block away he saw a refurbished barn, painted with a weathered brick pattern, and twin panes of glass that filled the front and stared at him like a myopic giant. Three pink neon diamonds flickered in the right window. Beneath them in glowing calligraphy was: *Three of Diamonds Bookstore.*

On the other side of the glass, fliers advertised future book signings.

There were writers of mystery, science fiction, fantasy, westerns, and romance, names Larry recognized; some were legends, authors he had read as a child. Inside, the barn had two levels, and stairs descending into a basement. Shelves held books stacked to the ceiling: old cracked leather bindings, glossy hardbacks, and paperbacks, both pristine and unopened and ones with used yellowed pages. Light spilled in from skylights, and in one square of illumination, Larry spied the brass eagle of an espresso machine and a counter of thick green glass. The odors of roasted coffee beans, steamed milk, and chocolate were in the air. And among a dozen tables sat people reading, sipping cappuccino, and eating cheesecake. Others wrote furiously in notebooks, while some sketched or spoke to friends in whispers.

Larry wanted to go in. He wanted to spend the day reading and writing. But he didn't even have a notebook. Everything was in his van. Larry had to go to Spencer's first, get his computer recharged, then bring it here, relax, and write.

Maybe Dry Water wasn't the hick town he had thought it was. Maybe *The New Yorker* had been right when they called it the next Taos. Maybe he hadn't made such a big mistake in coming here. He must have walked right past the Three of Diamonds yesterday . . . only he had been thinking of lightning and a gas station attendant he had predicted would die.

When Larry was three years old his talent for prediction had surfaced. He knew his father was leaving. He knew when he drove off he wouldn't come back. It was *black ice*. The words meant nothing to a three-year-old, but Larry knew it was on the road, slick to the touch, and invisible. He knew that it would kill his father.

The car spun out of control and hit a telephone pole. His father went through the windshield—Larry felt it like an ice pick slammed through his skull. He cried until the police came and told his mother.

Since then he had known things, mostly when people were about to die. That was the strongest and clearest of his precognitive powers. But there were other things that popped up, not as often, and not as precise, like glass that was about to break, checks that would bounce, and white shirts that were fated to turn pink in the laundry.

Across the street, another building caught his attention, a real estate office. It was wishful thinking, but perhaps he could buy a house and settle down. It was too soon; he should rent a place first before he committed to living here. But . . . it was on the way to Spencer's, so he crossed Agua de Viva.

On a bulletin board outside the office were pictures of the local properties, each with a brief description, and the asking price. At the bottom were cabins described as ''fixer-uppers.'' Those were in his price range, if he got the second half of his advance, and if Linda was decent about splitting up their joint savings account. Half of the cabins listed had electricity and indoor plumbing. Some did not, and Larry took that as a good sign. There were writers and artists here, successful and struggling. He'd fit right in.

Slightly over his budget was an A-frame with an enormous fireplace; he'd have to get a loan to swing that one. There were many far out of his financial reach: chateaus with two kitchens, three-story mansions with fifty-foot timbers . . . and a tower of black volcanic stone. It was the tower he dreamed of last night. The tower where he had sex, where he had a stake impaled into his chest. Larry's heartburn came back. The listing said it had been sold. Maybe he saw it on the way up here and incorporated it into his dream. Coincidence, that's all. It still gave him the creeps to see it in the daylight, in reality.

Before he bought anything, cabin or mansion or haunted tower, he'd have to make progress on his writing—or there would be no advance money.

Two blocks of small restaurants, and souvenir shops with turquoise jewelry, and quartz crystals, incense, and T-shirts, then Larry was back at Spencer's Gas station. His van wasn't parked where he had left it. It wasn't in the garage either.

He stepped into Spencer's gift shop, worried what the old man had done with his van. Maybe he died working on it.

Shelves of kachina dolls stared at him behind ceremonial masks with glittering onyx eyes. Each wore a crown of flames atop its head, tiny rainbows of translucent color. Larry heard the whispers of chanting from them too.

They weren't alive, they couldn't be; they didn't move, yet Larry sensed there was something in each one, something not alive . . . but not dead either. He stared into their masks, and with a shaking hand he reached for their burning manes.

A ''ding'' sounded as a car pulled up to the pumps. The dolls fell silent, and their auras extinguished. Larry heard Spencer's voice behind him: ''Get on out there, boy. There's a customer waiting. Don't you dare let her pump that gas!''

A teenager with greasy hair to match his greasy coveralls brushed past Larry. He muttered something about a raise.

Larry turned and saw Spencer, alive, or at least he looked like he was alive.

''Morning,'' Spencer said, and adjusted his coveralls so he had more room for his extended stomach. A green gas flowed from his mouth. It was a heavy vapor Larry smelled across the store: bourbon. The old man was four shots closer to death. Larry took another look at the kachina dolls. They were normal, no flickering colors, and not a peep out of them. Larry squeezed his eyes shut and turned back to Spencer. He opened them. The vapors still lingered in Spencer's mouth, moving like seaweed in water, back and forth with his breath.

He had to tell him . . . what? That he was about to die of an ulcerated liver? That he was drinking himself to death? He probably had been told that. How could Larry convince him that he *knew*?

''You OK? You gotta problem with your eyes? I know a good doctor in town. He'll fix you up even if you got no insurance.''

''Yeah, my eyes,'' Larry said. ''Maybe I need new contacts.'' Or a good shrink. ''What happened to my van?''

''It's out back. I was clearing all that glass out, and didn't want to get any on my driveway. Besides, you left a bunch of your stuff there. I didn't want people poking around in your business. Come on, I'll show you what I got done.'' He led Larry out back. Parked behind his garage was a fin-backed powder blue Cadillac, a cherry red 1958 Chevy truck, and a bulldozer with a new coat of safety orange paint on it. The Econoline van was there too. Only it was different.

''What happened to my van?''

''Just a little primer. Don't you worry about that. When I pulled the glass out, I saw you had all these pieces of asphalt stuck into the body panels. Like shrapnel. I dug 'em out, sanded, and primered her. While I had my tools out I took care of all that rust you had by the wheel wells.''

''Look, I never said you could—''

''Don't you worry. I ain't gonna charge you for it. I just hate to see things get rusted, that's all. Now if you want to paint her over, then that's a different story. I have a cousin that can get her done real cheap. Any color you want.''

Spencer still breathed death, but the vapors were thinner. Larry got a hot flash in his abdomen, deep, where his liver was. With the heartburn he had, his insides felt as if they were on fire.

''I ordered them seals,'' Spencer said. ''Express. The warehouse told me they'd be here in three days, OK?''

''Great. I just dropped by to get a few things out of my van.''

''Don't let me stop you.'' Spencer pulled his silver flask out. He spun the top off, then held it out to Larry. ''Want a snort first?''

Green vapors fumed out. They formed skeletal hands and reached for the old man's mouth.

''No, thanks,'' —Larry changed his mind and grabbed it. ''On second thought, since you offered.'' He'd pretend to take a swig, then cough it out, spill the rest on the ground. That would buy Spencer time. It would give Larry time to figure out how to stop him, time to save his life.

Larry pressed it to his lips. He hadn't intended to drink the stuff, but the liquid grabbed him, flowed into his mouth by itself, tried to claw its way down his windpipe. It tasted like hot razors. It was acid that dissolved his tongue. Larry gagged. He coughed the bourbon out his mouth and nose.

Larry dropped the flask (not quite as planned). Spencer lunged for it, and missed. Brown liquid glugged onto the oily earth.

''Dang it all,'' Spencer cried. ''That was . . . Aw, never mind.'' He whacked Larry on the back three times. ''You'll be all right. Maybe we should buy a couple of beers to wash that down with.''

''Sorry . . .'' Larry hacked out between coughs.

''Don't you worry about it. Got plenty more.''

Larry wiped his eyes, and suppressed the urge to puke. He took a minute to catch his breath. ''What was that?''

''Just bourbon.'' He winked. ''And a little something special that I brew myself.''

Larry shook his head to clear it, then rummaged through piles of clothes and books in the van for his power supply. ''There was a cross on the side of the road on the way up here,'' he told Spencer, pausing to swallow and soothe his sore throat. ''It was stuck in the middle of nowhere.''

''They're put up for the folk who died on the road—drunk driving accidents most of 'em. Usually for kids.'' He shrugged. ''If the whole family gets wiped out, the priests up the road go and put one up for them. About the only good they do anyone.'' He spat. ''Hey, you need help rooting around in there?''

Larry found the power supply buried under a box of overturned manuscripts. "No, got it." He stepped out of the van, got dizzy.

Spencer grabbed his arm. "You don't look so great. Why don't you sit a spell, and have a soda. On the house."

"No . . ." Larry saw the spot where the booze soaked the ground; he smelled it; he felt breakfast heavy in his gut, twisting. "I feel fine. I have to get some work done this morning. I'll drop by tomorrow."

"They treating you right at the Silver Bullet? They better be."

"Yeah, just fine."

"You want me to talk to my cousin? About that paint job?"

"I'll have to think about it."

"No rush. I'll be here."

Maybe you will and maybe you won't, Larry thought. Depends if you refill that flask.

Larry stood on the raised wooden sidewalk downtown. The air was hazy. He didn't remember leaving Spencer's. A blackout? Or was Spencer's home brew part Sterno and LSD?

The adobe church was half a block down the road. Larry lurched forward. He wanted to lie down and sleep. It wasn't only his head that spun, but his stomach too, his liver, everything, and in different directions. In his left hand he clutched the AC adapter like his life depended on it.

The buildings in Dry Water were on fire. Ruby flames with emerald tips, sapphire fires that burned in the road and twisted like sidewinders. Napalm exploded in the air. Everything solid shimmered translucent, and where there should have been nothing . . . things appeared. People from spaghetti Westerns, with boots, and cowboy hats, materialized on the street; they overlapped the tourists in their Patagonia jackets, jeans, and sneakers. Horses trotted down Agua de Viva through parked Jeeps and minivans.

Larry blinked back tears. Everything spun, his insides, the buildings, the air. He reached for a hitching post and it slipped through his fingers like sand. He couldn't tell if he stood, or had fallen in the street. The fringes of his vision blackened, and he closed his eyes, squeezed the panic out of his mind.

He opened them. Nothing had changed: chaos and vertigo.

The church appeared solid enough though. Larry staggered to it. He touched the adobe. It was real, solid. Everything else danced and distorted.

He threw up chili relleno on the sidewalk.

The cowboys and tourists got out of his way. They gave him looks of disgust. He heard the word "drunk" whispered.

It was both day *and* night. Three suns floated overhead, one of them glowing black, and a dozen moons in various phases sped past—blue, and red, and yellow Swiss cheese. The church's bells rang. They tolled wedding choruses and funeral dirges and fire alarms, and they all rang together. Larry cupped his hands over his ears.

By the double door entrance to the church was a message board, black felt with removable white letters. It read:

DEATH COMES FOR PASTOR WOBERTY

Larry blinked and read it again:

PASTOR WOBERTY IS DEATH. HE COMES FOR YOU!

And again:

PASTOR WOBERTY SPEAKS ON: GOD IS LIGHT.
COME JOIN OUR WATERCOLOR CLASSES, WEDNESDAYS AT 7 P.M.
SEMINAR: THE HEALING PROPERTIES OF CRYSTALS. SATURDAY AT 3 P.M.

Larry ran, coughing, and stumbling up Agua De Viva. He ran through people that weren't there. He pushed over the ones that were there and got in his way. He ran dreamlike, moving fast, but not getting very far, trying to keep his eyes closed until he got to the Silver Bullet Bed & Breakfast. He swung open the door so hard the frosted glass cracked.

Paloma stared at him from behind the reception desk.

He ignored her—bolted up the stairs, three at a time. When he got to his room, he slammed and locked the door behind him, then slumped to the floor and cried. He was insane. He knew it.

A man sat on his bed. He had boots on, but only wore white flannel underwear. He reached over and put on his hat, wide-brimmed and dusty, with a rattlesnake skin headband. The stranger twisted his handlebar mustache and said, "Yer in a heap of trouble, son. Ya been goin' places ya got no business bein' . . . not yet no how."

"Who the hell are you? And what are you doing in my room?"

"First of all, it ain't yer room. It's mine. I'm Matt Carlson."

Chapter 4

RAJA WAS ANGRY.

She stomped through her garden. Living, green things usually calmed her thoughts. Not this morning. This morning anger boiled in the cauldron of her mind.

She was mad that she hadn't sensed Judzyas sooner—in the house of her friend, no less! She was angry that someone else was looking for the same thing she was. And she was mad at herself for murdering Judzyas before learning more about his mysterious prophet.

A dusting of guilt settled on her heart, but she brushed it off. No. It was the only thing she could have done. Judzyas was too powerful a necromancer to let loose in her domain. He wouldn't have hesitated had she got in *his* way.

Raja's garden overflowed her estate. It was sensitive to the witch's moods. Before dawn her foul disposition blackened a field of daisies and lupine. By midmorning her anger had cooled to annoyance, which was still enough to stunt an aspen grove.

A palm tree swayed in the breeze as she neared. Its dates swelled, ripened, and fell for her. She stuffed them into her mouth, spit the pits out, and, feeling somewhat better, sat in its shade to meditate. Cool logic quenched her rage.

First fact: Judzyas was dead. He would provide neither answers nor trouble now, so it was best to forget him.

Second fact: He had come to kill a prophet. A man who sought "a water that cannot be drunk." This meant he was either competition or an ally. Experience suggested competition. She had too little data to draw any conclusions, however. She needed to know more.

Raja stood, stretched, then walked through tall grasses and splashed through a cold creek. She inhaled the scents of ginseng and basil, purple sage and mint, and her mood improved. Perhaps this prophet was the key she had waited for. It was foolish, she knew, but optimism filled her soul nevertheless, and she smiled.

Where her bare feet touched the black humus, blossoms appeared: sunflowers and heather, the white starbursts of onions, the deadly violets of monkshood, and bright yellow snapdragons. Anything grew for Raja, even in Seco County: fig trees and ferns, giant white oaks and bougainvillea, cactus and wild corn, Japanese red pine and pineapple, it mattered not to them; all that mattered was that the witch, their mistress, was pleased. And, for the moment, she was. For the moment her mind traced memories, past to the present, a path meandering from Tibet to New Mexico, long in time and distance, spirals of lovers and friends, births and deaths, pleasures and sorrows four centuries long.

To her friends she was known as Raja, to her enemies, she was Ms. Anumati, and to three Tibetan monks, her real name translated roughly as, "Daughter of the Terror Winds." This afternoon, however, she chose not to dwell on Tibet. There was too much sorrow lurking in the shadows of her childhood. That was before she had become a witch, before she had mastered the Himalayan Bon-po spirits of ice and winter and granite.

When Copernicus declared that the earth was not the center of the universe, Raja left Katmandu and journeyed to Baghdad to learn mathematics and the dogma of the Middle Eastern kingdoms. Algebra and geometry, logic and rhetoric, and the names of two hundred and twenty-two jinni she memorized so they might be summoned or dismissed at whim.

And when the first permanent settlement was founded in the New World, Raja sailed up the Nile Valley. She embraced alchemy, and worshiped pagan gods, and gave blood sacrifices. She became one with the great river, intuited her ebbs and floods. She spoke with the water nymphs. She learned the songs of the fertile soil.

The American colonies declared their independence from England, and Raja traveled to Crete. She became the apprentice of the diviner hermit called "Sonopous with three eyes." She met Judzyas too, and fell in love. Sonopous taught her to scry the past, sometimes the future, and to listen to her dreams . . . and travel to realms unknown in her sleep.

Napoleon conquered half of Europe. Judzyas left her. And she departed for Ireland with a broken heart.

For two decades she was the darling of the Fairy Court. The Elven Queen called Raja "Princess of the Moon" because her powers waxed and waned with the seasons. Raja would have been happy there forever, but thunder came to the enchanted forests. Iron Horses tore across the land, belching steam, and throwing sparks with their metal wheels. Typhoid ravaged the county, then cholera. Half of the children died before their fifth birthday. And those who survived no longer sang and played with the fairies; they toiled in textile factories. A half million people raped the earth for coal. Black smoke suffocated the world. The Fairy Court departed.

Raja begged them to take her, but they would not. They shed tears for her and her world, then vanished.

If only she could undo the damage, return the land to its pristine state, then perhaps the fairies would come back. But when she arrived in London and saw the swarm of starving people, the clouds of soot, and open sewers, she knew it was too late.

She had heard a legend, however. A way to change what had already occurred. Raja trekked to France, to the ancient caverns of mankind, the Rotunda of Lascaux and Le Tuc d'Audoubert, searching for clues left in primitive wall paintings, and prehistoric clay bison statues, and the handprints of long-dead shamans.

To Lisbon next, then upon the steamship *Leviathan* to Rio de Janeiro to speak to aboriginal medicine men. She waited and watched two world wars pass; she watched more of her world die. Then on to New Orleans, to dance with voodoo spirits and hear secrets whispered upon breaths laced with rum. And last, to New Mexico, where she found what she had searched for: a way to alter the past.

Raja paused by a stand of mimosa trees and let the feathery leaves brush her hair. She had enchanted them to draw the lightning, smother it, and protect the remainder of her garden. One could never be too careful with lightning in Seco County.

She pushed her way through a dense patch of ferns. There was soft moss beneath her feet. Dew sprinkled her face and arms, cleansing her. That was the first part of the ritual: protection by water. She entered her sacred place.

Five white oaks surrounded her, their boughs heavy with mistletoe, making a web of greenery overhead. In the center was an artesian well, its edges lined with slate. It held deep black water that overflowed and trickled into the meadow beyond.

She lit amber incense and beeswax candles, then set them in red clay bowls between the oaks. The smoke curled up and gave the afternoon sunlight a silky texture. This was her protection by air and fire.

A layer of decaying leaves covered the roots. Raja swept them aside to reveal the pattern of crisscrossing runners that formed a pentagram. Beneath the soil, she sensed the buried roots overlapping in a similar fashion. This was her protection by the earth. It safeguarded her multifold with the arcane five-sided symbol; one point representing her head, two for her arms, and two for the legs—secure within the circle.

Here she would divine where Judzyas's prophet was. And here she would find the water that could not be drunk.

She knelt by the well's edge and brushed the surface of the water. "Let us see the familiar," she spoke to the well. Ripples obscured reflections of leaves and sunlight, smoke and shadow.

Raja read of a "water in between worlds" in Tibet. An ancient Chinese scroll from the Qin Dynasty chronicled the experiences of a priest who had a magic elixir. It allowed him to experience the life of any man, poet or general, farmer or emperor. He chose Confucius.

During Confucius's glorious life the priest rode along as an observer. Upon one occasion a water hyacinth caught his fancy, and although the historical Confucius never paused for the flower, the priest, through an act of pure willpower, *made* him. He altered history.

And in Baghdad's House of Wisdom, Raja overheard that the scholar al-Kindi had relived the lives of Ptolemy, Euclid, and Archimedes to recover their mathematical knowledge forgotten for centuries by the West.

Along the banks of the Nile, the alchemist Elias Ashmole whispered to her of a compound that linked the spiritual to the physical world.

He said that it was a water that was not water, and it pooled deep within the earth where there was no earth.

On Crete, Sonopous boxed her ears when she asked him. He said the knowledge was forbidden. It was too much power for any man. Of course, Raja knew he had meant it was too much power for any mortal man . . . and she was neither.

The Fairies of Ireland once had the elixir. The well they drew it from, however, dried millennia before she arrived in their court.

Lisbon, France, the Amazon, and New Orleans all had their legends of the water, but none had it. There were clues, though, a trail of bread crumbs that led to New Mexico.

Raja sighed. Glimpsing her past upon the pool's surface took little power. Directly seeking this man Judzyas wanted to kill would take more. It would be easier with Paloma here. Raja could draw upon her apprentice's youth and vitality.

She would wait.

"Let us see the past of this place," she told the well. "Let us see where the water has touched Seco County."

Raja slipped her hand beneath the surface and let the artesian well draw magic and warmth from her hand. The water muddied. Swirled dreams and fog appeared, visions and nightmares.

Water underground: flowing, channels, cold pools, drops that clung to stalactites, primeval water that the earth had never released, and oceans of night reflected upon the surface of Raja's well—then up through the gravel and sand of a dry streambed. In Lost Silver Canyon a river of blood had been spilled among the lechuguilla and the prickly pears, a massacre of miners by Spanish cavalry. There were bars of silver just beneath the dry riverbed (if you knew where to dig), and hidden in the hillside caverns sat tons of the precious metal.

She pushed forward in time.

Settlers came through the canyon, off the main trail, because they feared bandits. One wagon rolled over a log, and little Sally Wainwright fell off the back, landed wrong, and busted her leg. The entire procession of sixteen wagons, their mules, horses, and cows came to a halt. Her family didn't want to move her, so they all spent the night there.

That evening one of the group, Father Wilber, wandered off. When he didn't return by morning they sent search parties into the hills and up Seven Horseshoe Ridge. They found the hills riddled with caverns, deep labyrinths, some with petroglyphs and smoke-stained handprints on the walls, but no Father Wilber.

He showed up on his own four days later, confused and dehydrated. "I heard angels in the hills," he told the settlers. "They told me to follow 'em."

"Where did you go?" they asked.

"To purgatory," he whispered. "They gave me this." He took out his silver flask, not filled with his usual whiskey, but plain water. "Now you give this to Sally. They told me she'd be fine."

The settlers gave the girl a sip of the water. Her broken leg healed before their eyes.

"Jesus Christ is up in those hills," Father Wilber said, "and I was with him." He then fell asleep.

That night, with the exception of Sally Wainwright, everyone who slept had nightmares. Some said the devil had come to them and whispered of magic and silver in the hills.

Father Wilber died in his sleep.

Half of the settlers wanted to get out of Seco County. The other half were determined to stay. They said a miracle had occurred. So the village of Silver Waters was founded in 1859.

"What happened to Sally Wainwright?" Raja asked the water. No answers came. Instead more ripples. Her mirror to the past jumped years ahead.

Silver Waters was a boom town. It had tents, and saloons, and houses of ill repute, buildings with false fronts all. The stagecoach arrived every afternoon on the muddy streets to drop off a load of hopefuls. The legend of Father Wilber's healing water had spread throughout the territories, as far as Saint Louis, and lured the sick. Some had whooping cough, others dropsy, others TB, some had aliments they had no name for, and many were just plain old.

Another kind of folk came too—not to be cured, but to cure. Faith healers congregated with their gospel revivals, drunk doctors came who had been thrown out of every hospital east of the Mississippi, and old-fashioned snake oil peddlers arrived with their wagons of a thousand panaceas. It was a carnival of death.

Not one got healed, but there were plenty of silver-plate flasks of

Prof. Low's Liniment and Worm Syrup, Mother Clark's Sarsaparilla, and Dr. Flint's Quaker Bitters filled with alcohol, cocaine, and opium. For a while, everyone felt like they were touched by the hand of God.

A decade later only a handful of desperates remained in Seco County. Silver Waters was now called Dry Water, because of the hundreds of embittered still-sick who never found their miracle. The Civil War came and went, and no great battle was fought over New Mexico; still, the town of six hundred had three graveyards with four thousand dead and buried.

And some continued to come, hoping.

One of them was Yanisin. He was one of those "uncooperative" Indians that Kit Carson and his U.S. troops rounded up after destroying their homes and crops. Yanisin was a peaceful man, so he surrendered. They forced him and his wife to walk three hundred miles from Gallup to the Bosque Redondo near Fort Sumner. In 1868, the Navajos signed a treaty and got part of the Four Corners region. Yanisin came to Dry Water with his wife instead. He had to. His son, born in the detention camp, was dying of pneumonia.

They arrived one afternoon along with one of the worst thunderstorms ever seen in Seco County. The boy passed away despite the attentions and cost of the best doctor in town.

Yanisin wandered the hills of Seco County, tracking down the rumors of the healing water . . . and found it. He settled in Dry Water. When his wife died of old age, he took a second, then a third, and had three sons, two of which left to get educated in Boston, and the third, Niyol, remained to become a shaman like his father. Yanisin Rodriguez was over a century and a half old by the time Raja reached New Mexico.

"You, I know," Raja said to the reflection. "You said your water was sacred. That I meant to use it for evil. You were wrong."

He tried to drive her away with a horde of conjured dust devils. She turned them against him, brought Old North Wind down upon him, and forced him into the hills. He resisted her again—even after she explained her plans to change the land—and fought back. Raja summoned a black cloud on a sunny day, a cloud of a thousand crows that tore him to pieces. His son, Niyol, tried to stop her too. He had more power than any ten-year-old had a right to have.

''It had to be the water,'' she whispered. ''You and your father drank from it, did you not?''

Niyol's spirit had haunted her, so she pinned his ghost under an alder wood cross, just like she had Judzyas.

A breeze rustled the branches of her five oaks. Upon the wind was a song, a nursery rhyme. Someone was in her garden. She recognized the smooth liquidity of the voice. Paloma.

Raja cleared the pool and her mind. Paloma was a child (much like she was before she spoke to her first Himalayan spirits). She had a spark of power; she saw and heard things outside the normal realms, and had the natural grace of an angel. She belonged to a group of Dianic Wiccans in Seco County. They were well-meaning people, but they could not help her when her powers matured. Raja joined their circle and took Paloma under her wing. There had been more than friendship between them at first, but that had faded. Now there were only hard lessons in witchcraft.

''Mistress?'' Paloma brushed aside the ferns beyond the Shrine of the Five Trees.

''Come,'' Raja said. Paloma knew the circle of protection would not be broken if she stepped across. The trees liked her. She merely asked for politeness's sake. Raja liked that about Paloma. Polite.

She knelt next to Raja, gathering her denim skirt so it would not touch the water.

''We have much to do today. Is your mind clear?''

''Yes, Mistress.'' She gazed into the black water mirror and frowned.

''Then why can you not see past your own reflection this afternoon?''

''It . . . my mind, I mean . . . it's not clear. I met someone, and I can't stop thinking about him.''

Raja sighed and examined her apprentice. Her dark hair obscured her eyes, and she nervously twisted the lace fringes of her skirt. Indeed, a child, thought Raja. ''Very well. Why don't you show me this man? We shall use your lust to our advantage. It will polarize your thoughts.''

She blushed. ''Yes, Mistress.'' Her long fingers touched the water; circles expanded, crossed one another, and Larry materialized, checking into the Silver Bullet Bed & Breakfast.

Raja thought he was rather plain. Part Asian, acne scars, wrinkled clothing, and an unremarkable body. What was remarkable, what Paloma undoubtedly saw too, were the flares of energy that crowned his head. There were shots of silver and streaks of dark green that reminded her of imperial jade.

''Aren't they spectacular?'' Paloma said. ''I could watch his colors for hours if he'd let me.''

''His name?''

''Larry. Larry Ngitis.''

He had the sight, the third eye like Sonopous had. Raja saw the pattern of his mind. It suffused the air with threads of colors and light. There were, however, two parts that ended abruptly—as if they had been sliced clean through. Those parts projected into the past, and possibly the future. Sonopous, who only had one such eye, said the Oracle of Delphi had two, one looking back, the other forward. He told her that such prophets were exceedingly rare, and rarer still were the ones who survived. Most of them went mad.

This Larry was strong too. Not as strong as she . . . unless he was actively dampening his colors. It was impossible to tell.

''Show me more of Mister Ngitis.''

Paloma leaned forward to touch the water, but Raja set her hand upon her arm. Raja had spoken to the pool directly, not to Paloma. She would use her own power for this.

An inch of mist condensed upon the water, and through it Larry rode a white horse with hindquarters of dappled gray splotches.

A new image: a shadowy corner in the Three of Diamonds Bookstore, where Larry talked and sipped espresso. Raja could not see the man he sat next to, but she recognized his colors: Judzyas.

She waved her hand, and the fog dissipated. He had to be the prophet Judzyas had hunted. The two of them in the bookstore, was that the past or the future? The water was never specific about such things. She had killed Judzyas, hadn't she? He was slippery. He might find a way to wriggle free from the alder wood stake that pinned his soul to his dead body. She would send her ravens immediately to investigate.

As for Larry, he had the means to find what she wanted. At least, Judzyas had thought so. She would persuade Larry to help her. If he could not be persuaded, then he could be threatened. And if not threatened, then he could be killed. Raja would not allow him to take what she had waited so long for.

''Is something wrong?'' Paloma asked.

"No." Raja squeezed her hand to reassure her. "I am intrigued by your friend. I would like to meet him. Perhaps he would be willing to become my apprentice too? Would you like that, Paloma?"

"Apprenticed? Under you? I . . . I don't know."

Raja smiled. "Do not worry. I have nothing more than a professional interest in his abilities. He is yours. I promise you that. Tell me more of him."

"He had a Californian driver's license"—Paloma closed her eyes remembering—"home address in Oakland. And he's a science fiction writer. I bought his trilogy at the bookstore. It's good."

"A writer . . ." It was an unusual profession for a man with power. Perhaps he was not as skilled as she suspected. Or perhaps he was on the cusp of maturing. She could take advantage if that were the case. She could use his powers before he himself knew how to use them. "Is he better than our Robert Dolinski?"

"No. Poor Mister Dolinski. He's hardly buried and his place is sold." She paused to straighten her bone bead choker. "No, Larry's not better. He's different. More modern."

"I see."

"I got the impression that he is here for more than a visit."

"Why is that?"

"He looked . . . distracted last night, and this morning too. Not like a tourist."

Raja was silent a moment, then, "We must speak with Mister Ngitis . . . to Larry."

"How? He doesn't even know I exist. He's probably here to sign his books, and has hordes of fans waiting on him. Why would he talk to me?"

"We will throw a party. I shall invite the local writers and editors, and some people from New York. He will come. You will make him come, Paloma. Smile at him that special way. Tell him what he wants to hear. You know how."

Paloma shook her head. "It's different. I can't read him." She knit her brow. "That's what makes him so interesting."

"You will try," Raja suggested in a tone that was not a suggestion.

Paloma sighed, "Yes, Mistress."

"As soon as you have spoken with him, call me. We shall continue our divination lesson later. Now go. Your concentration is ruined for today."

Paloma rose, bowed to her, and left the circle.

Indeed she is a child—perhaps too innocent for this business, despite her natural abilities.

Raja snuffed the beeswax candles, then left her Shrine of the Five Trees. She walked to the edge of her property. Waiting for her, perched in the branches of a cottonwood, and scrutinizing her with their yellow eyes, were her ravens, Soot and Jim.

"Go to the black tower," she told them, "Dolinski's tower. Look for a man in the highest chamber. He should be dead. Make certain."

A flurry of dark feathers and caws and they were gone.

Raja then went into her house, grabbed a phone, and wandered back to the meadow. She settled under a weeping willow and called the Three of Diamonds Bookstore.

"Henry? It's Raja. Yes, fine thank you. How are the little ones? Good. I need to know if you have an author by the name of Ngitis in stock. N-G-I-T-I-S. Yes, I can wait."

A pair of moths, wings the color of sulfur, alighted on her toes. They trembled in the breeze, then took to the air again.

"You have it? Just the second in the trilogy? Could you send it over please? And the publisher? Perspective? Thanks a million, Henry. My love to the children. Oh, one more thing. I'm having a party tomorrow night. Could you invite the usual crowd for me? And give the people at *The New Yorker* a call? Yes." She laughed. "Thanks again. OK. Bye."

She dialed Manhattan next.

"Ms. Anumati for Mister Jacob. No. You may not put me on hold. Hello, Walter? Raja. Wait one moment please." She punched the scramble option on her phone. A layer of static buzzed through the connection.

"I have secured my end, please do the same."

A second layer of static blanketed their call.

"I wish to purchase a substantial amount of stock. You will want to cancel your other appointments. Yes. Find the corporation that has Perspective. Yes. Perspective. They publish books. Science fiction. No, I do not care what you think. I want it. Hello? Buy as large a block as possible. Everything they have on the open market. I don't care. Move some gold from Zurich if you have to. And stop complaining. It's not your money. Now get on it. I want the preliminary papers faxed this afternoon. Fly out tomorrow and we'll finalize it. Yes. My love to Jenny. Bye.''

She knew Walter Jacob stole from her. She let him. He was worth it. Capable lawyers were hard to find. Besides, he was fun at parties, and rather handsome. Raja wondered just how married he was to Jenny, then dismissed the thought. She had to deal with Larry Ngitis first.

Owning Perspective was just the beginning. Raja had charms both celestial and earthly, and threats not only to Larry's career, but his family and friends if he proved difficult. She would have his help one way or another.

Indeed, they would have much to discuss tomorrow evening.

Chapter 5

LARRY WAS INSANE.

Only the deranged saw visions of dead kids on the road, and dead cowboys on their beds—wearing boots, a Stetson, and flannel long johns. The light looked strange too. The brilliant New Mexico sun shot through the slats of the window and crystallized into rainbows. It looked solid—clear at the same time—like glass.

Madness. Had to be. He'd been losing his mind since he left Linda. That was the only logical explanation.

He closed his eyes and wished it would vanish, wished he had never left Oakland, wished this was a dream.

Larry opened his eyes. The cowboy still sat on his bed. Bile rose in the back of his throat. He would have thrown up had there been anything left in his stomach.

"You tryin' to say something, son?"

"You . . . you're Matt Carlson?"

"Yep."

Larry got dizzy like he had in the street. His mouth went dry. He whispered, "You're dead?"

"Deader than a can of corned beef. Old Johnny Law and his Texas Rangers came up here. Shot me thirteen times." Matt pointed at the mattress with both his index fingers like tiny guns. "Got me catawamptiously chawed up. At least, that's what it sez on that there fancy brass plate.''

''Don't you know?''

''Nope. I was drunker than a snake in a bottle o' piss. Just sounded like more thunder to me.'' Matt leaned forward and whispered, ''Lots o' thunder and lightning in these parts.''

Larry wanted to faint. He tried to scream, but all that came out was a wheeze. ''You-you-you said this was your room? How? Why are you here?''

''I'm gonna help ya,'' he said, and narrowed his eyes, ''and yer gonna help me. Yer goin' through a change. A change that can kill ya.''

''I don't understand this. I don't believe this. I don't believe in you. Go away.'' Larry flailed at the air, hoping it would dispel the ghost.

''Believin' ain't got nothing to do with it.'' Matt gave Larry a careful looking over, then, ''Yer part Chinaman. Is that why yer so thickheaded?''

The colors streaming through the slats in the window vibrated. Green tore apart like taffy stretched too thin. It left a residue of yellow and blue staining the air. The orange crackled, then shattered into fragments of red and yellow. Purple separated into transparent blue and red, oil and water.

''Yer losin' yer colors,'' Matt said, and stood. ''Yer drifting all over the place. That's bad. Ya gotta get a grip or I'm gonna lose ya altogether!''

''Get a grip? I've lost my mind. There's nothing left to grip. I'm seeing ghosts.'' He tried to laugh, but his windpipe constricted in panic. ''I'm talking to ghosts. I'm hallucinating. I'm—''

''Yer makin' more racket than a Sharp's rifle is what yer doing. Now listen to me. Ya ain't loony. And the things yer seein' ain't no hallucinations. They're real.''

''How come I've never seen them before?''

''I dunno.'' He twisted the end of his limp mustache. ''I ain't no sorcerer. I ain't no shaman. I ain't no witchy-girl. I'm just a plain ol' ghost tryin' to get ya outta this. All I know is that the living ain't supposed to see this stuff, but fer those of ya that can, the change comes on real sudden. Ya get me?''

''No. I don't.'' Larry stood. He tried to. The floor was sticky. It adhered to his skin, stretched along with him like rubber, then pulled him back down.

"Help me," he pleaded. "Make it stop."

"Yer goin' fast, son. Yer fadin' from where I can see ya. Ya gotta listen. The only one who can make this stop is you."

Larry struggled against the floor, but it held fast. This had to be a psychotic episode. He had to remain calm until the paramedics got here. And if it wasn't . . . if it wasn't, then he had to figure out what the hell was going on. "OK," he whispered, "I'm listening."

"There are other places 'round the ones normal folk live in, places they can't see, or they plumb refuse to believe what they're seein'. Get me?"

"No."

"Well, pretend that ya do. These places wrap 'round ya like a ball o' tangled yarn."

"You're talking about parallel universes? Higher dimensions? That's crazy."

"Now don't go and get uppity on me. Suits me just fine if ya want to dig yer own grave." Matt turned his back to him.

Larry would have laughed at the button flap in Matt's underwear, but an ice pick slammed through his skull, molten hot. "I'm sorry, Mister Carlson." He held one hand to his forehead. "I didn't mean it. My head is splitting apart. I can't think."

Matt spun around. "Don't call me 'Mister.' That's what decent folk get called. I was never decent to no one. It's what lawmen and lawyers and judges call ya just before they string ya up. I'm Matt. Plain ol' Matt Carlson, get it?"

The colors flooding the room dimmed, then stretched thin and creaked; they made the pinging noise of hot metal cooling.

"That's a bad sign there, Larry. Yer losin' the last of yer colors. That's real bad."

"Losing? What do you mean?"

"You don't want to know. In those layers 'round ya that normal folk can't see there's all sorta strange things, ghosts, like myself, lots of Navajo spirits in these parts too. And things get plain stranger the farther you drift from where ya started. Get it?"

Larry closed his eyes. He wanted to organize his thoughts, but closing his eyes only made the room spin. "Ghosts," he repeated. "Spirits. Stranger the farther you go out. Got it, Matt. Loud and clear."

"Good. I thought ya was touched there fer a second."

Larry remembered the brass plaque, remembered that Matt Carlson was a killer, someone who stole and raped and murdered a century ago. You didn't trust a man like that, living or dead. "Why are you helping me? What's in this for you?"

"I'm agettin' to that part," he said. "First, we gotta get ya back where ya belong or nobody's gonna be helpin' no one. Now listen, this ain't no made up thing in yer mind. What yer seein' is real—least, I reckon it's real where you are. That can get right problematical at times. Mostly, the things out there are friendly like, but once in a blue moon ya run 'cross something ya wish ya hadn't. Things that'll take yer mind."

The light that remained, the red, blue, and yellow pieces of fractured sunlight unraveled. Threads of illumination tangled, pulled, and snapped.

Matt threw his Stetson on the floor. "Now yer in a heap of trouble."

What was left, what made up those primary colors, wasn't white light, it was something Larry had never seen. His mind refused to process what it was. It was unrecognizable, a color missing in nature. Yet, at the same time, he recognized every color he had ever seen, swimming in its chromatic depths. His eyes watered. The color drew him in. It was entrancing. It was horrifying.

"Son? I can't see ya. Can ya hear me? Give a shout!"

"I don't want to see anymore. How do I stop?"

"They ain't never gonna stop. Even after yer dead they won't stop bein' there. But ya can get ahold of 'em."

Larry couldn't pull his gaze away from the color. He did, however, make it go out of focus. He tried rolling his eyes back in his head. It distracted him from the unfathomable. "What do I do? I can't keep this up for long. I can't stop watching."

"Don't try and not look. Lookin's the key. But ya gotta focus. It's like when yer eyein' somethin' smack in front of yer face. Ya can't see the other stuff beyond. That's what it's like fer normal folk."

"And I'm focused on another dimension? Farther out?"

"Dead straight. We gotta get ya back to where yer focusin' in front of yer face again."

"How?"

"Ya can't let yer imagination run wild with ya. No daydreamin'. All that nonsense just gets ya farther out."

Larry remembered the suite: the adobe fireplace built into the corner of the room, the smoke stains that curled along the wall up to the split timber ceiling, and the thick Navajo rugs on white pine floors.

The unknown color faded.

The suite did not reappear. Larry floated through space; stars peppered the black background, and galaxies spun silently about him. He panicked, then realized he was breathing normally. He was warm. There were voices in the vacuum: whispers and an alien music.

''I think yer closer,'' he heard Matt say. ''Try to remember yer breathin'. That might work.''

Larry's heart pounded. He concentrated on his breath, in and out, slowed the rhythm, deep and full.

The stars came closer. Thousands more, millions. They became the sky, solid radiance, save a handful of scattered dark dots. These points of darkness wore halos of white brighter than anything Larry had seen. Along the edge were convection rolls, curls and vortices, whirlpools that collided and shattered, spinning, mixing pure energy. It had to be a black hole. He had researched them for his trilogy. Would it be possible to travel inside one in this state? Go past the event horizon and come back? Now that would be something to write about. The temperature on the inner edge of the accretion disk was over a million degrees and charged with X-rays. Still, if he could breathe hard vacuum, then he might also be able to creep to the edge, take a peek, and—

Matt's voice was tiny. ''Tarnation, boy. Yer slipping again. Yer not payin' attention. Yer gonna get yerself into more trouble than if ya was tryin' to tie up a bobcat with a piece o' string.''

''I see stars,'' Larry shouted back.

''Ya gotta get yer mind to thinkin' of yer body and where ya belong. Pinch yer arm.''

Larry didn't see his body. He reached for where he thought his arm was and grabbed hard. ''I didn't feel anything.''

''Yer gonna need somethin' with a tad more bite to it. Ya got a girl?''

''Yes,'' Larry said. It was automatic. Three years with Linda. Three years and he thought he'd always have said yes. ''—No.''

''Well, we can use that pain too, son. Think about her.''

From the inside edge of the white-hot accretion disk, Larry saw the fire writhe, waver, and slip past the event horizon. Nothing could escape a black hole. The gravity was immense. Then again, he shouldn't be here either, breathing vacuum, or seeing any of this.

The fire settled into a vague shape. Cilia wriggling along its body, shivering sparks. It pinwheeled toward Larry.

It had to be light years away, yet it closed the distance between them at an alarming rate.

"Think of pain," Larry said to himself in a shaky voice. Linda was back in Oakland, probably sorting through the things he had left, deciding what to throw away and what to keep. He pushed that thought aside. He had left California to *not* think about her.

Paloma surfaced in his thoughts. He shouldn't dwell on her. It was too soon, he knew . . . too many sticky feelings had to be worked through first. He didn't want another relationship. Not now. Thinking of her came easily, though. She was back at the Silver Bullet, wearing a denim skirt, a bead choker, deep brown eyes, and wearing a crown of pink fire.

The stars faded. The suite reappeared.

There were more angles, particularly in the corners, as if another dimension had been added. He saw two bathrooms, three fireplaces, and counted sixteen corners. The door to the hall blurred. The west wall rotated. Larry looked up and down at the same time. He had vertigo even though his feet were firmly planted on the floor. The walls bulged toward him—a sudden flex—and every line bent away from him.

The fire from the black hole was there too, coiled and boiling in a corner that hadn't been there when Larry left. It oozed and spread through the air and across the floor, rippled over the rug, and went under the bed.

The thing smelled of molten copper. It hadn't set fire to the furniture yet, but Larry had the feeling that wouldn't apply to him. He had seen a supermarket tabloid last week: *Minister Spontaneously Combusts in Rectory. The Devil's Work?* Maybe he had seen this—and it him. The thing's heat, from across the room, made his skin redden.

"Matt," he whispered. "Something followed me."

"We'll get ya all the way back. Don't panic. I can't see ya yet, but I can hear ya real strong. Get to the fireplace."

Larry stepped to the side and blurred. He reappeared next to one of the bathrooms. The floor had stairs leading up, down, and sideways along the walls, paths that all seemed to spiral into the corners. He crawled to the fireplace.

"We best get ya some real pain, and fast. Grab them matches by the tinder."

Larry heard a faint knock at the door.

"I can see ya now," Matt cried. "Hot damn. Get a handful of those matches. They're blue tips. Strike 'em anywhere."

Larry fumbled with the box, slid it open, and got three matches before spilling the rest. He dragged them across the adobe. They flared to life: warm, clear fire, and the scent of sulfur. It was the only familiar thing in the room.

Another knock at the door . . . far away, like you might hear in a dream.

The fire that had crawled under the bed came out the other side. It paused, tendrils and vapors rubbing over the spot where Larry had sat. It stopped, then moved, fast, spinning and sputtering sparks across the floor, straight toward Larry.

"Quick, son. Grab 'em. Burn yerself."

Larry reached for the lit matches. He hardly felt their heat with the creature of fire so close; it was a bonfire, a furnace of boiling metal. His flannel shirt smoldered. The air became too scalding to breathe.

He smothered the matches.

Gone.

The temperature dropped. Larry was covered in sweat, and abruptly cold. The extra dimensions and the dizziness vanished. No strange colors. No alien music. No visions of galactic cores. No ghosts.

Larry dropped the matches. He held his burned hand. Three blisters flared in his palm.

Another knock at the door, then "Hello, Mister Ngitis? Larry? Are you there?"

It sounded like Paloma. "Just a second," Larry called out. He grabbed a piece of firewood and thrust it under the bed. It didn't burst into flames, and it encountered no resistance. He looked underneath. Nothing. Where had that thing gone?

He got dizzy and sat on the bed. His knees shook, so did his hands, and he smelled a smoky musk in the room. The light looked normal though; all the right colors were there, and no crazy angles. Had he dreamt it?

He braced himself against the wall, got up, and opened the door.

Paloma smiled at him. "We were worried about you, Mister Ngitis." She tentatively sniffed the air, then, "I hadn't seen you at breakfast, and no one had seen you in town for—"

The hallway lights were on, antique gas lamps, glowing red glass with velvet shades and matching tassels. It was before noon when Larry ran back here. How long had he slept?

"—Are you feeling well?"

Did psychotic qualify as "well"? "I caught a twenty-four hour bug," he said. "I'm better now. You caught me napping."

"I'm terribly sorry. I should let you get back to sleep."

Larry wanted her to stay. Her company would be welcome, especially now. He wanted to invite her in, or out to dinner, but he was so weak, and there were those dreams he had to sort through. "Yeah, maybe all I need is a good night's sleep."

His hand throbbed from the burn. He hadn't quite pieced together how that had happened.

"I'll send up some black bean soup from the kitchen, and let you rest." She turned, strode down the hall, stopped, and came back. "Oh, I came up here to invite you to a little get-together at a friend of mine's."

"That's nice, but I—"

"Since you were an author I thought you might want to come."

"No, I don't think—"

"All the local writers and artists will be there, editors, and a man from *The New Yorker*." She glanced to the space above Larry's head. "But if you're feeling ill . . ."

The insane don't make very good dates. That's what he wanted to say. But *The New Yorker*? Maybe they'd be doing interviews. He imagined his picture splashed on the inside cover. That would give his career a tremendous boost.

"What time were you leaving?" he asked.

"The party starts at nine, but we could go anytime you want. And if you feel bad just let me know. I'll drive you right back."

Larry already felt bad, but her smile steadied him. Women didn't smile at Larry the way she did, sweet, embarrassed, and something else he never saw in the smiles directed his way: lasciviousness.

From the foot of the stairs, a woman's voice called up: "Paloma? It's the pipes in the kitchen again. Should I call the plumber?"

Paloma sighed and shouted back, "No. Fetch my toolbox, Rosa, please. I'll see to it myself." She turned back to Larry. "I better see what's going on. Will you come with me this evening?"

His stomach twisted into a half hitch, both because of Paloma's enthusiasm and because of what he thought he had seen. "OK." The hand holding on to the doorframe, the one she couldn't see, trembled.

"You get your rest then. I'll send up that soup and check on you in a few hours."

"Thank you, Paloma." It was the first time he had used her name, and when she heard it her eyes lit up.

"My pleasure."

Larry retreated into the suite, closed the door, and collapsed on the bed. At least he hadn't seen anything strange about her this time. Maybe this was an acid flashback. He had dropped some in college—a decade ago. How long did it stay in your fatty tissues?

Sleep. That was the best thing right now. Sleep first, then he'd figure out what had happened. He closed his eyes.

He was thirsty, terribly so. He got up, had four glasses of water, then went back to bed. The blankets were warm. He slipped easily into sleep.

"I'm right glad you've taken to my bed. Firm, ain't it?"

Matt Carlson lay close enough to Larry so he could smell the whiskey on his breath.

Larry leapt out of the bed, and got tangled in the blankets. He crawled to the corner.

"Tarnation, boy. After what you been through, you'd think a plain ol' ghost wouldn't tickle ya. It must be that Chinaman blood makin' ya yellow."

"This is a dream," Larry said in a weak voice. "This isn't happening. I saw you when I ran up here. I must have passed out, or I hit my head. I dreamed you then, and I am asleep now, dreaming again."

"What about yer hand?"

Larry took a long look at it: heat blisters in the center of his palm. "I burned it sleepwalking."

"OK, smart Chinaman. Then how come it's six o'clock the day *after* ya came arunnin' up here?"

Larry examined his watch. It had frozen at four o'clock. "Watches stop all the time," he declared. "The battery must be . . . dead."

"Try that fancy book of yers." Matt pointed to Larry's laptop.

Larry plugged in the AC adapter and booted the system. The clock read 6:45, Tuesday, July 22. "I've lost a day," he whispered.

''The colors. Ya remember how they fell apart? Ya seen things that no man, sleepin' or not, has ever seen.''

Larry was going to argue, but the puzzling color stuck in his mind. It didn't fit into his universe, dream or real. He sat back on the bed, wrapped the blanket around himself, and curled into a fetal position. He just wanted everything to go away.

''Nothing makes sense. If it did happen, then where did that—that thing go? It followed me here. I saw it. The heat was so real.''

''It's like turning a piece o' paper sideways,'' Matt said. ''If it's thin enough, ya can hardly see it. To that critter yer so wadded up, and packed away—least from its perspective—it can't see ya.''

''Like a point in three dimensions?''

''Now yer gettin' it, Chinaman. Just like yer trin' to spot a speck o' dust. It fades in and out of focus. That's what yer like to that thing.''

''What are you then? Why can you see me?''

''I'm a ghost. And I've been stuck in this room since I died.''

''You're stuck here? I thought when you died you—''

''Ya thought what? Ya go to Heaven? Or Hell? Or there ain't no afterlife? Well, I can't speak 'bout no Heaven. But I sure can tell ya that I'm here, and I'm dead. Stuck where I was gunned down. Can't explain it. Just is.''

''For over a hundred years,'' Larry added.

''Yep. Tain't so bad. I pass the time. The folk that come up here once in a blue moon bring newspapers or books. I read as much as I can, but unless they turn the pages all I can see is whatever's layin' face up.''

''You read?''

''I was the only one in my gang with a spit's worth of brains. I did all the readin', the writin', and''—he winked—''the countin'.''

''My laptop. You read over my shoulder yesterday—the day before yesterday.''

Matt tipped his Stetson and nodded.

''Let's say that you're real,'' Larry said and uncurled himself, ''and I'm not dreaming. How come I don't see any more colors, or stars, or extra dimensions?''

''Ya got yerself a firm grip on reality, at least, son, this reality. That Miss Paloma, who came acallin' on ya, she's what brought yer feet back down on the ground, I reckon. But if ya want some advice, ya better watch out fer her. She's got power too.''

"Paloma can see these things?"

"Don't know 'bout that. But ya see the colors 'round her head? That's how ya tell a person with power."

Larry hadn't seen any light around Paloma this time. Whatever prophetic visions he had had, they were at best erratic, at worse, dementia.

"Ya gotta watch yerself around her. Gotta watch yerself 'round a lotta people in Dry Water. They're out to get ya, son."

"My name is Larry, not son." He went into the bathroom and turned on the faucet. The pipes rumbled, then air and rusty water sputtered out. "No wonder I'm so thirsty. I've been asleep for a day." Larry's stomach growled. "And hungry too."

"And weaker than a kitten. Don't go to that party. They'll be awatchin' ya. They might even bushwhack ya."

"Who are 'they'?"

"I shouldn't be tellin' you nothin.' " He crossed his arms. "Specially since ya don't even think I'm real. But there's a witch, and she's got her finger in every pie in town. Ya can bet that she's lookin' for you, her and her spirits. They're all over this territory."

"New Mexico is a state now," Larry said. "And how do you know all this? I thought you couldn't leave this room."

Matt looked at his boots, then, "That lets the cat out of the bag. I guess I oughta play it square with ya." He looked directly into Larry's eyes. Matt's were hazel, and bloodshot from a hangover a century long. "There's a shaman in these parts. He's been awatchin' ya too. He and I talk. He said I should keep an eye on ya."

"I don't think I want your eye on me."

"Now looky here, son. I ain't tryin' to hornswoggle ya."

"Why should I trust you?" Larry said. "You're an outlaw. You robbed and killed people."

"I ain't denyin' what I did. And I ain't denyin' what I am. But I'm the only one in these parts who wants ya alive."

"Why?"

"Ya can see me. And ya got the means to get me outta this room."

"I'm not doing anything for you. How many did you murder and rape? You deserve to be locked in here. I'm going with Paloma to her party, and you can go to hell." Larry wasn't scared anymore, not of this ghost anyway.

''Yer walkin' into a den of rattlesnakes, ya thickheaded Chinaman.''

''Maybe. But I'm hungry, and there's going to be a man there from *The New Yorker*. I'd risk seeing a dozen ghosts and witches to be interviewed by him.''

Matt stomped around in a circle. His hands clenched and unclenched, then he faced Larry. ''OK, so yer gonna go. If ya don't take me, and ya start driftin' again, who's gonna talk ya back? No man or woman, with or without the sight, can go as far out as a dead man can. I was the only one who coulda got ya back when yer colors went. I'm the only one who's gonna save ya if somethin' else follows ya home.'' He paused, then, ''It'll be a worse death than I got, if ya get stuck out there.''

He didn't say anything else. He didn't have to. Larry knew he was right. Madness awaited him in those other dimensions. Things he could never understand, alien colors, and spaces—things he never *wanted* to understand.

''OK,'' Larry whispered. ''You can come.''

''Now yer thinkin' straight. This shaman friend of mine, he told me ya gotta get close to the way I died. That's the only way I can hitch a ride along with ya.''

''You want me to get shot thirteen times?''

''Nothin' like that. It's what he called 'sympathetic magic.' Ya gotta get one of the bullets that killed me into yer body.''

''First, I don't think lead inside my body is healthy. Second, you were killed over a hundred years ago. You want me to dig up your body? Cut it up and get the bullets?''

''It's a whole sight easier than yer thinkin'. If ya pull back this mattress, I'll show ya.''

Larry pulled the mattress off the bed, then the box spring.

''See that frame? Real oak. Old Shorty Wainwight he owned the Silver Bullet—only then it was called the Silver Star—and he was a cheap cuss. He had to throw away the mattress on account it was soaked with blood and other juices, but the frame he done kept. Now see there?'' Matt pointed to the corner of the headboard. ''That scar in the oak. That's one o' the slugs that got me.''

Larry tilted the lamp to get a better look. The wood had been splintered. Deep inside was a black chunk of metal. He tried to pry it out with his fingernail. It wouldn't budge.

''Use that fancy pick ya got in yer shavin' stuff,'' Matt suggested.

Larry got a nail file from his shaving kit. He wondered just how closely Matt had been watching him. Had he seen him in the shower? On the toilet?

He used the file to dislodge the metal. The tiny shred of solid black metal weighed no more than a paper clip.

''Doesn't look like lead,'' Larry remarked.

''It is. It's just old. Gets tarnished like silver does.''

''Now what do I do? Stick it in my pocket?''

''Well . . . not exactly, son. Ya gotta get it inside yer body. The way I see it ya got two choices. Ya can stick it in yer mouth. I think it's small enough so ya can bite down on it. That'll squish it into yer teeth real good.''

''Lead is toxic. I'm not putting it in my mouth. It gives you blue gums and damages your brain. What's the other way?''

''Ya can stick it up yer ass.''

''What!''

''Ya heard me. I seen lots of things in this room here. I seen those gloves ya guys stick on yer little fellows. Ya can wrap that slug up in one, then stick it on up there.''

Larry rolled the piece of lead between his fingers, wondering if Matt the too-friendly ghost was worth it.

''Tarnation, son. I've had to do worse things out on the trail. Don't be such a sissy.''

Larry smiled at Paloma across the crowded ballroom. She was by the bar, her back to the atrium. Larry was stuffed into the corner by the library. He listened with half an ear to a writer named O'Donald. He scanned the crowd for the man from *The New Yorker*.

O'Donald stepped away from his wife, closer to Larry, and whispered, ''Can you believe my agent suggested I put a dinosaur in my magic realism novella? Said it would sell better. Science fiction is no longer a bastion for ideas. It's pure pop culture.''

Larry smelled gunpowder on O'Donald's breath, and for a split second saw his face as a mass of blood and raw tissue—then normal.

''This puke has more wind than Missouri,'' Matt muttered, and peered down O'Donald's wife's dress. He still only had his long underwear, Stetson, and boots on.

Larry sipped his seltzer, then clamped down on the lead wedged in his back molar. It wouldn't sit tight no matter how hard he bit. He was afraid he'd swallow it. He was afraid it would cause him brain damage. By the time he passed that bullet he knew he'd lose a dozen IQ points.

He had been careful at the hors d'oeuvre table, but the first rumake almost took the bullet along with it. He hadn't eaten a thing since. If not for the soup Paloma had sent up to his suite earlier, he would have starved.

''Do you know Ms. Anumati?'' O'Donald asked.

''No,'' Larry replied without looking at him. ''Should I?''

''Ms. Anumati.'' Matt hissed, then spat. ''She's the witch I told ya 'bout.''

''Without her,'' O'Donald said, ''many of us in Seco County . . . no, most of us, would not be writers. She treats her favorites very well. You should talk to her, tell her about your trilogy.''

''She throws a nice party.''

''Oh, I don't mean the party. I mean money.''

Larry stopped looking for the man from *The New Yorker*.

''Martiniez over there won a grant from the MacArthur Foundation last year. Rumor has it that was Ms. Anumati's doing. And there have been several gifts. Cash gifts, if you get my meaning, Mister Ngitis.''

''If she likes your work,'' his wife chimed in, ''and if she likes you, then things happen. You get noticed. Editors call you.''

''I thought you had to see that fellow from New York City,'' Matt said. ''Find 'em. Speak yer piece, and let's vamoose. I'm gettin' a bad feelin'.''

Larry wanted to hear more about Ms. Anumati, but he too had a bad feeling, a feeling of being watched.

He excused himself from O'Donald and drifted to the spot he had last seen Paloma. He wanted to leave. He wasn't going to find the man from *The New Yorker* in this crowd. But that wasn't the real reason he wanted to get back to the Silver Bullet. He needed to write. The images of the unknown color, the black hole, and the creature from the other dimension were fresh in his mind. He had to get them recorded or lose them. They were perfect for his book, precisely what he needed to get back on track.

Above the crowd Larry spotted a flash of color, pink fire, Paloma.

''Larry,'' Paloma said, and wrapped her arm through his. His skin was clammy. Her skin was warm. She wore a little black dress, dark stockings, and high heels. Ethereal flames the color of peach blossoms flickered in her auburn hair.

''Watch yerself, son,'' Matt whispered, and pointed up to the chandelier. ''We got company.'' Perched in the lead crystal ornamentation were two crows. One cocked his head and examined every person below. The other rested its yellow gaze on Larry.

Didn't anyone else see them? Two crows, soot black against all that light? Maybe not. And if Larry and Matt were the only ones to notice them, maybe they were ghosts, or something worse.

''Come,'' Paloma said, and pulled him toward the atrium. ''There's someone you have to meet.''

''Can we leave soon?'' Larry said.

''Of course. Are you feeling sick?'' She set her hand on his forehead and frowned. ''I'll get the car as soon as we've said hello to our hostess. Then we can get you back into bed.''

Paloma dragged him across the ballroom, smiling at everyone, waving to authors Larry recognized from their dust jackets.

Matt followed, saying, ''I got yer back covered, son. I wish ya listened to me and got yerself a pistol back in town.''

At the south end of the ballroom, the marble tile was replaced by terra cotta, the chandelier by arched glass ceiling panels that revealed a million stars in the night sky. There were rows of planters filled with night-blooming jasmine and cactus with pale yellow blooms. Palm trees towered above Larry, brushing the glass roof. It was a desert oasis.

Sitting next to the jasmine in a rattan throne was a woman. She was regal and poised and watching him. Green fire crowned her head. Unlike the pink flames that he had seen on Paloma, this was a blast furnace; the heat made Larry flinch.

Circling her were crows, hundreds of tiny crows that danced and cavorted in the thermal currents above her head, flying through the glass, through the floor, even through the woman. Larry saw nymphs peering from behind their palm trees at him.

''Good evening, Mister Ngitis,'' the woman said.

Larry felt a compulsion to kneel before her.

''Straighten out yer backbone, son,'' Matt whispered.

''Ms. Anumati?'' Larry stammered.

She stood and held out her hand. Fire flickered in between her fingers. ''Call me Raja.''

Chapter 6

PAIN, SHARP AND SUDDEN. NICK'S HEART SEIZED—BURNING AND GUSHING warmth. A long life flashed before his eyes, a thousand places and lovers and enemies, then he died.

It hadn't been the first time.

The usual ebb and flow of death in the netherealms did not touch him. He tried to slip down and away, but could not. He floated, helpless, between the realm of the living and the dead. His aura was nonexistent. Shadows smothered him, velvet to the touch. He screamed. The blackness absorbed the sound.

He chanted Seneca's Unearthly Plea:

> "I summon the spirits of the dead and thee who rulest the spirits of the dead and he who guards the barriers of the stream of Lethe: and I repeat the magic and wildly, with frenzied lips, I chant a conjuration to appease or compel the fluttering ghosts."

His invocation went unanswered. There was no magic. No power. Nothing.

He had to concentrate to remain aware in this emptiness. How long had he been here? Moments? Days? Forever? Terror crystallized within

Nick. It could not end like this. He grabbed at the void, shouted into the oblivion. Useless. Logic was his only tool remaining. He had to think.

He remembered that last moment with Raja had been bliss. Their energies intertwined, ecstatic radiance, then she lunged—a flash of wood, glowing, the taste of blood.

His blood. Betrayed.

He had not thought her capable of such viciousness. A warning, yes. A threat, perhaps. But not butchery. Time had been his mistake. He had known Raja two hundred years ago. To him two centuries was fleeting. Wars, disease, progress, and change, he had seen them countless times before, and remained unaltered. He had assumed it was the same for her. She was young, however, and still susceptible to the world and its evolutions.

Sleep came for Nick, but he resisted. That would be the end. It was not sleep in this blackness; it was not even death. It was nothingness.

Seven runes blazed on Raja's alder wood stake; they burned in his memory, impaled upon his soul. Perhaps there was a flaw in the enchantment he could exploit. Three were runes of power: the sharp square edges of *Confinement,* the lacy spiral patterns of *Oblivion,* and the mosaic seven-sided tiles of *The Castle*. The next three were fairy magic, which he understood poorly: the silver filigree of *Arachne's Web,* the boiling pink and chartreuse and lavender fractals that were the *Jester's Chaos,* and the disappearing, reappearing smile of the *Cheshire Cat's Disvanishment*. The last rune was darkness cloaked in shadows: *Eclipse*.

It was a shrewd piece of magic.

He drifted, weakened, dissolved. Time passed—or no time at all—he could not discern, then a faint voice, "Master?"

"Here!" he cried. "I am here. I exist!"

There was no reply. Had he dreamed the voice? Had he gone insane?

"Master?" the voice said again, stronger. It was Dempsey.

"Yes."

"Is that you? I can barely hear you."

"Do not leave me, Dempsey, but come no closer. The bewitchment that has trapped me has the power to imprison you as well."

Nick considered his next words carefully. There was a mystical bond that held Dempsey here, but not to him. If the ghost discovered what it was he could leave. "Do you recall where I found you, Dempsey? Trapped in the auxiliary generator that took your life? Spinning two thousand times per second? Caged by sparks and copper wire? Do you recall?''

''Yes, my Master. I do.''

''Now I am the one trapped. I require your help.''

There was a moment of hesitation so long that Nick thought Dempsey had left, then, ''I shall help you, Great One. But I want something.''

Nick was in no position to bargain. ''I'm listening.''

''Magic. Teach me to capture and bind spirits, to tap them for their powers as you do, and . . . and how to release them.''

''This I shall do, Dempsey. I give you my word. Now, tell me what you see.''

''The Italian we obtained in Venice is dead. A stake has been thrust into his chest.''

''Is anyone else present?''

''No, but there were others here. After you dismissed me, I waited a day, then became worried why you had no further orders. I found the body in the tower's study. There were crows here, hundreds of crows. Some flew in through the open balcony doors, but two, I saw them fly through the walls. They didn't see me. I hid in a lightbulb. They have done terrible things to the body—picked the bones clean.''

Ravens and crows were sacred spirits in all the Indian legends he knew. Had Raja captured them from the Navajos in the region? Or had she aligned herself with them? On the other hand, European witches routinely used birds as familiars. Whatever they were, and however she got them, it was one more thing she controlled in Seco County. It was one more ally for her and the prophet, and one more enemy for Nick.

''You must remove the stake, Dempsey.''

''I am without form, Master. I cannot.''

''You have the power. Gather clouds. Call the lightning. Destroy it.''

''I do not know how. You must give me the power.''

''The tie that binds us has loosened, Dempsey. This has several consequences, one of which is that you no longer require my power to control the electrical forces you know so well. You must do this for me or I shall perish.''

''Will not the lightning touch you as well? Your essence?''

"I am dead. It cannot touch me."

Nick, however, was not entirely certain about that.

* * *

Haze appeared in the sunny sky over Seven Horseshoe Ridge.

The tourists on the wooden sidewalk of Agua de Viva Road grew thirsty and licked their chapped lips. In the Silver Bullet's kitchen, Paloma tinkered with the pipes, searching for a clog, and found nothing. The stream in Lost Silver Canyon slowed and turned to silt. Mud coagulated.

The mist that had been translucent at nine in the morning solidified to an iron gray mass by noon. It blocked the sun. The winds howled, but could not disperse the condensing vapors; they revolved in place, drew tighter and tighter, increasing density, until it was a whirlpool that towered a thousand feet high, utterly opaque and black, a thunderhead, Cumulo Nimbus Ominous.

Dempsey plundered the moisture from the earth. He summoned clouds from the Rocky Mountains, marshaled them into an orderly array, then piled them atop one another. He had never known such power.

He could wash the grime from New York skyscrapers, or shower the drought-ridden plains of Kansas, or bring cool summer sprinkles to San Francisco. First, though, he had to free his master.

He checked the flowchart on his clipboard: separate charge, increase voltage, consult the dielectric breakdown table, then filamentous cascade. Dempsey laughed and threw the clipboard away. The papers whirled through the air, white birds on the wing.

He whispered to the clouds and instructed them to brush against one another. He milked them of their charge—a handful of electrons slipped through his grasp—heat lightning flashed and lit the thunderhead inside.

He beckoned to the local dust devils. They came to him, screeching at one another, and poked the clouds with their pitchforks, agitating the storm to a boil.

Dempsey licked his lips and savored the ozone taste. Below, he sensed the opposite charge building, aching to be released, accumulating in the highest point, the tip of the black tower. Any discharge would strike the metal rebar reinforcement. It would never go through the open balcony door nor hit the stake that held the Great One. He would have to guide it himself.

His thunderhead turned toward the tower, attracted to the opposite charge building there.

He could hold it no longer. The lightning began its trickle cascade through the atmosphere. Fingers of electricity probed and pulled and ionized the air.

A connection.

Dempsey flashed downward, a blur of energy that stretched jagged across a mile of sky.

The leading tendrils of charge had already attached to the tower's metal structure, searching for the cool countercharge in the ground, pulsing with the return stroke. He created a shunt.

Pain burned along the edges of his soul as he forced the brilliant river to alter course. It overflowed, choppy with one hundred million volts. He struggled not to be swept aside.

Through the balcony doors he crashed, melting, exploding the wood and glass and stone in his way, setting ablaze paper and cloth, and detonating the air. He accelerated toward the stake, attracted to the enchantment. It drew him into a dark vortex. It captured the lightning as well.

The alder wood didn't have time to burn. It charred to ash. It flashed, vaporized, and left Raja's enchantment glowing by itself in the air for a split second.

Thunder shattered everything.

Nick was disoriented. The lightning had shattered him as well and expelled his soul deep into the netherealms. There was no up or down that he could sense. The space was filled with creatures and shadows that defied characterization. He had never been so far from the world of light. There was movement next to him, creatures compressed upon one another, slithering like layers of oil, touching him.

To orient himself, he incanted: ''Dreadful in aspect are they, their forms in appearance fantastic. I will that the demons shall once again become angels, whence to their nameless distortion I speak, never fearing: I shall impose my will for a law upon them.''

There was sound and power. His magic made him shoot up like a diver desperate for air. Up through the suffocating layers of death and madness, through murders, and fatal accidents, through the rippling echoes of gunshots, the stretching of a lynch mob's rope, and the quiet sobs of a thousand funerals.

He knew these layers of pain, for they were close to the surface. Among them he sensed another presence in his tower: a suicide. Nick came as close to the world of light as he could. He could not cross over, however. For that, he would require a new body.

He was outside. The rain passed through him. He could not feel the wet sandy earth beneath him, nor smell the mesquite or lechuguilla or purple sage that crowded the hills.

Nick drifted to his tower. Mail had been stuffed through the slot in the front door, and spilled into a mound on the other side. Junk all: expired coupons for pizza deliveries, credit card applications, and subscriptions to magazines. One flier caught his eye—from the Church of the New Age. Father Woberty and classes on the healing properties of crystals. A toll free number to call. Only major credit cards accepted. Perfect.

He floated upstairs, pausing in the doorway of the library. Faint letters hovered over the spare Underwood in the corner. Commas performed somersaults (some paired to make distorted yin-yangs); semicolons scooped up periods and flung them into distant orbits; an exclamation mark danced wildly, bouncing off the collection of murmuring consonants and vowels; and a question mark cowered, hiding in the keys. A man had died here—these visions were echoes of his life. It intrigued Nick, but he continued up. There were more urgent matters to attend to.

The study was in ruins. The lovely stained glass roof was gone. The books were ashes and scattered bits of paper. The Franklin stove was a twisted lump. Nothing remained of the Italian body he had worn. Nick did, however, spot the copper wire that had wound about his pinkie. It had spattered on the far wall, a solidified droplet of metal. Neither Raja nor her crows had taken it. That was good.

Dempsey stood on the balcony. "Great One? You survived?" Electricity crawled across Dempsey's skin. His hair stood on end, blazing white, and his eyes were wheels of sparks.

"Of course I survived. And I am in your debt."

"You saved me from that generator. I saved you from whatever it was that held your essence. We are even."

They watched the storm. Lightning touched the distant mountains. Veils of rain shrouded the valleys and made the red earth dark. Thunder rumbled low and long. Nick shuddered because he knew what it was like to be close to the thunder and have it whisper to your soul.

"I have not forgotten our arrangement," Nick said. "I shall honor it and teach you necromancy."

"I think I'd like that," Dempsey said with a voice full of static. He smiled, but he had no teeth, only arcs of current.

"But I require one more thing. I need you to tap into the phone lines. I need you to give me a voice."

Father Woberty bumped along the gravel road, up Seven Horseshoe Ridge in his Range Rover. He had debated if he should have taken the Rover rather than the church's Ford pickup. He wanted to make a good impression on Nick, but he had no desire to appear ostentatious.

This Nick character sounded sick on the phone. It could have been a poor connection, or perhaps he was asthmatic, or possibly he had tuberculosis. TB would be better, because the terminally ill always gave more. Father Woberty expected a large donation. Nick wanted to see him in person. What else could he have meant?

He heard that the Dolinski Tower had been purchased with cash. Father Woberty needed cash—not for his Church of the New Age—that made a tidy profit all by itself. He had other religious projects.

He rounded the final switchback, shooting gravel and wet red mud over the embankment with his rear tires, then rolled across the cobblestone driveway of the black tower. Dolinski had been wealthy, but he never gave a cent to the church. Father Woberty had tried to engage him in discussions of theology. Dolinski refused. He said there was no God—at least, he had never met him. Blasphemy. Father Woberty was glad he was dead. Too many atheist writers in Dry Water.

It was clear and cold on top of the ridge, an island surrounded by clouds and fog left over from the morning's storm. It smelled clean. From the distant mountains thunder rumbled.

Father Woberty grabbed his briefcase and zipped his parka snug around his throat.

The front door was twice his height, pointed at the top, with sixteen panels of thick black walnut.

A coiled Chinese dragon served as the knocker, so polished Father Woberty swore it sparkled in the shadows. Dolinski had a sense for the fantastic. Too bad he had squandered his wealth on this foolishness. There was a canto in Hell reserved for such extravagant wasters.

Father Woberty noticed the heap of wet newspapers on the stoop. Strange that they hadn't been cleaned up. Perhaps Nick had just moved in and not had time. He made a fist and knocked twice, hard. The thick wood absorbed the sound. He waited. Nothing.

''Damn Dolinski and his door.''

He reached for the knocker.

The dragon bit him. A flash and sparks. Ten thousand volts.

Nick flexed his new hand. It had been burned and scarred with the reverse imprint of dragon scales. This, however, was not the only wound on the late Father's body. A careful examination revealed crisscross scars across his back, precise incisions along his penis, welts on his inner thigh, and countless bruises. From the pattern of the injuries he believed them to be self-inflicted. They were everywhere save his hands and face.

Nick did not approve of his new features. They were too thin, pale, and long. He was ugly.

He spread Father Woberty's possessions out on the study's floor: a driver's license, social security card, credit cards, cash, and legal documents for the disbursement of monies to the Church of the New Age, but no pictures of family or lovers. That was good. If Nick was going to use this body in the community, the fewer close to Woberty the better.

One card had been tucked beneath a secret flap in his wallet. Embossed upon it was a crucifix wrapped in barbed wire. The image repulsed Nick. The juxtaposed symbols were simultaneously familiar and alien to him. He ran his finger over the silver embossing and detected no magic.

''Again, thank you, Dempsey. I will continue my search for the prophet.''

Dempsey turned from the balcony's view. A flurry of sparks shook off his body, and circled him like tiny fireflies. ''You're welcome, but it wasn't for free. I want more power. I want you to teach me necromancy.''

''I have not forgotten.'' Nick ran his new hands along the rough volcanic stone walls of the study.

''What is it you seek?'' Dempsey inquired.

''You have grown powerful in my absence,'' Nick replied without answering him.

''It is ecstasy,'' Dempsey said, and looked out to the clouds and sky.

''It will not last.''

He spun about. ''What?''

''You are dead, Dempsey. Your power will fade. You can be as a god here only for a short while. In the end, though, your spiritous nature will betray you. You will sink into the netherealms, and be one among many as powerful as you.''

''Lies,'' Dempsey said. Blue Saint Elmo's fire outlined his body. ''I can stay. I served you for decades. I never sank into the netherealms.''

''I bound you to this world.'' Nick found the copper, a drop of spattered metal on the rock, and he pried it loose. ''The price was a reduction of your powers.''

''There must be another way.''

''There is.''

''Show me. I control the clouds and the lightning. I can bring rain, or snow, or warm winds to the Arctic. I want to stay.''

He held the bit of metal out for Dempsey to inspect. ''This is the key.''

The ghost drifted closer. ''How can a piece of metal help?''

''It is not just any metal. It was a piece of wire that wound through a generator, the one that electrocuted you, the one that snared your soul.''

Dempsey floated back. ''It can keep my essence here?''

''It held your soul before.'' Nick took two steps closer to Dempsey. ''It overlapped its electrons with your spiritous matter, trapped you within its conductive energy bands.''

''I don't underst—''

Nick thrust his hand into the ghost.

Dempsey screamed and clawed at Nick, sending arcs of electricity crawling across his skin. Current jumped through Nick's heart, then found the copper in his hand and was grounded.

The ghost shrank and spun, accelerated, whirling two thousand times per second. With one long fading shriek he vanished.

Nick kept his fist clenched tight about the metal while the ghost bonded to the copper. The light was intense. It made his flesh glow pink.

''It held your soul once. Now it does so again, my Dempsey.''

The copper globule buzzed angrily in his hand, stopped, then let out a low lamenting vibration, which faded to silence.

Nick hadn't lied; ghosts did vanish. The tides of death were strong and forever pulling spirits deeper. There were only two things that kept ghosts in this world: an enchantment to capture their souls or their own pain.

Nick had had six captured ghosts when he arrived in Dry Water. He sensed none of them in his tower now. When he had died they departed. Nick needed servants. Fate was on his enemy's side, perhaps Raja as well. He required information. He had blithely assumed the prophet was the only one in Seco County with power. It was a mistake caused by his haste. But where to gather facts? Nick trusted no person. This was Raja's domain.

There was one being, however, that she could not influence: the ghost in the library. Raja's powers were attuned to life. She could not speak to the dead—at least, Nick hoped so. If she could, she might learn that he had not perished. No. Raja could no more speak to the dead than Nick could make things live and grow. It was an acceptable risk.

He went down the spiral steps to the library. There, he concentrated and listened and sensed the man's lingering death. There were echoes of paramedics, CPR, electrical shocks, and cardiac injections. They marked the time of death and listed the cause of his demise as heart failure, but Nick smelled the distinct scent of suicide, sharp and acrid among the rows of dusty bookshelves with their own stale papery scents.

Those who took their lives were powerful. Their pain and anguish often turned to hate when they discovered there was no peace in death. Nick would take precautions in his weakened state.

In the books he saw the man's lifethread—where it ended, where it turned ethereal, and where it led to. It wound through paperbacks, through the occasional leather-bound and gilt-edged volume, then curled through the yellowed pages of pulp. It meandered deep into the netherealms. It was curious. Most suicides dwelled in the means of their demise, remaining in the knife that cut them, or the gun that scrambled their brains. His books must have had a more profound effect upon him than his own death.

Nick removed the volumes and set them on the wool carpet. There were dozens of titles by Dolinski, science fiction and fantasy and horror novels with bright covers of spaceships and castles and mounted knights. There was Robert A. Heinlein and Edgar Rice Burroughs, Jules Verne and Isaac Asimov, C.S. Lewis and H.G. Wells. He spread them in a circle, then in the center he laid down five connecting lines, a pentagram of paperbacks.

He found a first edition Dolinski. Splashed on its cover was a warrior dispatching a creature that was a hybrid between giant alligator and anaconda. An anatomically improbable girl clung to the hero's shoulder for protection. Absurd. Nick tore the title page out and with a fountain pen wrote:

Dolinski
olinsk
lins
in

and set this in the center of the circle.

He whispered: ''Dolinski. Come. Come, Dolinski. The world of your birth calls to you. I summon you, and make my will into law that you manifest. Come.''

Nick repeated this chant in Arabic, then in Gaelic, and in Latin. He took the fountain pen and pricked his finger. Blood welled into the nib. He inscribed the square runes of *Confinement* at each point of the pentagram.

He chanted again. With every word his tingling connection to the netherealms strengthened, dove through the layers of death—then twisted suddenly, veered away, and revealed a place Nick had never seen. On the other side was a world with two suns, blue and red. A warm breeze from this place brought the scent of pine, the burbling of running water, and the calls of blue jays into the dark library. On the distant alien mountains, a glint caught his attention: a city of aquamarine with tall towers that diffracted the setting red sun and glowed purple.

Shadows spilled into the center of the pentagram. They oozed to the borders, repelled, then coalesced in the center. ''So few men speak Latin these days,'' it whispered. ''Such a shame. '*Lamque opus exegi, quod nec Iovis ira, nec ignis, Nec poterit ferrum, nec edax abolere vetustas.*' ''

Nick translated: '' 'And now I have finished the work, which neither the wrath of Jove, nor fire, nor the sword, nor devouring age shall be able to destroy.' I knew Ovid well, and I knew his *Remedia Amoris* that you quote.''

In the shadows sat a ninety-year-old man. His eyes were blue and clear, but his body, wrapped in a wool cardigan sweater, trembled. He was no ordinary suicide. Nick would not be deceived by this apparent fragility. Dolinski was from outside the netherealms.

"Where did you come from?" he asked the spirit.

"From? Ah, yes, the concept of locality. I am not from here." He squinted at the shelves of books, then pushed up his bifocals. "I recall this place. I had a life here once. Sad little life."

"You have cheated death. The netherealms do not pull at your soul. How?"

"What do you want?" Dolinski asked. "Am I dreaming? A nightmare of your boring lectures on your equally boring God, Woberty? Spare me the details."

"I am not Father Woberty. My name is Nick. I have only appropriated his shell for a time."

Dolinski took off his glasses and leaned closer. "Indeed. Well then, as one enlightened man to another, I shall answer your query, Mister Nick. The netherealms, as you call them, will never capture my soul. I have learned how to elude their attractions."

"The netherealms snare all souls," Nick declared. "You and I can only cheat death momentarily."

Dolinski laughed and ran his fingers through his thin white hair. It grew longer, and strands of the silver-gray turned black. "You are death, so I have no doubt that is what you believe. Your netherealms are only one in a collection of subspaces that overlap the mundane world. There are other places, and other realities, that are equally as potent."

He rubbed his eyes and smoothed away the wrinkles in their corners. "But you did not bring me here to discuss where I came from. Speak your piece, necromancer. *Absit invidia.*"

"Yes. Let there be no ill will. I summoned you to tell me of Dry Water. You have power. You can see. And you navigate the realms of death as a master would. I wish to know who else in Seco County has such abilities." Uncertain how powerful this spirit was, he added, "Please."

Dolinski pulled a handkerchief from his pocket and blew his nose. "I am old," he croaked. "I am tired in this place. Let me go back."

"My need is urgent. Fate aligns in Dry Water. There is a man here that I must kill."

"Murder?" Dolinski removed his glasses, folded them, and set them aside. "Life is so very precious. I cannot help you kill."

"If you are reasonable, Dolinski, you will listen first why I must."

Dolinski stood straighter, and his bones popped. His eyes shone a darker blue than they had a moment ago. "Proceed. I shall listen."

"This is no ordinary murder. I have hunted such men before, tracking them with my divinations and silencing their souls. They bring disastrous change to the world. They bring war and disease and terror. So many have slipped through my fingers." Nick curled his hand into a fist. "Machiavelli, Hitler, Nietzsche, Nobel, Rockefeller: dangerous men with dangerous ideas. So much death and misery, because I was weak.

"Even close to you in your tower, Dolinski, close to Dry Water, I have failed before. I missed Oppenheimer when he was at Los Alamos. I was too slow, and he was smarter than I imagined. The consequences of that failure may yet destroy the world."

"I see," he said, not looking entirely convinced. "And this one you seek now, he is as dangerous?"

"More. I have failed under ideal conditions. I have seen him with my magic. He has luck, and skill, and cunning. What he will bring to the world I cannot dream. But I do fear it."

Dolinski scratched his beard. It retracted into his face, and left smooth taut skin. "I see why you believe this matter urgent. However, the moral implications for me are more awkward than you realize. Still . . . if you only seek information . . . I suppose there is no harm in revealing who has power in Seco County."

"Excellent."

Dolinski paced the confines of the pentagram of books. "The first I saw here with the power was my English teacher, Miss Wainwright. She saw things. She taught me to read and to write. She taught me everything. Sadly, she is dead."

"Let us please concentrate on those who are still here then," Nick hissed.

Dolinski's hair grew jet black and gathered itself into a ponytail. A slim mustache sprouted on his upper lip. He pulled a pack of Chesterfields from his sweater, tapped one out, and stuck it in his mouth. The tip ignited by itself. "There is Raja Anumati. She has power. Any fool can see that. But there was another in town, a Navajo shaman and his son. They both could see."

"Is he an ally of Raja's?"

"I do not believe so. They fought over something, quite a quarrel as I understood it. He left a few years ago. The boy, however, stayed in Seco County. Niyol, I believe his name was. He sees very well."

A boy. Another threat? And Raja must have killed the shaman if she had his crows. "Is there anyone else?"

Dolinski removed his cardigan. Underneath he wore a white shirt, lace cuffs, and a saber at his side. He stood six feet tall and had the muscles of an Olympic athlete. He could have been twenty. He could have been ageless. "I used to read bedtime stories to a little girl. She saw other places with me, had a small amount of ability. She is a charming thing, sir, two long pigtails and lovely brown eyes. You shall not harm her in this machination of yours, or I shall hear of it. Her name is Paloma."

"She is not whom I seek, I assure you."

"Good. Then"—he drew his blade—"if that is all. There are princesses to be rescued, and evil to be defeated. I wish you luck with your quest."

"Thank you, Dolinski."

He saluted Nick with his saber and vanished.

The runes of *Confinement* smoldered, then flared on the books, burned as fuses do when overloaded. Nick examined them and saw on one of the paperback covers a sword-wielding hero that looked suspiciously like the young man Dolinski had become.

He sat down, exhausted from summoning the ghost.

Good. Only Raja and the prophet were significant threats. Perhaps this boy, Niyol, as well. He would deal with them all—eventually.

After his death, possessing Woberty, and squashing his rebellious Dempsey, he required rest. It would be months before he could confront Raja and the prophet, but he would. He had a body again. He had a purpose. Winter would come to Seco County.

Death would come for them all.

Chapter 7

RAJA STOOD AND HELD OUT HER HAND. THE HUNDREDS OF TINY CROWS that flew about her vanished. Fire flickered between her fingers, and a second ghostly hand stretched toward Larry. The heat reddened his skin.

"You don't want to shake my hand," he said, and took a step back.

Raja did not withdraw; rather, she took a step forward.

"I've got a cold."

She dropped her hand. "I am sorry to hear that." She retreated, and settled back into her seat, adjusting the silk blouse that clung to her glistening tan skin.

One of the two crows from the chandelier glided, circled once, then alighted on her shoulder. Its weight made no imprint upon her blouse. No one in the ballroom noticed.

"Indians in these parts thought them crows were awful potent magic," Matt whispered. "They're unpredictable critters. Always starin' at ya like they know something. Wish I had my iron. There'd be nothin' but spit and feathers left of 'em."

"Paloma tells me that you are an author?"

"Let me get us something to sit on," Paloma said, and left.

Larry watched her, admired her figure and the bounce of her thick black hair. He glanced to Raja and saw she followed his gaze with her mirror green eyes. He quickly looked to his feet, embarrassed. "Yes. Three books. Science fiction."

"You are a prophet then," she said. "A man in the business of predicting the future." Her hands flitted back and forth like a Balinese dancer. Grace. Precision.

"Hardly. My books are light adventures. There's a bit of hard science in them, but more action than speculation."

She raised an eyebrow, smiled slightly. "I've read your books, Larry."

"Read them? I didn't think—"

"You do not give yourself half the credit you deserve."

Larry wanted to leave. He didn't want to see any more crows or ghosts or women veiled in flames. If he was losing his mind, he wanted to do so in private. He thought of excuses: illness, food poisoning, or an urgent call to his agent, but when he opened his mouth he saw death. His death.

It wasn't like the premonition he had with Linda, a vision of him crushed by forty years of marriage and work. This time he saw four paths into the future, three dead-ends, and one that meandered into fog. Along the first path he left the party and lightning struck him. He tasted ozone, and felt his flesh char, his bones splinter. Simultaneously, he took the second path, and again he left the party. A storm of living crows smothered him. A thousand rips and probing beaks, and they left his bones picked clean. The third path, he left the party, made it back to the Silver Bullet, and as he drew a bath, he burst into flames, spontaneously combusted. On the last path, the one obscured by mist, he remained at the party.

Larry shut his mouth and decided to stay.

Paloma came back, dragging two rattan chairs. She offered one to Larry.

"Your first book came out six years ago," Raja said.

Paloma sat next to him. She smelled of gardenias. It distracted Larry. "Six years sounds right," he said.

"You wrote of a bureaucratic empire crumbling under the weight of its own authority."

"It was just a backdrop for my main character. He had to—"

"Your 'backdrop' predated the crisis in Europe, with which it has amazing parallels. Ethnic cleansing, mass rapes and murders, the shelling of peaceful cities, and religious stupidity. It is a timely topic, and I admire you for sneaking it into such a popular novel.''

Larry's Captain Kelvin did work for a galactic empire on the verge of collapse. True there were concentration camps, and countless, pointless deaths over absurd holy values, but that was to give his hero motive; it was to make his villains obviously evil. He never predicted anything. Yet, he had known when things were about to happen to him personally. Why not with his writing?

Matt stepped between Raja and him. ''She's tryin' to sweet talk ya. She must want somethin'. I've dealt with women like this. Every one of 'em rooked me.''

Larry saw Raja's crows. Could she see Matt standing in his underwear?

He waved his hand through the ghost and made him step aside.

''Mosquito,'' Larry said.

Raja's jade eyes gazed where Larry had looked, approximately where Matt now stood.

She said, ''Paloma, could you find Mr. Jacob for me? He and Larry should be introduced.''

''Of course.'' Paloma touched Larry gently on the arm, then left.

''We shall be in the gardens,'' Raja told her. ''Meet us there.''

Larry didn't like the way Raja ordered Paloma.

''Come, Mister Ngitis.'' Raja stood. ''Can I call you Larry? Let me show you my garden. I am rather proud of it.''

''It's a trap,'' Matt cried. ''Don't go with that witch. Yer beggin' for a bushwhackin'.''

Raja strolled through the open glass doors and waited for him.

Larry didn't want to be alone with a woman who had invisible crows for companions and burned with a living green flame, but he trusted the visions he had had of his death. All the things that had happened since he arrived in Dry Water, the lightning, the child ghost on the side of the road, his nightmare in his suite, and now Raja, were woven together. They had the same unearthly characteristics. Larry had to find out what they meant. He had to find out or die—he had seen that clearly enough.

He watched Raja stroll down the path. Maybe her abilities were similar to his. Maybe she could show him how to control them. She also had other things he wanted: an interviewer from *The New Yorker,* influence, money.

He walked through the open glass doors after her.

"Dang fool idiot Chinaman," Matt muttered, and trailed behind him. "Yer walkin' to yer own funeral."

The clear desert air magnified the moon and made her three-quarter face fill half the sky. The stars were huge too, more than he had ever seen on the foggy California coast.

Raja had gone ahead into an orchard of almond trees that had both moonlit pink blossoms and green nut husks—neither of which belonged on the trees at this time of the year.

He lagged behind her and caught glimpses in the shadows of naked nymphs with almond blossoms woven into their silver hair.

"We got company," Matt said, and pointed up. "Next time we bring guns." Underneath his mustache he gritted his teeth.

The other crow from the chandelier circled above them. Its eyes glowed yellow and fixed upon Larry.

"She's got more firepower than ya do," Matt said. "Flames 'round her head brighter than a pile o' flash powder. Yers looks like a couple of lightning bugs, sick ones at that. Let's duck outta here."

Raja was a dozen paces ahead of Larry. He halted, then whispered to Matt as softly as he could, "I have fire?"

"All ya shaman fellows got the fire."

"What does mine look like?"

Matt twisted his mustache. "It's kinda blue-green like dirty turquoise. But dim."

"How do I make mine as bright as hers?"

"I ain't a magic man, but I can tell ya this: it got brightest when I almost lost ya."

That was when Larry had seen the colors beyond his senses, and when he was in the stars. He gazed up into the night and remembered how he had floated among them, and how they looked up close, unimaginably luminous. He thought of the black hole and its accretion disk, a whirlpool of superheated gases and dust; he thought of the stars crowded together in the core of the galaxy, a solid band of light, blue and yellow and orange suns, and clouds of interstellar hydrogen glowing red.

In his peripheral vision, and beyond the blackness, the stars appeared. They surrounded him and welcomed him back among them. His equilibrium vanished. The world spun.

"Chinaman, yer gettin' away from me again. Are ya daydreamin' in the middle of an ambush? Pull yerself together."

Matt's voice snapped Larry awake. The stars vanished, and he stood again with feet firmly planted in the desert evening.

"What do I look like now?"

"Yer head's full o' sparks. Kinda like flowers on fire."

"How do I keep—"

"Larry?" Raja called to him from beyond the trees.

Whatever he had done, it was going to have to be enough. He walked through the almond orchard, smelling the heavy perfume of the blossoms. There was more light now. When he glanced at the wood nymphs, they hid behind their trees. The light came from him, silver illumination and gold sparks.

On the other side of the orchard was a meadow surrounded by willow trees that sighed in the breeze. A stream meandered through the grass. Raja removed her sandals and dangled her feet in the water.

Larry joined her, sitting not too close on the bank of the stream.

"You no longer have your cold," Raja said without looking at him. "I suppose I should have expected more from you." The green flames that licked her skin cooled and wavered near invisibility.

What could Larry say? He had no idea if Raja perceived his strength, or Matt, or even if he lied. He nodded and stuck his fingers into the water. It was cold and made his skin ache. He wiped some onto his face and hoped Raja didn't see his hand shake.

"Ya fooled her," Matt whispered, and crouched next to Larry. "Now let's skedaddle before she gets smart to ya."

Larry couldn't think of anything clever, so he said, "Nice garden."

"Thank you, but you know I did not bring you here to smell my flowers, or taste water from my stream."

"No."

His stomach churned. The thought of being picked apart by crows wouldn't leave him. His future paths contorted in his mind. Which one was he on? How did he navigate? How did he pick the one that did not lead to death? His visions had showed his demise, but not how to avoid it. He had to figure that out himself.

Raja splashed a bit of water toward Larry with her toes. "I know little about you," she said, "but I know that we have a common purpose in Dry Water."

"I suspected as much," he lied.

"So the water that cannot be drunk is what you seek. Nick told the truth."

Perspiration beaded on Larry's brow and under his arms. Water that could not be drunk? What did she mean by that? Who was Nick? His pulse throbbed in his neck; his throat and tongue dried. He scooped up a handful of stream water and sipped it.

"I want you to help me," she said. "Better we join our forces than serve cross-purposes."

This was it. The crossroads. He sensed it. Move slow, he thought. Take the middle path. Walk with small steps.

"I came to Dry Water to finish my fourth novel, Ms. Anumati. Whatever help you need, I'd be happy to give you, but first I must write. I have a deadline in December." Larry held his breath.

Raja narrowed her eyes. Her dim flames flared like a bonfire, then relaxed, and she said, "I could see that your deadline is extended."

Larry wished he knew how she did that—both the trick with her fire, and his deadline. He knew she could, though; she wasn't lying. But it felt wrong, like signing his name with his left hand. It was a trap. He had to stall until he learned what was happening to his mind. He had to stall her until he figured out what the "water that cannot be drunk" was.

"The deadline doesn't matter," Larry whispered. He had to whisper. He hadn't the courage to say the words louder. "I have to keep my momentum going or I'll block. It's happened before."

Raja considered this, then said, "I can give you Paloma."

Larry held his surprise inside. "Paloma can make her own decisions."

"She does as I tell her."

"Paloma is not a part of this." Larry sounded like he knew what he was talking about. He was grateful for that.

"She is now," Raja said. "You may be able to shield the depth of your abilities from me this evening, but you cannot hide your torn heart. Not from me. It shows with every beat. Paloma can ease that pain. She would be happy to help, happy to heal one I considered an ally."

How did Raja know about Linda? Maybe she didn't. Maybe she just read his emotions.

"She's slippin' the noose 'round yer neck," Matt whispered. "Stop barkin' at the knot and get outta here."

''The water that cannot be drunk will still be here,'' Larry said, using the words she had given him. ''Let me write, then I will be able to help you.''

''Your writing is so important to you?''

''More than money or fame,'' Larry said. ''It is what I am. A storyteller.''

''Then that is your strength,'' she said. ''It is where your magic lies. I shall not interfere.''

Magic? Larry believed he saw into the future, and maybe, possibly, he projected some of that talent into his writing, but there was no magic, and certainly none of it came *from* his writing.

Raja brushed the surface of the stream, making ripples. ''Very well, we can negotiate the details later. Enough has been discussed this evening. I shall take your pledge, for now.''

Larry exhaled the breath he had been holding.

Raja turned her head and looked into the orchard. ''Paloma and Mister Jacob have arrived.''

Paloma's pink flames flickered through the almond blossoms. There was a man with her.

''Mister Jacob is my lawyer,'' Raja told him. ''He has recently arranged the purchase of a large block of stock in Crystal Media.''

''Crystal Media. Sounds familiar.''

''It should. Crystal Media owns Troubadour Incorporated, and they, in turn, own Perspective Publishing, who, I believe, own you, Larry.''

If Raja had enough stock, she could talk to the publisher, who could twist the arm of his editor. She could extend his deadline. Or if she wanted to, she could have his fourth book killed.

''Hello, Walter,'' Raja said. She gave him a light kiss on the lips. ''I'd like you to met Larry Ngitis. He's our newest author in Dry Water, and a very special friend of mine.''

''Pleased to met you,'' Walter said, and shook Larry's hand. There was something oily covering his skin.

When the lawyer released his grip, there was an explosion—from behind—a blast that went through Larry. The wind was knocked out of him, and he coughed. He tasted sulfur and smoke.

Matt spun around. ''Didja hear that, Chinaman? A shotgun, sure enough. Ya can smell the gunpowder. Gotta be close.''

''You OK?'' Walter patted him on the back.

''I must have swallowed wrong,'' Larry said. It had been closer than Matt realized. Larry knew it was a shotgun blast. And he knew it would be going through Walter's spine. His wife was going to murder him. Soon.

''Walter,'' Raja said, ''can you arrange a lease for the cabin on Ferrocarril Mountain? I think the isolation would do Larry's writing a world of good. If that is acceptable to you, Larry? It is a wonderful place. All the amenities. No rent.''

Money was tight. The advance on Larry's fourth book was nearly gone. He had wanted to move to Dry Water—although that was *before* he had learned there were ghosts and witches here. Still, it was a place to write. A place that was rent-free. But accepting meant that he'd owe Raja a favor. How big or small a favor he had yet to determine.

''It is an extremely generous offer,'' he said to Raja.

''Then you will take it.'' It wasn't a question.

The cabin was a bribe. Larry didn't need precognitive powers to see that. His vision of the crows tearing him apart left no doubt of what the consequences of refusing were. If he took it, then Raja and he were friends. It would buy him time to figure out what she wanted, why, and if he could deliver.

The trees rustled, but there was no breeze. The leaves and the pink almond blossoms had turned black, thick with shadows that had not been there a moment ago, silky black like ebony feathers.

''OK,'' he said.

Walter took Larry's hand and pumped it again like they were old college buddies. ''Great. I'll bring the paperwork over tomorrow for you to sign.''

No shotgun blasts this time, but Larry saw blood soaking through the front of the lawyer's suit, and his back smoldering from the powder burns.

''I'd be countin' yer fingers,'' Matt said. ''Makin' a deal with a witch and a slick Philadelphia lawyer—together they're worse than the devil.''

''I'm glad you choose to stay with us,'' Raja said. ''Paloma shall show you the place tomorrow afternoon. Let me know if there is anything you need.''

A cool breeze made the orchard shiver. The shadows were gone. Pink almond blossoms floated in the air.

''Thanks,'' Larry said. He smiled and clenched his teeth, squishing the lead securely into his molar. He had plans for Matt.

* * *

Larry dropped from the top of the chain-link fence into Spencer's lot. The crickets stopped chirping.

Matt squinted into the shadows. ''No dogs guardin' the place.'' He looked up at the sky. ''None of them crows either. Looks deserted. But that's when ya gotta watch yer backside the most.'' He scratched his underarm. ''Ya shoulda let that Paloma kiss ya. She wanted to. Why'd ya take off like a jackrabbit?''

It was past midnight, and Spencer's shop was closed. A fluorescent light had been left on and long flickering shadows fell on his '58 Chevy and his orange bulldozer.

''Paloma's being used by Raja,'' Larry whispered back. ''She's a bribe like the cabin was.''

Parked in the corner of the lot was Larry's Econoline van. The new windows were in. It was locked.

''So what? The gal was willin'. Ya like gals, don't ya?''

''I'm not going to take advantage of her,'' Larry replied. He didn't admit to Matt that he probably couldn't. His memories of Linda would get in the way.

He didn't have his keys. Spencer did. He could go back to the Silver Bullet and get a coat hanger to jimmy it open, but if he did he'd lose his courage. He'd find a dozen excuses to stay there. Instead, he took off his sweater, wrapped his fist, then busted the vent window out. Larry paused and listened. Nothing. ''And even if Paloma knows, she probably doesn't have a choice. Raja treats her like a slave.''

''It's like findin' a silver nugget in the river and sayin' it might be some feller's upstream. Yer a dang fool.''

Larry dug through the a box marked ''old tax papers'' and found the spare keys. They were still attached to the maglight key chain that had been Linda's. It had been a gift from Larry so she would be safe, so she wouldn't have to fumble around in the dark. Cold guilt twisted his stomach into knots. He had promised her he'd mail it back.

Matt scrutinized the paperbacks scattered in the van, moving his lips as he read the titles. He muttered, ''Why we're thievin' yer own buggy?''

''It's called a van,'' Larry told him. ''I can't wait till morning. Raja's lawyer and Paloma will be all over me. I've only got tonight to get this done.''

''What?''

Larry got into the driver's seat and stuck the key in the ignition. Matt was already in the passenger's seat and examining the underside of the dash.

"I need an explanation for what's happening with my mind," Larry said, "and why, and how I can control it."

"I've told ya 'bout that," Matt said.

"No. You've just passed along information. You don't know any more about what I'm going through than I do."

"Now yer callin' me a liar? I oughta leave ya on yer own."

"You *are* a liar, Matt. You're a murderer, a rapist, and a thief too."

Matt's pale face flushed. "I reckon that's right." He snorted and spit. "So what?"

"So, just like I don't like Raja giving Paloma orders, I don't like you telling me what to do. I don't trust you."

"Tough. I'm all ya got."

"No. You mentioned a shaman. He told you how to escape the Silver Bullet's suite. He'll know what to do with me as well. I want you to take me to him."

"Yer givin' me orders now? I don't take no orders from no one—especially no Chinaman."

"You do now." Larry spit the bullet out. It landed on the dash. It was deformed by his chewing and sticky with saliva.

Matt vanished.

"And I'm sick of you calling me 'Chinaman,' you Anglo-Irish piece of crap."

Larry eased the van into neutral and coasted to the locked gate. He grabbed a hammer from his tool chest and struck the padlock until it popped open. He pulled out, then closed the gate after him, making certain it looked like it was locked. Wouldn't want anyone to steal from Spencer.

He turned north onto Agua de Viva and went through town. He'd have to check the maps, but he was certain the Navajo reservation was in the Four Corners region.

The neon diamonds flickering in the Three of Diamonds Bookstore window reflected and smeared on the asphalt. They made the adobe church across the street blood red.

He finally picked up the bullet fragment, blew it clean, and stuck it back in his mouth.

Matt reappeared, his mustache stiff, and his eyes solid red. Mad. "That was a dirty trick, son."

"It was no trick. You'll show me where this shaman is or I'll go to the Silver Bullet and put the bullet back. It may be another hundred years before someone comes along that can see you. Maybe a thousand. Or maybe I'll just flush it down the toilet."

Matt's mustache drooped and his red eyes dimmed. "Ya wouldn't."

"Try me."

"And after all I did fer ya—yer nothin' but a snake-bitin' son-of-a-whore." He twisted the tip of his mustache. "Guess I kinda admire that, though. OK. Only a fool argues with a skunk. I'll show ya the shaman."

"Good."

"But ya ain't gonna like it. Ya got a pick or a shovel with ya?"

"I can improvise. Why?"

"You'll see, Chinaman. Turn around. Ya need to be going south on this here Agua de Viva trail. It's gonna take ya to more than ya bargained fer."

In New Mexico you often see crosses erected alongside the road, especially on tight curves, steep embankments, and near liquor stores. It is a Hispanic tradition to make a shrine to honor the death of a family member. It is believed they protect the dead's soul and speed it to Heaven. No one is buried there. The crosses only mark the site of the fatal accident.

It is common for these crosses to be tended for decades. They are adorned with flowers, fresh or plastic, candles placed inside cut-in-half beer cans, bells that sprinkle notes onto the wind, and statues of Jesus or the Blessed Virgin. If the cross is for a child's death, then sometimes toys are left: sun-bleached Barbies and rusty Matchbox cars that no one plays with.

There are stories of ghosts appearing by the shrines on rainy nights. It is said they warn travelers of the perilous conditions.

But these sites are not graves.

Larry dug with a tire iron. He dug in the dark. He could have left his headlights on, pointing into the creosote bushes alongside the road, but then someone might have stopped. It would be awkward explaining to a state trooper why he was digging up a roadside shrine at two in the morning.

He stopped and twisted the maglight on.

The whitewashed cross he had seen five days ago stood firmly planted in the ground. He listened intently for a child's laughter. Nothing. The only ghost here was Matt, but Larry had the feeling he was being watched. The only other eyes watching him, though, were those on the faded statue of the Virgin Mary.

''This is crazy.''

''Ya wanted to see the shaman,'' Matt said. ''He's there.''

''A kid? A dead kid?''

''Yep.''

''I swear Matt if you're lying—''

Matt laughed. ''I ain't lyin'. That's what makes it funny.''

Clouds covered the moon, and a light drizzle fell.

Matt scanned the horizon. ''Better get a move on, son. I don't think we were followed, but ya never can be too careful with them crows.''

Thunder rumbled and echoed off Ferrocarril Mountain. Larry stared overhead a long time, looking for lightning, then, ''If the shaman is buried here, and you were in the Silver Bullet, how do you talk to him?''

''There are places that I can get to 'cause I'm dead that normal folk can't. Same with the shaman here. We're both stuck in one place, but places ain't the only spots to go, ya get me?''

Larry went back to his digging. It had something to do with the weird dimensions he had experienced earlier. Places that were not places. He didn't want to know.

He was three feet deep when he hit a layer of clay. He pushed the cross, but it wouldn't budge. It must be sunk into concrete.

More digging, and when the moon touched the mountain, Larry hit something solid. He turned the maglight back on and saw roots growing from the wood. They anchored it fast.

''That's the witch's doin' alright,'' Matt said, peering over Larry's shoulder. ''She put this livin' cross on the shaman to make sure he stayed put.''

Larry chipped at a root with the tire iron. It bled sap and wriggled deeper into the earth. The other roots moved together; they all pulled at the cross and held it with a steel grip.

''I've had enough of this.'' Larry went back to the van and got his wire cutters. The breeze turned freezing. The creosote bushes rustled and swayed with a disturbing rhythm.

He held the tiny maglight in his teeth, then snipped the roots with the cutters. They squirmed like snakes, curling and flexing.

Larry threw his weight against the wood. It budged.

The wind blew faster, and somewhere far off he heard bells and a faint crow's caw. He pulled and pushed on the cross. It loosened.

The maglight dimmed. The wind stopped. Larry stopped too. He was being watched. He knew. He had never felt so many eyes watching him.

He looked up.

Every shadow that clung to the creosote bushes, every black spot on the asphalt, every sliver of night, every piece of darkness moved. They all became glossy, the ebon silk of feathers. A hundred thousand pairs of yellow eyes opened, perched in the brush, upon the telephone wires next to the road, in between the stars, and filling the clouds—mean stares, feral and hungry.

''Tarnation,'' Matt whispered. ''Didn't see that one acomin'. They done bushwhacked us. Hurry, son. Get that cross out, before yer dinner.''

The crows took to the air—a hurricane of beating wings. They circled Larry, and the wind from their wings made the wet sand and twigs fly. He held up his hands in a futile gesture to fend them off.

No. The cross. The shaman was there.

He kicked the cross and it twisted. He yanked it with all his strength. Splinters cut deep into his hands.

The cyclone of crows tightened about him, then dove.

Larry pulled.

The cross came free—six feet of wood with small animate roots. He fell over. A child's laughter filled the air.

The rain exploded. A boy in bloody pajamas appeared. Crows scattered, trying to turn in midair from him.

The child stopped laughing. He clapped his hands thrice, and chanted:

> *''Brother North Wind.*
> *Brother North Wind.*
> *Hear my call.*
> *Feel my breath upon your skin.*

Come drive our enemies away.
Take them where it is cold.
Take them where it is always night.
Take them across the world.''

The rain danced and spun and became a whirlpool about Larry. The crows in the air blurred. They screamed like no animal he had ever heard before. The wind whipped at Larry, lashed his face, and drove the rain so it stung like needles. All he saw in the sky was black feathers, countless drops of water, and the ferocious wind, moving past him, looking like a huge beast with silver scales.

A flash and the rain ceased. The clouds vanished, and the stars again winked above him. He heard a distant crow's caw, long drawn out, then that too vanished.

Larry stood, drenched and dripping.

The boy held out his bloody hand to shake. ''Holà. I am Niyol Rodriguez.''

Larry suppressed the urge to run away. He did not shake the boy's hand.

''My father told me you would come to Dry Water.''

''He saw me?''

''Just as you can see into the future, my late father had the ability to see possibilities, ripples in events, consequences and repercussions. He saw the arrival of a person who would change the world. You.''

''I'm just a writer.''

Niyol wiped the blood from his rain-washed face. ''Not anymore.''

''Those crows—''

''They were the witch's. They will not harm us now. By the time they return from where the North Wind took them it will be spring—next year.'' Niyol nodded to Matt. ''Hi, cowboy. You escaped.''

''Yep. Looks like I'm saddled up with this Chinaman, leastways till I find someone better.''

''I thought you could help me,'' Larry said. ''I am seeing things I can't explain or control. Do you understand?''

''Oh, yes,'' said Niyol. ''The change. It happens to those who see other parts of reality.''

''Can you help me? I'm losing my mind. I'm seeing things I can't understand. I don't want to understand.'' It struck Larry that talking to a ghost by the side of the road at two in the morning qualified as one more thing he didn't understand, but Niyol was different. He had a calming presence.

"I will help you," Niyol replied, "but there is more to consider. I am an enemy of the witch Raja. She is strong. Allow me to teach you, and allow me to tell you the truth, and you become her enemy as well."

Larry scrutinized the boy. He looked like he was ten years old, but he spoke with authority, confidence that ten-year-old boys didn't have.

"I don't know," Larry whispered.

"Aw, Chinaman, don't be thickheaded," Matt cried. "Let the shaman teach ya what to do."

"Let him decide," Niyol said. "He must follow his instincts."

Niyol's eyes were black. Not the solid black that Larry had seen in Matt's dead eyes; nor did they contain the raw power that was in Raja's gaze. They were simple eyes. Honest eyes.

But there was Raja's free cabin to consider, and her block of his publisher's stock with which she could blackmail him. Larry rubbed the bridge of his nose. If he agreed and joined Niyol, then how long could he fool Raja? Could he fool her at all?

Raja wasn't going to teach him anything. She wanted to use him. Larry had a hunch if she knew he understood nothing, he would be expendable.

"OK, I'm your man," Larry said. He reached out and took Niyol's bloody hand.

It was solid.

SECTION TWO

a u t u m n

Chapter 8

LARRY STARED AT THE CAMPFIRE OF BURNING BONES. YESTERDAY, HE had cut up a dead cottonwood for the fire, but every time he set a log on the coals it became a rib, long and pale, or a staring skull, or a thighbone that sputtered marrow from its broken ends.

Niyol said it was a hanging tree, and spirits still clung to it.

Larry accepted that. It wasn't the strangest thing he had seen in the last ten weeks.

When he had moved into Raja's cabin his visions intensified. Every stray thought swelled and solidified. Old memories and lovers visited him; his father's head shattered the windshield of his van; childhood nightmares, bogeymen, and things under his bed became real with pulsing tendrils and razor teeth and skeletal bodies. The earth dissolved beneath his feet. Impish faces stared back from every shadow. He saw all his possible futures. He saw a billion alternate existences. He heard the stars whisper among themselves. It was chaos. Madness.

It had taken Larry ten weeks to stop his thoughts. Niyol coached him in breathing techniques, taught him Navajo chants, took him running for miles, and gave him Zen word puzzles to tie his mind in knots. Larry had great motivation to learn—it was keeping him sane.

He had control now. Some.

When the nightmare visions had started Larry had wanted to end it all. He would have killed himself, but Matt said it would be just as bad dead. He told him living, at least, he had a fighting chance.

Matt had stayed at the cabin, reading the newspapers Larry had laid out for him. That left Larry alone with Niyol. Larry didn't know if the kid was a ghost or real or something in between. He had seen him move objects, he had shaken his hand, and felt his breath, but sometimes Niyol was ethereal and part of the wind. Niyol said he was solid because Larry believed in him. Larry didn't buy that Tinkerbell explanation. He didn't believe in Niyol any more than he believed in Matt. He wasn't being told the entire truth.

Niyol sat cross-legged next to Larry. He no longer wore his pajamas, but jeans, a Grateful Dead T-shirt, and Keds. The blood that had covered his head was gone. He handed Larry a stick, which Larry used to poke the fire. The bones hissed and moaned. Ghostly fingers and faces writhed in the flames.

Niyol occasionally talked like a ten-year-old. Most of the time, however, he spoke with the eloquence of a professor, or the wisdom of a Buddhist mystic. Larry knew that whatever Niyol really was, it wasn't a ten-year-old boy.

Larry gazed at the arroyos that zigzagged through Kongsberg Valley, then vanished into distant Seven Horseshoe Ridge. In a half hour the sun would rise and wash the land with orange and red, flooding the crevasses with shadows.

''Am I going to live?'' Larry asked Niyol.

''It is likely,'' Niyol replied. ''You have experienced the worst, I believe.''

Niyol inched closer to Larry, and whispered, ''My father told me a tale on this mountain. He said a hummingbird told the story to him, and the hummingbird heard it from the winds.''

He pointed at the sky, and said, ''Those three stars in a row. See them?''

Larry squinted. ''Alnitak, Alnilam, and Mintaka—Orion's Belt.'' He knew their names because his Captain Kelvin flew between them on his patrols in the Space Guard. ''But we shouldn't be able to see them until November.''

Niyol ignored this. ''My father called those stars the Canoe. They are the bottom of the Hunter's boat. He floats upon a dark sea, peers down, and watches us. It is said that he was the one who showed the people how to hunt and fish.''

Larry imagined the dome of the night sky rippling with waves like a giant inverted ocean. He blinked, and the illusion vanished.

"One day a girl was born with a lame foot. Her parents could not afford the burden of another daughter, one that would take from the others and return nothing, so they took her into the woods. They left her to die.

"The Hunter heard the little girl's cries and descended. He raised her as his daughter and taught her to gather honey from the bees without getting stung. He showed her which berries and mushrooms were safe to eat as well, so she would never be hungry. He taught her how to move without moving to be safe from the bears and great cats that roamed the woods."

Larry wanted to ask what "move without moving" meant, but he remained quiet, and kept his mind still.

"No rain fell during her thirteenth summer. The berries shriveled, and the bees gathered no nectar. The Hunter told the girl that she must cut off his head. He told her she must plant it in the meadow where the stream flowed from the mountain snows.

"She refused, but the Hunter forced his knife into her hand and demanded she do it.

"Her eyes full of tears, she cut off his head, and buried it in the meadow. When she returned to his body, it was gone. The three stars had returned to the sky.

"The girl sat into the meadow and wept until she fell asleep. When she awoke tall grass, as high as her waist, had sprouted in the field.

"The bees told her to eat the grass instead of their honey. They showed her how to gather it, how to separate the seeds, and prepare them."

The soil around Larry shifted; it strained, and burst. Green shoots wriggled up in a ring around their fire.

"The Hunter watched the girl from the stars," Niyol continued. "She found her mother and father, her sisters and brothers. They gave her an honored place among them, for with the knowledge of the grain and the berries and the mushrooms they rarely went hungry again. She had her own family, seven daughters and seven sons. She grew old. She died.

"The Hunter took her up into the stars with him. There"—Niyol pointed—"that is her star. That is her, the Star Maiden."

The star was unnaturally bright, brighter than Venus, a small moon in the sky.

"She watches with the Hunter. When her sons and daughters die, she goes to them and takes them to the stars. She watches all the members of her tribe, and if they use her gifts wisely, she takes them too."

Niyol spread out his hands. "They are all there in the sky," he said.

The band of the Milky Way shone brighter than Larry had ever seen. Stars that had been too faint to perceive twinkled with colors. He saw faces within them, some looking upon him with compassion, others frowning. The starlight threw hard shadows on the ground. Their campfire dimmed.

"The Navajo call it the Path to Heaven, but to me they are the souls of my ancestors, forever watching and protecting me."

A star fell—not like a meteor, though; it fell slowly, ignited, and took the shape of a woman. She looked as if she had come from a New York ballroom, wearing an off-the-shoulder gown of black velvet with sequins in a constellation pattern. The top flared like the petals of an orchid, while the hem trailed infinitely behind.

She had a phenomenal inhuman beauty. Her eyes had no pupils. They were a solid blue that Larry had only seen before in underwater photography. Instead of hair, she had silver and golden stars orbiting her head. Her skin was perfectly white and shone with such an intensity that Larry had to shield his eyes.

He blinked.

The Star Maiden stood in their campfire of bones. She was ten feet tall, slender and regal, and as bright as an electric arc. She held out her hand to Larry. Tiny stars like dust fell from her fingertips.

"Do not," Niyol whispered. "You can see her, and she has mistaken you for dead. She wants to take you to the stars."

Larry withdrew his hand and shook his head.

The grass around them grew taller. The tips swelled, blushed red, and split open with ripe seed. A flock of hummingbirds appeared, circled the Star Maiden, and transformed into tiny blue stars.

She spread her hands apart, and the space between them became a labyrinth, twisting three-dimensionally. In every turn Larry recognized a different place: the interior of his van, Spencer's shop with the Coke machine and the shelves of kachina dolls, his A-frame cabin, the dry gravel bed in Lost Silver Canyon, the Three of Diamonds Bookstore, and Matt Carlson's suite in the Silver Bullet.

She whispered into his mind: *You shall protect my people from the bears and great cats that roam these woods.*

"She gives you a gift," Niyol said, amazed. "How to move without moving. Study it. Quick."

The maze of shapes and places had four quadrants, in each a dizzying ensemble of turns and corridors, and as Larry studied them, they slid into a new configuration.

He strained to memorize the patterns. He concentrated but saw only disorder. He relaxed, and took the entire shape in one glance. Indeed, it was like a vine twisted into knots, patterns resting upon patterns, identically repeated, layer upon layer, complicated, but comprehensible.

A flash, and darkness again. The Star Maiden was gone.

Larry looked up and saw her star. She was there still, watching him. He knew.

"It was more than a story." Larry grabbed a handful of the grain. "This was more than hallucination."

"Describe what you saw."

"Didn't you see her?"

"Please," Niyol said. "Tell me what *you* saw."

Larry told him, then said, "She wasn't what I expected."

"She wouldn't be." Niyol traced spirals in the dirt, and they glowed a pale red. "Magic is a perception-biased art."

Larry cringed. He had distanced himself from the word "magic" since this began. Magic seemed implausible to him. Primitive. "I don't believe in that," he said. "This has something to do with my mind."

"You make my point," Niyol replied. He drew his legs into a lotus position and floated two inches above the sandy soil. "What we do is so individualized that we cannot even agree what to call it."

Larry nodded. He had learned not to expect answers immediately. Doing so set his mind into cyclical questions. What is it? How did it happen? Am I crazy? In this state of mind he inevitably saw things he wished he hadn't.

"Magic is based on subjective perceptions," Niyol explained. "There exist dimensions and other realities surrounding ours. Some people have insights, flashes into the nature of what envelops them, but it is largely indecipherable. Therefore, to work magic we must call upon the natives of these other realms."

"You mean ghosts like Matt?"

"Ghosts, some, yes. Others are the stuff of myth like the Star Maiden. To me they are animal spirits. Still others wear different names: fairies, demons, dragons, or creatures of shadow."

Larry remembered the creature of fire that dwelled in the accretion disk. How did it coexist in a universe with the Star Maiden and the Hunter? With Matt and Niyol? He quieted his dangerous questions.

"You have saints in your mythology. They have insights to the other realms. They pray to the natives of those dimensions, angels, to work miracles."

A flicker in the fire vied for Larry's attention: horns and a pitchfork and a flutter of bat wings. He told himself it was a moth and didn't look. "How are they supposed to help me?"

"Have you read Edwin A. Abbott's *Flatland?*"

Larry shook his head.

"He described a flat-plane world inhabited by two-dimensional creatures. When a sphere visited this flatland only an infinitesimally thin cross section of it fit into the plane. From the flatlander's perspective the section of the sphere in their plane appeared to be a circle."

Niyol brushed his bangs out of his face. They immediately fell back. Larry didn't understand how the ten-year-old understood philosophy and mathematics and magic and how they fit together. He had been dead only a decade. How did he know so much?

"The sphere moved through the plane," Niyol explained, and slid one ghostly hand through the other to demonstrate. "From the flatlander's view, the circle expanded, then shrank, then vanished as the sphere rose above their plane."

"So to spirits we live on a flat plane? One in which they can vanish and reappear at will?"

"It is a crude analogy. Reality is more complicated. While you must conserve your energy, momentum, and mass, these creatures do not. They can shunt or gather such quantities from sources you cannot perceive. They can make it rain fish or stones from a clear sky."

"Or spontaneous combustion?"

"Yes."

"Or what the Star Maiden showed me, how to move without moving?"

"If you ever found such a folded path of space again, yes, you might risk using it."

"I can't find anything," Larry complained. "I'm barely able to stay here in the real world."

"That is what spirits are for," Niyol said. "Stay here in the world you know. Let them navigate the netherealms for you."

"Is that the only way?" Larry wrinkled his nose. The only spirit he had access to was Matt Carlson, and he was no guardian angel. "Can't I do it myself?"

"Yes, but you risk encountering malevolent entities, or worse, losing your way. Our world is a speck of foam upon an infinite sea. Become lost and your physical shell can fall into a catatonic state, or if you retain partial consciousness, insanity."

Larry almost had a nervous breakdown when he had drifted in the Silver Bullet's suite. What would it be like to spend forever there? Despite the warmth from the burning bones, he shivered.

Niyol swept his dark bangs aside, so he could stare at Larry. "To reiterate my first point: magic is subjective. Because you glimpse the true nature of reality through the imperfect filter of your mind, you fill in what you cannot comprehend. For those with strong wills, they see events and people from their mythology."

"And for those with weak wills?"

"They go mad. Or perhaps we are the ones with the weak wills, obscuring the truth of what is out there. Perhaps the madman sees everything. The difference between reality and illusion is blurred for us."

The sun peeked over the horizon. Blood red light washed through the valley.

"Come," Niyol said. He passed his hand over the fire and sniffed the flaming bones. "The lesson is over. I hear Paloma's Jeep. It is Monday. And she always comes to spy for the witch on Mondays."

Larry put on deodorant and a clean shirt, and hoped he looked presentable. There were no mirrors in the cabin. Larry had thrown them away. He couldn't see himself clearly in them; his reflection twisted into grotesque shapes. He saw things in them, out of the corner of his eye, whenever he turned away: motion and shadows that weren't on his side.

From the top story of the A-frame he saw Paloma drive her Jeep up the gravel road. For the last ten Mondays she had brought leftovers from the Silver Bullet's kitchen. What they didn't eat for breakfast lasted Larry days. Niyol insisted that he see no one while he disciplined his mind, but Paloma was different. When she was around his thoughts didn't drift; he focused only upon her.

Raja's crows had vanished ten weeks ago, and Niyol assured Larry they couldn't have told the witch of his escape. Paloma's visits backed that theory up. Raja was using her to check on him.

He trotted downstairs, careful not to disturb the newspapers that covered the floor, then opened the door.

"Morning." She stepped in, handed him a stack of takeout boxes, and went back to her Jeep for more. Larry took them out back to the picnic table so they could eat and enjoy the view.

Paloma joined him and poured the coffee. "How's the writing?"

"Good," he lied. "Two chapters done this week." In ten weeks he had produced a dozen pages of illegible fiction.

Paloma had been riding this morning. Larry noticed the flecks of rust-colored mud on her boots and jeans and leather vest. Her hair was back in a clip, and her ears were wind-burned. Her aura was radiant and brushed against him. Larry heard her mother's voice, smelled chocolate chip cookies in the oven, and fresh wash drying on the line. Paloma inadvertently let him have a glimpse of her soul. It was more intimate than sex.

"You should have taken Raja's offer of a maid," she said, and spooned black beans onto his plate, then opened containers of red and green salsa. "You could slip on those papers and kill yourself."

"It's research in progress," he lied again, and sipped the coffee. It was Jamaican Blue Mountain, warm and sweet without sugar. Perfect.

The adobe structures in Dry Water blended into the hills. Larry could only discern the red brick of the Three of Diamonds Bookstore in the distant glare.

"What are you doing tomorrow night?" she asked, and passed him a square of corn bread.

Larry tasted it. It had bacon bits inside with honey butter drizzled over the top. With a full mouth he replied, "Nothing. Writing."

"I have tickets to the Santa Fe Symphony. Grofé's *Grand Canyon Suite*."

Larry stopped chewing. "I'd love to. I can—"

"Say no," she said.

"What?"

She pushed a dish of flan to him, then repeated, "Say no. Say you're too busy. Say you're at an important point in your writing."

"OK," Larry said, not understanding why, "I can't. My tux is dirty. The toilet's clogged and has to be snaked. I have to clean the cat's litter box."

"That's too bad," she said, and sipped her coffee. "Raja will be there."

"Oh."

"I had to ask you. So I did."

Larry wondered if Paloma would have asked him on her own. "I know Raja wants to see me," he admitted. "She's been up here twice in the last week."

"You've spoken with her?"

"No. I was out for a walk both times. She left notes."

"Convenient."

"Yeah." Very convenient, with Niyol and Matt watching for her.

"Larry, you don't have to play games with me. I know Raja intimidates everyone . . . for good reason." She stared across the valley, then added, "I don't know what she wants from you, but whatever it is, she's losing her patience."

Paloma didn't ask Larry what Raja wanted, but he knew she wanted to know. He wished he knew so he could tell her. Instead, he sipped his coffee. It no longer tasted good. "How impatient is she?"

"Fuming. She could revoke the lease on this place or worse."

Larry wondered why "worse" hadn't already happened.

Paloma stabbed a tamale. "I don't know what you agreed to, but I'm scared. You don't know what she's capable of. I . . . I don't want you hurt. Couldn't you give her what she wants?"

"I might," Larry said. If she or Niyol would explain what the hell the "water that cannot be drunk" was. "I'll think about it."

The cat leapt onto the table. Killer of Crickets looked part raccoon, acted that way too. Instead of a black mask and feet, however, he had white socks and a mask of silver. He saw the flank steak and stepped toward it, tail high.

"Hey!" Larry pushed him off.

It hissed.

Larry wasn't a cat person. He wasn't a dog person either. Goldfish were more his speed.

The cat cried, then jumped back up.

Paloma gingerly grabbed him and set him on her lap. If Larry had tried that, it would have clawed his arms. The cat purred for Paloma, and kneaded her thighs as she cut some steak, spooned a dollop of molé, and a scrambled egg, then crumbled two slices of greasy bacon onto a paper plate for him. She set him and the plate down. ''There you go. Larry doesn't mind sharing. But ask next time.''

Killer of Crickets took the meat, shook it to make certain it was dead, then wolfed it down. She patted him on the rump. He raised his hindquarters in appreciation.

''You should get him vaccinated.''

''One of these days I'll take him into Grants. Get him his shots *and* get him neutered.''

Killer of Crickets stopped eating, looked at Larry with narrow eyes, then went back to his meal.

Paloma glanced at her watch. ''Sorry. I have to go. I just wanted to make sure you're OK and find a home for these leftovers.'' She stood.

''I am. Thanks.'' He gave her a kiss on the cheek—which was all he had worked himself up to in the last ten weeks, then saw her out.

At the door she dug into her pocket. ''Here,'' she said, and thrust what looked like a half-dollar into Larry's hand. It had a raised six-pointed star on one side made of thirteen smaller stars, and on the reverse was an eagle, wings spread, perched on a rayed sun.

''What is it?''

''They were minted in Dry Water during the silver boom. The government found out and put a stop to it. It's pure silver. They're suppose to be lucky.''

It was slippery in Larry's hand, but the weight felt good. ''I can't take this. It must be worth a fortune.''

''It is. But you already did,'' she said, and walked down the porch steps. As she got into her Jeep she called back, ''And think about what I said? About Raja?''

He nodded and waved while she drove away.

Killer of Crickets sauntered to the window, watched her go, then licked his paw and washed his left ear. He had shown up, starved and half-feral, the first evening Larry had come to the cabin. Niyol told him to feed him and accept his companionship as a gift. He said the cat would protect Larry while he dreamed.

Larry had not had any visions in his sleep since the cat arrived, but he had to tolerate its sprayings, and its clawings, and its bringing home birds, lizards, and crickets to devour in front of him. He had almost needed stitches when he tried to take one of the living morsels away.

The cat jumped down from the window, went over to the newspapers on the stairs, stretched, circled twice, then settled onto a sunny patch.

''Do I still need that?'' he asked Niyol, and pointed to Killer of Crickets.

Niyol reappeared in the living room. ''Absolutely.'' He brushed his bangs out of his face. ''We need to talk. Matt as well.''

Larry fished the piece of lead (which now had a coat of epoxy) out of the ashtray on the mantel. He wedged it into his molar and tried not to gag on the taste of the plastic resin. Matt materialized hunched over the newspapers, trying to read around the cat. ''Skedaddle, ya no good critter!''

Killer of Crickets looked up, yawned, and went back to his nap.

''Come on, Matt.''

''I heard 'em,'' he said. ''I was just readin' about these senators. I can't figure why someone don't stretch them fellers' necks.'' Matt gathered himself up and followed Larry into the kitchen.

As Larry put the food away, he asked Niyol, ''You heard?''

''I eavesdropped, yes. I apologize. May I see the silver piece she gave you?''

Larry set it on the table. It was in mint condition. He should put it away someplace safe, but that didn't feel right. He wanted it close to him.

Niyol looked it over. ''I sense nothing of a sinister nature. I am sorry, Larry, I had to check. The witch is impatient. I am afraid we must postpone the remainder of your education and secure the dry water.''

''That's this 'water that cannot be drunk' that both you and Raja talk about.'' He picked up the silver piece. ''What is it?''

''I shall do better than tell you,'' Niyol said. ''I'm going to show you how to use it. But first we must retrieve it. The dry water is held in a cavern. And it is a dangerous climb even for an experienced spelunker. You must first acquire training with ropes and caving, and you will need a partner.''

''Raja will know the instant I start asking for those things in town.''

''Not everyone in Seco County reports to Ms. Anumati. Not the Lobos sin Orejas.''

"What's that?" Larry asked. "A cult? More witches? Druids?"

"Not witches," Niyol said, "but dangerous nonetheless. You shall require a method of gaining their confidence."

"I ain't followin' whatcha want with them old-timers," Matt said, "and I ain't followin' whatcha want with me neither. I gotta newspaper to read out there."

Paper rustled. Larry leaned over and saw the cat bat an imaginary rodent under the newsprint. He pounced on it, then tore it apart.

"Not anymore," Niyol remarked. "Larry, get a pencil, a legal pad, and, if you have one, a map of New Mexico. It may not be accurate enough. We may have to go into Albuquerque and copy a U.S. Geological Survey map as well, before we drop in on their meeting tonight."

"I can't wait till that critter dies," Matt muttered, and glared at the cat. "And I still don't get what hole yer pokin' yer nose into, kid."

"Silver," Niyol explained.

Silver is the reason the Lobos sin Orejas exist.

In 1598 Don Juan de Oñate led his men up the Rio Grande River, claiming all the land he saw for the Spanish crown. In July he set up headquarters at San Juan Pueblo and proclaimed himself the first governor of New Mexico. Oñate then invaded the surrounding Acoma, Zuñi, and Hopi lands. The Acoma had the poor sense to attack Oñate and killed thirteen of his soldiers. In retribution, Oñate killed thousands of Acomas, cutting off their feet, throwing them off cliffs, and taking others as slaves.

On one of these explorations, a band of Oñate's men wandered west into a land of canyons and caves and mountain-fed rivers. One man drank from a stream, and saw the water gleam—below the surface. He fished out a handful of silver gravel.

The band swore each other to secrecy and vowed to kill any who spoke of the riches. The priest in their party, Father Hernnan Chavez, marked the incident in his diary. He also wrote *"Lupum auribus teneo,"* which means "I have a wolf by the ears." Thereafter in his journal he refers to the secret band as the "Lobos sin Orejas," the wolves without ears. Most of Oñate's men deserted to mine the silver. A handful returned to San Juan Pueblo, claiming they had been attacked by Indians, and their comrades slain.

In 1607 Oñate resigned as governor under mysterious circumstances and withdrew to Mexico City. Rumors claim his soldiers tried to poison him. Others say that priests were treated poorly under his rule and they threatened to excommunicate him. Still others say he was haunted by ghosts of the Acoma Indians.

In 1609 Don Pedro de Peralta was appointed governor of New Mexico. In the two years between governorships, however, the Lobos sin Orejas took more silver from Seco County than will ever be known.

That spring Don Pedro moved his headquarters south and started construction on La Villa Real de Santa Fe de San Francisco de Assisi, later called Santa Fe. He put every man under his command to work. When spies for the Lobos sin Orejas vanished for days at a time, he had them arrested and questioned.

One man confessed that thirty soldiers and natives worked a secret mine. They exchanged silver for gems with what remained of the Azteca Empire. They had a boat in the Gulf and traded Bahamian rum. They owned plantations in the Caribbean; and some of their silver made its way back to Europe through Dutch privateers.

Spurred on by tales of wealth, Don Pedro took his cavalry and mounted an expedition to hunt and capture the rebel miners and their treasure.

An army of Spanish Conquistadors charged fifty men on foot as they loaded a wagon with silver bars. Rifles discharged, horses trampled men, lances impaled, and blood clouded the stream. Screams of victory filled the canyon.

Don Pedro's men found sacks of raw emeralds and pearls, half a ton of turquoise, and nine hundred bars of silver that weighed twenty pounds each. They took all they could carry back to Santa Fe, then returned with more horses, a dozen carts, and a hundred slaves, but every trace of the silver had vanished. The rebel miners had been buried. Even their footprints had been erased. Thereafter, the canyon was known as Lost Silver Canyon.

Part of the captured silver went to the Spanish Crown, Don Pedro kept a fortune, and a portion was wrought into the legendary Santa Fe cross. It stood three feet tall, weighed over half a ton, and gleamed with encrusted emeralds and turquoise. It remained with the governor for a year, then it stood in the old church in Santa Fe until the Pueblo revolt in 1675, when it vanished.

Father Hernnan Chavez, however, survived. He was not there the day of the massacre in Lost Silver Canyon. He remained silent, and in Santa Fe, until he died in 1692 of syphilis. His possessions were transported to his family in Spain, and fifty years later his great-nephew found his diary.

The modern Lobos sin Orejas search for the lost treasure of those Spanish deserters. They are miners, geologists, historians, and opportunists with the necessary skills and tenacity to find their fortune. They have discovered new deposits of silver, and turquoise, but none of the vaults that Father Chavez's journal reports—rooms lined with a hundred tons of silver, piled with sacks of ancient Aztec gold and emeralds and jade and pearls.

Often they find clues mentioned in the dairy: painted handprints with fingers curled or pointing or clenched. The diary, however, only mentions that these signposts exist—not how to interpret them. The only rooms the handprints lead to are empty now or flooded with dark waters or bottomless chambers.

The diary also mentions a cavern with *agua seco de viva y muerte,* the dry water of life and death. The diary tells of ghosts and curses as well.

The Lobos sin Orejas are still looking, though. And they are prepared to protect what is theirs.

''Where'd you get this?'' Baxter asked. She didn't lower her sawed-off shotgun to look at Larry's map.

Larry shrugged. These seasoned miners would never believe this hand-drawn map was legitimate. Niyol may have been the expert on mysticism, but walking in here unarmed, with a treasure map drawn from Matt's shaky memory, was a stupid plan.

There were four of them in the back of Spencer's shop. There may have been more, but Larry wasn't in any position to ask. The woman with the shotgun, Spencer called Baxter. She had sharp features, was in her late forties, and kept the double barrels pointed at his gut.

O'Donald, the writer he had met at Raja's party, sat on Baxter's left at the poker table. He wouldn't meet Larry's eyes.

An Indian gentleman lit up a cigarette and examined Larry. He sat next to O'Donald, wore a gray suit, and had gold-nugget rings on four fingers.

And there was Spencer. Larry was astonished to see him still alive.

Spencer had been just as surprised to see Larry at his shop at midnight. More surprised when he had said he wanted to join their illegal activities.

Fumes of Anabuse caressed Spencer's lips, whispered into his ear, and contorted into vomiting mouths near the silver flask in his pocket. Half a dozen drinks and he was a dead man. A six-pack or a few snorts of his homemade poison. Larry's liver burned just standing close.

''Cut him a yard of slack,'' Spencer said. ''He's OK in my book.''

Baxter set her sawed-off shotgun on the table. ''I ain't sure I trust you much either since you climbed on the wagon.'' She turned to Larry. ''But alrighty. So you're being tight-lipped where you got the map, and where you found out about us—I understand that. What do you want?''

''Carlson and his gang hid their silver and gold all over Seco County,'' Larry said. He wanted to sound cool, in control, but his voice cracked, and his hands were sweaty. ''It's only the beginning. I have a source of information. Your group has the practical experience. I'm willing to split this fifty-fifty. No strings. Just let me in.''

''I do the research here,'' O'Donald said. ''Your map is a fake. The Carlson stash was recovered two decades ago in Real Canyon, Mexico.''

''That's a lie,'' Matt exploded. ''I never headed fer Mexico. Only yellow-bellied cowards head down there.''

''It should be easy enough to see if I'm right,'' Larry said.

''The ravine on your map''—the Indian pointed—''here, is Navajo land. That makes it not so easy.''

''I've been in that ravine,'' Spencer said. ''We can sneak over there tonight and check it out. Baxter's still got that low-light stuff so we can see. We oughta be able to get in and out before sunrise.''

''What if he's a spy for the Department of the Interior or the FBI?'' O'Donald asked. ''Have you all forgotten what happened?''

''Shut your trap,'' Spencer hissed.

''He already knows,'' O'Donald said. ''You can bet that's what this is really about. Those FBI agents never give up when one of their own goes missing.'' He paused, letting that statement hang in the air, then he snatched Baxter's shotgun off the table.

''Hey!'' Baxter lunged for him.

O'Donald pushed her away with one hand and stood from the table. ''We have to dispose of him like we did the other. There's no alternative.'' He waved the shotgun at Spencer. ''Step away from him.''

Why hadn't Larry seen this? He had seen when the lightning came after him. He had seen his own death half a dozen times. Why hadn't he seen O'Donald? ''Wait a second,'' Larry said. ''I don't think—''

"You should have done your thinking before you came here with your forged map and your lies," O'Donald said.

"Stop your foolishness," Spencer barked. "That first time was an accident. I ain't stepping away, and you ain't shooting no one."

"You're wrong," O'Donald said.

He fired.

Chapter 9

RAJA WAS NOT ANGRY. ANGER WAS A LUXURY SHE COULD NOT AFFORD. She had her chance to act and let it slip away. That was the laziness of summer.

She watched Melissa wipe the dust and fingerprints off the J.R.R. Tolkien bust in the Three of Diamonds' coffee bar. The girl was the only one in this morning, so she had to work the register and fill the customers' orders. The young redhead was one of the reasons Raja had come to town before the sun was up.

Melissa came to her table. ''Another mocha, Ms. Anumati? Or dessert?'' Her nose crinkled from the dust. Raja found it charming.

She closed her notebook so the girl would not see the mystic sigil there. Melissa had a bit of fire within her. She might perceive something.

''Not right now. Thank you, Melissa.''

The girl took her empty cup, went behind the green glass counter of the coffee bar, and straightened triangles of baklava into uniform rows.

She had a spark of power that one. And so young. Next spring if Paloma was no longer with her, and if the girl did not lose her intuition in a flood of hormones . . . she might do as Raja's next apprentice. She made a note to investigate the girl's parents in case they proved difficult.

Such decisions would have to wait until winter had passed. She had to be conservative. Fall was not the time for untempered actions.

Raja opened her notebook again, careful to smooth the six platinum buttons on the cover. Etched upon them were fanged grimaces to bite unwelcome hands, slanted eyes to watch for intruders, pointed ears to listen for silent footfalls, and two buttons mirror smooth with senses that transcended the mundane. They recognized her touch. The leather binding warmed to let her know it was safe to unseal its gilt pages.

Larry must have known her power cycled with the seasons. What other reason for his delays? Why else would he risk her anger? He had put her off until it was too late for her to react. Shrewd. She should have guessed he was responsible for her missing crows and destroyed him then. She had hoped too much for his help to find the dry water . . . but that was summer, and hope had been everywhere.

She sighed. The vase on her table held a carnation whose pink ruffles were brown and wilted. She touched the blossom. It blushed with fresh color. A hint of cinnamon perfumed the air.

What did Larry want with the water? It was unlikely he would restore the land as she planned to. He would probably use it for personal gain, more power or wealth. Foolishness. He had to be eliminated—not, however, before he led her to the magic.

Outside, leaves blew up Agua de Viva Road, a swirl of orange and red leaves, newspapers, plastic cups, and dust. In a month snow would cover everything, erase every trace of the warm summer.

This year she and the land had been closer than ever. She experienced an ache of pleasure when the yuccas blossomed, felt the soil loosen and thaw, roots tingled from a long sleep, and new leaves uncurled; her blood surged with life and power and freshness. Her spirit soared. She had woven magics more complicated than she could have dreamed a decade ago. But as the air chilled, and the sun dimmed, she moved slower, her thoughts became muddy, her vision dulled, and she napped twice a day. Autumn. It grew worse every year. Come winter she would sleep most of the day and slip into deep depression. What would it be like in a century? Would she die and be resurrected with her land?

And every year there were more roads and people pressing upon the earth, water tainted with sewage, exhaust and steel everywhere. She felt herself suffocating, trod upon, and strangled. It was a slow death. She must redouble her efforts.

Raja's enchantments made her immortal, but it took all her reserves to survive the cold months. It was not a time to war with Judzyas's prophet.

Had it been a mistake to kill Judzyas? His powers of death flourished in winter. He could have removed Larry for her.

No. Judzyas had been a danger to her as well. His motives were a mystery—chasing visions and future ghosts. He had been obsessed with things she would never understand.

As for Larry, Raja would have to outthink him. She would move with slow, sure steps . . . and use Paloma.

Raja inhaled deeply—breathed in the scents of pulp paper, strong coffee, and steamed milk—then turned to a page midway in her notebook. She ran her finger across the lines of her enchantment: thirteen tiny stars arranged to make a larger six-pointed star. Solomon's Seal. Common enough magic to be on every American dollar bill. Her stars, however, were held in place with delicate filigree, Celtic knots braided thirteen times. They glowed with the pale smoke blue of fairy magic. It was a rubbing of the charm she had cast in silver. Sprinkled with moon dust and water from her sacred pool and a drop of her blood, she had then sculpted and polished it to appear as a coin.

Whoever carried the coin left a trail. Every footprint, every overturned stone, and every broken twig Raja could observe in the reflection of her sacred pool. When Larry found the dry water, she would too.

Raja told Paloma it was a charm for luck and love. She knew she would not keep it for herself, but give it to Larry. Paloma's attraction to him was as strong as her loyalty to Raja. It took no magic to see that. She detested using her apprentice in such a calculated manner, but it was the surest way. Larry trusted Paloma.

She traced the outlines of the stars and knots with an 8B graphite pencil. The rough texture reminded her of stone. She sensed that Larry was still on Ferrocarril Mountain, still in her cabin. The coarse charcoal lines reminded her of her mountains as well, the Roof of the World, Gateway to Heaven, the Himalayas.

When Martin Luther began his Protestant revolution in Wittenburg, and when gold and silver from the New World filled Spanish coffers, Raja was eight years old, begging on the streets of Katmandu. Her family had abandoned her, but she had invisible friends to play with, friends that were part air, part smoke, and part whisper. She told her friends stories and sang them the lullabies her mother had sung to her.

Her invisible friends showed her warm places to hide, where to find food, and when the snows came and there were no warm places, they wrapped around her body to protect her from the cold. They told her what the words on the signs said, and what the symbols upon the shrines meant. They told her legends of their lands, stories of Xanadu, Shangri-La, the City of Brass, and the Black Jungles of Raymangal.

The merchants, priests, and other beggars of Katmandu called her Happy Rat, for she was forever smiling and singing to the winds. She always survived the harshest of blizzards, and for that they thought her good luck.

In her thirteenth summer a mountain man came to Katmandu. He purchased mules, barrels of salted meat, flour, and hundreds of candles. When he saw Raja he said that if she came with him, he would give her a warm home. He promised to feed her every day.

Her invisible friends whirled about him—a sudden gust of wind. They said he spoke the truth. They told her that she must go with him.

The man scared Raja. When he looked at her, she saw hunger burning in his eyes. She didn't understand why her invisible friends wanted her to go with him, but she trusted them. She went with the man into the mountains.

They walked for seven days through the snow, higher and higher, above the clouds, until they saw a temple called Tajloni, the Palace of Six Hundred Winds. Three holy men dwelled there. The man sold her to them.

When Raja entered the temple she no longer heard her invisible friends. She mourned for them, and every night cried herself to sleep. During the day, however, she was too busy to cry. The priests made her wash their robes, sweep their floors, cook, keep the incense burning, and polish the six hundred bronze idols of the temple. In return, as promised, she received a hot meal once a day, a bowl of steaming millet.

The idols whispered their names to her, Old Zariatnctmik, Blue Buer, and Ever-Leering Azinomas. They told her that no one would love such an ugly girl. They laughed and chanted her name endlessly to annoy her. She took to the habit of spitting upon them before polishing their gleaming surfaces.

Sometimes she heard her mother's songs or the whispers of her invisible friends upon the winds that drifted down from the Roof of Heaven. When she tried to return their songs, the holy men boxed her ears, and when that failed to quiet her, they beat her until she could not move her swollen lips. In Tajloni silence was the rule.

Raja stole scraps of food, saved rags to wrap herself, and one night, while the three priests slept, she slipped away into the wind-driven snows. She would never return to Tajloni as a slave, never go back to their hurtful touches. Better to freeze on the clean ice. She did not take the path to Katmandu; instead she climbed higher, and abandoned the trail. She followed the winds, and followed her mother's lullabies.

With frost on her face and frozen fingers she found her invisible friends. Here, however, they were more than invisible. On the mountaintops they were real. Only the shadows of their shadows had been with her in Katmandu, where to them it was unbearably warm, and too far from Heaven. They were the spirits of ice and wind and stone. They were the ghosts of lost travelers, the enlightened souls of gurus, sylphs with ice-blue skin, wings of silver silk, and sapphire eyes, and massive squat gnomes with granite shoulders to ride upon. They loved her, a living child to play with, to speak with . . . and to teach.

The ghosts showed her how to turn the cold into warmth. The sylphs taught her which songs excited the winds to typhoons, and which lulled them to sleep. The gnomes let her feel the pulse of the earth. They attuned her body to the cycles of nature. And the spirits of the enlightened ones took her to places that existed half in this world and half in others, worlds of crystal palaces, worlds of perpetual shadow, and worlds filled with stars.

Three years passed, then Raja returned to the Palace of Six Hundred Winds.

She unleashed the frozen storms she had collected on glaciers and screaming ghosts that tore the priests' saffron robes, and left them naked and shivering. Through chattering teeth they cursed her. Raja laughed. She let the snow and frost devour their warmth. Gnomes carried their frozen corpses to the top of Mount Karakal, where their spirits howled with the winds and were forever cold.

Raja read all the holy men's tablets and learned. Her spirit companions brought her food and kept strangers away. The six hundred bronze idols called her Daughter of the Terror Winds, and whenever she walked past them, they whispered their respect.

For two decades Raja sat perched atop the world, then she heard voices from other spirits in far-off lands, chanting in the Nile Valley, laughing on the Assyrian plains, and singing in the misty forests of Ireland. She left her mountains to see what wonders were in the world. She promised her friends to one day return with new songs.

Father Woberty pretended to examine the display case of rare Golden Age science fiction, a collection of Ballantine small edition pulp hardcovers. Every so often he stole glances at Raja.

She didn't like his stares. He wore dark sunglasses to shield his eyes. She couldn't tell what was in them. It was rude. Besides, he was a singularly unattractive man, thin, and unhealthy. He had always been timid. What made him so bold today?

Melissa opened the skylights that ran along the spine of the roof. Light flooded the store and reflected off the display case. Raja thought she saw the illumination flow *around* Woberty. He cast no shadow.

The light reflected from so many sources, however—the big windows up front with the neon glowing pink, from the overhead skylight, and off the glass case—that every side of the man was lit. It had to be illusion.

She blinked. He had colors: indigo flames, smoldering midnight, matte black, then the shades dimmed, flickered, and died altogether. Perhaps the man was borderline schizophrenic with a twin set of colors. Or perhaps she had been blinded by the glare. Father Woberty had no mystic powers. She had known him too long and too well. His classes on attuning crystals only bilked the tourists into buying cheap quartz rocks. And if his claims were true, if he really saw auras, he would not dare stare at her as he did.

He worked his way to the coffee bar, looked at the fruit tortes and cheesecakes, strolled to the local interest section, pulled out a volume, then wandered into the science fiction stacks, through Bester and Blish and Burroughs, rounded the corner and strolled by Orwell, Pohl, and Pournelle, stepped one aisle over to Zelazny, directly next to her table.

"Ms. Anumati," he said, feigning surprise. "How delightful to see you this morning. Would you mind if I join you?"

He sounded confident. Perhaps she had misjudged his rodent character. If she had not been so busy, and he so ugly, she might have considered it. She spied the title of the book he held: *The Natural and Recent History of Seco County.* "I drink alone in the mornings." She brushed her hair, and it crackled with static.

''I promise I will only take a moment of your time.'' He smiled, and it sent a shiver across her shoulders.

She drew her cardigan sweater tighter around and sipped her drink. Raja feared no man, especially Woberty. Then why did she feel like leaving? She touched her spirit to his. There was no warmth and no emotion. It was as if he was not there at all. Perhaps Father Woberty rated further investigation.

''Very well.'' She started to close her notebook.

Father Woberty caught her hand before the cover sealed and her mystic guardians activated. His skin was ice cold.

Only her friends touched her—and then only with permission. She would have slapped him, should have, but all she wanted to do was withdraw her hand from his.

He let go of her and turned the notebook to face him. ''A Celtic motif, am I correct? And this portion looks like a geomantic design that a thirteenth-century heretic might have experimented with. Intriguing. Is this a hobby of yours?''

''It is merely a doodle.''

Raja pushed her spirit deeper into Woberty. It was veiled in shadow and cloaked in a funereal shroud of fog. If Woberty had a soul, she could not perceive it. Perhaps he had sold it to some demon. That would explain much about the man.

Raja took her notebook from him and slammed it shut. ''What do you want?'' She kept her voice even.

''It occurred to me that as a leader of our community you should take an active role in its spiritual growth. I have never seen you at one of our services. There's one Wednesday night, and a seminar afterward on past-life regression. Why don't you drop by? We have free coffee and doughnuts.'' He inched his hand closer to hers.

Raja jerked her hand away. She disliked betraying her emotions, but the man repulsed her. ''Free coffee and doughnuts? So I will feel obliged by your hospitality and make a donation? May I be frank with you, Father?''

''Please.''

''I find your organization reprehensible.'' Raja set her hand in her lap, away from his ghoulish touch. ''You collect money from the community, my community, but no good comes of it.''

''My child,'' he said, looking sincere, ''we have overhead, and rent to pay. We have—''

Without raising her voice she interrupted him. "You have overhead? Let me tell you what you have. You have homeless people, and families on food stamps, because their crops burned up. You have children unable to go to college because our schools are underfunded. You have a government that wants to put a nuclear waste facility in abandoned mines on Ferrocarril Mountain. You have a community dependent on tourism. You have an infestation of parasites like yourself who would rather line their pockets in the name of spirituality than give a dime to the poor. That's what you have."

Her cheeks flushed, revealing her anger, but she didn't care. She wanted to tear this leech's heart out with her bare hands. Raja unclenched her fists, smoothed her sweater, and cooled her blood.

"I see," Woberty said. He looked away from her and drummed his fingers on the table. Raja noticed he wore none of his customary crystals, silver ankhs, or other gaudy accoutrements. Instead, he wore only a slim band of copper on his pinkie.

He stood and offered his hand. "I can see I have taken enough of your time. Perhaps we can discuss this another morning?"

"I don't think so."

He smiled. "We shall see." Woberty then wandered to the cash register, bought his book, and left.

Raja decided to have the man removed in an unpleasant manner—next spring when her powers rejuvenated. Today she had more important annoyances to tend to.

She opened her notebook. Static made the pages cling together.

Raja took a thick-leaded ultramarine art pencil and drew a spiral. She left space in its coils to trace a rune of *Heartache,* jagged like fractured crystal, a symbol of *Self-Loathing,* five arrows imploding inward, and where the spiral came to a single point, she printed a minuscule rune of *Shiva's Soul Disseverment* with precise lines and angles of hideous proportions that could pull apart ego from superego from id. Faint strands connected them, mixed their powers, and made the whole stronger than the sum of its parts. It was magic to drain a person's spirit.

Raja hoped it would not be necessary. No. That was a lie. It had been easy to lie to herself in the spring, when she believed the sun would shine forever. It was harder in autumn. Impossible in the winter. She *would* use this new charm after Larry found the water. She would make him kill himself.

First, however, a distraction for Larry. It was too dangerous to allow him to operate unhampered in her territory. She had to distract him while her powers waned. She took her phone from her suede backpack, then waved to Melissa. ''Another mocha please,'' she said. ''And a slice of strawberry cheesecake?''

''Yes, Ms. Anumati.''

She touched her phone and was shocked by the plastic case. There was an unusual amount of static in the air today. Odd electrical disturbances were normal in Seco County . . . still, Raja didn't like being on the receiving end of them. Perhaps there was a storm brewing.

She cautiously touched the phone again—nothing—then dialed an unlisted number.

''Ownes and Associates Investigations,'' a rough male voice answered.

''Hello, Paul? This is Ms. Anumati.'' The receiver buzzed with white noise.

He inhaled a cigarette, held the smoke, then blew it out, saying, ''Yeah, I'm here. We've got a bad connection. I can barely hear you.''

Raja listened to the hissing static. She imagined she heard breathing, a silent third party eavesdropping. ''Do me a favor. Check this call. Are we being monitored?''

''Hang on.'' There were three clicks and the noise ceased. ''Nope. It's clean . . . at least, it's clean now. You want me to call you back? Or you want me to fly out there?''

''No, just continue to monitor the line.'' That feeling of being spied upon hadn't gone away. The closest person was Melissa. She worked the espresso machine behind the counter, so she couldn't hear Raja over the squealing steam. There was one man in the travel section, and one sipping coffee in the loft. No one within earshot. The feeling persisted.

''Ms. Anumati?''

''I'm here. Do you have my information?''

''On Jasmine Imports? Yeah. You were right. They *are* smuggling Tibetan art. They're using a dummy shipping office out of Sri Lanka. I think I can—''

''I want the information on Larry Ngitis. Jasmine Imports can wait.''

''Ngitis?'' She heard the rustle of papers. ''He was a piece of cake. Hardly worth bruising my knuckles over.''

"I am not paying for your opinion." She turned to a fresh page in her notebook. "Hold on one moment."

Melissa arrived with a fresh mocha and a slice of cheesecake. She set them down and left.

"Go ahead, Paul." Raja picked a glazed strawberry off the top of her dessert and ate it.

"OK. Larry Francis Ngitis. Born in San Francisco. Masters degree in computer science from Berkeley. He spent one summer at Los Alamos setting up networks. Nothing classified. He was in the accounting division. He has three fictional books copyrighted under his name. Mediocre reviews. No big money involved. His TRW says he's piling up bills on his credit cards. With his computer background he might have falsified the database, but I've got a hunch he didn't. He's small potatoes if you ask me."

"Family?"

"His mother's parents were born in Akron, Ohio. Family name Brenner. His father's mother was an army nurse. Her family name was Sexton. His father's father was a soldier in mainland China. I'm still trying to find out how those two got together."

"What about his parents?"

"Dead. He lost his mother in the last earthquake. She got trapped underground. Father bought it in a car accident when your boy, Larry, was three."

"Friends?"

"No one important. College slobs. Lowlifes. No important acquaintances. He had a girlfriend in Oakland. Linda Becket."

"What happened?"

"Talked to the manager of their apartment. Looks like he left her. It was nothing the cops were interested in if that's what you're fishing for. Just left as far as I can tell."

"What else?"

"Arrested in a protest that got out of hand over that oil spill. Possession of marijuana when he was a student. No other criminal record. No major liquor or drug problems. Pays his taxes. Got lucky with the lottery three times for a total of two grand. A real square citizen. Like I said, a piece of cake."

"Give me the address and number of the girlfriend, what did you say her name was? Linda? And fax her picture to my office."

He recited the information, then, ''You want me to check her background too?''

''No. Keep on Ngitis. And keep on Jasmine Imports. I'll call you later about them.''

''Gotcha.'' He paused, inhaled from his cigarette, then, ''Too bad about Walter. He was a slick lawyer. I heard his wife didn't even cover it up. Then again, kinda hard to cover up opening a guy's rib cage with a shotgun. Wonder what he did to her?''

''Who can tell why a person does anything,'' Raja said. ''I'll be in touch.''

She disconnected. The channel popped. Static brushed her skin.

Raja turned to the next page in her notebook. She used a green ultra fine Sharpie to scribble an icon of *Yearning*. From its sensual S-shaped backbone curved spikes flared, concave inflections that caught the attention of the eye and heart.

Raja dialed Linda's number. There was no static this time. She checked her watch. It was seven in the morning on the West Coast.

''Hello?'' A tired female voice answered.

''Linda Becket? This is Raja Anumati. I am calling on behalf of Larry Ngitis.''

Silence.

''I am a friend of his. I was wondering if you could help.''

''Help? Larry? The bastard owes me money. Who the hell are you?''

''I represent Perspective Publishing. Mister Ngitis is in trouble, emotional trouble if you gather my meaning? He is not writing, and we may have to sue him for the return of our advance. We enjoy Larry's work. We would rather see him finish this fourth novel than pursue the matter legally, but his deadline has been extended twice.''

''Larry is always a little off. I don't understand what this has to do with me.''

''I was wondering if I could impose upon you to call Larry, or perhaps even visit him in New Mexico. Your expenses would, naturally, be covered.''

''No.''

Raja lowered her voice. ''Miss Becket, you do not understand the gravity of Larry's condition. I am afraid he is on the verge of a nervous breakdown.'' She let a bit of the land's power trickle into her sketch. The drawn lines thickened, and tiny jewels sparkled upon its sharp points—emeralds and cool jade and tourmaline—irresistible, impossible to ignore.

Linda was quiet a moment, then whispered, ''Maybe I could call. What's set him off this time?''

''He is blocked. I can only guess, but I believe he is not over his relationship with you. That is why I thought a call from you could clear this up.''

Raja heard her sigh. She pressed her. ''He is a lonely and deeply depressed man. Let me give you his phone number.'' Raja recited the number at the cabin. ''When do you think you could visit him? I will arrange the flight.''

''I work full-time, Ms. Anumati. I have a vacation in three weeks. I might be able to move it up, but I'd have to check with my . . .'' Linda's voice trailed off, then she firmly said, ''No.''

''I beg your pardon?''

''No. I'm not going to drop everything and everyone I have here just because Larry Ngitis is blocked. He didn't want anything to do with me before. He's just going to have to learn to get on without me now. That was his decision. Not mine. If he needs help, let him hire a nurse or a shrink or a baby-sitter.''

Raja nudged more power into her enchantment. The corners gleamed with diamonds, tiny rainbows of clear color that even she found herself attracted to. But this was as far as she was willing to take it. Any more magic and she risked not having enough to last the winter. ''I assure you he is more than blocked. I believe he is suicidal.''

''Suicidal?'' Linda's voice tightened to a squeak. Raja sensed the spikes of the *Yearning* icon catch. ''I had no idea. I'll speak with my boss. I'm sure she'll let me go.''

''Good,'' Raja purred. ''Let me give you the name of my travel agent in San Francisco. She can arrange everything you will need.''

''I'll call her right away. Thank you.''

''Good. If there are any problems ask her to call me. I can take care of it. Thank you, Miss Becket.'' She hung up.

Raja pinched the bridge of her nose and staved off her exhaustion. She had finished off her mocha and the cheesecake but not remembered doing so. With the previous two mochas she should have enough sugar and caffeine in her to vibrate. Instead, she was ready for a nap.

She turned to a fresh page and composed a haiku poem to relax

her mind. It had been a busy morning, but now Larry would have his ex-lover underfoot.

And if she had to, Raja would use Linda as bait—or as a hostage.

''Another mocha, Ms. Anumati?'' Melissa asked.

She handed the girl her empty cup. ''Coffee this time, I think. Black. I need a pick-me-up.'' She smiled at Melissa, who blushed beneath her freckles and smiled back. ''And call me Raja.''

Chapter 10

"YOU'RE WRONG," O'DONALD SAID. HE RAISED THE SHOTGUN.

Larry saw him squint down the length of the double barrels pointed straight at his heart.

He fired.

A flash and explosion. Fireworks detonated in front of O'Donald. Metal ricocheted off a tool chest, off the hydraulic lift, pinged against the steel oil drum, and whizzed past Larry's head.

O'Donald dropped the shotgun—blossomed like a metal flower, its stock blown to kindling. His face was a mass of blood and smoldering metal. He slumped behind the poker table.

Matt glanced at O'Donald's cards. "The snake didn't have no aces and eights," he said, grinning, "but it was a deadman's hand all the same."

Larry touched his face and patted his shirt. No holes. No blood. "H—How did that happen?" he whispered.

Baxter crouched next to O'Donald. "You got lucky," she said. "That's how it happened."

Larry touched Paloma's silver dollar. "Lucky?"

"The shells exploded like something plugged up the barrel," Baxter said. "I've never seen anything like it."

Larry tasted gunpowder. This was what he had sensed at Raja's

party, not a suicide, more like a grenade going off in O'Donald's face. "Should we call 911?"

Spencer and the Indian stepped closer and examined O'Donald. They exchanged glances, then Spencer said, "The idiot's gone. Calling the doc ain't gonna do him, or us, any good now."

"It's not my fault," Baxter told them. "I cleaned that thing two days ago." She looked at the gnarled metal. "Shot it myself a thousand times."

Matt sauntered over to Larry. "I'll tell ya what happened, Chinaman. Bullets done killed me. Thirteen slugs. That gives me power over them little bits o' lead. I nudged the ones in that barrel—wedged 'em in good." Matt slapped his knee and whooped, "The snake never knew what hit him." He stuck his face an inch away from Larry's. "Reckon ya owe me one. Don't forget it."

"He had a wife," the Indian said, and rubbed one of his gold rings. "She must be told."

"We'll say it was suicide," Spencer said. "That's the best way. He was a writer. Happens too damn often around here."

"No." Baxter told the Indian, "John, you get the sheriff. Tell him O'Donald was playing around with the shotgun, and it went off in his face. All the evidence will back that up, powder burns, my busted gun. He'll buy that. I'll call O'Donald's wife. She's a good woman. Too bad she married a fool."

"I'll tell the others," Spencer said.

"They're not going to like this." Baxter stroked her chin, then added, "So after you call them take your friend out for a long walk—about a week or two. John, you get Steve and Roger, and follow this map. And watch out, it might be a trap."

She turned to Larry. "Mister, if you and your map check out then you're in. If not . . ." She looked at O'Donald, then, "If not, you're going to wish O'Donald hadn't blown his face off. You're going to wish he shot you clean through the head."

Larry stared into the campfire—real mesquite, no more burning bones. In the last two weeks he had seen only a handful of hallucinations. Spencer had kept him too busy to think.

He dragged Larry across every mountain and canyon that Seco County had, giving him blisters on his hands and feet, teaching him to climb rocks with rope, carabiner, and piton, and avoiding any traces of civilization. They were in the hills twenty miles east of Ferrocarril Mountain. North was a desert full of prickly pear and spiny lechuguilla, tarantulas and translucent green scorpions that lurked under every rotten log.

"What are you gonna do with your share of the Carlson take?" Spencer asked. He plucked the coffeepot off the fire, filled a blue-enameled tin cup, and handed it to Larry.

Larry took the cup, but his eyes locked onto the Browning strapped to Spencer's hip. He couldn't believe Spencer could murder him. When he thought about it he smelled gunpowder and hot metal.

"I'll write for a while with my cut," he replied. Larry wasn't sure how long that "while" would be. Baxter found them two days ago. She told them the map was genuine. The Lobos sin Orejas discovered a stash of antique firearms, reams of Confederate money, U.S. mailbags stuffed with silver Spanish pieces of eight, American double eagles, and a sea chest overflowing with gold Napoleonic twenty-franc coins. A fortune.

Baxter was still checking *him* out, though. She said a woman was in town, asking questions about Larry—looked like a government agent to her. If Spencer couldn't kill him, Baxter could.

"What did your pals do to that FBI agent?" Larry asked.

"I wish O'Donald had kept his trap shut about that."

"But he didn't. Answer my question."

Spencer scratched his stomach, then said, "Don't get the wrong idea about us Lobos. We got a smooth operation here. We just want to be left alone. No taxes. No regulations." He sipped his coffee. "And that feller wasn't FBI. He was from the Department of the Interior. Came out 'cause he heard there were caves here bigger than Carlsbad. Stumbled onto one of our mines. One of us got jumpy."

"And shot him?"

Spencer was quiet, poured himself more coffee, then, "He woulda messed it up. The Lobos know how to take care of caves. We treat 'em better than our girlfriends. Look what the government did to Carlsbad Caverns. They put a parking lot smack on the top of her. Dried her up and killed her. Now they're talking about putting nuclear waste down there."

His hand strayed to the silver flask—touched it—but didn't pull it out.

Nausea rolled through Larry. This close to Spencer, he tasted the

Anabuse coursing in his blood. One drop of that home-brew would make him violently ill. Larry too.

Spencer changed the subject. "I wonder how Carlson got those francs? He musta been trading in New Orleans."

"Carlson didn't trade anything," Larry said. "He robbed and killed. He was a bastard."

"Now you watch what ya say 'bout the feller that saved yer hide," Matt said, appearing next to him. He tilted his Stetson so his eyes were covered in shadow.

"The way I figure it," Spencer said, "Carlson was down on his luck after the Civil War. He took what he thought was his from the Yankee railroads and government."

Matt grinned. "This guy's a hoot. Wanna know 'bout that Frenchy money? There was a feller who traded New Orleans to Saint Louis. He got itchy to come out West, hearin' all them stories 'bout silver and gold and turquoise just layin' on the ground." He pointed across the desert. "See that canyon? Got steep cliffs five hundred paces in. Nice place to camp. Nice place fer a bushwhackin'."

Larry squinted and saw six men on horseback and two wagons roll into the canyon. Gunshots crackled, then their echoes, screams . . . silence.

Spencer hadn't heard a thing.

Larry closed his eyes and made the vision go away.

"Didn't put up much of a fight," Matt said, disappointed. "He had beaver pelts and lotsa gold and silver. Had a pretty daughter too." Matt's smiled widened.

"Matt Carlson was a bastard," Larry said. "Take my word on it." He reached into his mouth and dug out the bullet.

"Hey! Chinaman. Don't—" Matt vanished.

"Your bridge giving you trouble again?" Spencer asked.

"Yeah. It's a real pain in the ass."

Spencer tossed his coffee into the fire. "So where do you wanna go today?"

"My cabin. I need my laptop." Larry wondered if Paloma was there, if she had brought him breakfast the last two Mondays.

"You know I can't let you. Baxter wouldn't like that."

His manuscript was due at Perspective. If they wanted to, they could demand their advance back, money that he had already spent.

Spencer had found him a notepad in his backpack. Larry filled its pages the first day. On the second day he wrote in tiny block letters between his sloppy cursive script. By the fourth day he resorted to writing on toilet paper, delicately so as not to rip it. He needed to organize his notes, run them through a spell checker, and print them. One accidental sneeze or wipe and two weeks of his prizewinning prose would be lost.

''How about a hike in Lost Silver Canyon?'' Spencer suggested. ''Afterwards, we could take a swim in the creek.''

''That sounds—''

Niyol waved to Larry from a stand of piñon pines. It was the first time he had seen the boy ghost since he had devised this scheme.

''Give me a second while I get rid of this coffee.'' Larry got up and headed for the trees.

''Don't go and wander too far,'' Spencer said, without turning around.

''You want to watch?'' Larry asked.

''Don't get your feathers in a ruffle. Just do your business, and let's get a move on.''

Larry stood by a pine where Spencer could see him, but far enough away so he couldn't hear him whisper. ''Where have you been?'' he hissed at Niyol. ''I've been stuck out here for two weeks.''

''Has the cat guarded your dreams? I sent him, but he is lazy.''

''The cat is everywhere in my dreams, sleeping, eating, licking himself. I wake up with his hair all over me. Yeah, he's around. Where were *you?*''

''I apologize for leaving.'' Niyol looked away as Larry unzipped his pants and peed. ''But it was safest.''

''Safe with Spencer and his buddies? They're going to kill me.''

''They will soon be satisfied that you are not a government spy. You will be one of them. They will protect you.''

''From Raja?'' He snorted.

''No. Not from her.'' Niyol sighed. ''And there is another presence in Dry Water.''

''Another witch?''

''Something different. I sense it grows stronger as the witch grows weaker.'' Niyol glanced over his shoulder. ''We must move first, and quickly. Go north. I shall guide you to the sacred cavern and the water that cannot be drunk.''

''Dry water,'' Larry spit the words out. ''Look, Niyol, no offense, but I can't play this game with you anymore. You've gotten me involved with criminals, a witch with powers I don't understand, ghosts, and God knows what else. I'm leaving Seco County. I've got to get to a safe place . . . a normal place.''

''There is no longer any safe place for you,'' Niyol said, ''nor any place normal.''

''But I'm not hallucinating anymore,'' Larry lied. ''I don't need you. I'm leaving. I have a novel to finish.''

''There is more at stake in Seco County than your novel . . . or your life.'' Niyol's eyes were two black mirrors. ''What do your prophetic powers show you? Drive back to California. What then?''

Larry swallowed. Saliva stuck in his throat. Back to Oakland. That was easy to think about. He'd get his old job and write at nights—

Three cinder blocks slammed into Larry. The first crushed his forehead. White-hot fragments of bone penetrated his brain and broke the world like a pane of glass.

He stood on the beach. Black water lapped his boots. It was sludge with trash floating on top, and things half-alive squirming in the oily layers in between. Drops of acid rain made his skin smolder. A city stretched across the horizon, rising like a mountain range: cold fluorescent lights, a blanket of brown fog, people and machines pulsing corpuscularly through tubes. The enormity of it crushed Larry's spirit.

The second stone cracked his left temple. He saw death, a skeleton of the city: twisted ruined buildings, concrete gravel, and glass. Human bodies with bar-code tattoos on their foreheads lay on the streets, in the water, and at his feet. The scent of decomposition, ozone, and singed hair was overwhelming.

The last cinder block snapped his spine. Electrical shock, then Larry floated in shadow. He had never been. He didn't exist. He was nothing.

Niyol's voice, distant, called: ''Larry?''

He leaned on a pine tree; the rough bark was the first thing he sensed. Then the odor of vomit. The world snapped back into focus. A mosquito buzzed in his ear.

''What the hell was that?'' he whispered.

''What will happen if you do not finish what has started,'' Niyol replied, and crossed his arms.

''It's not what *I* started,'' Larry hissed. ''You and Raja are the ones fighting over this damn dry water. Not me.''

Niyol pressed his lips together, and the color drained from his features. "You are in this. When you took my help to wrestle with your new perceptions, you chose a side. Accept responsibility. Do not walk away."

Larry wiped bile from his mouth. He spit. "Maybe I picked the wrong side."

"You have seen what Raja's world shall look like if she wins."

Larry didn't trust Niyol. He wasn't lying, but he wasn't telling the entire truth either. "How do I know your world won't be worse?"

Niyol laughed. "You have never understood. The water that cannot be drunk is not for me. It is for you."

"What the hell am I supposed to do with it?"

"Enlightenment cannot be explained, only experienced."

"Everything OK back there?" Spencer called.

"Give me another minute," Larry shouted back.

"Assuming I've got nothing better to do today," he whispered to Niyol, "and I go to this sacred cavern of yours, what do you want me to do with Spencer? He doesn't even let me out of his sight to go to the bathroom."

"You will need Spencer," Niyol said. "Tell him the cavern has gold and silver. It is the truth."

Larry didn't buy any of Niyol's Zen Buddhist enlightenment crap, but he did trust his own visions. If he left he was dead—by lightning, by crows, or by . . . by whatever he had seen a second ago.

"OK, Niyol. You win for now. But once I get this dry water you're going to answer my questions."

"As you wish. We must move with alacrity, however, and cross the desert before nightfall."

"What's the rush?"

"Tonight is All Saints' Eve, Halloween. Tonight the dead are as real as the living."

"What's in this place?" Spencer asked. "More of Carlson's loot?"

Larry stopped, kicked the mud off his boots, then continued to march through the desert. It must have rained recently, although Larry recalled no storm last night. "Not Carlson's loot," he replied. "Something better this time."

Spiny cycads and palm trees grew here instead of the mesquite and pine Larry had seen in the hills. The image of Niyol wavered over the sand like a mirage.

"I gotta tell the other Lobos about this," Spencer said. "I ain't gonna cheat 'em outta anything."

"I wasn't asking you to."

Spencer took off his hat and scratched his head. "Couldn't hurt to check it out first, though. Wouldn't want to get 'em all excited over nothing."

A dragonfly buzzed overhead, and scarab beetles scuttled with authority over the sand, unafraid in their glistening green armor.

"You know where you're going?" Spencer asked.

Niyol pointed north to the hills with streaks of white rock, and answered Spencer's question even though the old man couldn't hear him. "There, through legend and history. Pay attention to the path, Larry. You may have to find your way back—alone."

"I know where I'm going," Larry said. Wherever it was, it wasn't Seco County. Ferrocarril Mountain was sharper and taller this morning. The rim of the sky had too much pink and orange, and the air glistened crystalline.

The sugar-fine sand absorbed their footprints. They weren't blown away; they faded out of existence.

There were other footprints, however, and it was difficult to tell if they were real or hallucination. Larry didn't ask Spencer if he saw the three-toed marks that were larger than anything that lived in Larry's world. He'd only seen footprints like them before in museums, in fossilized river bedrock.

"Sure is humid." Spencer wiped his forehead. "I've lived here forty years and it's never been so . . . so tropical. Where is this place?"

Larry stopped and scanned the desert. Obelisks of green stone towered on the horizon, cities of odd geometric glittering glass, muddy rivers the color of blood, and black pyramids. They flickered in the wavering heat.

"Do not delay," Niyol urged. "There are creatures and places that branch from the main trail. You would not wish to meet them."

Larry turned away and gazed at the hills. Quartzite sparkled in the sun.

"I know where I'm going," he told Spencer.

A slim path switchbacked up the hill, steep, and strewn with crushed limestone. Larry paused to examine the tiny fossils of trilobites and coral and spiral nautilus encrusted in them.

Niyol led him to two massive rocks that leaned on one another.

There was a crack between them that widened at the base. Turned sideways, one person could slide through.

Spencer went in. "There's a door," he called back. "The lock is rusted off. You coming?"

Larry hated small places. He wasn't claustrophobic, but whenever he could touch three out of four walls he got nervous.

Spencer poked his head out. "Come on." A smile cracked his leathery skin. "There's all sortsa stuff in here. You gotta take a look."

"Give me a second to catch my breath."

Niyol stood behind him wearing the pajamas Larry had first seen him in. Blood soaked a pattern of flannel elephants and giraffes and matted his hair. It was as if he had just stepped from the car wreck that killed him. "I cannot make you go in. You must trust me."

Larry ignored him and drank from his canteen.

"Then trust yourself. Your instincts. Your vision."

Maybe his visions were wrong. How could he prevent what he had seen? It didn't make sense.

The desert was normal, gray and tan, no palm trees, and no obelisks. It was not the land he had walked across this morning. Creeping over Ferrocarril Mountain, a thunderhead loomed, solid black mass that smothered the setting sun; wisps of rain brushed the earth, and within its shadows lightning flickered.

"Happy Halloween," Larry muttered. Death was coming, for him and for the rest of the world. The feeling was a cold lump of iron in the pit of his stomach. "OK. I'm going."

He held his breath and squeezed between the rocks.

"Whoever built this place was ready for anything," Spencer said.

In the last hour they had searched the small cavern room. There was a dusty couch, a folding card table with three chairs, a portable toilet, crates of Civil Defense rations, drums of chemically treated water, ropes, a Geiger counter, a dozen acetylene lanterns with pounds of solid fuel, flashlights, scores of corroded batteries, and a lead-lined suit and helmet.

"This has to be for radiation," Spencer said, and tried the helmet on.

"It's someone's bomb shelter," Larry replied. He tried the Geiger counter. No clicks. Dead.

In the corner was a steel door with a compression seal that looked like it belonged in a submarine. Larry spun the hatch and pulled it opened. A blast of wind erupted from the other side and knocked him down. A rumbling noise spilled out, continuous, deep, and resonant. Inside was a lift, hand-powered by rope and pulleys.

"That's a cave down there for sure," Spencer said, and slammed the door shut. "Big difference in pressure. And you smell that air? It's wet. That means a living cave. It's gonna be slippery."

"What's the noise?"

Spencer shook his head. "Dunno. Guess we're gonna have to find out." He spent the next hour disassembling the lift's rope and pulley system, rethreading the rotten line with a new one, and oiling the moving parts.

Larry hooked a handheld acetylene lantern to his belt, tested the batteries in his flashlight, and checked the fit of his climbing harness—snug. It kept his hands from shaking. It kept him from thinking about what waited down that hole.

"Technically we're breaking the rules," Spencer declared. "You need at least four people to go into a cave."

"Four?"

"So you're never alone. If one guy breaks his leg, you got one to stay with him, and two go for help. No one ever gets left alone." He glanced at the lift, then said, "But to tell you the truth, I'm real curious to see what's down there."

Larry donned a hard hat with a lamp on the crown. "Then let's get it over with." He looked for Niyol. The ghost had vanished.

Spencer unbuckled his gun belt and set it in the corner. "Never liked taking a pistol into a cave. Them ricochets will kill you." He looked Larry straight in the eye. "I'm gonna trust you."

"Don't worry," he replied. "You can."

They opened the submarine door, braced against the wind, pushed in, then slammed it shut behind them.

Larry flicked on his flashlight. Air whistled through the cracks in the door. Beneath his feet it felt like a continuous earthquake.

Spencer whispered, "That rope I used was new, but I wish we had a backup line. Keep an ear on it."

Larry nodded, then Spencer let the rope wind through the pulleys.

Ten seconds down and the air became noticeably hotter. Water vapor steamed through the cracks in the floorboards. Sweat trickled down Larry's face. He closed his eyes, and pretended he was outside instead of trapped in this closet-sized sauna.

Thirty seconds down, and Spencer stopped. ''Maybe we should go back. I got a bad feeling about that noise.''

Thunder vibrated through Larry's calves. Overhead, the rope creaked and stretched. The frame of the lift groaned. He wished Niyol hadn't disappeared. He didn't know what to do. ''Let's try a few more feet. I think we're close.''

Spencer shook his head, sighed, then slowly let out more rope through the pulleys.

The lift reverberated and made Larry's teeth buzz. Below was the sound of a hundred rolling bowling balls, steel drums that smashed together, and angry gods. He leaned against the wall, and heard the straining of the rope and the squealing of the lift's rusty mechanisms. It got hotter too. He imagined they were being lowered into a pot of boiling water.

They hit the bottom—hard, and Larry dropped the flashlight.

Spencer opened the door. The rumbling noise filled the lift, twice as loud as it had been before. He played his lantern's light down a corridor of roughly hewn rock. Water vapor curled like smoke in the tunnel. Larry saw timber supports, rotten and fallen, covered with fuzzy orange fungus.

Spencer shouted over the din: ''Lead the way.''

Larry wanted to lead the way back into the lift, back up and out into the open air. He felt smothered breathing this thick wet atmosphere. Stepping out, he discovered the gravel on the floor was slimy, and his footsteps unsure.

Twenty paces in, Larry ignited his acetylene lantern. A small flame sputtered, then blazed white-hot in the brass ignition chamber. It was three times as bright as his flashlight. Shadows leapt as if they were alive. He saw bones littering the gravel floor: ribs, femurs, and a skull. He wasn't certain if they were real.

Spencer squinted down the tunnel, held his lantern higher, then marched ahead. Larry followed.

Thirty paces and the tunnel branched. On the wall where the right and left passages joined was the outline of a handprint, fingers pointed down. Over someone's palm, red paint had been spattered.

''It's one of the signs,'' Spencer yelled. ''From the diary.'' He scrutinized the palm and held his hand over it.

Larry barely heard him over the roar. "What diary?"

Spencer opened his mouth, then shook his head. "Too much to explain now."

Larry looked at the print. The fingers shrank and fused, and the handprint melted into a red skull. Fingers turned into teeth, and yellow eyes appeared to glare at him.

"This way," Spencer said. He headed down the right path.

Larry grabbed his arm. "No. We go left." The path away from the skull.

"What?"

"The left path," Larry yelled.

Spencer looked down the right. He got close to Larry's ear. "You've been dead right so far, so left it is. I wanna check this tunnel on the way out, OK?"

Larry nodded. On the way out . . . if they came out.

Twenty more paces, and the tunnel twisted right, then left, sloped down—and ended. It opened into empty space.

Larry held his lantern over the edge, but the light was absorbed by the mist that rose from the blackness. Drops of rain fell from a ceiling he couldn't see. This was where the thunder was, grumbling and booming, and making his ears ring, the inside of a gigantic drum, the belly of a dragon: the sound of rushing water echoing off the walls of this enormous cavern.

Spencer pointed to his left. Stairs had been carved along the wall. They plunged at a sixty-degree angle and glistened with water. "You still think this is the right way?" he yelled into his ear.

Larry concentrated on the blackness. He was scared. He wanted to go back, but no ghosts rose out of the mist to warn him. He nodded.

"Then we get the others. Do this right with pitons and ropes. No money is worth selling your life for."

Larry shook his head.

Spencer frowned, creasing the lines in the corners of his eyes. He took off his hard hat and lit the tiny acetylene lamp on the crown. Larry did the same. "If you're going, then remember to keep your hands on that wall, but don't hug it. That'll throw your center of gravity all outta kilter. Three points of contact at all times. And I gotta tell you, I think you're mighty stupid."

Larry swallowed and took his first step. The rock was slippery with water and slimemold. There were handholds carved in the wall; they were just as slick.

He eased onto the next step—and slid.

Larry grabbed a handhold, and hugged the wall like Spencer told him not to do. His grip started to slip. He took a deep breath, shifted position, arched his back out, not in, and steadied himself, then forced his foot to take the third step down, then the fourth. Drops of water pelted his hard hat and trickled down his back.

Spencer waited until Larry was eight steps down, then followed.

Larry tested every stair and every handhold to see if it held his weight. He lost count around three hundred steps. He lost track of time as well in the darkness and the droning thunder below. It was hypnotic.

He extended his foot . . . but the previous ledge continued. There was no next step. It was the bottom. The floor vibrated and jangled his stomach; it made the hairs on his arms dance.

He looked up.

White frothing water roared through a jagged channel of eroded limestone, a liquid storm barely contained. It was a flash flood, a tidal wave, a sea serpent that flashed past his light. He took an involuntary step back from the edge. It was boiling.

Spencer marched upstream. He ignited both his lanterns, turned on his flashlight, then directed them to the far wall: water exploded out of the ground in a continuous geyser. A skyscraper of liquid shot up, half steam, splashed and collected in a cauldron pool, then cascaded down a three-tiered waterfall to become the great torrent that rushed into the absolute darkness beyond.

The remains of a bridge stood in the river: two rusting steel pylons, one on each side with cable tangled about their bases. Useless.

Spencer walked downstream.

Larry examined the river where it flowed smoothly. It smelled of sulfur and almonds and turpentine. Mats of black bacterial scum clung to the bank and six stones made a zigzagging hopscotch across the river.

Spencer returned. "There's no place to cross," he shouted.

Larry pointed to the steppingstones.

"You're not thinking . . ."

Larry nodded.

Billions dead; he had seen it. And him too, if he didn't find what was on the other side. Maybe his vision had been wrong. Hallucination and reality had merged since he had come to Seco County. How could he trust anything he saw? Why should he risk his neck to stop something that *might* happen? It was ludicrous. It was true.

"I have to," he yelled to Spencer.

Spencer frowned. "What's on that other side that's worth your life?"

"I don't know," Larry admitted.

"Damn it. I can't stop you, but I ain't gonna follow you neither." He took off his pack and dug out his silver flask. "Here. You'll need a slug of this."

Larry took it, and hesitated, remembering how he had choked on the stuff. He took a small sip, and let the liquor trickle down and warm him.

He held it out to Spencer.

"Naw, keep it. I gotta stop anyways, and that flask always brought me luck in poker. You're gonna need it."

Luck. Larry touched Paloma's silver dollar in his pocket. "Thanks."

Spencer clipped a rope to Larry's climbing harness. "If you get across . . . when you get across, tie this to the bridge on the other side. It'll help on the way back."

Larry nodded.

"I'm giving you lots of slack—don't wanna tangle you up. I figure if you fall in, the way this stuff is boiling, by the time I'd pull you out you'd be medium rare."

Larry checked the strap on his hard hat, tied the flashlight to his belt, pulled his gloves snug, then went to the edge, and stared at the first steppingstone.

Niyol had taught him how to banish all thought, to concentrate, to focus on one thing alone. The thunder faded. The dripping water stopped. The boiling water was not there. Only the rock. It had a flat top, smooth, covered in slime.

A step and a jump.

Before thinking, he had done it. The stone was solid. He didn't slip.

The next boulder was a full body length away. Larry swung his arms, and leapt. Both feet hit and slid an inch.

Adrenaline burned through this heart. He let it. He didn't panic. He glanced upstream to find the third rock, and saw the waterfalls, a wall of splashing violent water and steam. He jumped.

The stone teetered; his knees buckled to compensate, and he didn't overextend. He and the boulder rocked together and regained their balance.

The fourth stone was submerged. It was small, no larger than one of his boots. A thin sheet of water skimmed over it; ripples showed him where the edges were.

It was the halfway point . . . the turning-around point. Larry banished that thought and jumped.

He landed on one foot—firm—up to his ankle in the water. The splash scalded his arms. The waterproofing on his boots saved his foot. It was uncomfortably hot; Larry shifted to his left foot.

Rock number five was a jagged tooth jutting from the river, white froth on one side, a whirlpool on the other.

Larry pushed off, one hand caught the tip, the other a solid handhold, one foot landed square—the other slipped into the water.

It stung and soaked his jeans up to his thigh. He scrambled up the rock. His leg tingled with agony as if it were asleep. Larry flexed and it responded sluggishly.

Sweat drizzled into his eyes. His concentration was gone.

He had to move. The rock was unbearably hot through his gloves. The last rock was two body lengths away, but he had some height from this rock. It looked deceptively solid, a square of dark stone.

He coiled his body, held his breath—jumped.

The air was so thick with steam that Larry imagined that he could grab onto it if he had to.

He landed.

The rock tilted and slid into the river.

Larry spun on one foot. He twisted and grabbed at the air. In the corner of his vision he saw the bank, close. Without losing his forward momentum, he pushed off the falling rock, toppled awkwardly, arced his body like a pole vaulter, and landed shoulder first on firm rock.

He lay there a moment, numb and too scared to move, with a hundred thousand gallons of boiling water rushing past him, inches away.

On the other bank he saw a light: Spencer danced a jig and waved his lantern up and down in victory.

Larry got up and waved back. He tied his rope to the rusted fallen bridge, then limped to the far side of the cavern.

There were a dozen tunnels, natural fissures, ancient mine shafts, rough-cut stone passages, and organic orifices that disappeared into the earth. Larry investigated the first, and it branched three times, then each of those split again. This was a labyrinth.

He backed out into the main cavern.

"Niyol? Where the hell are you?"

Only the thunder of the river answered him.

Down every passage, however, footprints meandered, some booted, others barefoot, and some of creatures not human . . . and one pair of small sneakers.

Larry followed the imprints of the sneakers, down wormholes, squeezing through tubes, and down vast corridors where the ceiling was hidden behind rows of stalactite teeth. Niyol waited for him.

"The cavern of Dai Esthai is here," he said. "Come."

"I'm not going anywhere until you explain why you left me."

"There are traps and obstacles to test worthy mortals as well as spirits. Had I accompanied you, I would have had to deal with . . . unpleasant experiences. Instead, I took a shortcut."

"You could have warned me. You might have given me directions."

"That was part of the test. Besides, if I had told you of the difficulties, would you have come?"

"No," Larry said. Then he caught himself and snapped, "I don't know. Maybe."

Niyol turned and vanished through a crack in the wall.

"You little creep," Larry muttered. He turned sideways, and pushed himself down thirty feet of crevice. It got cold fast. The fissure opened into a grotto. He panned his light down and saw no bottom.

Frost covered the rock. Icicle stalactites and stalagmites glistened in his light. The cold condensed the water in the air. Fog and mist and steam coalesced and spun around a blob of water suspended below a single smooth stalactite.

Larry shivered in his wet clothes.

Niyol floated at the edge of the rotating cloud. "Follow me. The mist will support you."

"Tell me another one," Larry said.

"Touch it if you do not believe."

Larry found a good handhold, then leaned into the fog. It was semisolid like whipped cream. He leaned farther. It was taffy; he grabbed hold, and pushed.

The mass of vapor swept him along, but his weight dragged him down. He scrambled up, through pillows, and foam rubber, up into the center, where the air was solid.

Larry had seen the cloud accelerate as it spun into the center, but now inside, it slowed, and the walls of the cavern contracted.

Droplets shone in his light. When he turned away, the illumination remained in them, sparkling like diamonds in air.

They were stars.

There was Orion, and the three stars that made his belt, what Niyol had called the Hunter's Canoe. Larry stared at it, and saw the Hunter appear in his boat, staring back at him. He saw the Star Maiden blow him a kiss. A swarm of iridescent blue hummingbirds circled her, dispersed, and darted through the cloud. He saw fish and scorpions and heroes and dragons—every constellation in the sky, galloping and shooting arrows and swimming and leaping—all alive.

He spiraled into the center, toward a glistening ball of water no larger than his closed fist. It vibrated, not frozen, more gelatinous than liquid.

"Take it," Niyol whispered. "Take it and save yourself. Save your world."

Larry grabbed Spencer's silver flask and dumped the booze out.

He pressed the lip of the flask to the water. The sphere shrank by half, yet Larry did not feel the flask fill.

"Drink it," Niyol urged.

"What's going to happen?"

"Life," he said. "Death. Everything between."

Larry hesitated. This was what Raja had wanted? All he had to do was give it to her and she'd leave him alone. Maybe pay him. But if she had it . . . if he left Seco County, he had seen what would happen: the darkness and death. It would be his fault.

He pressed the flask to his lips and drank.

Chapter 11

NICK CUT ACROSS FATHER WOBERTY'S ARM WITH A SCALPEL, DEEP enough to draw blood, and deep enough to scar. He had hundreds of such marks along his thighs and arms.

A breeze stirred the piñon pines about the meadow. Thirty monks had gathered here for midday Mass.

He set the knife upon the altar, staining a white linen cloth that had countless other stains upon it, then took a silver chalice and collected his dripping blood. He held it before his brothers. "That I have sinned exceedingly in thought," he said, "in word, and in deed, through my fault, through my most grievous fault."

They disrobed and flogged themselves with whips made of yucca until welts appeared; some struck so hard they drew blood. They wailed: "*Mea culpa*. My fault. All blame is mine."

Nick's assistant handed him a red-hot iron rod.

He reminded himself this was not his body, even so, he hesitated before pressing the scalding metal into his palm.

Stay in the role, he told himself, and blotted out the pain. One more evening as Father Woberty was all he required.

The odor of charred flesh, his flesh, made him gag. He swallowed bile, then spoke: "Lord, have mercy upon us. Christ, have mercy upon us."

Father Woberty was not the greedy man Nick had thought he was, nor the parasite Raja believed, nor a New Age priest with quartz crystals and a Land Rover. He led a secret religious organization, *Los Hermanos Penitentes*, an order of monks that practiced self-flagellation to rid themselves, and the world, of sin.

Under Father Woberty's guidance the Penitentes had taken their practices a step farther: electrocutions, thumbscrews, impalement, genital disfigurement, and burnt offerings. They had assault weapons and secret bank accounts. They believed the end of the world was near. Now Nick was their leader.

He knew all the rituals of the Catholic Mass; he had lived through the Spanish Inquisition and the Crusades. He had participated in more breaking of bread and bones and drinking of blood than he cared to remember.

In a private sanctuary beneath Father Woberty's church was a silver cross three feet tall that weighed half a ton, and gleamed with encrusted emeralds and turquoise. In the floor under this cross were fifteen burial vaults. Every Good Friday one Penitente had the honor of reenacting the crucifixion, an honor bestowed only on the most worthy. He despised their ignorance. No holy powers flowed from their tortures, only senseless pain.

Nick finished the Mass, then said to his congregation, "Brothers, tonight we venture into this darkest of all nights. Let not your desires or fears tempt you from the right path. *Pax Domini si semper vobiscum*—the peace of the Lord be always with you."

He tasted bitter hypocrisy in his mouth.

Nick's assistant, Jack, bandaged his hand. The boy was fifteen. He would receive his first scars this year and become one of them. "Father, is your foot well enough to walk on? Or shall I ready your horse?"

Last week, Nick had beaten his feet so badly the bones had cracked. He had healed the injury, but kept the limp.

"I shall ride tonight, I think."

Jack tied off the dressing, then whispered, "Why do we walk through the dark on this night?"

Nicked flexed his hand. "Darkness comes this night, Jack. We shed light upon it before it takes form. It is always a battle against the darkness. Good does not automatically win."

He almost sent the boy away, but the thirty Penitentes would not be enough, and he needed the strongest. Nick knew what he did was more important than Jack's life. He would feel better when the struggle ended.

"I'm frightened."

Nick rested his hand on the young man's shoulder. If there were another way, if innocents could be removed from the conflict, Nick would have done it. But they *were* involved, all of them, whether they knew it or not. "I am scared as well." He gave him a squeeze, then said, "Ready my horse. Check the lanterns."

Jack ran to Father Woberty's gray and white leopard-spotted Appaloosa, then brushed and saddled it.

Nick found the prophet when Dempsey had eavesdropped on Raja's conversation. This Larry Ngitis prepared his evil magics in her cabin, isolated, or so they thought, from danger. Dempsey traced the location through the phone line: Ferrocarril Mountain. Regrettable that he had not picked up the receiver. A simple electrocution, and it would have been over.

He would assault the cabin. Tonight, on the night when the lands of the dead and the lands of the living overlapped, his powers would be at their greatest until the winter solstice. He saw the dark currents of death swirl in the lengthening shadows, death so close to life, he had to but touch the surface, and ripples distorted reality.

Tonight he would be Death. And tonight death would come for Larry Ngitis.

When Dry Water was called Silver Waters, and stagecoaches arrived with loads of sick passengers who sought the miraculous waters there, a second settlement appeared thirteen miles to the west with its own hot springs that cured broken legs, cleared clouded vision, restored poor hearing, and returned vitality to the flesh.

Or so claimed Malchom B. Weavelson. He was a medium, a card reader, a brewer of medicines, and a con artist. Weavelson made his living with lies, but it was true that he had found a small cavern with a hot spring, and true that the water did have some power to heal.

While searching the hills for buried Spanish silver, he fell into a hole and sliced his leg to the bone. Using the springwater in the cavern, he cleaned the wound. His injury healed without infection.

Weavelson spread rumors of the miracle water, and within a week he had dozens of families and squatters, his own tent city: Serendipity.

What Weavelson didn't know was that the water had sterilized his cut. It came from a volcanic vent that plunged deep into the earth where it dissolved minerals and salts: lead arsenate, lead carbonate, mercuric chloride, and potassium isolate. It killed the bacteria. It was poison.

He sold baths in the cooler portions of the spring, or if your ailments were less severe, you could buy one of his distillates (pure springwater and a dash of opium to sweeten the taste) in a genuine glass bottle.

The people who drank his water asserted that their hands and feet tingled, and their skin flushed with vital energies. In two days they all had gastric fever: yellow skin, flaking rashes, vomiting, and bloody diarrhea.

Weavelson said they were lucky. They had come just in time. He claimed there was a plague in Silver Waters, and they must have contracted it. He sold more water to cure them.

That evening the seventy-three inhabitants of Serendipity experienced holy visions, they saw shadows moving, they hallucinated that death walked among them. They fell into convulsive fits and died.

Weavelson disappeared. Some folk say he killed himself—that seeing so many people die at once, because of him, drove him over the edge.

In the center of Serendipity is a mass grave. A wooden marker reads:

HERE LIES SERENDIPITY.
GOOD FOLK THAT CAME LOOKING FOR THE GRACE OF GOD.
FOUND THE DEVIL IN A BOTTLE INSTEAD. DON'T DRINK NO WATER HERE!

But others say that Weavelson wasn't the kind of man to linger at the scene of a crime. According to *The Natural and Recent History of Seco County* by Hoover James, he tried to sneak out of town when he realized the water was no good. Local legend says that the dead rose up, dug their own graves, and dragged Weavelson in with them.

These days, most folks stay away from those hills. The forest service barred up the entrance to the hot spring cave, and the occasional hikers that venture there claim the water in their canteens takes on a garlic odor. No one camps overnight. And no one has ever thought of digging up the cemetery to see if Weavelson is there.

Nick led his Appaloosa through the woods, followed by a procession of Penitentes, each carrying a candle or a lantern. They chanted:

"*Kyrie eleison. Christe eleison.* Lord, have mercy upon us. Christ, have mercy upon us."

He broke into a clearing, dismounted, and let the horse graze. It was late afternoon; the shadows from the pines fell twice their height; they bisected the earth into light and dark. A cluster of false morels grew in the shade. Their burgundy brainlike caps were lethal. It was a good omen.

There was little left of the town of Serendipity. Souvenir hunters had picked clean the area. Only a few rusted nails and pieces of weathered silver pine lay in the grass.

Nick gazed deeper, and veils of the past intruded upon the present. Tents had been hastily erected. People limped on crutches, while others scrambled blind to line up and buy healing baths or pint bottles of miracle water from a man with wire-rim spectacles.

Scattered in the sandy soil were bits of glass. He spied a whole bottle, stained cobalt blue by decades of sun, and within, an echo of the liquid death it had held. It frothed, boiled out, strands of heavy fog that poured into the dry stream bed.

Jack caught Nick's arm and distracted him. The vision faded.

"Father Woberty, is it true this place is haunted?"

"Those who perished in this town came to be healed," he replied. "Instead, they were poisoned. They died in delirium. Their spirits are restless . . . insane."

"Do you really think—"

"We shall ease their pain," he lied. "Fear not."

Nick stopped at a patch of dirt where not a weed, not a sand spur, nor a blade of grass grew. In the center was a grave marker. The writing upon it was too faded to read.

Nick sensed it was a pit of death, so deep, the pull so strong, that if he stepped upon it, his soul would plunge to the bottom.

"Come, brothers," he said, "make a circle. Sing with me. Guide the souls of these unfortunates to the Almighty."

The Penitentes quietly spread around the grave site. No one stepped on the poisoned earth. Candles flickered and died although there was only a slight breeze. The flames were quickly relit by their neighbors.

The sun set.

Nick felt the tide of death rise and pulse about him. Overhead clouds congealed. The sky chilled to iron gray. He touched the band of copper on his little finger.

He led them in chant: "Grant them eternal rest, O Lord, and let perpetual light shine upon them. *Requiem aceternam dona eis, Domine, et lux perpetua luceat eis.*"

Nick unfocused himself from the world, and sank into the nethe-realms, while the Penitentes prayed. On this Eve of All Saints, death was equal to life. He moved with great care; he could sink to the bottom and never rise.

He settled into the first layer beneath the world of light, the place where death began. The people of Serendipity arrived in wagons and on horseback, led over the pass by the man with the spectacles. Their auras were pale and flickered.

Nick dropped another layer, through fog and coughs, through breathless cries for help, and thick phlegm. The land distorted as if viewed through a lens; it rippled, and nausea rolled through him. With his right hand, he traced the nacreous emerald lines of an *Isolation* rune, a prism that cast four-dimensional shadows. The discomfort faded.

This was where and when they died. They limped and crawled into the street, back to the town's only building to buy more miracle medicine. They were desperate for life. They vomited blood. Coma took the lucky ones; others went mad, days of feverish nightmares that were half imagined, and half real.

Nick slipped—sudden—pulled from below through the odor of decay and slippery, half-coagulated blood.

Even the shadows of living things faded on this echelon. A spring of mercury burbled across a field of broken pint bottles. There were dense arsenic vapors in the air that smelled of garlic. The hills glowed as if hot metal.

Where the mass grave was, the people of Serendipity gathered about the man with the spectacles and fed him bits of his own broken bottles. He screamed from a misshapen orifice, so lacerated it was without lips, without tongue.

"Give us the cure," one woman demanded of him.

This was their hell: bound to finding an antidote to their sickness. In seeking to avoid death, they had assured it.

"I have your cure," Nick called to them. "I can give you life."

They turned, scrambled toward him, over the glass and burning metal. "We will pay any price," they wailed. "Heal us."

The poison had eaten their insides; madness for life consumed them.

"You will, in return, serve me," he said.

"Yes." They drew close, and even through the rune of *Isolation,* Nick gagged on the fumes of their desire.

He stepped away and willed himself to rise. Hands clutched him, pulling him back. "The cure," they cried. "Help us."

He incanted: "I shackle thee, cruel spirits, with knots knotting knots: entwine thy eyes, thy mouths, thy tongues, thy throats, and thy venomous bowels. Life will be thine, I invoke it; enter this ascending. Breath shall be with thee."

Up he shot through the layers of death, leaving behind a shrinking hole through which they followed.

Nick opened Father Woberty's eyes. He drew clean air into his lungs.

The clouds that had been overhead settled into a dense fog. The Penitentes' candles were murky globes of light that flickered perilously.

They continued their chant: "*Requiem aceternam dona eis, Domine, et lux perpetua luceat eis.* Grant them eternal rest, O Lord, and let perpetual light shine upon them."

They did not suspect the words were for themselves.

"You shall have your cure," Nick hissed. "You shall have your lives."

The Penitentes stopped, bewildered at his proclamation.

From the mist, hands and faces of the citizens of Serendipity materialized. They probed the ears and eyes and nostrils of the Penitentes. They wanted to enter their bodies.

Nick leapt back and covered his face. "Now Dempsey," he cried. "Bring their light."

Lightning crackled, shook the monks like rag dolls; connected body to body, an electrical arc that chased its own tail; round and round, lightning crackled.

Two moons floated over Raja's cabin, one waxing three-quarters, and the other a ball of blue flame that gently descended to where Nick stood in the pines. The globe of lightning unfolded: two arms, legs, a head capped with hard hat, and a black beard shot with white sparks.

''Speak, Dempsey.''

''There is only a woman in the house. Do you wish me to ring the phone? Electrocute her, Great One?''

She could be dangerous, an enchanted servant of Larry Ngitis. On the other hand, if the woman was what she appeared to be, she was a source of information. ''Do not kill her. What else of import?''

''A rune,'' Dempsey replied and made a check on his clipboard. ''It is tacked over the door, and has lines of power to places I cannot see.''

''Anything else?''

''No.''

Larry Ngitis might have been able to hide from Dempsey. Nick would be prepared.

''Master,'' Dempsey whispered, ''may I wear a Penitente body?'' He grew brighter and shadows sprang from the trees.

''Every monk has a spirit,'' Nick said. He held up three fused pieces of cobalt glass. ''I have had to bind the extra spirits in these.''

Dempsey dimmed and shrank.

''You would not want one of their bodies. They are poisoned by the fever of their desires, and the earth will reclaim them come spring.''

Nick slipped out of his robe and into a pair of jeans and a flannel shirt. He snapped a glass shard, drew out one of the captured souls and squeezed it until it screamed. With an iron gaze he froze the sound and grasped it in his left hand.

He pocketed the two remaining souls and marched up the gravel driveway.

''Tell my slaves to move closer to the house, Dempsey. Wait for my signal.''

''As you wish, Master.'' Dempsey sucked in his limbs, streaked over the cabin, then camouflaged himself as a star in the sky.

Nick had prepared wards to protect him: rare ambergris mixed with the water from a mirage, then rubbed into his skin to deflect physical harm, a spiderweb veil woven with deadman's hair to repel spiritous attacks, and a midnight fog distilled and anointed upon his eyes to protect his sanity from inconceivable visions.

He mounted the steps of the porch and saw the clear lines of power attached to the *Yearning* rune over the door. The spikes and curves had precision and artistic flair—Raja's handiwork. Curious that she would display her magic so openly . . . unless it was a trap.

Into the first layer of the netherealms he dove. Raja's rune glowed like firelit amber, pulsing, and rooted in the living earth. Nick could have snipped the lines of power, but that might trip an alarm. He scanned the area.

A cat on the roof stared at him with feral green eyes and hissed. Nick hissed back, and the feline vanished—gray haunches faded first, then the tail lashing back and forth, its white sock paws, and last, its silver raccoon mask.

Nick returned to the mundane world. He braced himself to do battle and rang the doorbell.

"I'm not passing out candy tonight," called a woman's voice.

Nick rang the bell again. "Miss? I'm looking for Larry Ngitis."

He heard steps over a hardwood floor, then saw her peek through the curtains. She unchained and opened the door.

Nick thought her a mousy woman. Her hair was cut too short for her round face, and her business blazer and permanent press skirt identified her as one of the compulsive working class.

"He's not here," she replied, and crossed her arms. "I'm waiting for him myself. I didn't catch your name?"

Nick held out his left hand. "Father Woberty. And yours?"

"Linda." She glanced at Nick's bandaged right hand. "Linda Becket." She uncrossed her arms and clasped his extended hand.

The frozen scream exploded on contact with her skin, wailing and gnashing its teeth, seizing her heart, and distorting her face with terror. She inhaled sharply. The breath caught in her throat.

Nick pushed past her. He glanced in the kitchen, the bathroom, and the loft, searching for the prophet. Every room was empty and smelled of pine cleanser.

He returned to Linda. Her aura was pale yellow smoke, drifting and dissolving. She had two minutes, then she would lose consciousness and die of fright. This was no lamia, nor familiar, nor servant of Larry Ngitis's creation. She was but flesh and blood and spirit.

From the kitchen counter Nick grabbed a pen, ripped open her blazer, blouse, and bra, then scribed the seven squares of a *Confinement* sigil over her heart.

Nick snuffed the frozen scream that boiled in her blood, then commanded: "Sit."

Linda folded her legs and crumpled to the floor.

"You will obey my orders. Do you understand?"

The muscles on her neck tensed as she fought the magic. The corners of the rune sparkled silver and counterbalanced her will. Linda nodded.

"Where is Larry Ngitis?"

"I—I don't know." Tears brimmed in her eyes.

"Then why are you here?"

"He needed me. He's depressed over his writing. I thought he might kill himself."

"That's all he is? A writer?"

Linda nodded.

He tore through the cabin, searched the dresser drawers, ripped out the cabinets, turned sacks of garbage baskets inside out—nothing with even a residue of power, no charms, no talismans, no wands, nor crystal balls. Either the prophet had outmaneuvered him again, or Nick had the good fortune to find him before his abilities had matured.

He relaxed and sat next to Linda on the sofa. He took her stiff hand, and told her, "He has powers. I have seen this with my divinations. Can he levitate objects? Can he talk to animals? Does he walk through walls?"

Linda hesitated. She tried to squirm away from Nick, but couldn't move unless he ordered her to.

"Speak," he commanded.

"He knows things," she stammered. ". . . It's nothing, though."

"Knows what kind of things?"

"When the tea water is about to boil, or when the oil is low in his piece-of-crap van, or . . . or, when I tried to get pregnant without him knowing." Tears spilled down her cheeks. "It's nothing."

"It is everything. Nostradamus had such a gift. Had I not twisted his sanity into knots so none could unravel the truth, the world would lie in ashes now."

Nick got up from the sofa and eased Linda onto her side. He stepped onto the porch. "Dempsey."

A star appeared before him; lines of static electricity licked the earth.

"I shall require a few hours of privacy. Please see that I am not disturbed."

"As you wish, Great One."

"And Dempsey . . . it appears that you may be acquiring a body after all."

Nick sat in the center of a pentagram burned into the hardwood floor. Encircling his five-pointed star were the articles that resonated strongest of Larry Ngitis.

Nick had disassembled his computer and arranged its inner workings along the lines of the mystic inscription. The LCD screen sat before him with:

LarryNgitisLa
rryNgitisLarry
NgitisLarryNg
itisLarryNgitis
LarryNgitisLa
rryNgitisLarry

flickering in a continuous column. The trackball rested in the top of the star. He had painted an eye upon it to help him search for its master. The chips and tiny resistors from the modem made a rune of *Connection*, patterns of interlinked squares and triangles.

Other items had been sacrificed to the divination, a mosaic of Larry Ngitis: pages from Strunk and White's *The Elements of Style* torn into strips, shattered bits of *Roget's Thesaurus* on CD-ROM, the ashes of burned notes, fragments of chewed pencils, nail clippings and black hairs found in the bathroom.

Nick drew power from the netherealms, let death pump through him and flow into the arcane construct. Lines and runes and inscriptions cast multifold shadows.

A thread of magic, trembling and mortal in stature, appeared. Two other threads, silver and blue, braided about the gray line that Nick sensed was Larry's. He untangled them.

Wriggling free from Father Woberty's body, and with the thread in one hand, he soared over a moonlit Ferrocarril Mountain. Dempsey's storm had drifted into the valley, and in distant Dry Water he saw jack-o'-lanterns and flashlight beams under umbrellas, trick-or-treaters escorted by their parents.

Over hills and ravines, through the scattered clouds, through deserts, and along rivers Nick followed the thread. A twist and a kink in the line and it vanished.

Nick backtracked.

He had lost Larry's trail in a desert where three sets of footprints meandered along in the sand, then faded to nothing. Nick sank through the netherealms, and picked up the trail two layers down. A drastic shift for one who was "only a writer."

Nick settled deeper into the layers of reality to find help. The spirits in the Penitentes would rather be destroyed than lose the flesh they wore; he could use them later to deal with Raja. Tonight, however, he would have to find other slaves.

He could afford to summon the most fearful spirits to aid him, suicides and the damned. Usually he chose his servants with care, as the powerful ones tried to impose their wills upon him, but on this night he could tolerate their presence.

He sank through smothering layers of carbon monoxide, through the screams of babies, and emerged in a place he loathed. A city stretched across the horizon, fluorescent lights, a haze of brown fog, people and machines pushing each other through tubes, and the entire place surrounded by a wall of iron. A river of oil and water and phosphorescent toxins flowed sluggishly. There was only smoke to breathe. It was the entrance to hell.

It wasn't *the* hell. There was no one particular hell, but it was a place for those who thought there was. Only the self-tortured were here, consumed by guilt or rage or insanity.

Nick incanted: "I summon the spirits of the dead and thou who rulest the spirits of the dead and he who guards the barriers of the stream of Lethe: and I repeat the magic and wildly, with frenzied lips, I chant a conjuration to appease or compel the fluttering ghosts."

Spirits bubbled from the depth of the sewage, gibbering, and gesticulating wildly. Nick captured the powerful ones: an arsonist with jars of napalm, an autopsied corpse with a gaping hollow chest, a swimmer covered with jellyfish, and a woman's head, floating free, preserved by cryogenics.

He let them occupy a niche in his spirit. Their insane shouts filled his mind; they wrestled with his consciousness, and struggled to possess him. Given enough time they would wear his sanity to dust. Nick dared carry them only an hour, perhaps two. He returned to the trail.

Larry's path corkscrewed into a land where nightmares had form and substance, where old gods lived in cities of green stone and lay sleeping in tombs. Then the thread rose along a hyperbolic trajectory back up to the mundane world, into hills of limestone.

The tracks were fresh.

He descended through layers of stone, and sand, and emerged in a tunnel. There was a mystic construct where the passage branched: the outline of a hand.

Nick traced a mirror plane in the air, copied his form, and sent it along the right path. The hand uncoiled and grabbed his shell; it caged the copy, melted into a skull, and crushed him with leering teeth. Nick turned left.

Down a chasm, and across a river of boiling water, then he halted where the thread frayed into a thousand different strands, and into a thousand different tunnels.

Nick had seen this before in the Minotaur's Labyrinth on Crete. A center path split into three, then seven, then thirty-one, then one hundred twenty-seven, then more than he had patience to count. They were Mersenne prime numbers, two raised to an integer prime, then one subtracted from that number.

He calculated the integers: two, three, five, seven, and if he guessed the pattern correctly, thirteen, followed by seventeen. Simple.

Down the middle path he went, took the second right, the third left, the fifth right, and the seventh left. The trail did not falter.

An old man wandered the maze. Nick sensed his soul had little fire left. He brushed past him and felt the terror pounding through his heart. Nick could have taken the lost man's life, but he decided to conserve every drop of his power for the prophet.

He tracked Larry's thread down a passage of stalactites, then through a crack in the wall, and into a frozen chamber.

The prophet was there. He lay prone and had no aura. He breathed, but the body was soulless. Above him spiraled a conduit between worlds, a vortex of power. It collected reality in a swirling disk about a center that was blackness made solid. Whatever the prophet's involvement with this power, Nick didn't like it.

"I've been waiting for you, shadow," whispered a voice.

Nick turned, saw motion in the crevasses of the chamber, then it moved, and in a flash stood over Larry's body. It was a boy in pajamas.

"I have seen you before," Nick said, "in the afterglow of lightning, by the side of the road. It was you who protected the prophet then. Why?"

"He will save the world."

"He comes to destroy it. I have seen."

"Then we are of different minds on this matter," Niyol said, and crossed his arms.

This boy's stance and affectations indicated he was not a boy. "Show me your true form," Nick demanded.

Niyol laughed. A ripple, and his shape peeled away. He stood seven feet tall, with strong shoulders. A mane of black hair ran down his back. The man resembled the boy; the nose more crooked, and the eyes wider apart.

In his right hand he held an eagle feather, in the left a branch of red manzanita wood. He wore a mountain lion cloak, the cat's head crowned his own, and its eyes gleamed like emeralds while they watched Nick.

"I am Yanisin," he said; his voice carried thunder in it. "You come to my hogan, where I am strongest. Go. You cannot kill me. I am already dead."

"I cannot kill you, but I can banish you." Nick threw the soul of the swimmer stung by a hundred tiny jellyfish. It splashed across the chamber and engulfed Yanisin in a globe of seawater frothing and swarming with quivering gelatin creatures.

Yanisin drew his right hand up, sliced the water in half with the eagle feather, then thrust the stick through the opening. The branch grew, its red bark split, and it touched the icicles overhead. Frost glistened down the length of the wood.

Jellyfish attacked his arm with lacy tentacles. Red welts rose and erupted in pus.

He grimaced in pain, but held on to the frozen wand. Filaments of ice crystallized and shot through the liquid, pierced the body of the swimmer, and encapsulated the stinging invertebrates.

Yanisin stepped free of the ice. His lionskin cloak clung to him, not wet, but part of his body. He grew nine feet tall, fur sprouted on his chest, and the head of the lion fused with his own face.

To Nick he appeared as an Egyptian god, with the features of a beast and the body of a Titan.

Yanisin leapt at him. With cat's claws he rended Nick, tore at his abdomen, ripped into his throat.

Nick released the soul of the arsonist.

A ball of fire detonated between them, gasoline and detergent. The arsonist laughed, and with burning hair, he tried to set them both aflame.

Yanisin ignored the fire and sank his fangs into Nick.

Nick squirmed, and the teeth penetrated his shoulder instead of his neck. Yanisin bit through his protective ward. Nick panicked and released all his spirits.

The frozen head flew up and bounced off Yanisin, leaving sizzling burns where it touched. The arsonist melted the ice around the swimmer and his jellyfish—they sloshed and splashed and enveloped both Nick and Yanisin, stinging, and filling Yanisin's lungs with fluid. The autopsied cadaver had half her skull cut away, no brain within, and an empty gutted abdominal cavity; she made a careful incision in Yanisin's navel.

Yanisin raked his claws into Nick, through his soft stomach—then the water solidified between them. The frozen head cackled insanely inside a ball of ice, covering the shaman's arm and shoulder.

Nick pushed away, struggled out of his hold.

Yanisin thrashed and moaned, engulfed by ice, by fire, stung, and cut apart with scalpels.

"You were right," Nick whispered. "The dead cannot die again. But you can be destroyed."

Yanisin lashed out at the spirits. His left arm was solid ice. Jellyfish covered his face. He swung at nothing. The spirit of the arsonist burned the tips of his ears. Yanisin roared in frustration, and the ghost of the autopsy crawled through his open mouth to dissect his insides.

"Take him," hissed Nick. "I unravel the knots that bind you—return whence you came!"

Yanisin faded, bit by bit, as the spirits stole his essence. They evaporated back to the hells they came from, and took the shaman with them.

Nick sighed. At last he was alone with the prophet. At last this would be over. He had but to snuff the prophet's breath and the world would be safe again.

He set his hand over Larry's mouth to capture the air escaping his lungs—and doubled over in agony. Nick released the breath, and collapsed to his knees. The cavern dissolved into waves of nausea and blackness.

Nick awoke with a start. He had underestimated Yanisin.

He clutched the cat-claw slashes in his stomach, tried to stand, fell, scattering the pentagram design and the components of Larry's life across the hardwood floor . . . along with Woberty's disemboweled intestines.

Chapter 12

LARRY WASN'T SURE IF HE LOST CONSCIOUSNESS OR DIED. WHEN HE pressed the flask to his lips, the dry water flowed into his mouth. It was air, nothing, an inhaled breath. It diffused through him, warped his awareness, then gelled, and he found himself staring into a perpetual twilight filled with stars, each as bright as a full moon.

He was walking alongside a river—not the underground river of boiling water, this river was muddy, stretched a mile wide, and moved with the smooth silent unstoppability of deep water.

How long had he been walking?

There was a feather in his hand. It was as long as his forearm, chestnut brown, and glistened in the starlight. He hadn't seen this before either.

There were three possibilities. First, this could be a hallucination or dream. Second, he could be dead, and this was purgatory. Third, Niyol's "water that cannot be drunk" might have worked. And did what? Transport him to another dimension? Let him see things even his new perceptions could not?

He marched over the gray gritty mud of the riverbank, under a sky that never changed.

Larry couldn't get a feel for how much time was passing. He counted his steps and lost track. He could have been walking for seconds or centuries.

Upstream he spotted a boy sitting on his haunches, scrutinizing the dirt.

''Hey Niyol!'' Larry shouted and waved.

Niyol looked up, then returned to watching the mud.

Larry strode up to him. ''Where the hell are we?''

Niyol shuffled a half step away. ''Stay away from me, weirdo. And don't mess up my painting.'' He took a pinch of black sand and sprinkled it onto the lighter dirt, tracing a stick figure, then a cluster of wavy lines that looked like a flock of crows, and in the corner, a thunderhead with sugar white sand lightning, and beneath it, a box with wheels, Larry's van.

''That's what happened when I arrived in Dry Water. The lightning and my van.'' He pointed to the stick figure, and asked, ''Is this supposed to be me?''

Niyol looked up. ''Who are you?''

''Is that another Zen question?''

Niyol narrowed his black eyes. ''Get lost, moron. I'm trying to finish this.''

''Stop acting like a jerk. You sent me here. You said it was the only way to stop Raja. What am I supposed to do?''

''I don't know you, slimeball.'' His eyes fixed on the feather in Larry's hand. He grabbed it. ''Where'd you get this? It's my dad's.''

''I woke up with it.''

Niyol looked at his picture, then at Larry. ''Did he send you?''

''This is crazy. You sent me.''

''I did not. I've been stuck here for . . . for I don't know how long. It had to be Dad that sent you. This is his feather.'' He touched his design in the sand. ''And this is his dream. He musta given it to you so I'd know.''

''I'm telling you, you sent me.''

''You're not very smart are you?'' Niyol stroked the fringes of the feather. ''I came here to get more power, to help fight the witch. Dad didn't know I drank his sacred water. He was afraid to use it. I wasn't.''

He wiped his nose on the sleeve of his pajamas and looked at his bare feet. ''But I messed things up pretty good. I couldn't get out.''

Niyol was quiet a moment, then added, ''Maybe Dad is wearing my body to fool the witch. Maybe that's why he looks like me.''

''Your father put his mind in your body while your mind was here?''

''That's what I said, dirtbag.''

It would explain why the Niyol he knew in Seco County was so articulate. He was the boy's father. Larry didn't mention that Niyol's body was dead and buried under a cross. Apparently his father's trick hadn't fooled Raja for long. ''Why can't you get back?''

''I got stuck in a loop. I already told you.'' He kicked the mud. ''Time and what I remember are all tangled up because I didn't make it to the other side of the river. I had to use the magic Dad taught me to get back here.''

The river was a mile wide. Larry was a good swimmer, but the river's currents were fierce. He couldn't swim across. ''Maybe a raft,'' Larry said.

''Not that way,'' Niyol said, and pointed into the water. ''Down. That's the only way out.''

Larry swallowed. ''Down? How deep is it?''

''It's more than deep and more than water. I'll tell you what it is if you let me keep Dad's feather. Deal?''

This Niyol acted like he looked, ten years old. Maybe it was a trick, and maybe he needed the feather to get out. Larry concentrated, focused on the future. No visions came.

''OK,'' Larry said. If he had to, he'd wrestle the feather away from the little punk.

''This is the Dai Esthai,'' Niyol explained. ''It's where time gets divided into the past, and the present, and the future. Every life that has been lived flows in there. Look.''

Larry stared into the water. It wasn't smooth. There were bumps and ripples that didn't coalesce like liquid ought to. It had a million clear threads, some as thick as tree trunks, others as thin as hairs that braided and frayed and faded and wove an endless flowing tangle. He squinted. In each filament frozen moments resonated: biplanes and square-sailed galleons, women in togas, Neanderthal men spearing an antelope, a ballroom waltz, men and women in white powdered wigs, peasants planting rice, a smoky battlefield with cannons flaring and cavalry charging, a cathedral with rapt audience listening to a pipe organ, and an orgy.

He reached out.

Niyol grabbed his hand. ''Not yet. I haven't told you the important stuff. If you just jump in you could end up as anyone.''

''End up? You said this was the way out.''

"It is, but you have to go through someone's life, top to bottom, birth to death."

"Death?"

"That's the tricky part. You can die along with them. Like I said, I chickened out. I'm looped. I'm stuck."

"But I don't have sixty years to live another person's life." Larry ran his fingers though his hair and pulled a few strands out.

"It doesn't take any time. Time flows downstream, not across."

Larry sighed, then, "OK. How do I start?"

"Not how," Niyol said. "Who. Anne Marie is the only one I know. You'll learn a lot from her, if you make it to the other side." He pointed into the river. "There she is."

Larry saw an image reflected—beneath the water: a cottage shaded with bay willow trees, a barn to the side, cows and pigs and pigeons, a garden on the left, grapevines, rows of lettuce and roses.

"If you make it, say hello to my dad. Tell him to visit me." He looked at his sand painting. "It gets kinda lonely here."

"How do I . . ." Larry asked. But Niyol had vanished.

This was ridiculous. Swim to the bottom of this river? He could drown.

Larry walked inland. There had to be another way out. Gray mud stretched to the horizon. He walked until he found the river again. It must have doubled backed on itself. He marched over the mud, and the river reappeared, blocking his path.

He sat on the bank, skipped a few rocks, waited, maybe days, maybe years, maybe minutes. He focused his precognitive powers, thought about the water, and swimming, or what would happen if he just sat here. No visions. Static.

"I really hate ghosts."

He took a step into the water.

The surface was elastic. It deformed, but held his weight, jiggling. Under this clear film the river flowed. Though he had only taken one step, he was in the middle of the river. Both banks receded when he stared at them—horizontal vertigo. So much for just crawling across.

He located the thread that Niyol had pointed to, took his index finger, and shoved it into the surface; the river distorted. He pushed his arm in up to the shoulder and broke the film. The water was warm. He took a deep breath and pushed his head in next, his left arm, then stopped because the tear in the surface had sealed.

With both arms underwater he flailed and tried to push himself out. There was nothing to push against. He was stuck.

Larry panicked. He thrashed and twisted, but that only got him stuck up to his waist. Niyol must be having a good laugh while he was drowning in this stuff.

He floated, relaxed, and collected his thoughts. His heart pounded, but he felt no impulse to draw a breath, nor any burning in his lungs.

Since he couldn't go back, he squirmed in deeper. He wriggled past his hips, and the water darkened. It pressed in around him, thickened.

It convulsed and sucked him in. It crushed him, became black, and warmer too. He tried to move, but the water had swallowed him whole. It was firm, hot, and pulsed around him. It crushed his head. The pressure was enormous.

The water squeezed him, drew him in deeper, smothered him, and pinned his limbs to his torso—then he emerged on the other side.

The pressure released. It was bright. It was cold.

That was it? Getting across had been easier than Niyol made it sound.

A film of gunk blurred his vision. Something grabbed Larry by his feet and hauled him up.

A hand spanked his bottom. He cried.

He was born.

Her name was Anne Marie Dubois. It took time before Larry could make her eyes focus. He tried to move her body, but the limbs responded with uncoordinated jerks. He was a prisoner.

Worse, he couldn't control the kid's bowels. It just happened—stuff just oozed out. It didn't smell half as bad as he expected, but he had to lie in it, screaming his head off, until someone came and changed him. By that time the stuff was cold.

Breast-feeding was nice.

When he got here, there was nothing else in this body, involuntary reactions and animal instincts, but once he, or rather she, felt and touched and fed, information was collected and organized: emotions and thoughts that were not Larry's.

Everyone spoke French. He picked up a few words. *Bébé* meant baby. *Maman* meant mother. And *couverture* was blanket.

Anne Marie had a warm crib, was fed often, but was left alone for long stretches. Larry thought he'd go crazy with boredom.

To pass the time he recited the adventures of Captain Kelvin to her. She seemed to pay attention to his stories. It was partly to entertain her, partly to entertain himself, and partly so he wouldn't forget he had a novel to finish.

He was recounting how Captain Kelvin got trapped in a black hole's gravity well—and he spotted them. They were unmistakable. Larry had seen them before on the covers of fantasy novels, and on the cereal boxes of his adolescence. They perched on the edge of his crib, hanging by their feet, making faces; others fluttered about with butterfly wings.

Fairies.

She was eleven. The year was 1858, and she lived in the countryside outside Dijon. Larry had lost control. He was a whisper in the back of Anne Marie's awareness, and fading every day. Sometimes even he forgot who Larry Ngitis was.

''Anne Marie?'' her mother called from the kitchen window.

She stopped pulling weeds in between the rows of iceberg lettuce and basil. *''Oui, Maman?''*

''Josette and I are going to the market. Be a good girl and make sure the pigeons are fed and the coop is cleaned.'' Without waiting for her reply, she disappeared into the house.

Anne Marie stood, brushed the mud off her knees, then kicked a head of lettuce, decapitating it. Clean the coop? The pigeons would only dirty it again. Josette always got to go with *Maman*. Philippe was always off with his friends. How come she did all the work? She was the youngest. The smallest. It wasn't fair.

Her secret friends never asked her to clean or pull weeds. They thought she was smart. They taught her important things. They were the only ones who really cared.

She looked for Philippe. He wasn't in the barn or on the porch, so she ran into the meadow, through grass that brushed her cheek, and into the forest. In the shadows lay a great oak. There was a hollow underneath; she squirmed through, and stepped into her private world.

In her forest there were golden oaks and feather trees, silver mists, blue-striped frogs and fire red salamanders that sang with the finches, toadstools with green veins, and caterpillars that sat atop them sipping crème de menthe.

She paused by a stone that was as tall as she was, carved with knots and curls and runes. The inscribed faces glared at her as she put her hair up with a red ribbon. The stone knew she wasn't supposed to be here.

She curtsied to the hallowed stone, then followed the path into the forest.

Mixim flitted past her ear. "Hi." The fairy darted ahead. "Catch me if you can, No-wings!"

Anne Marie chased her through a patch of ferns and peppermint, then stopped and panted at the stone bridge that crossed Drowsy Stream.

"You won," she said, and fell onto the velvet moss.

A puff of smoke and the leprechaun, Tommy, appeared on his mushroom. He bent his long nose out of the way and sucked on his corncob pipe. "You need to grow wings, lass. Mayhaps that be the next thing the gnome teaches ye."

The ground trembled, footfalls in unison, and in the distance echoed the low buzz of Wart Trolls singing war ballads and marching in formation. They carried rifles, barbed with glistening black scorpions lances that shot angry bees. The Wart Trolls were best avoided.

Mixim waited until the noise subsided, then landed on Anne Marie's shoulder. "Come on. We're late."

Anne Marie admired the fairy's porcelain skin, the topknot of flame-colored hair on her head, and her butterfly wings of silver-and-gold swirls and emerald spots. She wished she wasn't so plain.

Tommy puffed on his pipe, and said, "Tardiness is an illusion, a plaything, a—"

A growl rumbled from under the bridge.

"Aye." He jumped off his mushroom. "We are late."

Anne Marie waded across the stream and sat in the shadow of the stone arch.

The gnome crystallized from the rock: two great arms that were river-smoothed stones; his body melded with the bridge, and his eyes were two rough rubies. "Have my pupils studied?"

"Not exactly," Tommy said, and looked at his hairy toes. "I got busy showing the caterpillars how to spin their cocoons."

The gnome sighed and blew the ribbon out of Anne Marie's hair. "Mixim?"

"Yes, sir. I'll try." She landed and sat cross-legged on the ground, wings quivering.

Anne Marie felt the static as Mixim pulled the power from the earth; it made her skin turn to gooseflesh. Sparks appeared and spun about the fairy . . . then faded. Mixim's wings rippled in frustration. "Let me try again. I know what I did wrong."

"Rest first," the gnome said. He turned to Anne Marie. "So, you have chosen to join us this morning . . . late. Have you practiced?"

"Yes, sir. The twinkle of the will-o-wisp."

"No. I know you can do that. Summon Veracity's Blade."

"Veracity? That's . . . that's hard."

"I must be harder with you," the gnome said. "Our time together is measured in spoonfuls. You track the mud from your world when you come here. The Wart Trolls are shadows from your tumultuous realm. To stay longer is to court disaster. One day in five you have to memorize all I teach you. Only then will you be able to bring the Fey's magic to your world. Only then will it become a brighter place."

She sighed, having heard this lecture before, then sat, spread her hands on the moist earth, and held her breath. She listened, not with her ears, but with her heart until she heard the rhythm of the land, until she matched her pulse to it. She drew the power into her with a sharp inhale, then traced a spiral in the mud, a series of concave arcs that hugged the curl, then a dot on each point.

Veracity. That was truth that the earth knew. It had seen everything. It touched everything. It had no feelings to be fooled by, and was too wise to believe a lie.

Her sketch in the mud ignited with smoke gray flame. From it she drew forth a blade of mirrored fog. Holding it before her eyes, she gazed into its razor edge of truth—saw how part of the land was in her, and part of the Fairy lands too. She intuited how they connected, overlapped, and she saw that they were pulling apart. Light and magic pooled in the Fey realm, while gloom collected in hers.

Anne Marie relaxed and smiled. The blade turned to smoke. "I did it!"

Tommy clapped his hands. Mixim somersaulted in the air.

The gnome gave her a nod, which was his highest praise. "Practice," he said, "and you will see more truth, and, perhaps, understand what you see as well. After you have learned—" He cocked his head and listened.

Her mother's voice drifted on the breeze: "Anne Marie? Where did you go?"

"Don't leave yet," Mixim pleaded. "You said you would stay all day. I wanted to take you to Buzzing Nectar Meadows. The elves were going to make it rain and build rainbows.''

''You have yet to learn how use the blade,'' said the gnome. ''It is critical. You are the only one who can save your land.''

''OK,'' she said, ''I guess I can—''

''Anne Marie?'' Her mother sounded worried.

Stay, Larry whispered. *There will be plenty of time for chores, but there will never be time for this again.*

''Anne?''—her father's voice. That meant trouble.

''I . . . I better go. I'll see you next week.'' She kissed the gnome's pebbled nose, and patted Tommy's head. The leprechaun turned his back to her.

''Walk me to the edge of the forest?'' she asked Mixim.

Her shoulders slumped. ''Sure.''

They marched over the bridge, strolled through the forest, past the sacred stone, then Mixim tugged on her sleeve. ''Things are different,'' she whispered. ''We can't stay so close anymore. The Fairy Queen said we have to look for a new place to live. I'm scared, Anne Marie. I don't want to go.''

''Don't be silly, Mixim. I'll be back soon. I promise.'' She ducked under the log and waved good-bye.

Mixim waved back and shook jeweled tears from her cheeks.

Anne Marie placed the flat iron back on the stove to heat, then picked up little Remi and set him on the changing table. She almost dropped him when she saw Mixim sitting there cross-legged, butterfly wings beating, not aged a day in a dozen years.

''You're different,'' the fairy declared.

Anne Marie laid her son in the crib, then trembling, asked, ''Who . . . ?''

''Don't you remember me?''

The enchanted forest, Larry murmured. *The magic you have forgotten. Mixim who read us stories and checked under the bed for monsters.*

Anne Marie had thought that a childhood fantasy. Nothing more. The blood drained from her face, and she sat before she swooned.

''I've tried to play with your children,'' Mixim said, and brushed the hair out of her eyes, ''but the older one wanted to pull my wings off, and that brat''—she pointed to Remi—''spit up on me. Together, they're not half as smart as you.''

Anne Marie remembered her imaginary friends, but she also remembered what her mother had said about fairies: they stole human babies and replaced them with changelings. She squeezed her eyes shut and wished the fairy away.

Mixim fluttered to the open window, alighted on the sill, then inhaled the scent of baking bread. "Why don't you play with me? The path to the forest is still open for you." She scrutinized Anne Marie's hips. "You can squeeze under the log. The gnome says you have a lot of catching up to do . . . and he misses you." She looked away. "We all do."

"I can't. My children need me. My husband's uniform has to be ironed. I have responsibilities."

"What about me? Don't you have a responsibility to your friends? We are still friends, aren't we, Anne Marie?"

"Of course we are." She eyed the flat iron and wondered if she was quick enough to grab it from the stove and smash this child-stealer.

Mixim crossed her arms and her wings shimmered, iridescent. "It's not only you that's changed," she whispered. "Your world has changed. Men on horseback trample the fields. They have guns. Cannons shake the forest. It scares me."

"Don't be silly," Anne Marie said, stood, and stepped closer to the stove. "There is nothing to be scared of. The Prussians will be defeated."

"You humans throw away your lives for bits of paper, and who gets to sit on some old throne. It's silly. Come back to the forest. It's not too late for you."

"You do not understand the politics involved, fairy. Bismarck will strangle France's independence if we let him." She shook her head. "I am needed here."

From upstairs a man's voice yelled down: "Anne Marie? Is my uniform ready?"

"It is almost done," she cried back. She reached for the iron.

Mixim took wing and landed on the rail of the crib.

Anne Marie froze. She could not hit the fairy with Remi so close.

"This one is ugly too," Mixim remarked.

"I think it best if you leave. I don't want you near my children again. Stay away. Do you understand me?"

Mixim's eyes grew wide, and she took a step back. "You had

magic once,'' she said. ''You and the land were one . . . maybe you still are.'' She fluttered out the window.

Anne Marie threw the iron at her. It clipped the frame, bounced, and shattered her best serving platter.

Remi screamed.

She scooped him up and rocked him. ''I won't let anything harm you,'' she cooed. ''I promise. I promise.''

Anne Marie and her brother Philippe waited for the train. Philippe could not stand with her on the platform. He had lost his leg forty-six years ago in the siege of Paris, the same battle that took Anne Marie's husband.

She prayed Remi was on the train. He had been at Verdun when it fell. Her other children had been on the Western Front, somewhere in the wasteland that stretched from Switzerland to the Channel. She had not heard a word from them in a year. ''Missing in action'' was the official report. She knew in her heart they were gone. But not Remi. He had to be alive. He was the only one left.

The train was a kilometer away. She could not see it because of her cataracts, but she heard its shrill whistle. The platform trembled beneath her feet.

She coughed until her throat was raw and her lungs could draw no more air.

''You should see a doctor,'' Philippe said.

''Oui.'' They both knew there were no doctors for civilians.

Philippe and she had come every day since Verdun fell, every day waiting for Remi, and every day they went home disappointed.

The engine crept into the station, billowing clouds of steam, pulling cars that held human cargo. The men stumbled out and looked about, then ambled to the depot. They advanced in small steps, taking a zigzag path as if drunk. Some had only one leg like Philippe and teetered on crutches, and others had bandages over their eyes and had to be led. Their skin and uniforms had no colors; layers of mud obscured them. They said nothing to one another.

Philippe hobbled to her. ''This is no army,'' he whispered, ''it is a funeral march. These are men to be buried.''

She ignored him, and strained to see if one of the men was her son.

Few of the passing soldiers met Anne Marie's gaze. They looked away ashamed or angry or too tired to gaze at the hope in an old woman's milky eyes.

After they left, Philippe put his arm around her waist, both to comfort her and to support himself. "Come. Perhaps tomorrow he will be here."

"There were fewer today," she said. "Tomorrow even fewer. One day no more will come. He is dead, isn't he?"

"Who can say? The Germans captured thousands. If he is with them, they will release him when the treaty is signed."

She shrugged off his arm. "Go after the soldiers. Tell your stories to them. Listen to theirs. Ask if any knew Remi."

It was what she always asked of him. He sighed, kissed her, and followed the parade of dead men.

Anne Marie walked home. The fields had been tramped into a swamp of mud and broken trees by cavalry and tanks and a thousand pairs of boots. Her home still stood. The garden had been confiscated, the pigeons eaten, cows and hens slaughtered.

She settled before the fireplace, and threw a handful of coal onto the flames. The heat soothed the pain in her bones.

"Hello?" said a small voice from the mantel.

"Who is there?" She squinted and saw a flutter of gold and silver, spots of emerald flash in the shadows.

"It's Mixim."

She was quiet a long time, then, "I remember. You played with me when I was a girl. You came once to steal my children too."

"I wasn't going to steal them. I just wanted to play with them. I never stole you from your mother."

"No." She added more coal to the fire, but could not get warm.

"I've seen your son, your Remi."

Anne Marie drew her shawl tighter around her throat. "You lie, imp. Go away. You came to torment me."

"He was at Verdun where the land is not Land anymore. There are only skeleton trees and barbed wire and trenches filled with rats . . . walls supported with corpses. There are clouds of mustard gas and dead horses, thousands of lives thrown away to gain a few yards. That's where your Remi was."

Anne Marie was silent, then, "Was?"

Mixim floated to the floor. The fire made her silver-and-gold wings glow pink and orange. ''Your Remi is alive. He deserted and surrendered. I think that was smart.''

''My son would never desert. He is an officer. It would shame everything his brothers and father fought for. I would not want him back if that were true.''

Yet, he was alive. Her son was alive. Anne Marie finally grew warm in front of the fire.

''Thank you for telling me, Mixim.'' She coughed until she ran out of breath, then said, ''If I had one wish, I would wish for a bowl of cream and sugar for you. That is what fairies like to eat, isn't it?''

''And if I had one wish,'' Mixim whispered, ''I'd wish that you could come back with me to the forest. The path is so tiny now, though, I can barely squeeze under the log. I have to go before it closes.''

Anne Marie coughed again and tasted blood in her mouth. She scooted closer to the fire.

Mixim hugged her arm; that was the last thing Anne Marie felt. Then, through blurry eyes, she saw the fairy fly out the window and leave this world forever.

Anne Marie sank through crystalline water. She did not struggle. It was cool, and soothing; it lulled her to sleep.

A part of her squirmed inside; Larry tore himself free.

The water caught him and dragged him down. It was a vortex, a funnel that wanted to suck him to the bottom. The water grew murky; he didn't know which way was up. Larry panicked. He paddled in random directions—desperate for air, desperate to reach the surface.

Bubbles streamed out of his nose, precious oxygen lost. They swirled in the current, then floated up.

Up.

He chased them, clawed through the water, stroke after stroke until black dots filled his vision—then light, the surface, and he inhaled sweet air.

The shore was inches away. Larry was in water that was only knee deep. He crawled up onto the bank and collapsed.

He was Anne Marie. He had lived her sixty-nine years. He knew how to bake bread, hem pants, when to plant tomatoes, and how to change a diaper. He even knew the magic she had forgotten: how to summon a will-o-wisp light, and maybe, with practice, Veracity's Blade.

He had done everything she had: run through enchanted woods, made love to her husband, given birth to her sons, and attended their funerals.

Remi had survived the Great War. He wept for joy.

Memories shifted, rearranged, and perspective scrambled his thoughts. He was Larry. Those recollections weren't his. They lost something when he had left her. He remembered the experiences, but they lacked the spirit of Anne Marie.

He mourned her death.

"You made it," said a voice from the water.

Larry raised his head from the mud.

Niyol bobbed in the river. "I can't tread water much longer," he said, panting. "I'm tangled in Anne Marie's death and getting dragged down. I'm going to move without moving, and shift back."

"Let me help you." Larry crawled toward him.

"No. If you help me, then I'd have never seen you on the other side. I'd have never sent you, and you'd have never rescued me."

"Then move to this side."

"Can't." He submerged, then struggled and surfaced again. "Not strong enough to break through death that way. Gotta back out."

"*Quand êtes-vous lá?* How long have you been here?"

"The question means nothing. We are both at this moment, forever."

Larry knew why. His mind interpreted this phenomenon of the collective human consciousness as flowing water, but it was really time. Move along the bank of the river and you moved into the past.

Niyol dipped below the surface again, longer, then bobbed up. "Look, I have to go. Tell my dad I'm sorry. Tell him that I love him."

With a soft plunk he slipped back beneath the surface and did not return.

"Au revoir," Larry said.

Niyol would be trapped in time forever on this river, "looped" he had called it.

The far bank, the side Larry had started from, came into focus. Strange that he had not been able to see this shore from that side before. Maybe it was easier to see the past than the future. He saw himself talking to Niyol, then handing him the feather. Niyol vanished. Larry stepped onto the water, then wriggled in.

That was the definitely past. Twenty-twenty hindsight. And he was definitely here, on this side now, in the present. He touched his face. Yes, he was Larry Ngitis.

His breath caught in his throat. Another Larry appeared on the far side of the river. It waved to him!

Had he been here before? Or would he be here again? It might be either. Or neither. A headache pounded in his temples.

A second figure winked into existence on the far side: Raja.

She glared at that other Larry, pursed her lips, then plunged into the river.

Why would Raja relive a past life?

Larry understood. That was how she would cause the future his precognition had shown him, the world of darkness, and pollution, and death. She was going to alter the past.

He had to stop her.

The gray sky and stars faded to black.

Larry woke up.

Chapter 13

RAJA TOOK A STEP INTO THE DARKNESS. HER BARE FEET FOUND THE EDGE of the chasm that contained a sound that shook the earth. Mist rose from the blackness below, condensed in the shadows above, and fell as rain in the cavern.

Her three fairy lights caught up to her. The first settled on her left hand, the second overshot her position and executed a wide turn before it found her again, and the last flitted ahead and illuminated a tortuous line of stairs.

She descended the slick rock steps with confidence. The earth had never betrayed her—not on the frozen cliffs of the Himalayas, nor upon the muddy banks of the Nile, nor would it allow her step to falter now.

She had tracked Larry across the desert, through a hole in reality, and into this cavern. It was not the best time to engage him, November, close to winter, and the nadir of her powers. She dared not wait, however. Upon the surface of her scrying pool she had seen him. Larry had discovered the dry water. Discovered it, drank it, then departed.

At the bottom of the chasm she paused to appreciate the boiling river, its frothing waters and primal rumble. She sat cross-legged and set both her hands on the flowstone. Her pulse matched that of the sleeping earth. The lazy vibrations lulled her. She resisted the temptation to doze and called to the gnomes of the earth.

The largest of their kin ignored her summons. They dreamed of volcanic eruptions when they would awaken and dance and mate. Raja heard their resonant snores and left them alone. She focused on the smallest ones.

They awoke with a start, annoyed, then pleased when they recognized Raja.

"Hold on to one another in the river," she told them, "so I may cross."

Pebbles and rocks churned in the water, limestone in the channel crackled, and a band of stone appeared beneath the surface, solid and smooth; the fragments welded into a walkway for their mistress. Water rippled over the surface, then swirled under as an arch rose from the boiling river.

She stepped lightly across the path, and thanked the gnomes.

They returned to their slumber. The bridge crumbled, dissolved, and washed away.

Larry had carried her silver dollar charm that left an indelible trail of smoke for her to follow. It wavered like spidersilk in the air, curled and knotted into Celtic filigree . . . then bifurcated. Where the tunnel split into three passages the magic split as well. It branched again, and only a thin ribbon of vapour remained for her to track him. When the trail split a third time, her magic fractured—shattered with a tinkling.

This evasive magic had the feel of a Navajo trick. Was Larry shaman-trained? Or perhaps there was another involved?

She backtracked, marking her path with limestone chalk. After seventy-three tunnels and wormholes and fissures, she found his spoor. It twisted through a crevice in the wall.

Raja paused, and exhaustion seeped into her body. Better to rest a moment. Every minute that passed, though, was less autumn and more winter. Rest was impossible. She took a deep breath, centered her spirit, then squeezed into the crack in the wall.

Frost made the stone slick; she breathed on her hands, warmed them, touched the ice and melted it.

The fissure widened into a grotto. Raja sent her three lights ahead, and their pale illumination lit the cavern: glistening ice stalactites like dangling blades, delicate patterns of frost etched upon the walls, and clouds of mist that swirled in the center, a silent cyclone.

She climbed to the bottom and saw patches of stone aglow from the recent expenditure of magic . . . great quantities of it. The musty scent of death lingered in the air.

Larry had been here.

Overhead, in the center of the vortex of mist, Raja spied a globe of silver. The dry water.

She stepped gingerly upon the fog, ascended. Like a bead of mercury it clung to the roof, water that was not water, the water that seeped through the cracks in reality, water that could not be drunk. The legends had been true. That meant Larry had been to the river. What damage had he caused?

She took a wineskin and sucked in the water. A drop touched her skin and was absorbed; it was Himalayan glaciers, the first stinging droplet of a cold shower the morning after, and lime sherbet. It was one part memory, one part ice.

She took all the water that remained. The wineskin weighed no more, but it bulged with two, perhaps three, mouthfuls of the elixir. All there was left in this world.

She held it to her lips, inhaled, drank. The dry water transformed her thoughts, transported her mind to a world outside time. It had no taste, but quenched her thirst.

Raja beheld the river Dai Esthai. It was black and cool, and color flashed upon the surface like an oil slick. When she peered into its depths she saw businessmen eating lunch on Wall Street, Greek peasants pressing olives, explosions and swirls of mustard gas in the trenches, a couple making love in a castle under attack with burning oil and arrows and siege machines crashing together outside.

The gray mud of the riverbank oozed through her toes. She was alert and refreshed. It was as if spring had returned.

She eased onto the bank. The river was a representation of the collective experiences of humanity, and the shadows they cast in time. It was what she had searched for. Her pleasure extruded into the magical metaphor and made wild strawberry and primrose sprout in the mud and bloom.

Larry had left a handful of the dry water—either by carelessness or by thinking it would be safe in the cavern. It would be millennia before another drop appeared, if ever. She had, however, more than enough for her purposes.

Raja intended to alter history. She intended to make her land pristine again.

She drew a map in the mud, Europe and the Americas, then connected them with a line. First, she would prevent Columbus from discovering the New World. She crossed the line out. This would give her time to advance the Native American tribes with technology and magic. She brushed the Americas with her fingertips, and applemint grew there.

Without gold from the new worlds, Europe's wars would be difficult to finance. Scientific development would be slowed. The Industrial Revolution, if it occurred at all, would be significantly delayed.

That was just the beginning. Everything could change. Perhaps the Fairy Court would return . . . or perhaps she could make it so they never left.

She wandered the bank of the river, leaving a trail of roses and jasmine and juniper, then halted when scenes from the fifteenth century reflected in the water.

She scrutinized the currents and located a tangle of lifethreads that flowed through Spain and Portugal, sailors in ports, ships upon the waves, hard lives worn by wind and sun and ocean. Columbus was there, but she passed over him. He had persevered for years convincing the Spanish Court that his quest was worthy. His will was too strong. No. Raja had to be subtle. She needed a lower route to her goal.

There, one of the sailors to make the voyage with Columbus, his path would do.

She bit her lip. So much could go wrong. Friends, lovers, cities, even countries could be undone by her tampering. Yet, if she did nothing her land would be choked with poisons, overcrowded, crushed by a humanity too prosperous.

Raja stepped onto the water.

Delano's parents had abandoned him when he was ten years old. A priest had pronounced him possessed. He was, but not by the devils they thought.

The streets of Lisbon were different from the streets of Raja's Katmandu; they were warm, scented with ocean air, and alive with the trade from a hundred foreign ports. They were similar enough, however. She taught Delano how to steal fish from the mongers, where to hide from the other boys, how to pry up the cobblestones and use them to protect himself, and to never trust anyone.

She sang her mother's songs to comfort him, then had to stop. Raja found his dark eyes and cherub face irresistible, but he had to fail. He had to be miserable and commit horrible acts.

From the banks of the Dai Esthai she had seen him volunteer for Columbus's voyage because he had been in prison. Going on the dangerous journey meant his sentence would be commuted. She had been able to bend his will when he was younger, but he was twelve, and with each day her voice grew fainter, and his will stronger. She could not risk taking him on another life path. He was guaranteed to be where and when she wanted in twenty years. She could not lose that opportunity . . . no matter what it cost Delano.

He begged for Raja's voice. He thought she was an angel sent to protect him. He cried and beat his head. He promised to do anything for her, enter a monastery, serve God, as long as he didn't have to be alone again.

Raja was silent.

Delano withdrew, and part of his spirit turned cold. He hid from other people. He lived with the rats in abandoned buildings and ventured forth only under cover of darkness. He stole food when he could; more often, he went hungry.

Every night he waited until the tides turned, and watched the ships unfurl their sails, catch the moonlight, and glide out of the harbor. He wanted to sail ships like those to Venice, Athens, the coast of Africa, all the places he had heard the sailors speak of, and all the places he could but dream of.

Raja watched him for two years. Delano spoke to no one. He had no need to. Then one afternoon whispers woke him.

The rats with whom he shared an abandoned warehouse rustled and squeaked in alarm. They had heard too. Delano cracked open his eyes. Through the slats of the rotting boards he saw shadows swarm in the alley.

The door slammed open and seven boys tumbled in. Two grabbed him and shook him awake.

"Hold him still," said a boy with a wide scar across his nose, then punched him in the gut.

Delano tried to speak but had no air to make words.

Scar-Nose was older than he, and twice his size; another boy stood as tall and had only one eye. The rest were Delano's age. They all looked mean, dirty, and hungry enough to eat him alive.

''We know you got food,'' Scar-Nose said. ''We seen your carcass poking around the wharves. You've been here two winters, so you're eating something. Where is it?''

''I don't have—'' His stomach hurt too much to speak. He wanted to curl up into a ball and disappear. One-Eye held his arms pinned behind his back.

Scar-Nose shoved his face into Delano's: ''You're either selling your butt on the piers, or you steal your food. Doesn't matter to us. What you got is ours now.''

They tore his den apart. They ripped into his pile of rags, smashed the crates, terrifying the rats inside; they pried the floorboards up, and dug through the ashes in his crumbling fireplace.

''Here!'' said a Sicilian boy who had climbed into the rafters. He waved a canvas bag. ''Six loaves of bread, a quarter wheel of cheese, and salted pork.''

''Don't have any, huh?'' Scar-Nose asked.

''I need that food.'' His knees faltered. One-Eye released him and let him slump to the floor.

Delano pushed his hands under the straw of his sleeping nest, searching. He found what he wanted. He grabbed it.

''Just starve,'' Scar-Nose said, and laughed.

Delano lunged up—punched Scar-Nose in the throat. From the boy's neck came a sickening pop, and his windpipe collapsed.

The others stood and watched as Scar-Nose grabbed his throat, blood streaming from his lips, then fell over, gasping.

With his fist still clenched, Delano said, ''The rest of you want some?'' No one saw the cobblestone hidden in his hand.

One-Eye glanced at the fallen Scar-Nose, then to Delano. ''You'll pay for that, Rat. You can't take all of us.''

''No. But I'll take you first if you try.''

One-Eye stepped back.

The Sicilian boy climbed down from the rafters, jumping the last four feet. ''Don't fight.'' He grabbed One-Eye's arm. ''We need his strength. He knows where to get food.''

The boys exchanged glances, then Delano spoke: ''I ain't gonna join anyone.'' He paused to look at each of them. ''But if you want, you can join me.''

Delano smiled, and within him Raja smiled too. He was on his way.

"Idiot!" Delano hissed. He looked down the corridor of the warehouse, past the stacked barrels of the olive oil they had come for, and miles of coiled hemp rope, stood on tiptoe and squinted over the crates of dried smelt from the Aegean Sea, and cords of cedar from the Middle East. No guards.

"It was your plan," one-eyed Castillo whispered. The scar that covered his eye had become glossy and bone white over the years.

Delano held a finger to his lips. He heard nothing save the lapping water of high tide on the pier.

"We'll find a way to move it," Marco the Sicilian said. Worry lines crinkled his forehead, and the corner of his eye twitched.

Delano cast him a sharp glance, irritated by his optimism. He hadn't known the oil would be shipped in such large barrels. He had six men, but only three could grasp the barrels that stood as tall as his chest, and half as wide. They rolled it a few feet, then stopped, exhausted. "Lower it onto its side," he said.

"It'll bust," Castillo declared.

Castillo enjoyed Delano's foul luck. He had been leader once. And if Delano couldn't get this barrel out and sell it, Castillo might be leader again.

"Better than waiting for the guards to finish their wine," Delano replied.

His six men glanced up and down the rows of merchandise stacked to the ceiling. They had observed the warehouse of the Mariposa Trading Company for a week, and knew how many guards there were, five, and knew every night they "borrowed" wine imported from Marseilles, exchanged lewd stories, then returned to their posts.

Delano had lined up a buyer for the pure virgin olive oil from the hills of Verona. This quantity could keep them all in women and booze for a week.

But he never dreamed the oil would be shipped in containers so large.

They eased the barrel onto its side. It creaked and oozed from the joints on the bottom. Delano pointed to Castillo, who was the strongest, and to three others. "Roll it. Quick."

They pushed and slipped in the slick fluid.

''From the ends, fools,'' he hissed. ''You're getting it all over you.''

Grabbing the top and bottom, they rolled it. In the corner of the warehouse they had pried loose the boards of the wall—enough for a man to pass through, and perhaps large enough for this barrel.

From behind them a loud bark: ''Hold!''

Delano spun. A guard stood twenty paces from them. He unsheathed his saber and jogged closer.

''Scatter,'' Delano ordered.

Six men could take one, even if he had a sword. Delano knew, however, had he ordered them to fight, they would have run anyway. They were cowards all.

Castillo had already disappeared. The rest of them bolted. Young Marco joined Delano, jumped over a mass of netting, and sprinted down a towering aisle constructed from sacks of sponges and crates stamped with foreign calligraphy.

''Thieves!'' the guard cried. Then another voice: ''Get to the door. Find the city patrol. I saw four of them.''

Delano grabbed Marco and ducked into a cul-de-sac. The air was heavy with the aroma of the cheese wheels that had been stacked there.

''We need to get to the back and escape,'' Marco whispered.

''Wait until they find one of the others. Then we make our move.''

The creak of a boot—close. Delano drew a thin blade from his belt and crouched low.

The point of a saber eased around the corner.

Delano didn't wait for the guard who held it to appear. He jumped, knocked the blade aside, and tackled the man. He held his knife at his throat, and put his left hand over the guard's mouth. ''Make a sound,'' he hissed, ''and I slit your neck.''

The guard reeked of wine. He nodded. The point of Delano's blade pricked his chin.

''Go,'' he whispered to Marco. ''I can take care of this.''

Marco studied him a moment, then ran.

Delano waited three heartbeats and listened: echoes of far footsteps, the creaking of crates piled too high atop one another, the endless lapping of the water in the harbor. He cut the man across the neck—quick and deep. The guard jerked, but Delano had his knee firmly planted in his chest.

Raja knew violence was Delano's life. For survival at first. Then for food. Then control. It was how he manipulated his gang and gained respect. There was no other way than ruthlessness for Delano. It was what he was.

She understood because they shared a common desperation, and they both used drastic means; they had, however, different goals. Raja meant to save the world. Delano meant to save himself.

Delano ran to the back corner, where they had loosened the boards. He tumbled over a pile of oiled rags, kicking slabs of Grecian beeswax across the floor . . . skittered into three guards with their sabers drawn.

He backpedaled and fell.

They grabbed him.

When they found their dead comrade they beat him. Delano let them, going limp with the first blow, and crumpling to the ground. They kicked him, and spit on him, and hauled him up to start over.

He awoke after a time to throbbing bruises, busted ribs, and a cracked lip. Through swollen eyes he saw he was in a dim cell, mud and his blood on the floor, two candles, no window. A new set of guards was with him.

"You killed one of the duke's own men." A metal rod cracked his jaw and black stars swarmed in his vision. "Confess, pig. Or we slit your belly and make you watch as we burn your guts."

"I killed no one," Delano lied. His words came out slurred. Three of his front teeth were gone. "I swear. It was the others. They make me steal for them. I saw them kill the guard."

"Then tell us where they hide." He kicked Delano in the groin.

He choked back the nausea and told them where their hideout was. "They made me do it. You must protect me from them. They will kill me if they know I told you."

They laughed. "Protect? Your thug-friends will dangle from the end of a rope. You will rot in jail forever. What more protection could you want?"

Delano slumped against the wall. He had no strength to cry. He had surely killed Castillo and Marco. They were not friends; they were not family, but they were all he had.

In a low whisper, so faint he wasn't sure if it was really there or his imagination, he heard his angel sing to him.

*   *   *

''At least it's better than a stinking hole of a prison,'' Delano whispered to himself, wanting to believe the words. He clung to his hammock and swung back and forth with the waves of the storm.

A row of men huddled against the hull.

At midnight they were woken by the change of watch. They were seasick, and had no view save the empty horizon. They were sunburned, crammed belowdecks with the stench of vomit and sweat and farts. There were lice, cockroaches, and rats that outnumbered the crew ten to one.

Given the choice of prison or sailing to the Indies, Delano had thought this the better option. Now he didn't know. He wasn't certain sailing west would get them to the East.

''If we don't see land soon,'' said Juan, ''I will talk to the pilot. We have gone far enough to sail past China.''

''Forty leagues yesterday,'' someone in the darkness said.

''Has anyone added the full distance?'' Juan asked.

''Too far,'' Delano replied. He knew the answer, though he had never been able to add. That scared him. Many things scared him.

Last evening they had seen a bolt of fire in the sky. It streaked across the heavens, a finger of flame that burned the stars. It was a warning, a sign from God they should turn back.

''Maybe the *Santa Maria*'s rudder will slip its gudgeons like the *Pinta* did,'' someone whispered from the shadows.

''Shut up,'' Delano hissed. ''If the officers hear that, they'll string you to the mast.''

A decade ago, Delano would have beaten the man. Fear had been an effective tool for gaining respect before. Now, however, the crew respected his opinion because he knew things. He knew the names of the constellations. He knew how to use a quadrant and an astrolabe—things he had no right to know. The pilot of the *Santa Maria* had him double-check the latitude readings, and snuck him extra food and wine.

He knew other things. The *Pinta* had been sabotaged. They had put into the Canary Islands to repair her rudder. In the middle of nowhere, though, a lost rudder would mean abandoning the *Santa Maria*, and a cramped journey with a double crew. Delano wasn't willing to do that, yet.

And from the same place in his mind this information came, doubt welled up that they would reach the Indies. The distance was the key.

It was wrong. It was certainly recorded in Admiral Columbus's log . . . not that he had any right to see it, nor if he could, would he be able to read the writing. Where these thoughts came from, and what they meant, puzzled him.

Still, the feeling persisted, and his sense of wrongness prevailed.

From above deck came a single cannon shot and a cry: "Land!"

Delano clawed his way up the stairs. Sunlight stung his eyes, and he saw the sky on fire with the setting sun. "Where?"

The pilot, Peralonso Nino, pointed to the left of the sunset. "There," he said. "The *Pinta* has signaled for land ahead. Climb into the rigging. Tell me if you see it."

Delano cursed as he climbed. There was a reward of ten thousand maravedis to the first to sight land. He wanted it. Already he schemed to rob the money from the cursed son-of-a-whore who stole it from him. He glared at the horizon, southwest, and, yes, there was a strip of land. Perhaps. It was faint: mountains covered with snow, twenty-five leagues distant.

Admiral Columbus was on deck, shielding his eyes, straining to see his precious Indies. There was a satisfaction in his posture, back straight, smiling, and perhaps a touch of relief in his eyes. He ordered the crew to sing *Gloria in excelsis Deo,* then the pilot, Peralonso, snuck a double ration of wine belowdecks. A fine fellow that Peralonso.

Delano wouldn't mind if the high and mighty admiral took a long swim, and Peralonso took command. Still, Admiral Columbus had brought them to the Indies as promised, but the wrongness he had tasted before remained with him despite the wine. A voice in his thoughts whispered that this was a lie.

They sailed through the night. No one slept. They all wanted to see the land and feel its firm, unmoving texture beneath their feet again.

Dawn came, and there was nothing. Delano and Peralonso checked the distance. Thirty leagues. The land had been a mirage.

Columbus appeared unshakable. "It was merely a cloud," he announced, then retreated to his cabin, no doubt to record the incident in his bloody log.

The log. Delano had an indescribable urge to see it. He spit over the rail, then went belowdecks to listen to the grumbling of his mates and sleep off his disappointment.

Three days later, the *Nina* fired her gun and hoisted a flag. The crew assembled on deck, and strained to see another distant strip of land. Columbus ordered that they sail together, even though the *Santa Maria* was the slowest of the three.

Half a day chasing the land, then it vanished.

Belowdecks the crew gathered. ''Enough,'' Juan said. ''We take action. The devil plays tricks, raising land, then sinking it. No man was meant to come this far.''

They waited for Delano to speak. He thought a long time, then, ''We will do something. We will talk.''

''Talk?'' Juan hissed. ''We take the ship and—''

''We talk,'' Delano repeated. ''We talk first, then fight . . . if we need to.'' He climbed above deck and found Peralonso. The crew followed him.

''Get below,'' Peralonso whispered, ''before the officers see this.''

''No,'' Delano said, loud, so everyone heard him. ''We have gone too far, and seen nothing but clouds. It is time to turn back before we run out of water and food, before the sea swallows us.''

The crew murmured their agreement.

Columbus and the officers emerged from his cabin. ''What is this?'' he demanded.

''You have sailed too far,'' Delano said.

''Who is this man?'' Columbus let his hand drift to the pommel of his sword. ''Take him below.''

The crew surged forward, grabbing pins and lengths of rope—anything they could use as a weapon. The officers drew their steel.

''Wait!'' Peralonso shouted.

The crew hesitated.

''Let us hear his words first, Admiral. He has knowledge of navigation. He has double-checked my readings and often has found my errors. He is worth listening to.''

A flicker of an amused smile flashed across Columbus's face. ''Speak then.''

The smirk rattled Delano. Maybe he was wrong. Columbus knew what he was doing. The king and queen had believed in his plan. Who was Delano to question them?

''We have gone too far,'' he repeated. ''If the Indies or China were here, we would have found them.''

''But we have seen signs,'' Columbus protested, now addressing the crew. ''Green twigs in the current. I know you are as disappointed as I, but my calculations have been checked and rechecked by the finest navigators in Spain. We are close.''

The crew appeared unconvinced.

''Three days,'' Columbus said. ''If no land comes to sight, I swear by the Almighty God that I shall turn the ships about and declare the voyage a failure. Give me three days. I will find the land. I shall find you riches and glory.''

This sat better with the crew, and they lowered their weapons.

''Your log,'' Delano insisted.

''What?'' Columbus said.

''Let us see the log,'' Delano repeated, ''to add up the distance.''

''Insolent wretch. You cannot even read. You will make the words and numbers up to suit your cowardice.''

''The log.''

''Throw this man in irons,'' Columbus ordered, and turned to his officers. His face had drained to bone white. ''I cannot command the fleet with traitors shouting their insanity and inciting riots.''

''Why do you hide it?'' Delano demanded. The officers stepped toward him.

''Show us the log, Admiral,'' Peralonso said, and stepped in between Delano and the officers.

There was an uneasy silence, the creaking of the ship as it rose and fell, a slight breeze fluttering the sails, then Columbus said, ''My journal is for the king's and queen's eyes alone.''

''I know this man,'' Peralonso said. ''If he says the distance is wrong, and if it bothers him so that he places his life in danger, then I too would see your logs and discover why.''

''No.'' Columbus unsheathed his sword.

Delano and Peralonso and a dozen of the crew rushed him with rope and pin and gaff.

Columbus stabbed Juan in the leg, and slashed an arc of steel in front of him to keep the rest at bay.

Delano threw a pin at his head.

Columbus deflected it with his sword.

Peralonso dove into his legs and brought him down. The others grabbed Columbus's wrists and tied him to the mast.

The officers hesitated. They made no move to rescue their admiral. Delano saw there was doubt in their eyes as well now.

They searched Columbus's cabin. Delano found an iron-banded

chest. Within was the ship's log, a second, private journal, and a glass jar sealed with wax.

He paged through the log while Peralonso looked over his shoulder—he had not known he could read. The log indicated they had set sail on August 3, forty-eight miles on course to the Canaries. On August 6, the rudder of the *Pinta* slipped off its gudgeons. Columbus wrote he suspected Cristobal Qunitero, the owner of the vessel. There was nothing amiss. The distances and dates were neatly recorded. Delano's heart thundered with panic.

He set the log down and leafed through the journal.

Passages of glib optimism. Pure confidence that Columbus knew what he was doing. Then, on September 9, a change of tone. It was what Delano had heard from the whispers in his mind. Columbus had shorted the distance.

He wrote that he was afraid the crew would mutiny if they knew how long they had traveled. He logged sixty-three leagues, but told the crew they had traveled but fifty-one. The next day he logged twenty-one and told the crew seventeen. Every day he shaved the distance by one league in five.

Delano smashed the sealed jar. Inside were green branches, the specimens they had found in the currents—what Columbus had claimed was evidence of land. Faked.

He read the log to the assembled crew and showed them the cuttings.

''I can explain,'' Columbus cried.

The crew beat him bloody, then dragged him below for more.

Delano examined the officers. Had they known? They appeared shocked, angry like the crew. ''Master Pilot, do you read the same words as I?''

''Yes.''

''You agree that the distance is too great? That if the Indies were on this side of the world we would have found them?''

He thought, then said, ''Aye.''

''Then, Captain Peralonso, what orders?'' The officers had no objections with the pilot succeeding Columbus. He was the only one who could get them back.

''Turn the ships about. We sail for home.''

Delano smiled. He had escaped prison and stopped this suicidal voyage. He was a free man. He was a hero.

*   *   *

Delano sank through the murky river. He was disoriented, confused, smothered; he choked on inhaled water. A powerful current pulled him down. He paddled against it. A part of him struggled inside. It peeled away and tore free.

Raja clawed her way to the surface. The water thickened with each stroke—gelatin, mud, concrete. It wanted to pull her down with Delano, into death.

She broke the surface and gulped air. She crawled to the shore of the Dai Esthai, then lay in the mud, and savored the taste of oxygen.

She had nearly drowned with Delano. A storm had caught them on the return voyage, and broken the heavy *Santa Maria* into kindling. He had never found his freedom.

His death weighed heavy on her soul. She could have given him a better life. They were both orphaned children. They both had invisible friends, only Delano's had abandoned him—*she* had abandoned him.

Delano had been dead five hundred years, and there was no one left to mourn him. His miserable life was part of hers now. He had taught her things she had not learned in all her centuries. He had shown her failure and desperation.

A twist of fate sent his life into a downward spiral, and hers to glory. So simple a thing, a comforting friend, to make such a difference. Were all lives thus? Perhaps. And perhaps she ought not to tamper with them.

Still, it had been done, and Raja would not risk death again to undo it.

The river was no longer smooth. It churned and frothed and rapids sent white water splashing. She gazed into the depths and saw that only the *Pinta* had returned to Spain. The crew was starved and dehydrated and told tales of sea monsters and ghosts.

Good.

But something else caught her eye on the opposite bank.

Raja saw herself gazing into the water on the far side. She expected that. That was herself poised at another time. Farther downstream, however, she saw something that made her heart skip a beat: Larry.

He watched the image of her past self, and clenched his fists when she stepped upon the water and into Delano's life. He scanned the river, gazed at something held within his hand, then he too stepped upon the water.

"No," she cried.

Larry squeezed into the water, close to Delano's life. Was the fool attempting to undo what she had done?

Raja flushed with anger. She could not afford to waste the dry water going back and forth through history playing chess with Larry.

He would have to die.

Chapter 14

LARRY TOUCHED THE FLOOR OF THE CAVERN. IT WAS SIMULTANEOUSLY hot and cold, part black ice and part molten. His vision flickered and there was only limestone.

Static caressed his skin, lines of magnetic force. He caught the scent of almonds and spice. Her magic hung in the air. Raja had been on the river. Or she would be. He wasn't certain—his sense of time was blurred.

"Larry?" Spencer's wrinkled face appeared and cracked into a smile. He helped Larry sit up, and said, "I tried to wake you, but you were dead to the world."

He was in the grotto the shaman had led him to. There was no fog, nor cyclone of stars, only a film of mist overhead. Veiled there was a globule of silver, the remaining dry water.

Larry touched the flask in his pocket. Good. It was still there. "Th—Thanks," he said, shivering. "How did you get here?"

"Waiting for you six hours is how I got here. Couldn't just up and leave without knowing what happened." Spencer glanced about the frozen cave uneasily, then, "I leapfrogged the river—it was a sight easier with that rope you strung across."

"I'm glad you came, but—"

"I ain't done telling what I got to say yet." His smile vanished.

Burning acid pooled in Spencer's stomach; Larry felt it. It wasn't booze eating a hole through him. It was fear.

''Past the river your footprints done strange things . . . they split. The right headed one way, the left the other, then they multiplied, two and three feet together, wandering through every rathole. I got lost.''

He wrung his hands and glanced at his boots. ''But that ain't the strangest thing.''

Had Spencer seen the cloud of stars in the cavern? Or the dry water? Or Niyol's ghost? How could Larry explain without sounding psychotic?

''Death was in those tunnels,'' Spencer whispered. ''It rolled right through me. There were five ghosts, and one God-almighty black demon from hell holding 'em all together, pushing 'em on. Death.''

Larry set his hand on Spencer's shoulder.

He flinched. ''You got to believe me. I ain't touched a drop of hooch in three months.''

''I believe you,'' Larry said. ''What happened?''

Spencer's tanned face turned pale. ''They weren't after me; they were after you, kept calling your name.'' He licked his lips. ''There was frost on the walls where they touched, so I followed it—figured if they were gonna kill me, they woulda done it before. It led me straight to this hole. You were in a coma.''

Spencer stared at Larry. ''Am I crazy? Was it real? What did it do to you?''

''Let's find out what it was you saw first.''

Niyol, or rather Niyol's father masquerading as his dead son, was nowhere to be seen. Larry had questions for the shaman: how sending him to the Dai Esthai would stop Raja, why he hid in the body of his son, and what the hell Spencer had seen.

Larry dug into his pocket for Matt Carlson's bullet. The outlaw might have a clue where Niyol went. He set it on his molar and bit.

The Stetson appeared, then boots, and his long-john underwear. Matt had his back turned to Larry, with his arms crossed.

''Matt?''

''There someone else here?'' Spencer asked, and held up his lantern.

''That's part of the explanation. Give me a second.''

Matt still had his back turned to him. ''I ain't gonna help ya none, ya stinkin' Chinaman. I'm madder than a peeled rattlesnake, and ain't gonna take yer spittin' me out whenever it suits ya. I'm sick of sittin' in limbo.'' He turned. His eyes smoldered red, and the tips of his mustache smoked. ''Go ahead and chuck that bullet. I don't care beans 'bout my soul no more. I may be dead, but I still got my pride.''

''Come on, Matt.'' Larry brushed the dust off his pants and stood. ''We can compromise. Keep your racist remarks to yourself, and I'll keep the bullet. I'll get newspapers for you. I'll even turn the pages of books.''

''Books?'' Matt's eyes dimmed to black.

''You feeling OK?'' Spencer asked Larry.

''Television too. You never had that in your room. They're pictures that move.''

''Yer different,'' Matt said. ''You smell of fancy French perfume and yer colors are a sight brighter. You been with a woman?''

''No . . . well, yes. Kind of. I'll tell you about it later.''

''If I stay we gotta be partners. I ain't gonna be no slave to a China''—Matt frowned—''to you.''

Larry wasn't certain what a partnership with Matt meant. He'd worry about that later. ''OK. What's this death Spencer saw? Why is it after me?''

''Did you bump your head?'' Spencer asked. ''I got a first aid kit.''

''That's the heap o' trouble yer in,'' Matt whispered. ''The shaman was here when it came alookin' fer ya. It wasn't no witch. It wasn't nothing I seen the likes of before. That Spencer fellow is right. It was Death. It was full o' ghosts, and they killed the shaman deader than a can o' corned beef.''

''But he was already dead.''

''Dead ain't the half of it,'' Matt said. ''His soul got dragged off to Hell. Them ghosts chawed him up, and they woulda done the same to ya if the shaman hadn't ripped into the one aleadin' them—that one hightailed it to lick his wounds. But he'll be back alrighty. Ya can bet that fancy silver dollar of yers on that.''

''You best sit a spell,'' Spencer suggested, ''and tell me what you think you're seeing.''

''We have to leave,'' Larry told him. ''I'll explain on the way out. And after I'm done, you may think we're both crazy.''

Between Ferrocarril Mountain and Lost Silver Canyon lies Terranegro Gorge, a scar of volcanic rock with fissures and razor-edged spikes.

White petroglyphs decorate the black walls of the ravine, figures of men, snakes, and spirals.

Anthropologists claim these symbols tell the same story, with slight variations, and span a period of three hundred years. They tell the legend of Spirit Warrior and his challenge to Fire Woman who could summon volcanoes and rains of destruction. Fire Woman wanted to destroy the earth, and remake it a better way.

They battled. They died. And the earth remained unchanged.

There are variations, though.

Some petroglyphs say Spirit Warrior lived to lead a new tribe of men, while others tell that he died and Fire Woman changed the land, while still others say that they battled, then compromised. Several versions recount that they fell in love.

In Hoover James's thesis, *The Natural and Recent History of Seco County,* he asserts the Anasazi called this a living legend. They believed it repeats over the ages, not only in this world, but the spirit worlds. He cited anecdotal references from the shaman Yanisin Eagle Feather Rodriguez.

Respected anthropologists and tribal leaders never heard of this mysterious shaman, and declared Hoover James a fraud.

During his thesis defense Hoover James vehemently stated the petroglyphs predict that the conflict will occur again. That next time it will end the world.

Spencer halted in the black sand, and shielded his eyes from the noon sun. "Let me see if I have this straight. Ms. Anumati is a witch. You're haunted by the ghost of Matt Carlson. A dead shaman was teaching you magic—but the ghosts I saw in that cave took him to Hell. And it's all over a magic potion?"

"It's true," Larry said, "or I'm crazy. But I'm not lying." He sat on an outcropping of basalt and shifted to get comfortable on the jagged surface.

They had hiked for five hours, climbed out of the cavern, through the desert of mirages, and into this canyon of pumice and lava and faded petroglyphs. Larry couldn't shake the feeling that Raja followed him. He rubbed Paloma's silver dollar for luck.

He should have been worrying about this "death" Spencer and Matt had seen, and if the dry water was safe where he had left it in the cavern. Instead, he examined the silver coin and thought of Paloma.

He traced the raised stars on its surface. Anne Marie would have laughed. It was obvious how Paloma had tried to win his favor. Why hadn't he seen it before? All her breakfasts, her body language, her perfume, the good-bye kisses that ached to turn into something more. He had been a fool.

"I ain't certain which is worse," Spencer said, "believing that story or making up one of my own that fits the facts." He sat in the shade and examined a stick figure traced onto the cliff wall.

Larry listened to the gurgling stream that zigzagged though the canyon, meandering in between sharp rocks and twisted piñon pines and manzanita bushes. "Probably better if you think I'm crazy and stay out of this business."

"So show me some of that magic you say you know. That'll put to rest if you're telling the truth or if you're crazy. What do you say?"

Larry bristled. He had no reason to show Spencer anything. It was dangerous. Yet, part of him didn't believe either. Part of him thought that Matt and Niyol and the magic were delusions. Maybe if he convinced Spencer, he would believe too.

"OK," Larry whispered. "Give me something you know like the back of your hand."

Spencer thought a moment, then got out his Swiss Army knife and handed it to him. It had one blade, a screwdriver, scissors, and tweezers and a toothpick that slid into the end.

Matt inspected the knife and declared, "Couldn't slice up a horny toad."

Larry stared at the red plastic case and the white cross trademark. He pulled the blade out. It had scratches along the edge from being sharpened. He opened the scissors and worked them. The spring was firm.

There was no outside world, no rocks, no Matt or Spencer—only the knife.

It blurred.

It cast seven shadows in seven other directions he hadn't noticed before. There were six attachments, not three. He rotated the knife so the parts that existed in the other dimensions came into view, then folded the old blade and screwdriver and scissors into shadow.

Larry set the knife down.

He scattered his concentration, tracing the angles of a snake petroglyph on the wall, retying his bootlaces, then counting from one to ten, filling in the numbers at random.

He wasn't certain what he had done. By shifting the parts of the knife that existed elsewhere, he might have bent the metal, or reversed one of the attachments—something that would prove his story to Spencer.

The sky was blue. Spencer and Matt were there. Everything was normal. Without looking he closed the parts of the knife and handed it back to Spencer.

"OK," Larry said.

"OK, what? You stared at my knife, played with it for a second, and nothing happened."

"Are you sure?"

Spencer opened the big blade.

The metal was golden and had a sand-blasted texture. There were eight slices of diamond, each half an inch wide, set to make a serrated edge.

Spencer's mouth hung open. He tested it on his bootstrap, and cut the thick leather like tissue paper.

He opened the screwdriver and found a silver fountain pen. The scissors had twisted into a double-helix corkscrew. The toothpick was flat with elegant scrimshaw carved upon it: ships that sailed in the clouds. The tweezers had eight prongs.

Larry hadn't expected this. The knife was like nothing in this world. It scared him. It intrigued him too.

He knew this time it was real. The look of shock on Spencer's face was real. The trembling of the old man's hands was real. Everything that had happened had been real.

Spencer was quiet. He reexamined his altered knife, rubbed his finger over the pentagram that had replaced the white cross. "I know I ain't crazy, and I know this is my knife. I see where I scratched the blade."

He folded it and slipped it into his coveralls. "So I guess I'm sold on your story." Out of habit he reached into the pocket where he had kept his silver flask. The pocket was empty. Larry had the flask, and Spencer's booze was gone. He frowned, wrinkling the worry and laugh lines on his leathery face. "I want to know more about this dry water. It takes you into the past? Is it like peyote? A drug?"

Larry regretting telling Spencer that part of his story. He wanted to trust him. But not with the dry water. He sighed, then, ''The water lets you live a past life. It's not a time machine.'' A spiral on the far canyon wall caught Larry's eye. Had it moved? He shifted his attention to a chuck of limestone embedded in the rock he sat on.

''So if you wanted to you could be a Spanish Conquistador? Maybe one that hid the silver in these hills?''

''Not a bad idea,'' Matt said, ''if you live to tell the tale. That's always the trick when ya get rich. Some weasel always waitin' to take it, and yer life, from ya.''

Spencer took out a pouch of tobacco and rolled a cigarette. ''I can't speak for the other Lobos, but count me in. I got guns and places for you to hide. Anything. Just ask.''

''I appreciate the offer, but what you saw in the cave isn't going to be stopped by a gun. Neither will Raja.''

''A gun wouldn't be such a bad idea,'' Matt said.

''I still want in,'' Spencer said, struck a match, and lit his cigarette.

Larry couldn't afford to alienate Spencer. He needed the help, and he needed to keep him quiet about the dry water. Besides, his lost silver treasure was at stake, and Spencer might do anything to get it—including shoot him. ''OK.''

''So what's our next step?'' Spencer still held the lit match, oblivious that it burned close to his fingers.

''We go to town and have Paloma find out what Raja has been up to. Then, we—''

The petroglyphs twitched, maybe a trick of the heat and the sharp shadows in the gorge. Larry ignored them and hoped they would go away.

They didn't.

Stick figures danced around whirling spirals. Geometric suns rose and fell. Angular birds and clouds dove, cavorted, and circled. A swarm of symbols glowed lightning bright, left trails of fire in the stone, and set the rock in the canyon ablaze.

Larry concentrated. He willed the molten images to fade. He focused only on the rocks, but there were too many images, too many figures that waved and shouted and fought one another. He couldn't fix on any one of them.

The sky ignited with blue acetylene flames that consumed the air and left only twinkling stars. Ferrocarril Mountain exploded. The edges of reality charred black, curled, warped, and disintegrated like smoldering newsprint.

Spencer blurred . . . then unraveled along with the rest of the world.

Larry lost his focus. Adrenaline flashed though his blood. He spun around looking for something that wasn't on fire.

Everything was gone.

There was nothing for Larry to touch, no ground under his feet, not even himself.

Seven heartbeats, then Matt whispered, "This is what happens when ya take the bullet out. People and places and everything kinda fades. After a time, when there's nothing left, yer in Limbo."

Larry tried not to panic. The shaman wasn't here to guide Larry. He had to guide himself. "Where are we?"

"It 'taint a place to be called 'where,' " Matt replied.

"Then how did we get here? What happened? How do we get back?"

"I ain't got none of them answers."

Larry took three deep breaths—though there was nothing to breathe. This wasn't any more implausible than a black hole in his hotel room or an alien city in the desert. The world had simply disappeared. He could handle that.

Had manipulating Spencer's knife caused this? He had scattered his concentration afterward. He hadn't been focused on anything in particular. No. This shift to Limbo had to be triggered by an outside source: moving without moving, stumbling through a hole in reality like when the shaman led him through the desert, or . . .

"It was Raja. She found the dry water."

"I reckon leavin' it behind wasn't such a smart idea," Matt said.

Larry remembered the world the shaman had shown him, a world of megalithic cities, trillions of people, oceans of polluted sludge. Raja's world. "She must have been right behind me, got to the Dai Esthai, and changed the past. She may have changed the world so that you and Spencer and me never existed. And if we don't exist—"

"Then we're plumb sunk," Matt answered.

Larry grabbed the silver flask from his pocket—felt nothing—and unscrewed it, or thought he did. "We're not done by a long shot." He drank.

* * *

"Looks like a river to me," Matt stated. "Big and muddy. Smaller than the Mississippi."

"It's not," Larry said. "It's a metaphor, the way our minds interpret the inexplicable. If we had a real look at what it was, we would lose our minds."

"What am I doin' here? Last time ya drank that water-stuff, I stayed put."

"The bullet—where your twisted soul is—was in my mouth when I drank. Its magic affected you as well."

Matt snorted. "Yer makin' that up. Ya don't know what's goin' on any more than a preacher in a cat house." He looked upstream, pointed, then yelled, "It's the witch. Hide. She might see ya."

Larry watched as Raja drew in the mud, pondered the design, then stepped onto the water. She wriggled beneath the surface and vanished.

"She can't see us," Larry told him. "Time works different here. It's a shadow from when she was here in the past—or the future. Look further up the river, and you'll see me when I was here."

Matt squinted. Another Larry stood up the river from Raja, talking to Niyol. "Tarnation. Yer there. If that don't beat all."

"And I'm on the other side of the river." Larry couldn't see across, but he knew his other self, the one that was emerging from Anne Marie's life, could see him. He waved to himself. "Come on. We've got to find out what Raja was up to."

Matt and Larry marched to where she had been. There was grass growing in the riverbank mud, patches that looked like North and South America, and to the right, Europe and Africa. A line traced Spain to the Caribbean.

"A pirate map," Matt said. "Maybe she's alookin' fer gold."

"Raja has all the money she needs. She's changed history for another reason."

Larry gazed approximately where Raja had entered. He saw glass-blowers in Venice, merchants wearing brocaded velvet cloaks, the first printing of Chaucer's *Canterbury Tales,* and three-masted Portuguese carracks upon the waves, merchant ships armed for war.

There were too many lives tangled in the currents, clear threads of existence that he could never unknot. It was a million to one shot that he could find the life she had lived. Even if he did, would he live that life with Raja? Would they be trapped together in the same person?

Would they emerge together on the other side? He didn't want to find out.

First, though, he had to discover what she had done. There had to be a way to know the truth.

Truth . . . truth was veracity. And Larry had Anne Marie's Blade of Veracity to cut to the heart of Raja's scheme and see the truth. Anne Marie had forgotten the magic, but Larry remembered. Would the old gnome's divination work for him?

He sat in the mud and tried to recall the lesson. It was so long ago, but this place was full of memories. The river was memory. He recalled the afternoons when she snuck into the barn and practiced, ever afraid Philippe or Maman would find her.

''What are ya doing in that mud? Playin'?''

Larry ignored Matt and felt for the pulse of the earth. There. Slow, strong, steady. He concentrated and tugged on it, drawing the power in with a sharp inhale. With two fingers he traced a double spiral upon the bank, then a series of concave arcs that hugged the curve, and a dot on each point.

The sketch in the mud ignited with smoke gray flame.

Larry reached into the design. It was hot. It was cold too. It was a furnace to forge the truth. His found a handle and pulled. His hand appeared inside a basket hilt; he yanked it free, and drew a slim rapier, a wisp of razor manufactured from mirrored fog.

''Fancy piece o' work,'' Matt said. ''Can ya fetch me a pistol outta there too?''

''No.''

Larry held the edge of the blade before his eyes. Not too close. The truth could blind him as well. It was a line that blurred his perspective; he focused on it and on the river simultaneously. Gray fog. Muddy waters.

Ripples broke the surface of the water where Raja had entered. They were half arcs that only rolled downstream—forward in time. He saw Delano's life unfold: orphan, thug, sailor. He saw the one change. Columbus failed.

The ripples did not fade, but grew and accelerated.

Larry focused under the wavelets. The French sponsored the navigator, Bartholomew Diaz, to lead an expedition two years later. He discovered Florida.

Waves churned. The river turned black.

Downstream fifty years, France possessed the Caribbean islands, Central, and South America. The gold from the New World made them rich. They conquered the interior of Europe by the end of the sixteenth century.

Waves slapped against the shore. Eddies swirled. Whitecaps danced.

The French Revolution occurred a hundred years early and Marseilles was burned to the ground. The new government made peace with the Native Americans. They granted them full rights in Parliament. The French colonies never revolted.

The bank eroded; slabs of mud and dirt tumbled into the water.

England allied with France. The rest of Europe fell into a war that left thirty million dead.

Whitewater covered the river. It cut a gorge into the earth.

The Industrial Revolution came fifty years ahead of schedule. Paris disappeared under a blanket of coal ash and smog. At the Institution de Technologie in Nice a spark flared deep inside a graphite vault. Nuclear power was discovered a hundred years early.

Light under the water. It seethed and splashed into the air. Whirlpools appeared. It roared. It boiled. It was oil-slick black and picking up speed.

Larry could see no more. He didn't want to see any more.

He traced Delano's lifethread from birth to death. He had to find a way to get him off the *Santa Maria*. Killing him might precipitate another change. There had to be a subtle way to nudge his life.

Larry found a thread that crossed Delano's. It was a gamble. He'd take it.

"That's quite a swim ahead of ya," Matt said.

"We have quite a swim ahead of *us,*" Larry corrected.

"I ain't going in that stuff."

"You wanted to be partners. So now we're partners. If you stay here, you stay forever. It's better than Limbo but not much. I need you, Matt. You're the only one I have to watch my back. You're the only one who can see the magic Raja has. Don't be . . . so . . . so yellow."

Matt twisted the ends of his mustache. "You been down there before?"

"Yes."

"Then I reckon if you can make it, so can I."

* * *

To say Arturo Baldovino had power did him injustice. Arturo Baldovino was power.

He held no political office. When grants or writs were required, he obtained them subtly, with bribes, with blackmail, with the occasional twist of the arm, or with the odd poisoning that afflicted so many new uncooperative bureaucrats.

He was a silent partner of the Mariposa, Gilbert, and De Von trading houses, held six thousand acres of vineyards along the Mediterranean coast, and possessed one hundred thousand gold florins hidden in vaults, bedchambers, and banks across Europe.

He had a charming wife half his age whom he sent abroad whenever she fancied, which happened to be whenever she was not pregnant. He kept seven mistresses and had his eye on three more.

He had family to comfort him. There were his delightful daughters, his charming sons, his aunts and uncles, cousins, and others whom he simply called "friends." He was forever changing his will, and forever playing them against one another. They were his private, living, chess set.

He had everything any man could want. But Arturo Baldovino was not any man. He was Arturo Baldovino. He wanted more.

Which is why he supported Columbus's venture when his friend, business partner, and puppet, Count Luis de la Cerda, explained the matter to him over dinner. He urged the count to introduce Columbus to the Royal Court.

It wasn't that Arturo was a romantic explorer at heart or that he believed at all in Columbus's theory of a round world. It was because it was an investment in his future.

If Columbus was wrong, then Arturo had lost nothing more than the prestige of Count Luis de la Cerda.

If Columbus was correct, albeit however long the odds, then the count would be handsomely rewarded by the Crown for bringing them a new route to China—and Arturo would own the first, possibly the only, trading company to capitalize on it.

Arturo's instinct guided his strategy. It was rarely wrong. And on this matter it virtually shouted inside his head that this was a once-in-a-lifetime opportunity.

A snag in the design, however. Arturo had extorted Cristobal Quintero into selling Columbus three ships, but no sane man would be part of the crew. He had a solution, one that he had to personally convince Columbus of: criminals.

Count Luis de la Cerda had seen to the legality of the scheme—freedom extended to any man who went on the voyage. And today Arturo Baldovino would be there to personally help Columbus handpick his new crew. They both had so much invested in the venture.

''This is absurd,'' Columbus said, as he stepped from Arturo's carriage and strode quickly up the cobblestone street of Palos, perhaps trying to outrun his misfortune.

Arturo caught Columbus's arm, slowed his pace, and said, ''It is the only solution. If you wait, the tales of sea serpents and falling off the edge of the earth will only grow. Already many whisper that you are mad.''

Columbus's jaw clenched. ''I have heard that many times before.'' He halted at the prison and pounded on the tiny door set into the gate.

''Trust me. I shall marshal all my intellect to help you select the finest men.''

The guards led them inside, to the courtyard, where three dozen men stood in manacles, blinking in the sun. They smelled of offal and disease. Arturo covered his nose with a handkerchief. They were filthy rags of men. Eager to do anything to escape. Desperate. Disposable.

They went down the line and inspected them. Arturo rejected three out of the first dozen; he said, for the nature of their crimes. They were weak specimens.

Columbus objected to the arsonist. Arturo agreed.

The thirteenth man caught both their attentions, Columbus's because he had sailed before, and he knew the names of the constellations, and Arturo's because he saw a halo about the prisoner's head, a crown of verdant flames. He blinked. The light vanished.

''Name?''

''Delano.''

Arturo's stomach soured. This man was wrong. Everything in his being screamed it to him. ''We should pass on this one,'' he whispered to Columbus.

''Why? He has experience.''

Arturo glanced at the parchment record. ''He is a thief, a murderer, and worse, he betrayed his compatriots. Would you want such loyalty aboard your ship?''

Delano must have heard because he stepped forward. ''I know

how to work an astrolabe, and a quadrant.'' Desperation shone in his glassy eyes.

A guard cuffed his ears and knocked him to the ground. ''Speak only when spoken to, pig.''

Arturo saw death in that man. His. Columbus's. The world's. His instinct had never been so potent before. So vivid.

Columbus said, ''He can navigate. I must have him.''

Arturo took Columbus aside. ''Don't you find it rather convenient that this felon has precisely the skills you desire?''

''Luck,'' Columbus stated.

Arturo shook his head. ''There is no such thing as luck so close to the royal court. Count Luis de la Cerda warned me this might occur.''

''What?''

He glanced about, then whispered, ''Spies. Saboteurs. Certainly you have made enemies in the court? It is inevitable.''

''I . . . I do not wish to discuss my experiences in the Royal Court.''

Arturo had his confidants. He knew Columbus had many enemies at Court. ''No matter. It is inevitable.'' He continued, ''There are many men to choose from. Allow me to investigate this''—he glanced at the parchment again—''this Delano. If he has no ties to the Court, and he is who and what he claims to be, then take him with my blessing.''

Columbus glanced back at Delano, who struggled to rise with his hands chained together.

''Otherwise, you could find your mission compromised in a variety of fashions. Misread charts. Fire. Poison.''

Columbus exhaled. ''I am fortunate to have your counsel.''

''Indeed.''

Arturo sank like a rock.

Larry struggled. The water was choppier than when he had emerged from Anne Marie's life. He swallowed a mouthful of the muddy liquid, gagged, coughed, and went under.

Matt floundered next to him. Within the river his ghostly presence apparently had form and mass. Maybe every soul did. Matt flailed with his arms, splashed.

Larry tried to tow him. Matt panicked and grabbed onto him. They sank together.

The pull of Arturo Baldovino's death dragged them deep. The light became diffuse, dim, gone, and currents slithered by, slippery, brushing his face and arms and legs, tugging him down.

Larry seized a handful of Matt's hair. He kicked toward the surface. Black dots clouded his vision. He exhaled the last of his air as they broke the surface.

Matt was limp.

Larry was too tired to haul him all the way to the shore. He should leave him. The ghost was already dead. Why should he risk his life?

No. That's what Arturo Baldovino would do. Humans were disposable to him. Larry had learned much in the last seventy years: medieval Italian, Spanish, Latin, Greek, logic, rhetoric, a wide array of diplomatic skills, and just how cheap human life was.

Larry slipped his arm under Matt's shoulder and kicked toward the riverbank.

Twice he stopped to rest, treading water while holding Matt's head. The current pulled at both of them. Death wanted them.

His legs and arms burned from exhaustion; one last burst of energy, seven quick strokes, and he touched the riverbank.

It had been too easy to manipulate and kill. He had to sort through Arturo's life, sift the evil from his mind, and separate his knowledge from his belief. He wasn't Arturo Baldovino. He could never share his values. Never. Life was precious to Larry. But part of him had enjoyed the wealth. The power. Part of him was Arturo Baldovino.

Matt lay faceup in the mud next to him. He vomited, eyed Larry with a glassy stare, then, "I reckon I owe ya one fer that." He laughed. "We were poisoned. Who woulda thought his nephew had the guts?"

"That's not important now. It's centuries in the past. We're going back to Seco County."

"I figured as much." He rose to his hands and knees. "Too bad. Haven't had so many whores since the Civil War." He gave Larry a wink. Apparently *he* wasn't having any moral difficulties incorporating Arturo's life.

Matt squinted across the river. "Looks a might smaller from this side. I can see the two of us on the other bank." Matt waved back. "There's the witch, and there's another one of you."

Arturo's life was not wasted on Larry. Seeing the duplicates of Matt, Raja, and himself in time aroused his tactical instincts. It was obvious. "If we can see copies of ourselves on the river," he told Matt, ''then Raja can see what we have done as well. She will know we stopped her.''

''She's got the rest of the dry water, and she's gonna be wantin' to use it.''

''Then she will try to kill me,'' Larry said.

''It's an all-out fight now. You gonna be ready fer that, partner?''

''Of course.'' Larry was more than ready. He was eager for his turn.

SECTION THREE

winter

Chapter 15

LARRY WRINKLED TIME.

When he and Matt returned to Terranegro Gorge, it was mid-December, not early November. By keeping Delano, and Raja, off the *Santa Maria,* they restored history: Columbus discovered San Salvador. But Delano had never sailed to the New World like he should have. It changed things. When Larry regained consciousness, he had the distinct feeling of riding the crest of a wave, the ripple they had caused in history.

He bounded down the stairs of the Silver Bullet Bed & Breakfast three at a time, refreshed after his scalding hot bath. It had taken half an hour to soak off the grit. Enjoyable as it was, he couldn't linger. Raja might stumble across him.

''I kinda miss that room,'' Matt said.

''You want to go back?'' Larry paused on the landing. ''I could nail your bullet into the bedframe. It would be safer.''

Matt's mustache stiffened. ''I ain't gettin' yeller on ya. A man just puts down roots after a while. That's all.''

''Watch that 'yellow' stuff,'' Larry said, and continued down the stairs.

''Tarnation. Do I gotta talk all genteel 'round every Chinaman and Darky and Jew? Might as well ask me to turn Confederate money into silver dollars.''

Paloma was at the front desk. She wore a long chamois skirt, hiking boots with good soles for navigating the icy sidewalks, a white flannel shirt buttoned all the way, and a teardrop topaz pendant that matched her warm eyes.

Killer of Crickets was there too. She had been feeding him scraps of flank steak and refried black beans while waiting for Larry.

"I didn't think it was possible." She smiled. "You look human again. You didn't leave all that dirt in my tub, did you?"

"The steel wool and bleach helped, but I had to scrape the mud out with a shovel."

Larry found her irresistible. Her nose looked a bit straighter today, and her cheekbones, a bit more pronounced. Maybe it was clear winter light that made them so. But what was inside hadn't changed. She wore a crown of pink flames. Alive and healthy. Her fire flickered and reached for him.

He trusted her. She was Raja's apprentice, but he knew that she would never tell Raja where he was. It was more than trust, and it was more than friendship. He loved her.

Larry had Anne Marie to thank for this realization. Arturo Baldovino too. Two full lifetimes he had known love. The merchant from Palos would have kept her as his mistress. Anne Marie would have proposed. Larry would settle for something in between: dinner, a movie, and a kiss good night.

Paloma stepped around the front desk. "How about breakfast? You can pay your debt while you eat."

Larry caught the savory odor of frying bacon and coffee from the Silver Bullet's dining hall.

Killer of Crickets leapt onto the counter. He was skinny; his fur hung in loose folds. He gave Larry a flash of his feral green eyes, then sat his gray raccoon haunches down, and rubbed his head against Paloma's hand.

"I've got to run. But thanks. And thanks for looking after Killer."

"Oh no, Mister Larry Ngitis. A deal's a deal. That bath wasn't free. You have to tell me what you've been up to." She stopped scratching Killer and crossed her arms. "You have to explain why there was another woman at your cabin. And why, when I went up the next week, the place had been destroyed."

Telling Paloma he had been searching for the dry water, and that he found it, was nothing Raja didn't already know. It would, however, draw her deeper into the conflict, place her squarely between Raja and him. Larry didn't want that. Even coming into town to bathe—who was he kidding? He came to see her—had been asking for trouble.

He told her about his and Spencer's trip across Seco County to the cavern, omitting the part about the Lobos sin Orejas, what happened to Niyol, his vision of Raja's future, and the dark pyramids he had seen in the desert of mirages.

"So you found this water you were looking for?"

Larry nodded. "Raja found it too. She was tracking me . . . somehow."

Paloma was quiet a moment, uncrossed her arms, then, "That explains a lot." She whispered to Larry, "Raja has a pool in her sacred grove. It shows her the past, the future sometimes, and the present. She must have watched you."

"Could she be watching now?"

"Raja tires easily in the winter. If she went to this cavern, and was scrying you, she'll be exhausted. She's slept the last three days. If I had to guess, I'd say she'll be asleep for at least three more."

Killer ceased his affections, scratched himself, then licked his white sock paws.

"Now," she said, and her eyes narrowed, "who was the woman at the Ferrocarril cabin? Why did she trash the place?"

"From your description it was Linda. How she found me, and what she wants, I haven't a clue."

Paloma drummed her fingers on the counter.

"Believe me, it's over between us. I haven't even talked to her since I left."

She stared deep into Larry's eyes. "OK." She dropped the probing gaze. "I believe you. But why tear the place up? Revenge? Is the woman psychotic?"

"I don't think Linda did it." CPAs don't get psychotic. They mess up your tax forms if they want revenge.

Yesterday Larry had gone to the cabin for a change of clothes and his computer. The place had been ransacked. Everything made of glass was shattered: windows, cups, plates, even the lightbulbs. His clothes were torn to ribbons. Books shredded. Pieces of his laptop were scattered across the living room.

Ritual marks and runes were carved into the hardwood floor. Some still glowed with power. Old bloodstains covered most of the design, smeared and dotted with bootprints. Larry took great care and skirted the magic.

Spencer couldn't stay inside for more than a minute. His arms and leathery neck turned to gooseflesh. He fumbled with his rolling papers, got a cigarette made and lit, then told Larry he'd stand guard outside.

Larry sensed it too. The cabin had a musty smell, and the air inside was too still.

He concentrated. Five black lines appeared under the bloodstained floor, a pentagram, and the eye that had been painted upon his trackball blinked and stared back; his partially disassembled modem chirped once, then fell silent.

What Spencer had seen in the cavern had been here. Not Raja. A new threat. One that Larry couldn't ignore. It had destroyed the shaman. Matt said it had been wounded. That might buy him some time—but not much.

He sat cross-legged next to the pentagram. Then, touching the wooden boards, he felt for the pulse of the earth beneath the cabin. It was there. Faint.

Larry would summon Anne Marie's Blade of Veracity and use it to see what had happened. Maybe it would give him a clue how to protect himself.

In the dust he traced the symbols of power, arcs, concave curves, and focused his thoughts. Smoke gray flames spread over the design, charred the wood. Larry reached in, grabbed the handle he knew was there, and pulled. The blade resisted. He tugged again, this time bracing himself against the floor. The blade would not come free.

His concentration wavered. The edges of the design flickered and dissolved. He released the handle, pulled his hand out, and the magic vanished. It almost took part of him with it.

Why hadn't it worked? Did Anne Marie's magic only function on the bank of the Dai Esthai, where her memories were strongest? Or was it Larry?

The reason could wait.

He grabbed a pair of jeans, a new shirt, a change of boxers out of the dirty clothes hamper—they were the only ones intact. He then checked under the lining in the sock drawer and found his backup disk. It had his journal, his notes, and the completed chapters of his fourth novel. Without it, he would have had to start over. He would have been doomed.

Sometimes it paid to be paranoid.

Killer of Crickets was under the back porch. When he saw Larry he jumped into his arms. He was cold, had lost three pounds, and his eyes were wild. His claws were still sharp though, Larry discovered, as the cat dug into his skin, kneading with gratitude.

Spencer and he then parted company. Spencer went to get a stash of guns and ammunition together, and stock his hideouts with food and water. Larry snuck into Dry Water before dawn and woke Paloma up—to borrow her bath, to see her, and to pump her for information on Raja.

Larry told her the story, leaving out only his failure to reproduce the magic he thought he knew.

"Then someone else is looking for this water?" Paloma asked.

"I'm certain. So I want you to stay away from Raja. And I want you to stay away from me. You could find yourself in the middle of something ugly."

"Why is it so important to you and Raja? Tell me." She met his eyes. "Trust me."

"Let's vamoose on outta here," Matt said. "Ya washed yer butt. Ya seen yer girlfriend. Now yer just beggin' fer a bushwhackin'."

Larry wanted to tell her everything. How he doubted his abilities. How he was so scared he could hardly move. "I can't. I know you want to help, but I won't risk you getting involved any more than you already have. This is dangerous. Raja is dangerous. This other person looking for the water has already killed a friend."

Her eyes widened.

"I don't want the same thing to happen to you."

Paloma opened the antique brass cash register and lifted the tray. "Here." She withdrew a bead dangling from a leather thong and set it on the counter for Larry to inspect.

Killer of Crickets jumped off.

The bead was Venetian glass. It was barrel-shaped, the length and width of the first joint in his thumb, and covered with tiny handmade patterns of amber and emerald and amethyst blossoms: illuminated purple roses, luminescent stems, and nectar of opalescent fire. The designs glistened in the light. They cast shadows deep into the matrix of the glass.

There was a flaw. When Larry held it up to the sun a dark cobalt fracture appeared, originating in the bead's black center; it spiraled out, a jagged coil that touched the flowers and splintered the light into variegated shards. It was symmetric. Part of the design? Why would the maker purposely ruin it?

It was a shame. The bead could have been a work of art. It was frustrating to see the blemish embedded there.

He scratched the surface with his fingernail. No. It was smooth and solid. The imperfection was inside. It bothered him. It reminded him of his life, one small thing after another, spiraling out of control. Linda, his writing, this move to New Mexico, Raja—everything was messed up. It all could have been perfect.

He set the bead on the counter.

Silly. He was getting depressed over a cracked hunk of glass.

''What is it?''

''Raja gave it to me. She said it would protect me, told me only to use it in an emergency.'' Paloma paused, then, ''I think this qualifies. I want you to have it.'' She held out the leather thong for him to take.

''I can't.'' Sunlight shone through the bead and made it glow. All Larry saw was the flaw. ''It's for you.''

''It can protect you. Doubly so from Raja, because she made it. Please. Take it.''

Larry wanted to bury his feelings, but they were too obvious. Paloma risked provoking Raja to help him. She deserved to know that he thought of her as more than a friend. He wanted her. As a lover. As a companion. As a partner. He wanted to tell her that he'd take her away from Dry Water, Seco County, and New Mexico, make a new life together, and explore the magic they shared.

First, though, he'd accept her charm. It would be a token of her affection that he would never remove. Imperfection and all.

He stared at her and reached for the bead.

The front door opened.

Without looking away, Paloma said, ''Sorry. We're full. Try the Ramada Inn back at Grants.''

''I don't want a room,'' the person behind Larry said. ''I want him.''

He recognized her voice and turned.

Instead of the practical leather flats she always wore, she had sheepskin boots, black jeans—she never wore jeans—a loose cotton blouse, and copper bracelets on her left arm made from Indian-head pennies. She'd lost a good fifteen pounds.

''Linda?''

''A friend gave me your number,'' she said, standing in the open door, letting the cold air flood the lobby. ''I tried to call, even stopped by that cabin of yours''—she glanced at Paloma—''but I can see you've been busy.''

He should have introduced them. That would have been the polite thing to do. But he couldn't speak. Linda was so different. Even the way she held herself, straight, not slouching the way he remembered.

''How about breakfast?'' Linda asked. ''We can talk.''

Larry's tongue thickened. He was dizzy, but it was neither hallucination nor precognition. His old life had come back to haunt him. A life with Linda, all their memories, and all his timidity and awkwardness. The only hallucination Larry suffered from was believing he had escaped it.

''Breakfast? I guess.''

''Didja slip in that tub and hit yer head?'' Matt cried. ''The witch is out there. Death is out there alookin' fer ya too. Ya can't go boozin' and whorin' in town. Listen to me. That's how I got killed.''

The life Larry had with Linda had been normal, save the occasional precognition that was easily explained away . . . then he left and the world shattered, cracks in reality appeared, and the dead came to life. Maybe he *had* gone crazy. Maybe none of this was real. Maybe as long as he was with Linda life would be stable.

Paloma slammed the register shut—so hard its tiny bell rang.

Larry's thoughts crystallized. No. He didn't want that life. Leaving Linda had been the hardest choice he had ever made, and the best. What he wanted was in Dry Water.

''Uh . . . Paloma, why don't you join us?''

''I have work to do,'' she replied, ''and breakfast to serve. Here. If you will excuse me.'' She brushed past Larry; marched into the dining room.

Killer of Crickets followed her, his tail high.

From behind the counter, Matt said, "Ya got that one to backfire on ya real good."

The bead was gone.

"Well?" Linda said. "Your friend seems busy at the moment. There's a charming little bookstore two blocks down. Espresso and dessert? My treat."

The Three of Diamonds Bookstore wasn't right. Sunlight filtered through the snow on the skylights and made the place appear dim and smaller, colder too. Several sections of the book stacks had empty shelves. A sign read: WATER-DAMAGED STOCK. SALE WEDNESDAY.

The people weren't right either. There should have been artists dressed in black and writers with their notepads, people browsing the stacks, sitting on the floor, reading, and chatting in the coffee shop. No one was drinking coffee. These people looked like they had come from Sunday Mass in their sport jackets, their polished dress shoes, and their hair combed back. Larry walked past one and smelled garlic and cheap aftershave.

While he waited for their order, an espresso for him, and a fruit torte and a grande mint mocha for Linda, the bust of J.R.R. Tolkien stared at him. It gave him the slightest, almost imperceptible, shake of his head.

Although Linda had offered to pay, Larry insisted on picking up the tab. He didn't want to owe her anything. He gave the redhead behind the counter his credit card, and when she handed it back, it seemed different . . . the numbers. Larry didn't have them memorized, though. He examined his social security card. The last four digits had been 9152. Now they were 9167. Changed.

Delano's life, regardless of how small, was significant. Keeping him imprisoned in Palos had altered the present. How much?

Linda was different too.

He joined her at a table in the far corner. She was reading the table of contents in a thick hardcover. Gold print on the spine read: *Basic Integrated Circuit Design.*

"I thought reading gave you a headache," he said.

Linda wolfed the fruit torte down and sponged up the crumbs with her fingers. "No." She looked up from the text. "I mean, yes. I'm just picking this up for a friend. A present.'' She spooned a third of the whipped cream off her mocha and into her mouth.

He shouldn't have come. Raja could be anywhere, despite what Paloma said about her sleeping habits. He should go back to the Silver Bullet and explain why he left.

Why had he come with Linda? Simple answer: guilt. He wanted to make amends for leaving her without warning. He also wanted to prove to himself that it was over. That he could walk away from her. Not run out the back door like he had last time.

Maybe they could be friends.

Linda quaffed her drink—three, four, five gulps, and the overly sweetened coffee was gone. Her upper lip was stained with froth.

Maybe not.

Had Linda lost the weight and changed her clothes to attract him back? Or was it just to show him what he was missing? One thing for certain: she hadn't just dropped by to say hello because she was in the neighborhood. Not unless Oakland had annexed New Mexico.

Linda leaned forward. ''Have you settled here permanently?''

''I haven't decided.'' He sipped his espresso. ''I want to tell you why I did the things I did . . . I mean, why I left.''

She traced the woodgrain on the tabletop with her finger. ''It's in the past. I'm willing to forgive and forget.''

That definitely didn't sound like Linda. Linda kept grudges. For years. Larry's right arm bristled with static.

Matt whispered, ''This is a trap fer sure. We're in a box canyon''—he glanced up to the second floor—''and lotsa strangers here. I can feel it all the way down to my boots.''

Linda glanced at Matt.

He stared back.

She shifted her gaze up to the second-story balcony.

Larry turned to see what it was she was looking at. In Eastern Religions, by a circular window, stood a man in a black suit with a reverse collar. A priest. His face had no features. It was a blur. A passing cloud must have covered the sun. The light dimmed, and upstairs, shadows collected, pooled, seemed to drip off the mezzanine.

Matt circled to Larry's side. ''I ain't gonna say it again: this is a trap. Look at this new girl of yers. Take a good, long look.''

Larry noticed that Linda's eyes weren't brown, but gray, the color of thunderheads. Contacts maybe . . .

Another body snapped into focus, a body inside Linda's. It was an older man with a white beard shot with electricity that stood straight out. He wore a hard hat, and held a clipboard with a checklist that read: *Linda Becket Dialogue: "Have you settled here permanently?" "It's in the past." "I'm willing to forgive and forget." "What are you doing for dinner?"*

The smell of ozone was so strong Larry coughed. He cleared his throat, then, "I've got to visit the rest room." He rose. "I'll be right back."

"Stay," Linda said. The ghost inside her reached forward—extended fingers that dripped sparks.

"Make a break fer it," Matt cried. He dove into Linda and tackled the other ghost. They rolled onto the floor.

Linda slumped on the table.

Larry ran.

Behind him was thunder, and out of the corner of his eye he saw lightning in the coffee shop. No one else noticed. The bullet in his molar buzzed and popped and shocked him.

Four men in suits stood at the front door, pretending to read the fliers for upcoming signings. Larry veered into the History stacks, ducked, then looked around the corner.

The priest was downstairs. He shook Linda awake, then spoke with her. Three men in suits approached him and reported.

Matt materialized next to Larry. He had a black eye, sparks arced across his skin, and his mustache was singed. "Got three things to tell ya. None of 'em good. First that girlfriend of yers has one mean ol' cuss inside her. Second, them fellers in suits got ghosts inside 'em too. Stinky ones." Matt looked over his shoulder.

"And?"

"And that priest ain't no priest. He's the Death that chawed up the shaman. We're in a heap o' trouble."

"Is there a back door?"

"Yep. It's covered by three o' them suits." He frowned. "Bet yer awishin' ya had that pistol ol' Spencer offered ya."

There had to be another way out. Another back door. A delivery entrance. A way to get past the suits. A way to move outside, but not be seen . . . a way to move without moving.

"Where's the Science section?" Larry asked.

"It ain't the time to be readin' no books."

"It is. Find out."

Matt poked his head up, then ducked. "They're alookin' fer us alright. Yer blasted Science books are three rows thataway"—he pointed to the corner of the store—"and one over, by the door to the basement. There's a suit there too."

"Can you sneak up on him and coldcock the spirit inside?"

Matt rubbed his jaw. "If there's one thing I know, it's how to be low-down and sneaky. I can do it."

"Meet me at the Science stacks, in Astronomy."

Matt vanished.

Larry let the outside world go. He teetered on the edge of panic. People after him. Linda possessed. Even Matt was scared. He couldn't lose his nerve. Later, he could have all the nervous breakdowns he wanted. First, he had to get to the Science section, and, hopefully, the way out.

He concentrated. Focused only on moving his body. His vision tunneled. He crawled through the History section. A volume on the Revolutionary War caught his eye—just for a moment. Musket fire and lead balls whizzed over his head. His mind strayed. Roman military campaigns waged on his left; chariots thundered by, broke on pikemen walls. Splinters and the spray of blood scattered on the carpet before him.

The Philosophy section was next. Larry slipped by books that whispered to one another, arguments on the nature of man and existence and perception, heated debates in Latin and German and Chinese.

When he entered the Travel section, Mount Everest towered in front of him, dazzling white reflecting the sun, snow blowing off its slopes and down the collar of his shirt.

He halted.

To get to the Science section he had to cross in between the stacks and risk being seen. If the priest was in the coffee shop, and if he looked this way, Larry would be spotted.

There was also no guarantee that the book he needed was there. So many shelves were empty.

The priest. He remembered he had read something about a priest, or a father, or . . . or a pastor. It was the day reality cracked, his first morning in Dry Water. He stumbled past the Church of the New Age and on their bulletin board: *Death comes for Pastor Woberty*. Then it changed: *Pastor Woberty is death. He comes for you!*

He had to know if this priest was there. He eased around the corner.

The priest he had seen on the second floor now stood in the coffee shop, shifting his gaze around the store, looking intently for Larry. Shadows leaked from him and stained the nubby carpeting like blood oozing from an artery. His suit lengthened, cuffs expanded, and pant legs melded, changed into a robe, tattered and flowing about him. Skeletal hands protruded from his sleeves, staring skull beneath the cowl—not the flesh of a man. Death.

Larry scrambled across the aisle.

Death was coming for him. He wanted to curl up in a ball, hide. No. Think. He had to find the book.

The sections for Chemistry, Physics, and Biology were empty. Water stains dotted the silver pine shelves. Geology was still there . . . and on the bottom rack, Astronomy.

He grabbed a volume with gilt pages, flipped to the star chart in the appendix, and found the constellations projected onto a circle, month by month. Lines connected the stars, made stick figures of them, and over these were sketched faint illustrations: Orion the Hunter, across from him, Pegasus the Winged Horse, and above them menaced Draco the Dragon.

Larry dropped the book.

These were the wrong images. Orion was the wrong hunter. They weren't the legends he needed.

He snatched another volume off the shelf.

Matt appeared, rubbing the knuckles of his left hand. "Got 'em."

Larry wrestled with his concentration, opened the second book and found a map of the winter stars in the northern hemisphere. No stick figures. No illustrations. It might work.

Orion's belt nestled between Betelgeuse and Rigel, three stars in a row, what the shaman had called the bottom of the Hunter's Canoe. And next to that, a scintillating sapphire, the Star Maiden. He could have reached out and touched them if he wanted, touched the band of the Milky Way, touched the Path to Heaven.

He linked the stars together like a connect-the-dots puzzle. A structure appeared. The map twisted, another dimension folded into Larry's perspective, and the flat page became a maze with walls and conduits, rectilinear halls and helical passages: a labyrinth.

Matt removed his Stetson, stuck his head around the corner, then pulled back. "They've got a posse aheadin' this way. Ya better finish what yer doing with them stars, partner."

He had to remember the pattern that the Star Maiden had shown him. She told him to protect her people from the bears and great cats. She had taught him how to move without moving.

The jumble of lines and convolutions had four quadrants, mirror images of one another. They were a dizzying ensemble of turns and channels, and as Larry watched, they shifted. It was a tangle twisted into knots, but there, a portion repeated itself, and there, it repeated again, smaller, and in other sections larger, layer upon layer reproduced.

He comprehended it in a glance.

Between the stars scenes formed, people and places that Larry knew, and some he did not: the Silver Bullet's dining room, empty now, waiting to be filled for lunch, the dry gravel streambed of Lost Silver Canyon, snow on the ground, more drifting from above, Raja's A-frame cabin with Larry's possessions scattered on the floor, Spencer cleaning an elephant rifle, the interior of his van, a city of black stone pyramids and green glass towers, and Paloma in a thick white robe drawing a bath.

He lingered on that last scene and willed himself closer. Nothing happened. He reached out—the vision shrank.

The labyrinth was the way in, not by observing from the outside, but by traversing the paths inside, solving the maze. There were a hundred different places, a hundred different solutions, a hundred different puzzles knotted together.

But he also lingered because something was wrong.

Paloma sat on the edge of the tub and rolled the bead between her thumb and index finger. The fracture inside ignited magnesium bright. It spiralled out of the glass, filled the air with jagged luminous barbed wire. It tangled in her aura.

She didn't notice. She slipped the leather thong around her neck.

Matt whispered: "Ya look a mite serious there, but I got to tell ya old Father Death is two aisles over. Ya gotta hurry."

Paloma crumbled dried lavender and mint into the water, then tested the temperature with her foot. She gazed at the charm again. Barbed magic coiled about her body head to foot; tendrils reached for the medicine cabinet and pulled her arm along. It made her withdraw a razor.

It was an old razor, one that used real blades. Paloma tested its edge with her thumb. The magic pulsed, matched the beat of her heart. She ejected the blade and eased herself into the water.

Larry knew this was wrong. That bead was not meant to protect. Just looking at it made the hair on the back of his neck stand.

He had to get to her. The only way was through the maze. He hoped. That's what seemed logical. But without the shaman to guide him, without the Star Maiden, he was only guessing.

Larry squeezed through the labyrinth, a twist, two left turns, then up and over. He knew the master pattern, but inside the sparkling curves it was harder to visualize the intricacies. There were paths he hadn't seen before, curls and bends and spirals and folded spaces.

Left and right, up and down lost their meaning. There were more directions than those. More dimensions. Incomprehensible disorientation.

No. This was the wrong path.

Larry backtracked.

"We gotta skedaddle," Matt said. "It's now or never."

There, a right that curved into a mirror-dimension where bent was straight, down was up, that's where he should have turned.

He was close enough to see Paloma. Ahead there were a series of deceptively simple right angles yet to solve. He halted. He had to see what was happening.

Paloma held the razor above her wrist. Tears welled in her eyes and clouded her vision. The jagged magic overlapped her fingers, forced them to lower the blade onto her left wrist. She turned the razor parallel with the direction of her tendons—sliced down and ripped up her forearm.

"No!" Larry cried, and dashed through the last of the maze.

She didn't hear him. The bead was white-hot. Its barbed wire appendages whipped through her artery like a band saw, tearing into the wound, making her blood drizzle into the tub. It splashed and stained the water pink, red, black. She slipped below the surface.

A shadow fell across him. The stars dimmed.

He found himself sitting on the bookstore floor, huddled over the map of constellations.

Woberty stood at the end of the aisle. His robe was a black suit again, white collar tight about his throat. There were no bones, only flesh. But Larry knew he was Death. He knew he had come for him.

''Mister Ngitis,'' he said. ''You have been the hardest man to kill since I poisoned Mohammed.'' He strode closer. Frost crackled beneath his feet.

Larry sat poised on the threshold, Death on either side. He reached for Paloma, reached into the book, and pulled himself through.

Chapter 16

NICK SAT CROSS-LEGGED ON THE FLOOR OF DOLINSKI'S LIBRARY. NO trace of the former occupant's ghost remained. There were only shelves with rotting paperbacks, an Underwood typewriter in the corner, and a blue-and-black checkered carpet.

New sutures pulled tight across his stomach. He had moved too quickly yesterday at the bookstore and torn the old ones open. Father Woberty's body, however, was accustomed to such inconveniences.

Four tallow candles burned and dribbled wax onto the stone floor. The top portion of a human skull rested in Nick's lap. It contained materials from this world and others: the frozen breath of a lie stolen from Pope Innocent III mixed with a lover's impassioned promise, grave dust and a bit of tarnished silver from the hand mirror of Lucrezia Borgia.

Nick examined a shard of cobalt glass. It glistened from the captive spirit thrashing within. He held it between his thumb and forefinger, and quoted Tennyson:

> " '*Be near me when my light is low,*
> *When the blood creeps, and the nerves prick*
> *And tingle; and the heart is sick,*
> *And all the wheels of Being slow.*

Be near me when the sensuous frame
Is rack'd with pains that conquer trust;
And Time, a maniac scattering dust,
And Life, a Fury slinging flame.' ''

The glass smoldered, ignited, and burst into clear flames—shrieking as it burned. Nothing solid was consumed, only the soul within fed the ethereal fire.

Nick set it in the bowl. The incense sparked. Thick ribbons of smoke curled over the edges of the vessel. Dense fumes slithered and circled him like an impatient cat.

He cleared his mind. Random thoughts led divination astray, and sometimes to visions no man was meant to see. Foremost distracting him was Larry Ngitis. Yesterday, when Nick approached him huddled over his book of stars, he had seen fear in Larry's eyes. It was an emotion no experienced sorcerer allowed himself. It ruined magic. His power manifested nonetheless.

Larry had been an implosion of color, a whirlpool of sacred Navajo black, white, yellow, and blue fused with lavender paisley and swirls of emerald and gold, fairy colors. A bizarre mix. He fluttered like a torch with too much fuel, blowing so fast it snuffed itself out. Wild flames. Then Larry had vanished.

This prophet had power. But power meant neither control nor experience.

Larry was no necromancer. The black in his colors was not death's black. It was neither shadow, nor cold indigo currents, nor the dark that dissolved light.

That was the best news.

It confirmed that Larry's teachers had been the Navajo shaman Yanisin and Raja. How else had could he have obtained such a strange combination of colors?

The Indian had been removed. Raja would be taken care of shortly.

Nick was the only necromancer in Seco County. His power would grow until the winter solstice. He would be more than a match for Raja and Yanisin and Larry combined. He would become the incarnation of Death.

The mist of his divination hovered an inch off the library floor. It circulated counterclockwise about Nick. Smoky tendrils crept up his arms and chest; they touched his face, tickled his ears. He breathed them in and out of his body.

He drew in death from the sleeping land with an icy inhalation that slowed his heart and wrinkled his skin. The divination started with him, familiar visions to build momentum and power. ''The past,'' he whispered. His words sent tiny waves through the fog, eddies that spun, collided, and dissolved. Episodes of Nick's life emerged in the mist: islands in the Aegean Sea and him the captain of a trireme, the Russian steppes on horseback, the Yangtze River on a junk, savoring loaves of salty bread on the streets of Pompeii, and in Paris smoking cigarettes and drinking coffee in the cafés near the railway station.

People materialized, faces in the fog, a sea of boiling mouths and noses, ears and eyes that stared at him, the past prophets that never were: the man who discovered plastics a century before John Wesley Hyatt, the woman who used the mold on oranges to cure her daughter's pneumonia, the little boy who would have been general and emperor of Prussia—he had removed them all.

It was not so easy now. The pulse of the world had quickened. There were billions of lives to think and to breed and to turn the wheels of the world faster and faster. It ran out of control.

He could do nothing but watch as more changes slipped through his fingers, more progress, more thinking, more pollution, more misery, more wars, more death, more births, more noise, more information, more philosophical thoughts and scientific advances—until this realm was burnt and sterile and cold.

There were times he wanted to die. He had to stay, though; his sin was the worst of all. Nick had caused the biggest change.

He waved his hand through the mist. ''Enough of these ghosts,'' he whispered. ''On to the present.''

The magic surged, the fog pulsed, and Nick's heart stuttered. The blood chilled in his extremities. He saw motion in the vapors, but it was murky, an impressionistic painting of smoke and dust.

Nick concentrated and the vision cleared: a man rode a gray-and-white horse at breakneck speed. It was the prophet's divination again. It was Larry. Nick had found his Econoline van, white with gray primer patches, as confirmation.

He perceived more. The horseman left a woman. He left her in a city by the sea. That had to be Linda Becket and Oakland, California.

The city limits sign of Dry Water appeared in the mist. Elevation 6580. Population 455. The horseman rode past it and spoke: "I will drink a water that cannot be drunk and bring a sea of change." The words sounded hollow, mechanical.

Nick pushed the magic. Frost crystallized on the walls. "More," he whispered. The winter solstice was close. He had the power. He had to see more. Death channeled through him. His left side went numb. He tasted blood in his mouth.

An image appeared, one he had never seen: a gauntlet rested upon a globe—no, not a globe; it was the earth, clouds and sparkling oceans and stars in the distance. One man with his hand upon the world. There had been others who thought they controlled the world, petty emperors, scientists, philosophers, popes, and sages. None of them ever had. This one might.

The prospect terrified Nick.

He quelled his speculations, his emotions. Random thoughts destroyed the divination.

"Show me Larry Ngitis in the present," Nick said.

The mist stilled, not a single quiver upon its surface. That meant the prophet was no longer in this realm. He had disappeared to another place . . . for now.

He had to see where and when Larry would return, where he would be on the winter solstice—where Nick could destroy him. He banished thought. Focused. The last part of a divination was always subjective and dreamlike . . . unreliable. "Show me the future."

His heart seized, trembled, and stopped. Pain shot through his arms. His vision blurred. Nick braced himself with one hand on the library floor.

The fog boiled, then took shape. Raja, Larry, and he stood in a ballroom. There was a glass atrium and garden attached with palm trees that touched the roof. It was Raja's home. He recognized her Degas pastel, *Woman Drying Her Neck,* on the far wall.

The image wavered and resolved. Raja and Larry sat before Nick. His future self was ablaze with shadow and power. Outlined with nothingness. Death. The magic distorted the air like heat rising from a furnace. His face was a blur.

Was that blood on the prophet? Yes. He was in great pain. Good.

Raja and Larry talked to Nick. Their voices were distorted. The tone was clear enough, however; they were defeated.

Larry collapsed. Dead? Yes. No pulse. No breath. No spark of life.

The divination dissolved.

The smoke was only smoke again. The incense was ash. Nick pushed Father Woberty's heart. He willed blood back into the arteries. Inhaled.

He knew where and when it would end. On the solstice. At Raja's estate. The details on how were murky, but he had five days to gather materials, to speak to the dead . . . and then pay a neighborly visit to the witch.

The moon was a sliver in the night sky. Stars shimmered, and Nick looked among them, wondering into which one Larry had vanished.

He dismounted Father Woberty's Appaloosa. The mare had climbed from the bottom of Lost Silver Canyon, up the gravel slopes of Seven Horseshoe Ridge without pause. He guided her to an abandoned silver mine, removed the saddlebags, then hobbled her to let her graze on the dry grass.

Nick had grown attached to the strong beast. He called her Dorinda, which meant beautiful gift. She had seen ghosts and spirits and lightning, yet she never shied away or bucked. Perhaps all the years of taking Father Woberty to his midnight rites of self-flagellation had hardened her.

The mine was a hole that twisted forty feet into the ridge. A cloud of Mexican free-tail bats flew out when Nick entered. There was no granite or quartz, just limestone and red clay. Whoever had dug it had been a fool.

He scratched two triangles in the dirt at the mouth of the cave, then connected their corners with straight lines to form a prism. With his mind, he traced the other parts of the *Isolation* rune, shadows that extended into other dimensions.

It flared then dimmed. He made the magic purposely feeble. It would not bar entrance, only alert him to another's presence. Nick had felt as if he had been watched for the last few days . . . with growing intensity. He had checked this realm, and others, but he saw nothing shadowing him, no spies, no ghosts, no crows overhead. This feeling, however, would not leave. He wished the other entity would show itself.

He gathered wood, unrolled his sleeping bag, and started a small fire. The smoke drifted out of the cavern, and the crooked tunnel shielded the light. It was a good place to camp.

From the saddlebags he removed a pouch, opened it, and emptied thirty silver coins into his hand. Nick had manufactured them by melting sterling from the Penitentes' cross, then pouring the metal into molds he had cast from a seventeenth-century Spanish piece of eight.

His Penitentes would not be enough. He required an army; so with the silver he had bought the services of thirty ghosts in the canyon below. They had deserted the Spanish Army to mine precious metal from these hills. They had been caught, killed, and their treasure confiscated.

They told Nick they needed the money to pay the ferryman to cross the Rio Del Muerto. It was an ostentatious lie.

Nick recognized Greed when he saw it. It dripped from their open palms; it glittered in their rotten eye sockets. Nevertheless, he had paid them. Their thirty souls were his.

The silver glowed in the firelight. Deceptively warm.

He had spent the last two days preparing for Raja and Larry. Nick could not take the divination for granted. Larry had escaped thrice before. Nothing would be left to chance.

Tonight he would rest, and think. Tomorrow he would kill Raja.

He wavered on that issue. There were other ways to deal with her, but her death held the least risk for him.

But it was Raja. True she had betrayed him, killed him, and banished his soul to nonexistence; yet paradoxically, she was one of the few in this world who understood him, and perhaps loved him. He still loved her.

Raja was the only one who had endured the centuries with him. He would sleep upon the matter, then decide tomorrow.

He caught a glimmer in the corner of his eye, and a gentle touch brushed his arm. The rune of *Isolation* had been breached. He removed his consciousness from Father Woberty's body—flashed to the mouth of the tunnel.

Linda was here. Good.

He returned to Woberty's shell. ''Come in, Miss Becket.''

She stumbled through the passage, flashlight in one hand, backpack dangling off her left arm. The seven squares of his enchantment glowed beneath her sheepskin jacket. She halted and waited for his command.

Nick stood and took the backpack. ''Sit,'' he ordered her. ''Please.'' He pointed to the sleeping bag.

She sat.

''You hobbled your horse? You made certain you were not followed?''

''Yes,'' she said.

''Excellent.'' He opened her pack. ''Ah, dinner.'' He emptied the contents: a tin of Brie de Meaux, a fresh loaf of Italian bread, and a bottle of Gewürztraminer.

She had endured remarkably well for a mortal—almost killed at the Ferrocarril cabin, possessed by Dempsey, and participating in the hunt for her ex-lover. She had unexpected strength. Nick liked that. He would erase her memory when this was over, send her back to Oakland, and perhaps use her again. Assuming she survived.

''Dinner then, please, Miss Becket. Serve me.''

She trembled while she opened the cheese and sliced the bread.

Nick wondered if she fought his enchantment. Perhaps she wanted to stab him with the knife. In her place, he would have tried.

He opened the wine. It smelled of peaches and apples and cinnamon, and looked like effervescent honey. He poured one glass for himself and one for her. ''Join me.'' He handed her the wine. ''And speak freely.''

The glow from the square runes upon her skin faded. Linda scrambled away from him, started down the tunnel, slowed, turned, then returned. Her face contorted, resisting the magic. She sat opposite Nick so the fire was between them. A small victory.

''I don't want your ghost inside me.'' Her chin quivered, but she did not cry. ''He eats like a goddamned pig. He makes me touch myself. I'd rather die than go through that ever again.''

''I can guarantee nothing. The need may arise for Dempsey to inhabit you, but it will not be long. Just enough to ensure that Mister Ngitis is dead.''

With both trembling hands she brought the wineglass to her lips, drank deep. "What has he ever done to you?"

"It is not what he has done. It is what he will do." Nick tore off a crust of bread. "I kill only murderers. Those history calls tyrants. Monsters. Abominations."

"Murder? Larry? He couldn't flush his goldfish down the toilet when it died. I had to do it for him. He's not exactly the next Hitler or Stalin."

"Precisely like them." Nick caught her eyes with his. "I removed Hitler too late in the game. Missed Stalin completely."

"The man can't balance his checkbook. You make him sound like the next conqueror of the world."

"He is. He has magic. He has luck. He has powerful allies. It is a deadly combination." Nick sampled the cheese, approved, and smeared it on his bread. "Have you not sensed a change in him since last you were together?"

"He never liked brunettes." She frowned, was silent a minute, then Nick's enchantment forced her to answer his question. "And he was never so confident. He actually articulated his emotions . . . or tried to in the bookstore. He never used to do that."

Nick poured himself another glass of wine. The alcohol warmed him for a moment, then his soul turned back to ice. This close to the solstice there was only cold.

"But you're talking about murder, taking a human life. It means—"

"It means nothing. I let others live whose work and intentions were noble. Circumstances twist their benevolent ideas into hatred and death: dynamite invented to remove stumps from fields, the atom pried apart for curiosity's sake, and monopolies created for stockholders' profits. I have seen it hundreds of times. And I have seen the millions of lives it has destroyed."

Nick pinched the bridge of his nose, took a long draught of wine. He could never explain to her that he was responsible for much of the world's misery.

"There are matters I wish to forget," he said. "Sit closer to me. Keep me warm."

"No." Linda got to her feet.

"It was not a request." The magic upon her chest flared neon red.

Linda came to him, struggling against every step her body took.

"It is not passion I desire, only warmth. Touch."

Linda dropped to her knees on the sleeping bag next to him.

"Please," he said. "Allow me to pour you another glass of wine."

Nick rubbed his hands together, but the chill did not leave him. His joints creaked when he moved. He pulled his London Fog trench coat tighter around him. There was a bullet-proof weave under the lining, but it did nothing to keep him warm.

He had ridden onto Raja's property just before sunrise, then decided to walk the rest of the distance. There was no need to endanger Father Woberty's Appaloosa. The mesquite and lechuguilla and purple sage crowded together, unusually lush. Things always grew wild near Raja.

He keyed his walkie-talkie. "Dempsey?"

"Yes, Master?" The ghost's voice crackled through a blizzard of static.

"Are the Penitentes in place?"

"As ordered, they surround the property." Dempsey's pen made a scratching noise as he checked this item off his clipboard.

"And Ms. Anumati?"

"Still in her house."

"Excellent. I am coming in. If she attempts to leave, disable her vehicle. And take care of the guard at the gate."

"Immediately, Master." A crackle of static, and the line disconnected.

Although it was three days until the height of his power and the nadir of hers, Nick would take no chances with the witch. He rubbed his chest, remembering her cleverness.

He marched until he came to the driveway of her estate. A massive black oak stood sentinel there. The limbs swayed, and the bark had a peculiar serpentine pattern. He looked deeper. There were scales, pits, and tails with rattles; it slithered and coiled and hissed at him. Each branch had a fat triangular head that watched him with golden stares.

Nick removed a roofing hammer and nine-penny nail from his right pocket, a silver piece of eight from the left—then leapt under the serpentine canopy.

They struck at him, snagging in the Kevlar weave of his coat; limbs slithered down, coiled around his legs, and constricted.

He pounded the nail through the coin, once, twice, three times, affixing it to the tree. The metal shimmered, and a Spanish soldier appeared with a spade in his hands.

A serpent struck at the ghost, but he laughed and pinned it under the edge of his shovel—beheaded it with a quick thrust.

The limb retracted, whipping wildly, as if caught in a typhoon.

The ghost hacked off snake heads, and severed their twisting bodies until they had all retreated back into the tree, or they were dead, dripping sap, and only wood again.

''Gracias,'' Nick said.

''De nada, Don Muerto,'' the soldier replied, and bowed.

He left the road and circled around the estate. That was where Raja kept her sacred pool. The forest thickened; piñon pines and aspens made a roof over his head. There was no snow on the ground, not even in the shadows. The soil was wet and black. It steamed in the early-morning light. There were aspens that still had golden leaves shimmering upon their branches. Some had green buds.

It was spring in Raja's domain. Her land dallied through fall, and hardly spent a day in the season of sleep. It did so to please her, to bolster her spirits through the winter, and so she might smell the perfume of flowers on New Year's Day.

Nick let the netherealms overlap this place. Dark currents broke the surface. He crouched to the ground, set his hand upon it, and the death oozed like blood from a wound. The shadows lengthened. Leaves fell: confetti and colored snow. Frost crackled.

He continued his march, but slower. The path was hard and slick with ice.

Farther into her grove there were English walnut trees and cherry plums, white willows, species that couldn't grow in New Mexico, and others with broad violet star-shaped leaves and trunks of glistening silver that Nick suspected did not belong in this world at all. He crossed a patch of ferns and moss. Beyond were five oaks in a circle and an artesian well. He squinted and perceived roots tangled beneath the soil, the lines of a pentacle, protection against unwanted visitors.

Winter swirled about him, frigid air and snow and ice-gray fog that settled upon the earth, froze it solid, cracked it open, and shattered the roots.

He stepped across.

Water nymphs scrambled out of the well and left their delicate footprints on its slate edge.

Nick took a bottle from his trench coat and poured half the contents in. A film of scum rose to the surface; the water clouded, and vapors bubbled forth that prowled the edges of the well, and scraped the stone with claws and teeth.

He walked back to the road, observed his possessed Penitentes in place with night scopes and hunting rifles, walkie-talkies and flak jackets. If his divination was correct, the prophet would get past them. Nick still had to try.

A gate blocked the entrance to Raja's manor. Wrought-iron leaves had rusted to the hues of fall. Steel reinforcements were supported on either side by twin columns of basalt and looked strong enough to stop a tank. A security camera eyed Nick as he approached. Beyond the gate stood a guardhouse, empty.

The gate rolled aside, and Nick walked up to the guardhouse. A uniformed man lay smoldering on the floor. The video screens within were black. It smelled of ozone.

Raja's manor was adobe the color of chocolate. Granite boulders were incorporated into the walls of the structure, part building, part earth. In places it was two, three, even four stories tall. Minarets rose above the central structure. Ivy clung to the towers, and spilled across trellises and covered walkways. It was a palace from the *Arabian Nights,* whisked from Baghdad to this New Mexican oasis.

Nick knocked on the front door.

The redhead from the Three of Diamonds Bookstore answered. Her face was puffy, and eyes bloodshot from crying.

"Father Woberty?" She tried to smile, failed.

"Ms. Anumati sent for me," he lied. "May I come in?"

The girl wrinkled her brow. "She did? I don't understand."

Nick stepped past her into the foyer.

"Well, OK, I guess. It was nice of you to come on such short notice, considering . . ." Her eyes welled up with tears.

"Yes, considering," he echoed, not knowing what it meant.

She led him past the ballroom he had seen in his vision, marbled floor on the north end, terra cotta on the south where the glass atrium attached, and vast gardens beyond. The Degas pastel was there too, hanging between twin gilded mirrors. This was where it would end.

Up two flights of stairs they went, past potted plants: poinsettias, night-blooming jasmine, and cacti with pale yellow blooms. There was an eighteenth-century Bavarian grandfather clock; a wall carving of bearded bulls from the Babylonian city, Uruk; a Grecian urn; Navajo blankets; and the black-on-black pottery of the Santa Clara tribe. It was an eclectic mix of past and present.

Nick had no need to disguise his soul from Raja as he had in the bookstore. That was October. This was December. He had power.

The girl knocked upon a door of rough green stone, then pushed it open. "Ms. Anumati? Father Woberty is here."

Raja stood up from one of the couches in her office. A slab of banded agate served as her desk, stone that looked like wood. There were two other couches of taffeta silk, mosquito netting that veiled a balcony, a wet bar, and in the corner a hibiscus tree in an oak barrel.

Dark circles ringed her eyes. She wore a black robe; Nick knew she hated the color. Her aura flickered low with dark green flames. She had overextended herself. There were wrinkles in the corners of her eyes, and her skin was porcelain white.

She set her coffee mug down when she saw him. Her only hint of surprise was the faintest twitch of an eyebrow. Her jade eyes flicked to the girl. "Thank you, Melissa. Please go home. You have done all you can for me here."

Melissa nodded. "As you wish, Ms. Anumati." She eased out of the room and pulled the door closed behind her.

"Father Woberty," Raja said. "Or do you still prefer me to call you Nick? Or Judzyas?" Her eyes narrowed, but the corners of her mouth curled into a smile. "How long have you worn his body?"

"August," he said, and sat. "After the Feast of the Crows."

"Then it was you in the bookstore. Had I known . . ." Raja mustered her power. The flames of her soul flared, wavered, dwindled.

Nick let winter flow through him. Cold winds tore the mosquito netting to tatters. The hibiscus shriveled. Shadows darkened.

Raja collapsed onto the coach. "Have you come to kill me?" She closed her eyes.

Nick could not imagine her dead. He touched the bottle within his trench coat. He had prepared for it, but he could not see her lying in a grave. The earth would reject her death. It would heave her coffin from the soil. "I do not know."

She tossed her head back and fixed her eyes upon him. She was regal despite her fatigue. "You are early. The solstice isn't for three days. It's not like you to be sloppy."

"I came to discuss Larry Ngitis."

"You came alone?"

"No. I have servants on your estate, and ghosts to occupy your spirits; I brought winter to your garden."

"Efficient as ever. And ironic. Last time you left me to chase your prophet. This time you return for the same reason." She leaned forward. "For my help?"

"Help?" He shook his head. "You are his ally."

She laughed. "Your divinations are dated. Matters have changed. I now desire him dead."

"I wish I could believe that. His magic is colored by the Fey. You are the only one who remains to teach him fairy sorcery."

"I did not."

He wanted to trust her, but her motivations were a mystery. Larry had slipped through his fingers three times, and he could not let her be the cause of another failure. "You may speak the truth. But he will be here. And whatever the situation, it will end on the solstice. This I have seen."

"So you did come to kill me."

"No." He sighed, and from his coat pocket removed a brown paper bag. The slender neck of a blue bottle protruded. "Perhaps."

"Glass stained by the sun," she remarked, never taking her eyes off him. "Lovely."

"I offer you a drink."

She rose and smoothed out her dress. "Then it is only fair that I offer you one as well." She took three steps to the wet bar. "I have Irish whiskey and ouzo—"

"I think not." Nick stood and set his hand upon his chest. "I have experienced your heartwarming hospitality before."

"As you wish." Raja smiled, returned to her seat, then, "You never answered my question. What shall I call you? Nick, Judzyas, or Woberty?"

''I do not know. Sometimes I forget who I was. Who I am.''

''I know who you are. Stay here. Be with me. I know the weariness and boredom, the burden of wisdom and a life too long. The earth forces me forward in time. Season after season. It will not let me die.''

He set his hand upon hers. She was warm. ''You cloud the issue.'' He withdrew from her. ''We were talking about Larry Ngitis. I must see to him first, and I cannot risk you stabbing me in the back . . . or the heart.''

He pushed the bottle closer. ''Take it.''

She reached down.

Clear lines of power drifted above the bag—and struck her as a sea anemone might capture its prey. It dragged her closer. With two fingers she pulled it free from the paper. Glued to the center of the bottle was a piece of parchment, water-stained and its edges frayed. In smudged green ink a sensual S-curve had been traced with spikes and flares.

''Your runes were always better than mine,'' Nick said. ''I severed it from the Ferrocarril cabin, and reattached it to this.''

''Why?'' Raja stared at the magic, snared by her own *Yearning* rune.

''I could never force you to drink it. Only your power could do that.''

She removed the ground-glass stopper, wrinkled her nose at the smell of garlic and sulfur. ''What is it?''

''Water from a spring. Near the ghost town called Serendipity. It is poison. Drink it.''

Raja slowly brought the bottle up, tilted it. Stopped. ''No.''

''It may kill you. It may not. It shall certainly incapacitate you for the next three days. Drink.''

She struggled against her magic, pressed the glass to her lips, and sipped. Her skin flushed. ''It is sweet.''

''Opium. For flavor.''

''Why this slow uncertain death?''

''The prophet's reason for coming here is hidden from me. I can only surmise it is for you, either aid or revenge or information. If you were dead he might sense it and never arrive.'' Nick sighed. ''So I will be waiting for him, with you, not dead, but not alive either.''

Raja doubled over and clutched her stomach.

He sat next to her, propped her head upon a pillow and held her hand. "I am sorry my Isis, my Moon Goddess, my Raja. Death has come. For you, and for Larry."

She dropped the bottle. It shattered on the floor.

Chapter 17

LARRY REACHED INTO THE BOOK AND PULLED HIMSELF THROUGH.

The maze behind him, the bookstore, the entire world turned inside out. Perspective inverted. The distant was near, and the near was far. Larry was everywhere at once: among stars and grains of sand, spread between vast galaxies and smears of electron probability, in blue nebula clouds and raindrops, and—

He stood perfectly still beside a claw-footed bathtub.

Paloma lay in the water up to her chin. Her right arm was draped over the edge, but her left was submerged in water so red it looked black. Within that hand she grasped the bead, which glowed a murky crimson.

His eyes caught on the razor blade next to the shampoo. Trails of blood red on porcelain white.

"No!" Larry shouted.

She breathed; he saw ripples on the water, but she did not respond.

He grabbed her, pulled her up, yanked a towel off the rack—knocking white candles and smoldering incense cones and dried lavender into the sink—and wrapped it around her wrist to slow the bleeding.

He saw the bead and halted.

It had three lengths of barbed wire magic coiled about her; one wrapped around her torso; the other two penetrated the incision in her wrist, long dark lines up her artery and vein. They pulsed and shifted. He had seen it whip through her like a band saw and draw her life out.

He grasped the bead, tugged, but it was stuck to her skin, the lines of magic embedded deep in her spirit. It wouldn't let go.

''She's got one foot on my side,'' Matt whispered.

She lifted her head. ''Larry?''

''I'm right here. Hang on. I'll call an ambulance.''

She clutched him with her right hand. ''Don't leave me again.'' Her eyes were glassy, dilated. Full of fear. The flames about her head were translucent and flickering.

Matt took off his Stetson and shook his head. ''I'll be outside if ya need me.''

Larry had to do something. He stood, started out of the bathroom, then stopped.

The future came to him. His pulse slowed, throbbed because there wasn't enough blood to pump. He gasped—couldn't get enough air into his lungs. This was how Paloma felt. Larry knew if he left her, she would die. In the minute it would take to tell the emergency operator where she was and what had happened, Paloma would bleed to death.

. . . Bleed to death. People didn't die so quickly from slitting one wrist. He tied the towel tight about her arm, just above the elbow, a tourniquet to slow the flow. Thick blood dribbled from the incision, then a stream. It didn't make sense.

The bead. Its magic sucked the life out of her. He had to get rid of it.

''I tried not to be jealous,'' she mumbled, and her eyes fluttered shut. ''But when I saw you leave with her . . .'' Her head dropped.

He touched the side of her neck. One heartbeat, two, three, each one fainter than the last.

''Linda and I aren't even friends anymore. You're the one I love.'' He shook her shoulder. ''Do you hear me?'' Larry's stomach twisted into knots.

''I tried,'' she whispered. ''I got my favorite things. Brought them with me. I thought a bath would help.''

There was a rubber duck in the soap dish, old yellowed paperback Dolinski novels, a bowl of poinsettia leaves, and a silver frame with a picture of a young Paloma and an ageless Raja.

''I remember the Dolinskis,'' she said. ''When I was a little girl he read them to me. I'd pretend to live in those worlds.''

The white glare of the bead's magic washed all the patterns and colors out of the glass. Larry saw the spiral fracture in the center, twisting out, sharp with hooks and barbs and jagged edges. Caught on them were pieces of Paloma, her memories and dreams, her thoughts and imaginings. It had ripped them from her.

There was the time her father spanked her after she broke a china cup. Larry smelled his aftershave. She didn't mean to do it. He relived a moment of anguish when they put down her horse. She remembered her mother's cancer and death, and the time she overheard her aunts whisper that she would have been able to afford chemotherapy if she hadn't had to pay for Paloma's tuition. There was a string of failed relationships. Awkward sex. The Silver Bullet Bed & Breakfast teetered on the edge of bankruptcy. It was land that had been in her family for three generations. It might have to be sold. She agonized over her mediocre talent as a witch. If only she could impress Raja, once. And Larry . . . losing him hurt the most. He was the freshest pain, on the surface, the straw that broke her.

Larry seized the bead again. He braced one leg against the tub, pinned her hand with his other foot, and pulled. The glass and Paloma were welded together, bonded by witchcraft that invaded her body and mind.

"Where did you get this?" Larry demanded.

"I told you," she murmured. "Raja. She said it would protect me."

Raja. The bead was meant for him. She must have planned for Paloma to give it to him, but the witch miscalculated, and Paloma was going to die.

"You've got to snap out of it. It's killing you."

Paloma slipped into the water. Larry pulled her back up.

If he couldn't physically remove the bead maybe he could destroy it with magic—shift it into other dimensions like he had with Spencer's Swiss Army knife. Alter it so it was brittle or soft or transmute it into liquid?

He focused, tried to change the shadows about the bead, but there were none. It was so bright. It appeared the same no matter how hard he concentrated.

Larry had failed. He was responsible. If he hadn't come to see Paloma, none of this would be happening. His whole life was a series of disasters. His writing was a joke. He had nothing to contribute to the world except misery. He could have prevented his father's death.

He knew it was going to happen. He should have warned him. His mother died in the earthquake. He saw it before it happened. He should have called the police. Told them that basement parking structure was going to collapse. It was his fault.

Right now, that razor was looking particularly tantalizing. He reached for it.

Motion in his peripheral vision made him pause.

Two tendrils of barbed wire had wrapped around his wrist. The bead wanted him too. On their barbs hung arguments with Linda, his dead parents, doubts that he could write, and his own hands covered in Paloma's blood.

"No," Larry whispered. "None of it is my fault." He wasn't worthless. He had things to say in his novels. His parents died before he could have done anything. He had dreams. His life had value.

He pulled the sticky wires. They were anchored to those memories, wedged deep. He yanked them with all his strength. They came free.

Larry knew how to move without moving. He saw into the future and into other realities. He had lived three lives. Why couldn't he untangle the magic of one bead? Why couldn't he close the incision on her wrist? He struck the tiled wall with his fist. All his power was worthless.

"Matt," he yelled. "Get in here. Help me."

Matt appeared. His mustache drooped and his eyes were dark. "Ain't nothing to help with," he said, "'cept to ask her what she wants. Then do it."

Larry wouldn't accept that. He wouldn't let her die. He twisted the towel as tight as he could to stop the flow of blood. The skin underneath pinched and blackened.

The blood dripping from her slowed . . . but not because of the tourniquet. Larry's mouth went dry; he tasted dust; he sensed only a trickle of blood was left.

"Larry?" she whispered. "Your friend is right." She gave Matt a weak smile. "You know what you can do for me? What would be nice?"

"I have to—"

"Read to me."

"Read? You'll die if I don't . . . if I don't . . ."

"Please," she whispered so softly he barely heard. "Please. Read to me."

Larry hung his head. He couldn't refuse her. He picked up an old paperback. The spine was cracked and the edges frayed. *To Sail an Amethyst Sea,* it was called. On the cover a man and a woman stood on the prow of a galleon. They were part pirate and part wizard, with sabers on their sides, red kerchiefs holding their hair, glittering amulets, and an aura of sorcery. They had adventure in their eyes.

He swallowed the lump in his throat, turned to the first page, and read:

> "It was the year the great comet struck and dragons boiled from the earth. It was the year of the White Festival when men skilled in magic and blades and with stories to tell gathered to share company and banish the dark.
>
> "Aquilina and I gathered our crew and set sail for the golden beaches of Bartabree. We had silver and jewels to trade at the festival, tales to hear, and tell, and, if we were lucky, a few new stories to discover along the way. Among our numbers were Peter the Brave, the red-haired archer, Marion, and the thief we called Pox because he never told us his name.
>
> "Dark clouds gathered on the horizon. Aquilina shouted, 'Raise the mainsail. We can outrun this winter squall.'
>
> "The wind rose as if it had heard her command. She flashed me a wry smile, leaned against the rudder, and set a new course.
>
> "I said to her, 'Our adventure begins early.' "

"You can stop now, pardner," Matt whispered.

Paloma floated on the water, peaceful. The bead's binding lines of magic darkened then vanished. There was nothing in her anymore. No flames. No life.

"What are ya gonna do?"

She was gone, and there was nothing Larry could do. The life he had thought he might share with her was gone. No one else would understand him, or his work, or the magic Niyol had taught him. He was hollow inside. He wanted to cry, but his body wouldn't. He was too tired.

Larry untangled the bead's thong from her hand. It was only Venetian glass covered with tiny amber-and-purple roses. He set it on the counter, grabbed the silver picture frame, then smashed it.

There was something he could do. He said to Matt: ''I'm going to get even.''

Larry followed Spencer's directions and turned off what he had described as the ''old Route 66,'' onto a single-lane dirt road that led into the middle of the desert. Spencer's hideout was an abandoned service station with a faded Texaco Pegasus painted on its cinder-block walls.

When he pulled up, Spencer came out to meet him—with an elephant rifle, which he slung over his shoulder once he recognized Larry's Econoline van.

They went inside.

The garage had three bunks, a pinball machine called *Eight Ball,* olive-green crates of ammunition, food, and liquor, a pair of antique gas pumps with glass reservoirs, and a restored Model-A with its doors missing.

Larry told him what had happened in town.

Spencer listened, nodded occasionally, but said nothing. He looked like he believed it, even though it sounded crazy: death personified in the bookstore, his ex-girlfriend possessed, walking through the stars, magic beads that killed people.

''You need a drink?'' Spencer asked.

''No. Thanks.'' It wouldn't help. No matter how drunk he got, it wouldn't change what had happened, it wouldn't bring Paloma back, and it might make his mind wander to dangerous places.

''I thought you gave up drinking.''

''Did.'' He rolled a cigarette, lit it, then pulled a crate of shotgun shells off a box of Absolut vodka. ''This stuff was here before I quit.'' He took a bottle out.

Larry watched the clear glass darken to cobalt blue. Inside he saw death swirling: a skeletal eel, all rib bones and fangs and empty eyes that stared back at him.

He blinked. The bottle and liquor were crystal clear.

Spencer gazed at it, sighed, then held it out. ''You sure? It'll take the edge off.''

''Really. I'm fine.''

Larry went to a cot in the corner and lay down. ''How safe are we here?''

''The place belongs to us Lobos. No one's gonna drop by. The only reason we ever come out is to plan an expedition or for target practice or a game of poker . . . or if there's trouble.''

Trouble. Larry squeezed his eyes shut. He had plenty of trouble. The woman he loved had just slit her wrist and bled to death. Raja wanted him dead. And whatever that thing was in the Three of Diamonds Bookstore was after him. It had Linda too. He had get her out of this mess. He wouldn't let another person get caught in the cross fire and die because of him.

One thing at a time. Paloma first. He had no way to bring her back. If the shaman was here, he might be able to tell him if such a thing was possible. But he wasn't. Larry hadn't even seen her ghost. She was gone.

Raja was responsible. He had to deal with her.

Larry sat up. ''I need a gun.''

''I got guns,'' Spencer said. ''You need a rifle, a shotgun, or a pistol?''

Matt appeared. ''Pistol,'' he said. ''Get two of 'em. And a scattergun. And see if he's got a Winchester. That's some mighty impressive iron.''

''Just one gun,'' Larry said. ''Something I can conceal.''

Spencer went to a metal cabinet with a dial combination, unlocked it, then returned with three handguns.

''You can take any of these,'' he said. ''First—'' He set a gun the size of Larry's hand on the tool chest. It was blue-black and had a plastic grip. It almost looked like a toy. Almost. ''That's a Beretta Model 70 Puma. Takes .32 ACP ammo and has an eight-round magazine.''

''That little thing couldn't slow down a mule,'' Matt said. ''Has he got a Colt Peacemaker? That's what I'm used to killin' with.''

''Do you have a Colt?''

Spencer nodded. He set a large revolver next to the Beretta. It was a nickel-plated monster with a six-inch barrel, walnut grip, and definitely did not look like a toy.

Matt whistled. The mirror finish glittered in his obsidian black eyes.

''That's a Colt Trooper MK V 357 Magnum. It's gotta heck of a kick.

''And last''—he set an automatic next to the Colt—''a Glock 17.'' It had a polymer frame, a barrel slightly longer than the Beretta, and was matte black. ''Takes nine-millimeter rounds, and holds seventeen in a clip.''

''Seventeen?'' Matt said. ''Bullets? They gotta be buckshot tiny.'' He twisted the end of his mustache. Larry looked at him, and Matt pointed to the Colt.

Larry reached for it.

Spencer grabbed it first, checked for a round in the chamber, then handed it to him.

It was heavier than he had thought it would be. It didn't feel right in his hand.

Matt ran his fingers over the barrel, and squinted at the intricate firing mechanism.

Larry set it down. ''Can I see the Glock?''

Spencer nodded, checked it, and gave it to him.

Larry tasted gun oil. He heard shots being fired from it, and saw ghostly smoke curling from the barrel even though it wasn't loaded. He knew he was going to use it.

''This is the one.''

''Take the big gun,'' Matt cried. ''I know my iron. It's gonna kill better.''

''If you want to practice,'' Spencer said, ''we've gotta range out back, and lots of ammo.''

''OK,'' Matt sighed. ''Take the one that fires tiny bullets if ya want, but don't worry none 'bout aimin'. Ya leave that to me. Guns done me in. That gives me the savvy with 'em. When I was livin' I could draw, shoot, and kill a feller quicker'n you could spit and holler howdy. Now that I'm dead, I'm better.''

''I think I can handle it,'' Larry said to Spencer.

Spencer wrinkled his brow, creasing his worry lines, then nodded. ''OK.'' He handed him a box of nine-millimeter ammunition and three clips.

''Get that thing loaded,'' Matt insisted, ''then let's skedaddle and give that witch a taste of her own medicine.''

Larry set the gun down. ''It's not right. Shooting her in cold blood.'' He went back to the cot, and sat down. ''It had to have been an accident. She wouldn't want to kill Paloma.''

''We gotta get her before she gets us,'' Matt cried. ''Save yer talkin' for the funeral.''

''It's like a Greek play,'' Larry said, ''everyone trying to kill each other, and getting sucked into schemes they don't belong in.'' He remembered his vision: a world black with pollution, acid rain, people squeezed together, nothing to breathe. ''Raja may not know the consequences of her actions on the Dai Esthai. She may not know how the world changes. The shaman died rather than let her have the dry water. I'm not going to die, or kill, without first trying to reason with her.''

''I knowed Sunday preachers with more backbone. It's kill or be killed. Any fool can see that.''

Logically and tactically, Matt was correct. Killing Raja was the prudent thing. They had both lived as Arturo Baldovino. They both knew any other action was a dangerous waste of resources. Larry could get himself killed with his good intentions.

But he couldn't kill because it was prudent. He knew more than Arturo Baldovino. He knew life had value. Even Delano's life mattered. Keeping him in prison had changed Larry's time line. With a slight nudge, Raja had used him to radically alter history. Every life had meaning and potential. Raja's included.

''No,'' Larry told him. ''I want to know a few things, for starters: what she's trying to do, and if she sent that thing in the bookstore to hunt me down.''

Matt threw up his hands, stomped in a circle, and pulled his mustache straight. He made a strangled sound of frustration.

Spencer drew smoke from his cigarette, made the tip glow bright yellow a moment, and said, ''And if she knows what she's doing?''

''I'll stop her. Any way I have to.'' Larry glanced at the guns. The weight of the nine-millimeter had given him a feeling of power. The solid reassurance was an illusion, though. Raja wouldn't be stopped by bullets.

He needed magic. The shaman was gone. And everyone that might have had power was dead and buried . . . in the past. That was the key: the past.

''I have to go back,'' Larry said, ''back in time to find a sorcerer's life to relive. I need to be on an equal footing with Raja, but I don't have the time to learn on my own. I'm going to steal someone else's experience.''

''A sorcerer?'' Matt cried. ''Yer askin' fer a heap o' trouble. Yer gonna get our souls sold off to the devil. Or worse.''

''Don't worry, you're not coming.''

"We're partners. Ya said ya weren't gonna spit me out no more. What happened to yer word?"

"I have to do this alone. It's between Raja and me. It's for Paloma."

Matt stared at him, then nodded. "If it's fer gettin' even, I reckon I understand that. It's the first thing ya said that makes sense." He frowned. "Probably gonna have yer nose stuck in some book fer years, anyway. When yer ready to do some shootin' ya let me know."

"I will." Larry removed the bullet from his molar. Matt crossed his arms and vanished.

"Were you talking to Carlson?" Spencer asked.

Larry nodded. It had been hard enough to pull Matt's spirit out of the Dai Esthai last time. If they were in deeper water or the current was stronger, they might both drown. He also didn't need the ghost learning magic. He was trouble enough without it.

"How much of the water is left?" Spencer asked. "If you do this, will we still have enough to go looking for that lost Spanish treasure?"

Larry didn't care about treasure, but Spencer had a point. He might need the dry water if Raja wouldn't listen to him, if he had to block her again on the Dai Esthai.

He took out the silver hip flask. It felt empty. He opened it, angled it so the light filtering through the dirty bay windows could get to the bottom. He saw water sloshing back and forth, flecks of illumination, less than half full.

"Two, maybe three more swallows."

Spencer nodded. "I'll watch over you then. Good luck."

Larry eased back onto the cot. He eyed Spencer, wondering if the old man was going to steal a sip of the water and try to find his lost Spanish silver. No. He trusted him. "I won't be long." He tilted the flask to his lips. It was like inhaling ice.

The world faded, blackness, stars, nothing.

The date of Robert Dolinski's birth is a mystery. Some biographers place it in the late nineteenth century because of fan letters from him to H.G. Wells and Jules Verne. Others claim the letters are fake, and use photographs of a young Dolinski with H.P. Lovecraft and Edgar Rice Burroughs to approximate his birth date in the early twentieth century.

He traveled extensively: on safari in Africa with Ernest Hemingway, jaunts to Caribbean islands, exploring the Australian outback by camel, and vanishing in China's Kwangsi Province for three years during World War II.

His first books, *A Mind Filled with Twilight* and *To Sail an Amethyst Sea,* were published in the United Kingdom after the war. They enchanted the children who read them with vivid adventures, and their parents with clever morals and unexpected plots. They have never gone out of print.

His career in America was, however, besieged with scandal. During a hiatus from writing in 1951, he allegedly became involved with several women, some of whom were married, and some suspected Soviet spies. Rumors abounded of Dolinski's dealing and double-dealing the Italian Mafia and the U.S. Intelligence community. None of the allegations were ever substantiated.

Dolinski moved to New Mexico, where he remained in seclusion, reportedly suffering from tuberculosis. He was unusually prolific during the next four decades, writing two novels a year—not only classic fantasies, but science fiction, mysteries, and horror.

According to *The Natural and Recent History of Seco County,* Robert Dolinski had more than scandals and spies to hide. Hoover James claimed the writer spoke not only of H.G. Wells and Jules Verne as if he knew them, but Bram Stoker and Mary Wollstonecraft Shelley. He provided Hoover James with details of their lives that made him either an expert historian, an accomplished liar, or a man over 150 years old.

Dolinski's ranch had an interior that Hoover James described as ''opulent beyond the imagination'' with rare art and artifacts: crystal statuary from the Minoan Empire, calligraphied tapestries from China's mythical Xia Dynasty, scrolls from the Library of Alexandria, and the titanic bronze face of the Colossus of Rhodes.

Within a year of that interview, Dolinski had his ranch house torn down and built a tower on the property. There were no reports from later visitors that matched Hoover James's account.

One last controversy surrounds Robert Dolinski: his death. The official cause was coronary failure, and given his advanced years few question this. But close friends report that he was despondent in the weeks before his demise. Dolinski himself remarked in the Hoover James interview that this life was dull and gray and that he wished to move on to something a bit more exciting.

He did not elaborate on what he had meant.

The Dolinski family had his body cremated and the ashes scattered over the Rio Grande. No autopsy was performed.

Larry woke feeling mud ooze into the fabric of his jeans, and soaking the back of his head. There was the sound of running water, a smooth mile-wide river.

He peeled himself off the bank and brushed as much of the muck off as he could, then watched the Dai Esthai—caught a glimpse of his life: Spencer explaining the caliber and capacity of his handguns.

What would happen if he traveled downstream, into the future? The river rolled on, widening rapidly into a delta, thinning, the flow sluggish, wider and wider until it lay flat and motionless against the horizon, an endless sea of possibilities.

A few small steps and he could see the future. Or could he? Once he knew his future, could he alter it, or would it be locked into place? It was foolish to tamper with time. Now anyway. Later he might return and experiment when there was less at stake. He'd stick to his original plan: find a sorcerer's life to live.

Larry drew lines and spirals in the mud and listened for the pulse of the earth. Gray fire erupted from his design, water sizzled along its edges, and the clay baked hard and cracked.

He reached into the center, through flames that were both hot and cold, and grasped the handle of the Blade of Veracity. The fire flickered. Last time at the Ferrocarril cabin the blade resisted him. Did the magic he learned from past lives only work on the Dai Esthai? Or was it a lack of confidence and concentration?

With one clean pull Larry drew the sword—basket hilt, then slim rapier blade, a wisp of razor.

He held it before his eyes, focused into the mirror reflection of the sword, shifted his gaze, and looked up at the river and the lives within. The edge reminded him of the razor by Paloma's tub. His mind wandered. He loved her. But she was gone forever. Lost. No. He had to concentrate; later he would mourn her death . . . and avenge it.

A sorcerer, he thought, a shaman or a witch, a person who understood mystic powers. Their life would teach him.

Images flashed in the water: a child answered the phone, a couple kissed on a front porch swing, a woman wolfed a gelatinous fast-food hamburger. None of them had magic.

He would look elsewhere and elsewhen. He stood and walked upstream.

Scenes from the past sparkled on the river, shimmered and vanished: a magician in top hat and tails did card tricks, made pigeons appear in a puff of smoke, then cut his lovely assistant in half. Not exactly the brand of magic Larry had hoped for.

He wandered further upstream and watched Doctor Franz Mesmer in the French Court wooing a young duchess with his wild stares and probing touches. The power of "animal magnetism," he claimed. He had no color in his aura. Lies. A charlatan.

Children ran through a street at night, screaming. Men with torches and faggots of wood. Terror and anger and mass hysteria. Three witches were burned at the stake in Salem, Massachusetts. No real magic, either good or evil.

Alchemists materialized in dark laboratories. There were fumes, and jars of preserved salamanders labeled "embryonic dragons," and furnaces full of green flames. No philosophers' stone, though. No transmutations of lead into gold. More lies.

Shamans danced wildly about campfires. Saints performed miracles and later collected silver in the name of God. The Oracle of Delphi chanted gibberish and got high on opiates and hemp and wine.

They all flowed past Larry.

How long would it take to find a person with real power? How long had he been searching? An hour? Days? There was no way to tell. Time had no meaning on the bank of the Dai Esthai.

His arm, though, trembled from holding the rapier aloft for so long. The blade was weightless, but the hilt and handle had mass.

The Blade of Veracity wavered; its ethereal smoke edges dissolved—gone.

Why was this so complicated? He had found Raja buried among a million lives in the sixteenth century. He had seen her first, however, on the other side of the river, where, or rather when, her future self had entered.

Could he find his future self the same way? Could he see where and when he was going to enter the river? Where he had already found a sorcerer's life?

If that was possible, how was he supposed to *originally* find it?

He sat, confused at the temporal logic of his situation, and found a stone to skip across the water. Three, four, five times it bounced, then plunked beneath the surface. Tiny ripples expanded, then disappeared.

On the other hand, what was the rush? He had forever to search. As long as he didn't give up, he could watch every life that had ever been, and no time would pass for him or his body in the conscious realm.

Larry froze.

There were dangers he hadn't thought of. Niyol got trapped on the river, looped in time, because he retraced his path across the river. The same thing could happen to him.

The river wasn't a river. It was only a metaphor his mind created to understand the concept of history and human life and the flow of events. It was time.

If he performed the same task twice, intersected his path, or maybe all it took was to accidentally step in his own footprints, he might find himself in a time loop like young Niyol. Trapped forever.

He examined the mud, spotted the impressions of his boots, and made certain that when he stood he was nowhere near them . . . then he saw another set of footprints.

They were smaller, perhaps a woman's or a child's, barefoot with a very high arch, and fresh. They marched toward where he had been sitting from upstream, stopped, then turned and marched back the way they came.

Someone had been watching his image at this time. Raja?

He followed them.

Larry wasn't staring into the Dai Esthai, so he noticed there were more stones and washes of gravel along the bank of the river, and depressions that held pools of water . . . and a small dam, a pile of mud and clay that diverted a trickle of water. A channel had been dug, so this water flowed along a path perpendicular to the Dai Esthai.

''Hello, Larry.''

He looked up.

Paloma wore blue jeans, a white flannel shirt, and was barefoot. She was alive. Vibrant pink-and-orange flames danced about her head, so strong his skin flushed standing close to her.

''I don't understand.''

''I love you,'' Paloma said. ''I wanted to tell you that first.''

A shadow fell over him, something behind him.

Larry turned.

The something that the shadow belonged to was a serpentine body longer than a train and as thick as his Econoline van. It had three heads and resembled a hybrid of *Tyrannosaurus rex* and a great white shark. Its long bat wings stretched, and one of the heads yawned, breathing smoke and brimstone.

Saddled atop the beast was a man in black leggings, white shirt with lace cuffs, with a saber strapped to his side. He took out a pack of Chesterfields, tapped one out, and the middle dragon head turned, snorted once, and lit it.

Larry's knees wobbled. His mind locked, terrified.

Paloma stepped closer, and took his arm to steady him. ''He can explain everything,'' she whispered. ''Larry, allow me to introduce you to my friend, Robert Dolinski.''

Chapter 18

DOLINSKI APPRAISED LARRY. HE BLEW SMOKE AT HIM, SWUNG HIS LEGS over the dragon's saddle, and jumped down. "Home," he said to the beast. The reptile sprang into the air, beating its tremendous wings and pelting Larry with gravel.

Larry sneezed. The dust settled, and he held out his hand.

"I would welcome you, Mister Ngitis." Dolinski drew his cutlass. "But I have yet to decide if I am going to run you through."

The sword pointed at Larry's breastbone was red-gold steel etched with roses. It was long as Dolinski's arm and tapered to a fine point. The crossguard bore scratches from past engagements.

"Please." Paloma pushed his blade aside. "He's not responsible."

Dolinski stepped around her and brought the point in line with Larry's heart.

"You think I killed Paloma?" Larry took a step back. "It's the last thing I'd want. I . . . I care for her a great deal."

He was embarrassed to admit he loved her to Dolinski. He'd had mistresses and a wife as Arturo Baldovino. He'd had a husband and children when he was Anne Marie Dubois. He knew what love was.

"I believe you did not wish to harm her," Dolinski replied, and lowered the tip of his cutlass. "That is why you are still alive." He flicked his blade in the direction of the siphoned stream. "Walk."

''I don't—''

Dolinski jabbed him between the ribs.

Larry grasped his side. There was blood. ''Are you crazy?''

''No!'' Paloma cried. This time, however, she did not step between them. ''Larry,'' she whispered, ''you'd better humor him.''

Larry wished he had Spencer's nine-millimeter or his Blade of Veracity . . . to do what?

Dolinski narrowed his eyes, and pointed with the tip of his sword. ''Move,'' he said, ''or I shall be forced to move you.''

Larry couldn't argue with a cutlass. He marched.

''The majority of the blame is Ms. Anumati's,'' Dolinski said, keeping his blade pointed at Larry's back. ''However, you are partially responsible for Paloma's death.''

Paloma interrupted, ''I'm the only one responsible for me.''

''Of course you are,'' he said and turned to her, ''but had Mister Ngitis and Ms. Anumati employed a civilized method of settling their differences, none of this would have occurred.''

Paloma exhaled an exasperated sigh. ''Sometimes, Robert, you go too far.'' She caught up to Larry and wrapped her arm through his to reassure him.

Her skin was warm. Real. She *was* dead, wasn't she?

The creek swelled, though no tributaries fed it. The water was a foot across. Smooth stones covered with moss littered the bank. Koi swam in the shadows; red and orange and white scales flashed underwater. A crane stood motionless, staring intently at the fish, its beak poised.

''This isn't the Dai Esthai?'' Larry asked. ''Is it?''

''This is my world,'' Dolinski answered, ''built of stories and imagination. Everything I wrote or dreamt is here.''

He lit another cigarette and lowered his blade. Larry considered making a run for it, but Paloma still held his arm.

''I have been told you are a writer.'' Dolinski picked up his cutlass. ''I shall see that you are given pen and paper. Or a typewriter if that suits you better? You must be bursting with ideas.''

Larry's eyes followed the sword. ''Ideas? Not really. I've got other things on my mind.''

''Come, come, Mister Ngitis, you are a writer; you must write. Imagination comprises most of what we are. Fail to exercise your creativity and you might as well be dead.''

The water was a stream now, too wide for Larry to jump across with a running start, and too turbid to see the bottom. On the opposite side stood a grove of acacia trees. Birds of paradise fought and dove in the branches, a flurry of shrill cries and trailing rainbow feathers.

Dolinski offered Larry a cigarette from his pack of Chesterfields.

''No thanks.'' Larry spied a city of aquamarine glass on the ridge of a distant mountain. It caught the sun's setting light and glowed. ''How did you do this?'' He tried to encompass the sky and the horizon with a sweep of his hand.

''When I was eleven,'' Dolinski said, ''my teacher encouraged me to express my thoughts, in song, with paints, or with writing, if I was so inclined. Miss Wainwright said I had the gift of communication. She told me it was too rare to waste.''

A swarm of dragonflies touched upon the surface of the river. They darted between Dolinski and Larry, all cellophane wings and bodies of electric blue—then gone.

''The day I graduated from her one-room school, she gave me a vial of water, a magic elixir. That was how this''—he waved with his cigarette extravagantly—''started.''

''Dry water? Where did she get it?''

''A priest gave it to her when she broke her leg. Where he obtained it, I do not know.''

''This place can't be real. Your mind fills in what it can't comprehend with hallucination. This has no substance.''

Dolinski watched his setting sun, then, ''Come.'' He motioned with his blade. ''We are almost home.''

Pale moons materialized, invisible before in the sunlight, a giant lavender globe accompanied by a swarm of silver, copper, and crimson orbs. The river was a thousand feet wide, and the moonlight glistened upon its surface.

There was a crash of waves in the distance, the rumble of ocean.

They strode through palm trees and emerged on a beach. The lavender moon transformed the water into an amethyst sea. The river roared into the surf, crashed, swirled, and mingled with the incoming tide.

A castle stood at the water's edge, with glistening white towers and silver domes; stained glass windows illuminated from within, flags fluttered on the ramparts, and gargoyles leered atop parapets.

''My palace is sand,'' Dolinski said. ''With every wave it erodes. With every beat of the earth's pulse it grows.''

A tower crumbled and fell into the surf: lumps of sand and white foam. A new minaret rose upon the far wall, with sharp edges, clear geometric reliefs, and sturdy, at least, for the moment.

''Don't worry,'' Paloma whispered. ''There are rooms hundreds of years old. It's safe.''

''I am afraid, Mister Ngitis,'' Dolinski interrupted, ''there is one more thing I must show you.''

''What's that?''

''The prison.''

Larry sat in a tower. It stood on the corner closest to the ocean—a corner whose base was eroding. From his vantage he saw statues grow and melt in the courtyard, neo-Gothic buttresses extrude from the walls, and Moslem scrollwork meander across blank archways. The chapel attached to his tower collapsed, a slow-motion cascade of sand and stained glass and gargoyles.

His cell had scrolls of papyrus and yellow legal pads, pencils, Mont Blanc pens, and sharpened quills for him to use, and, as promised, an Underwood typewriter. Larry had finished three chapters of his novel. How long had that taken? His sense of time was distorted. It took between a week and a month to write a chapter, unless he was blocked. There were no distractions here, though. It could have taken him three days.

There was a bed of straw, a wool blanket, and a chamber pot. Iron bars blocked the window. With a ballpoint pen he gouged the sandstone around the sill. When he paused to wipe the sweat from his forehead, his scratches sealed themselves.

Larry had a theory.

Magic was subjective—that's what the shaman had taught him. His mind filled in the parts it didn't understand. What if he filled in the blanks with his emotions? Projected his feelings into the magic? Paloma could be a manifestation of his guilt, and Dolinski his need to punish himself.

Larry couldn't explain Paloma's existence otherwise. She was vibrant, and stronger than he had seen her before, yet he had seen her die.

Or maybe it was real. Maybe all writers went into their novels when they died. Were hacks consigned to their invented hells of clichés and bad prose? Larry considered revising his Captain Kelvin novel while he waited.

A knock. A servant with another culinary delight, dry corn bread like last time, washed down with stale milk. What he wanted was coffee. Black and hot.

"Larry?" It was Paloma's voice.

The iron-bound door cracked open. She stepped in. Beyond stood a guard in chainmail with an unsheathed sword. He glared at Larry, closed, then locked the door.

Paloma wore buckskin leggings, a belt of seashells, and an empty scabbard hung on her hips. Her white silk shirt buttoned to her neck where a choker of garnets and black pearls clung. Two sterling pins held her auburn hair back.

She stepped up to Larry and kissed him. He smelled rice and black beans and piñon pine, and it reminded him of their Monday morning meals at the Ferrocarril cabin; he tasted her tears as she lay bleeding in his arms; he heard her pronounce his name when he stumbled into the Silver Bullet Bed & Breakfast for the first time.

He held her tighter. Memories of her mother's death, the horse that had to be put down, and the broken china cup were still there. It was Paloma.

He pulled back. Her eyes were darker than he recalled, almost black. The flames that crowned her head were brilliant pink neon that filled the cell.

"I don't understand any of this," he said. "I don't know what's real and what's not."

"It's OK." She took his hand and made him sit next to her on the straw. "Ask me anything. I'll do my best to explain."

"Where is this place?"

"It's like Dolinski said. This world is cobbled together from his stories. I've been to the White Festival at Bartabree. I've seen dragons playing in thunderstorms. There are things he never wrote of too, pirate grottos, and mermaid lagoons, and cities of ice. He's shown me the maps. It's amazing. Endless."

"You've been to all those places? How long have we been here?"

Paloma wrinkled her brow, thinking. "I'm not certain."

"The suns and moons have risen a dozen times, but I'm not tired. It's impossible to tell time."

She stared out the window a moment, listened to the ocean, then said, ''I don't think time exists here.''

Larry mulled that over. ''Are you real?''

''Touch me.'' She grabbed his hand and stared into his eyes with such intensity that he looked away. She pulled his chin up so he had to look at her. ''Don't I feel real? Stay with me. Stay and we can have a hundred lifetimes together.''

Larry pulled away and stood. ''It's not like I have a choice.''

''You can leave . . . if that is what you want.''

''How? Pry the bars loose and fly down? Even if I did, I bet I couldn't find my way back. This is Dolinski's world. He calls the shots.''

Paloma frowned. ''He likes you, I think. He says your writing shows promise.'' She bit her lower lip, then, ''He decided to release you. But he has this overblown sense of adventure. He wanted me 'accidentally' to reveal that in the dungeon is a vial of water from the Rio Grande. Drink it and you'll find your way home.''

''The Rio Grande, huh? It's that easy? Am I supposed to trick the guard into opening the door, then knock him out with a chamber pot? Sneak down to the dungeon, pick the lock, and steal this water?''

''Dolinski thinks everyone has the soul of a swashbuckler.'' She removed a slender crystal vial from her shirt. ''That's what I was supposed to do.'' Water glistened within, and upon the cut-crystal surfaces gleamed Agua de Viva Road, snow falling in Lost Silver Canyon, and Spencer pouring himself a cup of coffee.

Larry sat back down next to her, and asked, ''Why?''

''I would never make you stay.''

Stay. He hadn't even considered it. He had thought of only escape. Paloma was here, though, and there was no Raja, no incarnation of death haunting him, and no problems.

But this wasn't his world. It was fantasy and dream.

Larry had always run from his problems. He had left Linda and his job. He had left his parents when he was sixteen. Problems were best fled from, ignored, and stuffed deep in the abscesses of his guilt.

But his world would be destroyed if he didn't stop Raja. Linda was somewhere in Seco County too, possessed, used to bait a trap in the Three of Diamonds Bookstore . . . what had happened to her? Spencer was waiting for Larry to wake up. How long before the old man poured himself a shot of vodka? Matt Carlson would fade into Limbo if Larry didn't go back and ingest his bullet. Killer of Crickets had been with Paloma—probably been stuffed fat in the Silver Bullet's kitchen, but with her gone who would feed him? And his damn novel was due at Perspective.

"I can't stay. There are too many things that I'm responsible for. If I stayed with you, I could forget everything, but I'd never forgive myself for being a coward."

Paloma swallowed, kissed his cheek, and whispered, "I understand."

They were silent a moment, then Larry said, "I have to go."

"You still have the dry water? Will you come back?"

"There are two sips left." He held her eyes with his. "I'll come back. I promise."

"I shall wait for you, Larry Ngitis."

He reached for the vial of Rio Grande water.

Paloma snatched it up. "What's your rush? Time doesn't exist for us." She drew him close, and ran her fingers across his chest.

"No rush," he said, and kissed her.

Larry rolled over and reached for Paloma. Making love had never been like that before. It wasn't awkward touching and selfish pleasure. It was a melding of flesh, spirits, and passions, a joining of the physical world, and worlds he had been afraid to glimpse. They had shared perspectives and orgasms, then collapsed, tangled in each other's arms.

His hand touched rough cotton.

Where was she? Had it been a dream? Had he wasted the dry water? Paloma had to be real. She had to be alive.

Hot breath, rancid with cigarette smoke, blew across his skin. Larry opened his eyes: Spencer's face was four inches from his.

Spencer jerked back. "Sorry," he said. "I couldn't tell if you were breathing. You've been awful quiet." Spanish pieces of eight reflected in his eyes.

Larry touched the silver flask with the remaining dry water. It was still there.

"You get what you needed to done?" Spencer asked. He glanced at the flask—then away.

"Not exactly." Larry hadn't lived the life of a sorcerer, and he only had two sips of the dry water left. One he had to save to get back to Dolinski's world and Paloma. The other was for Raja. If she changed history again—erased Larry—he had to be able to block her, go back to the Dai Esthai and undo her mischief.

Could Larry trust Spencer? His eyes were back to their normal bloodshot brown. The silvery greed he had seen was gone . . . but for how long? Larry needed Spencer. He needed all the help he could get. Spencer had to be shown what was at stake.

Larry sat up and touched the concrete floor. It was dusty, and cold, and far beneath him the pulse of the earth thundered. He traced lines in the dust, spirals and fairy runes.

He centered himself. Banished thought. There was nothing save the design. There was nothing save the gray flames that erupted, hot and cold. Nothing save the center of the fire.

Larry reached in and grabbed the handle of the Blade of Veracity. No thoughts.

He drew it in one smooth pull. The blade was wider, double-edged, more saber than rapier. The basket hilt was etched with designs of rocket ships with filigree vapor trails and stars and moons and ringed planets. The balance was perfect. It was a natural extension of his arm. It was no longer the old gnome's or Anne Marie's magic. It was Larry's.

"God Almighty." Spencer took a step back.

Larry held the blade aloft, so both he and Spencer saw into it.

The metal rippled. Images resolved and reflected. Raja slept in a glass coffin, filled with rose petals and orchids, surrounded by candles and wisps of incense. Downtown Dry Water flickered upon the blade; a light down of snow coated the adobe buildings. Pink neon from the Three of Diamonds Bookstore made the lacy frost on the windows glow. A bathtub materialized next, porcelain and dried blood and yellow police tape. Linda appeared, sitting in a wicker chair, studying a chessboard. Her opponent sat in the shadows. She was losing.

No trace of Dolinski's world appeared. Nor Paloma.

The blade blurred.

Larry refocused his eyes beyond the metal, and focused his thoughts on the future. "Look and feel what tomorrow holds."

Mirages coalesced on either side of the saber's midline. The top half reflected New Mexico in the winter: snow fringes on red rock mesas, brilliant blue sky, and thick white clouds. Spencer was in the blade too; he pored over a U.S. Geological Survey map by the light of his campfire.

Upon the bottom of the blade: lakes of oil smoldered, forests burned, the earth was dry and cracked and dead. The sky was black and without stars. Cities covered the world. Spencer was there as well; he gnawed upon a human bone. Dust and ashes.

The visions vanished. Larry gazed only at a mirror image of himself, then the Blade of Veracity was smoke in his hand.

''That's why Raja has to be stopped,'' Larry said. ''That's why I'm risking my life. It's why Paloma died.'' He locked eyes with Spencer. ''It's more important than any Spanish silver. More important than either of our lives.''

Spencer backed into a crate of twelve-gauge shotgun shells, and half fell, half sat on it. Larry's throat burned. The old man wanted a drink—even if it killed him.

''So, are you ready? I could use a hand.''

Spencer swallowed. ''Yeah. I guess.'' His red skin blanched and his eyebrows wrinkled into creases. With a shaking hand he unscrewed the thermos and poured himself a cup of coffee.

Larry put Matt Carlson's bullet in his mouth, then bit it into place.

Matt stepped from the shadows, straightened his Stetson, then faced Larry. ''You look ready fer a fight.'' He glanced at the nine-millimeter across the room. ''Don't forget the pistol.'' Matt exhaled gunsmoke. He wore a belt and holster over his long johns.

Larry picked up the gun.

It felt the same as before, only different . . . he remembered shoot-outs in saloons, pressing the muzzle into unsuspecting backs, the flash and smell of gunpowder, blood, the recoil, and the ringing in his ears.

''Now ya know how it's gonna be,'' Matt whispered. A gun appeared in his holster, a Colt Peacemaker. The cylinder was as fat as his fist. He examined it, then pronounced, ''Yep, seventeen rounds. We gotta lot o' shootin' to do.''

The Glock 17 moved in Larry's hand. It was as if it had a gyroscope spinning inside, aligning it perfectly with his wrist. Larry trembled, but the gun was steady.

Matt holstered his Colt. Larry did the same with the Glock.

The smell of hot metal wouldn't leave his nostrils. Phantom recoil made his wrist flinch. How many lives would he take before he saw Paloma again?

On Christmas Eve in New Mexico there is a Hispanic festival of lights. Votive candles and a handful of dirt are set in paper bags. These are called *farolitos* or *luminaria.* The citizens of Albuquerque make half a million of them—a symbolic gesture to help Mary and Joseph find a safe haven.

Dry Water has a festival of lights as well, but it starts three weeks earlier. Every night two hundred candles are added along the raised wooden sidewalks, and the edges of the adobe walls and rooftops. There is a holiday theater, caroling, and vendors who sell hot mulled wine, souvenir T-shirts, and authentic hand-dipped candles. Flocks of snowbirds on their way home from Taos and Santa Fe stop for the festivities.

There is another purpose for the festival, however.

The original inhabitants of Seco County believed that evil spirits haunted the remote northern canyons, Terranegro, Lost Silver, and Dusty Knot. When the winter stars rose these spirits grew restless. It was whispered they came from those stars and wished to go home.

The spirits roused sleeping ancestors. They possessed the weak. Inexplicable events occurred: hailstones of frozen fish, rocks migrating across dry lake beds, and clouds that burned.

Acoma and Hopi shamans lit bonfires and blessed special lamps to keep these demons at bay.

When the Spanish came in the sixteenth century, the spirits attacked them. Children were consumed by tumors, young men grew old overnight, and their horses vanished and reappeared upon sheer Caemous Mesa. These occurrences faded as the winter stars set. The Spanish thought it was Christmas that drove the evil away.

One man, Father Hernnan Chavez, saw the Indians' lights. He saw how they protected them. He stole their fire.

The wind snuffed Father Chavez's candles when he tried to light them, so he shielded the flames in buckets, jars, and leather pouches. The custom of lighting *luminaria* was adopted into Christian ritual, modernized, and, everywhere but Seco County, truncated to a single evening.

Today, if you happen to drive through Seco County between Halloween and the New Year, especially near the remote northern canyons, you may see a dozen candles or lanterns burning on a porch.

Ask, and you'll be told they're for good luck. Offer to buy one, and you'll be politely but firmly denied. Try to steal one—and you may be shot.

It was noon, but clouds shrouded the sky, gray veils that shook loose snowflakes.

A crow circled and landed on the iron cross atop the Church of the New Age. It teetered on the perch, cawed once, then vanished again into the storm. One black feather fell and fluttered to the street.

Spencer drove his '58 Chevy truck through Dry Water, and, at the insistence of Larry, past the Silver Bullet Bed and Breakfast. No police cars. No yellow tape sealing the entrance. Nothing to indicate Paloma had died.

Maybe she hadn't.

Maybe Larry had hallucinated it. He had seen her alive, hadn't he? Or was that the dream and this real?

Spencer turned right on Agua de Viva Road. *Luminaria* stood in precise rows along the raised wooden sidewalks. The warm lights gave the snow a luster like gold.

A boy's choir sang ''Ave Maria'' in front of the Three of Diamonds Bookstore. Their paper bags had been decorated with Crayola crayons. Midnight blue Christmas trees with burnt sienna ornaments flickered in the candlelight. Stick figure families with violet red hair and peach smiles came to life as Larry watched. Periwinkle snowflakes fell on the luminous yellow paper. A navy blue Santa in a brick red sled pulled by cornflower reindeer flew through the truck and wished them a Merry Christmas.

Spencer drove on, not seeing any of it.

The children's pictures reminded Larry why he had come back. There was nothing abstract or heroic about it. It was survival. His. The world's. These people. Families. When Larry had lived with Linda in their Oakland apartment he hadn't known his neighbors' names. He hadn't cared to either. It was different now. He was different.

Spencer gunned the engine when he got outside the city limits and headed south toward Mount Taylor and the Cibola National Forest.

Larry looked for Niyol's grave along Agua de Viva, but didn't see anything under the snow except the tips of sage and the twisted limbs of mesquite.

They drove up the mountain, skidding onto the side of the road and sliding around curves.

"That's it," Larry said, and pointed at two giant black oaks on the right-hand side of the road. A gravel driveway ran between the bare trees.

They rolled closer. Spencer set his 357 Magmun on his lap.

"Go ahead and turn in," Larry said. "I still want to talk to her first. Face to face."

"You sure?" Spencer asked.

"Damn fool idea," Matt muttered. He sat sandwiched between them. "If yer askin' me it's an ambush."

Larry touched the Glock—to make sure it was still there. Matt knew about ambushes. Memories bled through the pistol's grip, polluting his thoughts. He had known the anticipation when he had watched settlers wander into a box canyon or he had followed a drunk prospector back to his secret camp. The thrill of surprise. The quick death. The easy money.

"I'm not sure about anything anymore," Larry replied. "Let's go in."

Spencer eased onto the gravel road. The temperature dropped inside the truck as if both the windows had been rolled down. Larry turned the heater on full blast, but it only blew cold air. The tires slipped.

"Gravel's frozen solid," Spencer said, and shifted into low gear.

They crept forward. Aspens and English walnut glittered with frost. Under the trees, where the ground had been sheltered from the snow, lay amber and flame and gold quilts of leaves lacquered with ice.

Spencer traversed a hairpin turn and stopped. The gate to Raja's property, a barrier of steel bars and wrought-iron leaves, stood ajar. A camera on the stone wall turned and tracked them.

"Stay here," Larry said. "I'll walk up to the guardhouse."

"I can drive—"

"Look, it's my idea to talk to Raja and straighten this out. There's a good chance she'll try to kill me instead. I'll go in alone." Spencer could get caught in the cross fire. Like Linda had. Like Paloma.

Spencer frowned.

''Besides,'' Larry said, ''if I get into trouble, I'll need you to get me out.''

''OK,'' Spencer whispered. ''I'll sit for a spell. But the first whiff of something wrong and we get back to my hideout to rethink this scheme of yours.''

''Deal.''

Spencer grabbed his arm. ''I figure none of this woulda happened if we left well enough alone—if you hadna showed up at my gas station, if you hadna dragged me into that cave, and if you hadna showed me what was in that blade.'' He whispered, ''But if it was gonna happen, then I'm glad it was you. I wouldn't want to be in trouble with anyone else.'' He held out his hand to shake. ''Good luck.''

Larry clasped his hand.

He opened the door, and stepped out. Frozen wind tore at his skin and made his eyes water. In his peripheral vision he saw impish faces, spindly legs and arms, and white bat wings swirling in the snowdrifts. He pretended not to see them and hoped they went away.

He clenched the automatic and marched thirty paces to the adobe guardhouse, shaking, half from the frigid wind, half from terror.

Matt shivered too. He walked on Larry's right side, brandishing his pistol. ''Tarnation. It's like Hell's done froze over.''

The guardhouse was empty. There were video screens inside: views of Spencer's Chevy and the front door of Raja's mansion.

''We're being watched.'' Matt cocked the hammer of his Colt.

The gate jerked and started to roll shut. Sparks of electricity jumped from the wrought-iron leaves to the steel bars to the grounded track.

Spencer jumped out of his truck, .357 in hand. He ran toward the narrowing entrance, hesitated, and the gate slammed shut.

''There,'' Matt said, pointing into the woods.

Five men jogged through a grove of skeletal white willows, crunching across the icy snow. They wore camouflage parkas and combat boots. They carried assault rifles with curved clips of ammunition. One halted and raised his rifle.

Larry ducked behind the guardhouse, slipped, and fell flat.

Adobe exploded and wood splintered as a spray of bullets hit.

Matt yelled, ''Get on up. That's only to let ya know they're there. Get yer pistol out and say howdy back.''

Larry used one hand to help himself stand on shivering legs. He peeked out. They were forty paces away with dozens of intervening trees to use for cover.

"Shoot 'em," Matt cried. "Them fellers couldn't hit a bull's ass with a handful of banjos that far away. We can."

Behind him three cracks of thunder erupted. Spencer crouched behind the door of his truck and returned their fire.

The Glock was level and steady in Larry's hand. He sighted down the barrel, lined up the sights, forced his eyes to stay open, and squeezed slightly to release the tiny lever safety built into the trigger.

Matt stepped inside Larry; his Colt occupied the same space as the Glock.

Larry knew what to do. His heart skipped a beat. He squeezed hard.

Blast and recoil—the round caught the closest man in the neck and he toppled forward spraying the snow red. Good. He got what was coming to him.

The others ducked behind willows. Larry squeezed again. The Glock aimed itself. Point, fire—no time to wait for a target. Squeeze. He stopped breathing.

The barrel of a rifle swung around a willow trunk.

Larry shot before the man stuck his head out. The bullet glanced through the bark of the tree, and the man fell back, clutching his face.

Adrenaline surged through Larry. He stood straighter, knees braced, eyes unblinking. Matt wanted him to fan the hammer of his Colt. This wasn't his old Colt, though. It was better.

Two men lay behind a mound of snow. They fired. The windows of the guardhouse shattered, and sheetrock detonated as the rounds missed and puffed into the snow inches from Larry.

He squeezed off four rounds—fast.

Bullets blasted through the snow, and their heads. They convulsed and rolled, and were still.

The last man turned and ran.

"We got 'em jumping like jackrabbits," Matt whooped. "Finish 'em off."

Larry grinned. This was the best part: when you couldn't miss. He stepped out and pumped three slugs into the air.

They tore into the man's back. He tumbled. Blood and down feathers from his parka burst into the air. He skidded face first to a stop.

Larry could have taken twice their number. Next time, though, he'd be the one doing the bushwhacking.

No. This was wrong.

The elation and anger weren't his. He wasn't the one who took pleasure in rape and shooting the helpless. It was Matt. He was a coward. A bully. A murderer.

Larry stared at the gun—half Colt Peacemaker, half Glock 17. Smoke curled from the barrels. He dropped it into the snow. It sizzled and hissed as if it were angry.

"Don't throw yer gun away," Matt cried. "There's gotta be more awaitin' for ya. Pick it up."

"No." Larry would never touch it again.

The bloodlust cooled. This wasn't murder. It was self-defense. His stomach twisted. He had killed. After living Anne Marie's life, enduring two wars, and surviving her children; after being Arturo Baldovino and manipulating people like pawns; after watching how even worthless Delano could change so much of the world, Larry knew every life was priceless.

Five deaths stained his hands. Blood pounded through his ears. The edges of his vision clouded.

"You OK?" Spencer called.

Larry steadied himself. "Yeah," he called back. "You?"

Spencer's left arm hung limp and his jacket was soaked with blood. "Got winged. Let's get that gate open and get outta here."

"Larry?" a voice from the woods called.

He recognized the voice and squinted.

"Get down." Matt crouched behind the guardhouse.

Linda stumbled past the dead guards and looked over her shoulder, as if someone followed her.

"It's that girl," Matt said. "I don't see no trace o' that other cuss inside her."

She stopped a dozen paces before the guardhouse. "Larry," she panted. "It is you, isn't it? They told me you'd come."

Larry ran out to her and grabbed her hand. "Come on. We've got to get out of here."

She resisted, then pulled free. "I'm sorry, Larry. I never meant to do any of this. They made me."

"Now's not the time for apologies. I know it's all Raja's fault. There's no need to—"

''No,'' Linda said and drew a chrome .38 from her coat. ''I'm sorry about *this*.''

A flash from the muzzle. Agony tore through his stomach and paralyzed him. He crumpled upon the snow, went numb.

She shot him again, straight through his heart.

Chapter 19

LARRY HURT. BITS OF GLASS GROUND AGAINST HIS HEART AND RIBS—AT least, that's how it felt.

Moonlight seeped through a tiny window and illuminated his frosty breath. He was in a room: four concrete walls, ten paces to a side, one door, and an earthen floor.

A woman lay next to him. Paloma? Was he dead? Dreaming? He didn't care. He touched her warm skin, but the memories and passion that had melded with him before were missing.

She stirred, turned; green-mirrored cat eyes flashed. Raja.

Larry scrambled away, wedged his back into the corner.

No fire crowned Raja's head, nor clouds of crows. Her eyes were jaundiced, glassy. "Conserve your strength," she whispered. "You were dead . . . and shall be again if you are not cautious."

"What do you mean, 'dead'?"

"Shot through the liver and heart. Your spirit clung to your body because it had unfinished entanglements. Nick threw you in here. And, I am afraid, that is not the worst of it."

His flannel shirt had two holes, burned around the edges. The skin beneath was scar tissue crusted with dried blood. Larry remembered: Linda, her .38, the shots. He had died. A current had sucked him under, smothering, irresistible, then warm hands had pulled him out. Raja's. "Am I alive?"

''Temporarily.'' She crawled to him.

''I saw you in a glass coffin. I thought—''

She stopped Larry with a finger over his lips. ''Divinations are oft metaphor. I have been poisoned.'' She looked at the door, then, ''We have little time. Listen.''

He nodded.

''We are locked in my basement. Nick has fouled the soil here, so my abilities are limited. I healed you with the last of my strength.''

''Why?'' Larry realized Matt's bullet was missing. Swallowed. Or removed. ''Who is Nick?''

''Nick is a necromancer. He is also your enemy.''

''I don't know him.'' He had seen Death, though, in the Three of Diamonds Bookstore. He had seen Father Woberty transform into the grim reaper. Was he this Nick? ''Why did *you* help me?''

''There is no time. It is the winter solstice, when Nick can banish your soul to the deepest reaches of the netherealms.''

''Why should I believe you? You tried to murder me. Remember your bead? Paloma's gift?''

Raja locked eyes with him.

This had to be a trick to get the dry water. Larry shifted on his haunches. The fabric of his back pocket stretched taut against the flask. It was still there.

''You were dead. I could have taken your dry water if that is what I desired.''

So she knew he had it with him.

''Nick divined you will be the prophet of this age, and that you will change the earth.'' She pinched the bridge of her nose, then shook her head. ''He believes us conspirators.''

''Hardly.'' Larry leaned forward. He wasn't afraid of her, not now.

''You can help me,'' she insisted. ''We both wish to change the world.''

''I don't. I want to keep it the way it is.''

Raja frowned. ''Perhaps, but you have the ability. Nick is rarely wrong on such matters. Tell me how you used the dry water. You have obviously stumbled upon something extraordinary.''

He hadn't, but he couldn't reveal that. It was the only card in his hand. ''I've seen what your changes do to the world. I'm not telling you anything.''

"You had only seen the first step: Columbus. I had not advanced the Native Americans. They would have repelled the Europeans, and no New World gold would have financed their wars. Technology could be delayed. The earth can be kept pristine."

"You're guessing," Larry said. "Altering history and stopping Columbus only buys you two years, then the French discover Florida. You're gambling with a hundred generations."

"Lies," Raja hissed.

"Change the past and you wipe out billions of lives. Don't those people have the right to exist? You can't throw them away like you did Paloma."

"Paloma was an accident. I never—"

"Never meant to use her?"

Raja's pallid skin flushed; emerald flames wreathed her head, flickered, and vanished. Her shoulders slumped.

"You were Delano," Larry whispered. "You have to know what it's like . . . to be a failure. To go hungry. To die."

"That is precisely why this world must change. It is not only the land that suffers, but the people too. They are chattel, commodities, numbers—soulless. I can change that." Her eyes were unwavering, intense. She believed in her plan.

"Then tell me more about your scheme."

The temperature dropped. The moonlight dimmed.

"Do you sense it, Larry? The nadir of winter is close. Minutes, seconds, heartbeats, and Nick will come for us. There is no time for explanations. You must tell me what you have discovered. What frightens him so?"

He didn't want to trust her. The air thickened; it was hard to draw a breath, and when he did, the oxygen did nothing to ease his growing apprehension. "We'll trade information. I went to the Dai Esthai to relive a sorcerer's life, and failed. Tell me how to find one, and I'll tell you what I discovered."

"Lives that change the world muddy the waters. Tell me first what you found, then I shall consider your puzzle."

"You found Columbus. It can't be impossible."

"I found Delano, a rarefied path to influence the past."

He withdrew the silver flask and unscrewed the cap. Water glistened within. Two sips. Raja hadn't stolen any. That much of what she had said was true.

Upstairs footfalls squeaked across the timbers.

Raja glanced at the ceiling. "Tell me. Hurry."

"There's nothing to tell."

"There must be," she insisted. "You searched for a sorcerer on the Dai Esthai. You didn't find one. What happened then?"

Steps pounded down the stairs outside the door.

"I wandered upstream and ran into Robert Dolinski."

"In the river?"

"No. I don't understand how, but he diverted part of the river and built his own world. Paloma's there with him."

Raja's eyes widened.

Keys jangled in the lock.

Larry coiled his body into his corner, and faced the door. The concrete walls were frigid. With both hands he gripped the flask.

"That is it," she whispered. "Thank you, Larry. I am sorry you must die again."

It was the deepest part of winter. Larry felt the world stop. Death had come for him.

The door opened. There were only shadows, black space without stars—the outline of a man. "Mister Ngitis," it whispered. "Ever full of surprises . . ."

Larry drank: one gulp that boiled down his throat and diffused into his soul.

Velvet black flowed across the room, reached out, smothered him, grasped his neck, and squeezed.

Larry's pulse pounded in his temples. His last breath hovered between them, a cloud of ice. Vertebrae crackled and popped. His vision blurred.

Larry's boots squished into the mud a hairbreadth from the Dai Esthai. It was a mile wide; mirror smoothness that became swirls and whirlpools, choppy and opaque, split into a million rivulets, then spread into an alluvial fan. The future.

He peered at his life, scenes frozen in the present: Raja speaking to him, the door opening, and Father Woberty strangling him. Silt and murk next—what followed, unknowable—although it wasn't hard to guess.

Raja hadn't told him how, but he *had* found a sorcerer's life. It was so large he had missed it. A current flowed around Larry's smaller life, and churned it into eddies and turbulence. He squinted and traced this current upstream. It was a slight shimmering in the water, otherwise invisible. It would be easy to lose.

If Nick was so powerful, then Larry had to become as potent. If Nick controlled Linda, then Larry had to learn how to free her. If Nick had the power to annihilate his soul, then Larry had to discover how to do it too.

He marched upstream, backwards in time, and caught glimpses of Nick's life: Raja drank his poison; Linda in a cave, trembling in his hands; a legion of dead men raised—a jump—Father Woberty's life bisected his. The priest's soul rippled, diffused, faded, and only Nick's thread continued downstream. He had stolen the life.

The necromancer could jump from body to body. How old was he? How far back would Larry have to go?

He slipped, skidded on gravel. Stones crowded the bank where before there had been only mud. They looked like pearls, gleaming with silver opalescence. He continued, careful where he stepped.

He had another option: go to Paloma. Just a brief visit. But would it be brief? Larry hovered in a state of non-being, fixed in time. It would be too tempting to avoid the death waiting for him.

Even if he returned to the Dai Esthai, he risked retracing his steps, getting looped as Niyol had.

There was another reason not to go: Dolinski's world might be an invention of Larry's guilt and longing. He wasn't willing to risk everything for a fantasy, no matter how enticing.

No. He'd live Nick's life first. If he survived, he'd return to Paloma. Too much was at stake. Living as Anne Marie and Arturo Baldovino had shown him how shallow he had been. Before he might have gone. Screw the world. Now, he understood too much.

Nick's life meandered back from Father Woberty to an Italian mobster. There were images of horses and rolling hills, olive trees and the Mediterranean.

He was a GI running through the streets of Berlin. The city was on fire. Explosions, and crumbling buildings. Larry sensed he searched desperately for someone.

A patch of oil made rainbows on the surface of the river. The jangle of colors undulated downstream to pollute an uncertain future.

Further upstream Nick was a minister to Czar Nicholas II. He signed the execution orders for a dozen dissidents, and sipped brandy.

Before that he was a captain in Napoleon's cavalry. At Waterloo, he made a suicidal charge against five cannons, destroyed his line, and escaped unharmed.

A flash of Raja. She was the same; Nick had a different body. They made love and drank ouzo and listened to the ocean from the cliffs of Crete.

Hundreds of lives, brief, long, but always, Larry sensed, with purpose. He ventured into the Sahara searching for a mythic oasis. He was an assassin for the Médici family of Florence, and a crusader sacking Constantinople. There were dark laboratories, secret meetings in graveyards, rituals, blood sacrifices, a series of endless wars through Baghdad, Egypt, and Damascus, marching upon Roman roads, his body racked by plague, a recital by Virgil, decades of drinking and orgies, and skirmishes with Spartan hoplites.

The river was narrower; there were fewer lives in the world. The bank of the river was fine black sand. Streaks of gold dust made lacy spirals. Larry wondered what Spencer would have given to pan here.

There was no more to Nick's life. Larry didn't know the date, but it looked ancient: men in chitons, collimated buildings, armies with bronze armor and iron-tipped spears.

He hesitated. He hadn't seen Dolinski's dam and siphoned stream, and didn't remember going this far back when he had found it before. He hoped he could find it again. He hoped it was real.

He stepped upon the water.

"Where is it?" Socrates hissed. "To keep death waiting is to tempt fate." He rinsed his hands in the scallop basin, wiped them on his beard, then strode to the marble slab where he would lie down and die. "How long does it take to prepare one cup of poison?"

The others clung to him with their eyes. None dared touched him, even now. He loathed to be touched.

Socrates cared, though he never showed it. He had cared enough to talk to Judzyas when he was a simple potter. What is truth? he had asked Judzyas innocently enough. What is beauty? What is justice?

Those questions infected the potter's thoughts. He left his clay and wheel and begged to be one of his pupils.

Judzyas sat in the corner and gathered his chiton to insulate him from the cold floor.

Plato glared at him with dull black eyes.

He stared back. It was unfortunate that Plato was not the one to die today.

Plato went to his master. ''Please reconsider,'' he whispered. ''You can still escape. All is ready.''

''No.''

''Then what can we do?''

Socrates stopped his pacing. He was the teacher, and he asked the questions, not his pupils. ''You can go. Give me a moment's peace. All of you. Take your long faces and drippy eyes and wait outside.''

''But Master,'' Plato said, ''we only wish to—''

''Go!''

They slithered out, weeping; young Kratos huddled against Crito. Plato too, although he lingered by the door. Judzyas hated them. They had stolen irreplaceable time with his master.

''What are you still doing here?'' he asked Judzyas. ''Did you not understand my command?''

''I heard, but choose not to obey.''

Socrates raised one eyebrow. ''You ignore my last request? Do I mean so little to you?''

He meant everything to Judzyas. He wanted to throw his arms around the old man. A display of affection, however, would only earn him contempt.

''I have asked you a question,'' Socrates said, and came closer. ''Answer me.''

Judzyas had unraveled his questions for two decades. He had been led through mazes of logic and deduction, oft left dumbfounded, and only rarely rewarded with insight. He formed his reply carefully, ''I shall mourn after you are gone. There is still much to be learned.''

Socrates's scowl evaporated. ''Indeed . . . what?''

Judzyas swallowed. He stood. ''You choose to die. True, you have enemies in the Athenian assembly, but you have more intellect than all of them combined. You could have reasoned for a lesser sentence. Instead, you goaded and belittled them in public.''

A smirk flickered upon Socrates's face, then withered.

''When you were required to propose an alternative sentence, you asked them for a pension and an apology.''

''What does this demonstrate? Why would a man seek death? It is illogical. Do you suggest I have lost my wits?''

Plato inched closer in the doorway, straining to hear. Judzyas stepped closer to Socrates and whispered, ''You are the wisest man I shall ever know. You have done this for a reason. You will profit from it.''

''How could a man gain from death?''

''If he wishes to martyr himself—but you are too smart to be a martyr. You must gain in another way.''

Socrates was silent. This was unusual. Judzyas was close to the truth.

He continued, ''You have oft claimed the existence of a personal daemon, one that whispers to you what is wrong but never what is true.''

Socrates sat, a gesture reserved for those he thought worthy of listening to. ''This I do not deny.''

''It is a thing beyond the sphere of man's abilities, a thing of the gods.''

Socrates nodded. He never acknowledged a pupil's statement. Indeed, Judzyas had uncovered a pearl of wisdom.

''If, then, it is a thing beyond man's experiences, and you have the privilege of its counsel, you must comprehend what lies beyond the realm of normal human experience.'' Socrates said nothing, so he ventured, ''You have insight into what lies past death.''

''A guess.''

''No. Truth. You seek death, yet you are sane. But you gain nothing by dying, that is, nothing perceivable in this world.''

Socrates locked his hazel eyes upon him. Eyes appeared within his eyes, another entity. A blink. It was gone.

Larry saw it too. It wasn't a ghost. It cast shadows from other realms. It was arms and legs, octopus tentacles and quivering antennae, clouds of silver and golden sparks, peacock feathers and nine-clawed talons, gears intermeshed, pistons, and spinning gyros, bat wings and cat whiskers, and pulsing rolls of luminous flesh that pressed, touched, stroked, and devoured itself.

Socrates got up, embraced Judzyas, and whispered quickly into his ear, "Correct! There *is* more after death, but few know how to navigate its treacherous paths. Seek the tomb of Alkibiades. There you will find all you require to summon those from beyond—if you have the courage. Be warned. It will enlighten you or it will drive you mad—or both."

Judzyas tried to pull away. The old man held him with a strength no seventy-year-old should have.

"One last thing: watch Plato. He will change the world, ruin it perhaps."

Socrates pulled away, stared at him again—this time with human eyes.

From the doorway, Plato announced, "The Bringer of Death has come."

The Bringer of Death wore gray robes, was shaved bald, and smelled of ashes. He held a copper chalice in both hands. The potion was oily and black. He handed it to Socrates.

"No." Plato said. "Give it to me. I shall take your place. Escape."

"Do not be ridiculous." He grabbed the cup, then addressed them all: "Remember my words and arguments. Remember that you will never know a fraction of what I do. And I am ignorant beyond reckoning."

He drank the poison.

They moaned. Gelusis tore his hair out. Kratos slumped in the corner. Plato and Crito clung to Socrates, though he beat them back.

He disentangled himself, and strode about the room until his legs failed.

They pawed at him as he sat upon the marble slab, and questioned him, pleaded with him to reveal his secrets, wailed their grief, and cursed the gods.

Socrates was silent. When he could no longer hold his head up, he beckoned to Crito, who came to his side and listened intently, ready to absorb his master's last words. The others gathered around him too.

"Crito, I owe a chicken to Asclepius. Will you remember to pay the debt?"

''Yes. Is there anything else?''

Socrates closed his eyes and was gone.

Judzyas watched. The pair of eyes within his master's opened. They winked at him and vanished.

Judzyas was no stranger to graveyards, from the tomb that Socrates had sent him to three centuries ago, to the maze catacombs of the mad Babylonian Zurtinni, to the mirage island of Lethos, but this was the grandmother of all barrows.

''Why this place?'' Arion whispered. He drew his cloak about his skinny frame. ''It is cursed.''

From their hilltop vantage the distant shore of the Mediterranean was a band of gold, and the slopes between littered with thousands of obelisks, statues, tombs, mausoleums, cold pyres, and lye-etched sarcophagi.

''The Necropolis of Cerveteri is not cursed,'' Judzyas replied. ''It suits our needs.''

He set a hand on his apprentice's trembling shoulder. ''Ignore the visions fleeting in the corner of your eyes, and they will not harm you.'' The boy had undeveloped talents. He had to be protected from them. ''Concentrate on more corporeal dangers. There are guards here to protect Rome's citizens.''

''They will see us.''

Judzyas opened a vial, whispered a word to the contents, and rolled out a drop of mercury. It sizzled and sent green fire and silver smoke to the heavens. Three heartbeats and the flames were exhausted.

He sat against an olive tree and watched the ocean. ''Rest. You shall need it. We enter at dusk.''

Arion huddled close to him.

Fog steamed from the sea. When the sun touched the water, the mist drew up onto the land. The necropolis wore a gray funeral shroud.

They slipped down silent streets, past ancient piles of stones, and a jagged rock that resonated with human sacrifice. Judzyas took the third left, a trail that wound around worn statues and vaulted tombs. Spirits paced within and called to them. Arion flinched. Judzyas took his hand and led on.

Domiciles of marble and granite crowded together. These were reserved for Rome's elite, tended, carved with caducei and curling ivy, and too often patrolled by soldiers.

"This is the one," Judzyas whispered. It was a block of stone with three false arches on each side. The inscriptions were indecipherable in the waning light. He removed two iron spikes from his robe, and handed one to Arion. "Dig."

"The tomb will have a stone roof."

Judzyas pried up cobblestones and hammered at the sandy clay. "Dig," he insisted.

Arion scraped at the soil, removed an armful of earth, then asked, "Who dwells here?"

"A general, but he is not whom I seek. When he sacked Carthage he enslaved a half-breed Jew, Hezekiah. He could see very clearly and very far. It is he I wish."

Arion suppressed a dust-induced sneeze. "Do you gather his bones for a ritual?"

"No. I wish to speak with him. Keep digging."

Arion shuddered, but obeyed his master. He tore into the dirt until the hole was waist deep, then carved out the side, angling under the structure. "Why is a Jew in a Roman tomb?"

"They were lovers. The general commanded that Hezekiah be sealed in the grave with him. Jealous, I gather."

Arion struck something hard. "There, as I said, solid."

Judzyas wedged his spike into the stone seam. "Years ago I was a mason." He grunted and rocked the stone back and forth. "I set this one without mortar." The stone rumbled out. "Thought an entrance to these catacombs might prove convenient."

He took a candle, held the wick between his thumbs, and a tiny flame winked to life. "You first." He handed it to Arion.

His brown eyes widened. "I—"

Judzyas pushed him toward the hole. There was just enough room to squeeze through. "Hurry, before the guards see our light."

Arion paused then entered. Judzyas followed.

Inside there were no rotting corpses, only smooth marble floors inscribed with names and dates.

"They are beneath," Judzyas explained, and covered the hole with his cloak. "Give me the candle." He traced four lines in the dust, a diamond whose points touched the middle of each of the tomb's walls.

''Stay within one of the triangular corners—outside the lines—and you will be safe.''

Arion scrambled into the opposite corner.

Judzyas drew Hebrew letters and Egyptian hieroglyphs. They smoldered like coals. ''Son of Israel,'' he whispered. ''Come. Come, Hezekiah. The world of your birth calls to you. I summon you and make my will into law that you manifest. Come.''

Candle smoke and dust took form in the inscribed square: a lion's body, white eagle wings, a human head with square beard, and a third eye that blazed like molten metal. The sphinx was motes of light and the shifting currents of exhaled breath. ''Who summons me from beyond?'' He regarded the mystic sigils, then, ''And by such mediocre capacity?''

Arion shrank in the corner.

''I did, Judzyas, potter of Athens, student of Socrates, and necromancer.''

''Socrates had never a student such as you.''

Judzyas's eyes narrowed. ''My name does not appear in Plato's discourses, but I was Socrates's best pupil, conveniently removed from history by his most ambitious.''

''I see.'' The ghost wavered from the intensity of Judzyas's words. ''What do you seek?''

''You had powerful clairvoyance in life, more so in death. I have seen the future with my humble talent. I require confirmation.''

Hezekiah glowered; his third eye fixed him in a cone of light. ''Personal futures are ever-shifting. You waste my time.''

''Not my future. Another's. My master warned me of men who change the world. He warned me to watch Plato, and I did. He founded the Athenian Academé, and stole Socrates's ideas. It was not his thievery, however, that changed the world.''

''What did?''

''Plato spurned his pupil, Aristotle. Armed with vengeance and too much knowledge, Aristotle tutored the boy-prince Alexander, showed him the world, and planted seeds of conquest. The Persian Empire fell before the boy-king, then Syria, and Egypt, and nearly the entire world had not his army grown weary. Aristotle returned to Athens, founded the Lyceum with more prestige and money than Plato's Academé, and had his revenge. But when Alexander the Great died his empire shattered. Hundreds of thousands were killed to make it; more died in the conflict to divide it.''

''You speak of history and the future as if they were the same.''

''They are. Rome has risen in the shadow of Alexander the Great. And it will happen again. I have seen another prophet with new ideas and more lives that will be lost.''

The ghost's tail swished back and forth. It flexed its curved talons. ''I find your cause worthy.'' Its mystic eye cooled to black, and filled with stars. ''I will seek the future, but demand tribute.''

''This I have brought.''

Flames flared from the protective diamond. In the curtain of fire, armies shot bows as tall as a man, and pushed siege engines that launched rocks carrying thunder and lightning. They crushed cities, leveled hills, and left death upon the field. Rome sacked. Alexandria leveled. Byzantium ashes. A new city rose, and a new emperor ruled it. Arion.

The boy gasped.

''As I feared,'' Judzyas whispered. He wished he had never seen the truth. All those lives could be saved. Wars stopped. One life. Was it too much? His conscience, usually overflowing with suggestions, was silent. Perhaps even it realized what had to be done.

''Master,'' Arion cried, ''I would never do such things.''

''You will,'' the ghost sphinx growled. Then to Judzyas it demanded, ''My tribute?''

''This I have brought.''

Judzyas whispered, ''Plato, Aristotle, and Alexander the Great meant nothing to me. They were led by fate. You, however, Arion, I taught how to see. Your future would have been my fault. And it is my responsibility to undo the wrong.''

He touched the diamond drawn in the dust, and smudged the line.

The ghost wheeled to face Arion.

Judzyas snuffed the candle, then pulled himself up the hole. ''Forgive me.'' He shoved the block into place, muffling the screams.

''There are better trees in the valley.''

''No,'' Judzyas replied. ''Bandits roam there.'' He eyed his hired compatriot, dirty, stupid, a thief certainly. Perfect.

The man frowned. ''Half now then. I walk no more without my money.''

Judzyas reached into his purse and handed the man a coin.

''You said three dinar.''

''How does one split three silver coins in half? Come. I overpay you for no work at all. We must find a proper tree before the sun rises.'' He stopped. ''There, on the hill. That one.'' The tree was dead, but as tall as four men. Brackets of mushrooms sprouted from the trunk.

''Hand me the rope.'' Judzyas wanted to keep his shaking hands busy. He untangled and knotted it, then passed it back. ''Climb to that branch and loop it over.''

The man grumbled about insane old men, but did as he was asked. Judzyas had a reputation. Those who failed him had been known to die while asleep or slip and crack their heads open.

''Now pay me.''

''Drink?'' Judzyas removed his wineskin, took a small draught, and passed it to the man. ''Indulge, my friend.''

He guzzled, letting rivulets of the dark wine spill from his lips and trickle down his neck.

''But before you are unable to stand,'' Judzyas said, ''help me secure the rope. My hands ache.''

The man tied it off. ''Tell me what the tree is for.''

''So I might hang myself. I am old. This body I have kept alive for four hundred years with spirits and ancient Egyptian alchemy, but it is time for a change. That or oblivion.''

Perspiration beaded on the man's brow. ''You are mad.'' The color drained from his face.

''Perhaps. Help me into the tree.''

He backed away.

''Help me, and you can have all the silver I carry.''

The man hesitated, then approached, and laced his fingers to give Judzyas a step into the branches.

''There.'' He slipped the rope about his neck. ''I killed a man last evening, a man with extremely devoted friends. They shall seek me. And my face is far too well-known to hide.''

''I still . . . I don't . . .'' The man swayed, braced against the tree, then fell.

''It is the poison you drank, hemlock and nightshade, that saps your life. It will not kill you, but it will bring you to the very gates of

Hades. I shall take your body then. At least, I hope to. I have never done this before.''

The man jerked his legs, but they wouldn't respond.

Judzyas slid off the branch. The rope snapped his neck. He concentrated, banished the pain, and slipped out of his dangling body.

The man struggled; he floundered in the currents of death. Judzyas wrestled with him, suffocating him in the rushing turbulent waters of the netherealms. He cast the man's soul into the void.

There was another death his conscience would not let him forget—a prophet he had betrayed to the Romans. His ideas were dangerous. Radical politics. Monotheism. Had he lived, entire civilizations would have died.

The decision had not been easy. It was not like Arion, for whom Judzyas had been responsible. It had not been like Ovid, whom he had exiled to a desert island. Judzyas had acted preemptively, killed a man for whom he had nothing but respect.

He wished he had never started this, never been a student of Socrates, never seen anything.

The man's legs, his legs now, tingled. Good. The poison burned itself out. He would go far from Judaea. The Jews here irritated him. They could never properly pronounce his Greek name—always shortened it from Judzyas to Judas.

Judzyas wept in the streets of Constantinople. French crusaders burned and raped and looted. Smoke covered the city like a blanket. There would be more killing, more crusades, Inquisitions, and suffering. He cursed Pope Innocent III. He cursed himself. If he had only seen what the death of Christ would bring. If only he had not been so eager to save the world. The responsibility was his to undo what had been done. ''*Mea culpa. Mea maxima culpa.* My fault. All the blame is mine.''

''See how your manuscript burns?''

Nostradamus stared at the embers that spiraled from the flames.

''Do you see?'' Judzyas asked. ''By the power and light and secrets of Thoth, I call upon the spirits of the future to remove the veils of fear and truth. Reveal what lies beyond. I make my will into law. Manifest.''

Nostradamus's eyes, bloodshot from the smoke, dilated, and tears welled, but he did not blink. ''I see,'' he cried. ''I see cities of metal, man flying through the air—to the stars. I see every corner of the universe!''

''Then write your *Centuries* again with your new sight. Write them with the clarity of a madman. Write them so none can comprehend.''

The edges of the prophet's beard singed in the fire. ''I see that too. And I see who you are.'' He laughed. ''And why you have done this.'' Froth covered his mouth. ''Defeated my prophesies you have, but there will be others.'' He clenched his teeth. ''You will miss him in Vienna, the one who bends the cross. No school for him! And in the desert you shall meet yourself and be undone. Even now it happens!''

''He must be burned,'' Judzyas said.

The head counsel of the Inquisition sighed. ''No. No. He has friends, and His Eminence, Pope Urban feels this situation requires a lighter touch.''

This was a mere formality. Burning Galileo would not remove all the copies of his *Dialogue* in circulation, nor would it erase the knowledge Judzyas had thought he buried with the Greeks. ''Arrest him then, at least. Let us have no more science for the church to contend with.''

''Agreed.''

He jumped over a flaming gas can. Shells exploded up the block. Tanks rolled over the asphalt and tore it to shreds.

He couldn't think of blame now—but he did. If he had been minutes earlier thirty-eight years ago, he could have altered the test scores, and gotten him into the Academy of Fine Arts in Vienna. Minutes! Instead a young man joined the army, became a war hero, a political leader, a prisoner.

An hour ago, when they found the bunker, Judzyas knew it wasn't him.

There. A group of Gestapo and Brown-shirts ducked around a corner. He sprinted after them, caught them in the middle of an alley, and opened fire.

They fell, shielding the one in the center, but Judzyas kept shooting.

He had taken two bullets, but kept this body going. He had to know if the prophet was there.

Under the pile of corpses he found him. The smudge of a mustache was missing, and the hair had been bleached blond . . . it was unmistakeably him. Dead, but too late. Far too late for it to do any good.

"My fault," he whispered.

Nick sipped Raja's ouzo and played chess with Linda. Stars shone through the glass atrium and reflected in his drink. The woman was a fair opponent, but she wasn't using her knights effectively.

He contemplated the prophet of Dry Water as he took her bishop. Thrice he had missed, with lightning, in the desert cave, and in the bookstore. Prophets had escaped him before, but none so many times. Larry Ngitis had magic and luck and powerful allies. What change would he have brought to the world? His visions were never clear.

"Your move," Linda said, and wrapped her sweater tighter.

Nick glanced at the grandfather clock. Five minutes till midnight. He blocked her rook's pawn. It had been too easy to lure the prophet, and too easy to kill him using Linda. He hadn't seen that in his divinations.

And the feeling of being watched still haunted him. He shifted in the wicker chair, looked over his shoulder, but only saw a dryad shivering behind her palm tree.

"Study the board, Miss Becket. I must attend to unpleasant business. I shall only be a moment."

He strolled to the basement stairs. The prophet's spirit still clung to his body, because it had unresolved matters to attend to in this world. Tonight he would banish his soul so deep into the void that no magic, no fate, nothing would bring him back. And Raja? He still had not decided what to do with her.

Down the stairs he trotted, gathering his power and spirits and shadows, unlocked the door, and pushed it open.

Larry huddled in the corner, clutching a silver flask in both hands. Alive.

Raja appeared more vital than a poisoned woman should have. Almost smug. The cat that just ate the bird. His mistake had been to underestimate her.

"Mister Ngitis," he said. "Ever full of surprises." He moved to him in three quick steps.

The prophet tipped his flask, drank.

Nick grabbed his neck, squeezed; vertebrae crackled and popped. A cloud of ice hovered between them.

Larry's eyes were open and staring into his.

Nick saw his reflection in them . . . and reflections of those reflections as if he and the prophet were two mirrors parallel—as if the prophet's eyes and soul were his.

Chapter 20

LARRY WAS JUDZYAS. THEIR HANDS WRAPPED ABOUT HIS NECK, AND squeezed until the pulse pounded in his temples. Vertebrae cracked. Power surged through them, negative energy, freezing magnetism that polarized into crystalline order.

A whirlpool of frothy water lay ahead in the Dai Esthai, sucking Larry in; behind, the vacuum of the necromancer's past tugged. Two vortices pulled them apart.

They were two identical charges, two north poles compressed.

The air rippled between them, pressurized. Exploded.

Judzyas bounced off the far wall, and crumpled to the floor, dazed.

Larry slammed into the corner. The impact left him dizzy.

He had spent centuries preparing for Judzyas, peering over his shoulder, watching and learning. Larry's fingers twitched, casting shadows in other dimensions. Seven squares of a *Confinement* rune materialized and wove through the spirals of the *Oblivion* sigil. Crimson right angles distorted hypervolumes with twisting edges. It was a shrinking web, digesting everything within its diminishing lines.

Judzyas stood, one arm against the wall; the neon geometry settled around him, cutting the air, collapsing space, glowing brighter as it condensed, shifting spectrum from red to orange.

Raja clutched Larry's arm and pulled herself up. Her eyes fixed on his.

He couldn't leave her. They had loved one another in Crete. He knew her unquenchable fire and quick temper, her long memory, her eternal beauty. But she had killed him when he was Judzyas, betrayed him, and murdered Paloma.

Raja peered into Larry's soul, took a step back, and whispered, "Judzyas?"

"No—Larry."

Judzyas struggled. His limbs deformed in the domain of the web, one thin and long, the other shortened to a stub. The magic was bright as an electric arc, distorting this world, and contracting. A wave rolled through the intermeshed magic, and Judzyas tugged at two knotted runes. They unravelled. His left arm was free.

Attack or escape? Larry's hair bristled with static. Dempsey was close. There were other ghosts as well. And Raja . . . Larry had to get her out.

He scooped her into his arms. She weighed nothing. He was a magus-necromancer in the deepest part of winter with more power than he had ever known. He bolted up the stairs three at a time and ran across the atrium. His pulse never rose.

Linda saw him and screamed. She knocked over the chessboard, scattering pawns and rooks and knights across terra cotta tiles. "You're alive?"

He set Raja down. She clung to him a moment, then let go.

Larry picked up a black rook, gazed at the tiny carved obsidian tower, and twisted it through dimensions and realities as he had with Spencer's pocketknife. He endowed it with form and mass, then threw it at the basement door—still shifting while it arced through the air—more rough stone, crumbling mortar, a staircase that ran up the center, steel reinforcement.

It splintered through reality. Became a real tower. A ton of granite.

It crushed the basement door, and smashed the surrounding adobe wall. The rumbling noise rolled though his body, shattered the windows of the atrium into a hail of glass. Rock choked the staircase and lay upon the floor like a giant's jigsaw.

"I know a place to go," Raja said, and tugged at his hand. "Safe, perhaps."

Linda's face was blank. She took two tentative steps toward the rubble. Plaster fell from the ceiling. She moved one stone aside, then another, digging debris from the staircase, breaking her nails.

"Linda?" Larry said, and started toward her.

"No." Raja stopped him with a hand on his arm. "She is Judzyas's."

Linda got squeamish when she had to kill cockroaches in their old apartment, but she hadn't hesitated to shoot him twice. There was no time to undo the magic that held her.

Raja pulled him into her garden.

The moon wore a double halo and made the world glitter. Frost covered the almond grove, white lace over skeletal branches. A rime of ice coated the snow. Raja jogged barefoot upon it without breaking the surface. She was the Daughter of the Terror Winds, Bon-po witch of the Himalayas.

She had betrayed Judzyas. Larry shouldn't trust her. He had thought her powerless upon the solstice, but she had resuscitated him, and now, in the fresh air, spirits boiled about her, not ghosts, but snowflake sprites and black silk crows of fragmented night. The northern winds caressed her.

Larry trudged through the icy crust after her. She promised a safe place. He needed to think. The winds cut through him, chilled him to the core. His blood neither pulsed nor kept him warm. It didn't bother him. He wanted to be as lifeless as the land. Still and calm and cold.

He kept his head down, running, and watched his feet. There was too much to see elsewhere. His vision had been multiplied with knowledge: two millennia among the netherealms. Behind every tree lurked ghosts, Spaniards who had sought silver, poisoned settlers, and a child who had played with a gun. Under every rock lay demons waiting to be called from the void. Around every twist and turn in reality lay things the living could not comprehend.

Raja halted in a circle of stones. Each was twice as tall as Larry with worn angles suggesting eyebrows, square noses, thick lips, and blank eyes. They were on a hilltop, and the mansion looked like a gingerbread house, wrapped with a blue-white blanket.

"Rest a moment here," she said. "Gather your strength, then we must flee. Judzyas may be buried, but that will not stop him long."

"I know," Larry whispered. "I know everything he does. I've lived his life."

He fell to his knees and rubbed his temples. He had assimilated two lives before, but Judzyas's had lived three dozen generations. It was too much. Larry's thirty-five years blurred, wavered, and bit by bit were washed away by the Judzyas's millennia-long existence.

Larry held onto what he was: his fears, his novels, his failed relationship with Linda, his lost Paloma, his visions and nightmares. He rejected Judzyas.

Images dripped from his eyes: tears blurry with visions of Rome sacked by Gauls, and the stained glass in Saint Paul's Cathedral. Sensation spilled from his fingertips: how to flick a rapier and disarm, a painting lesson from Michelangelo. He exhaled smells, the smoke from Joan of Arc being burned at the stake mingled with Lucrezia Borgia's perfume. Sounds rushed from his ears, Arion's last cry, and the premier of Beethoven's Fifth Symphony. Judzyas leaked from him, swirled in the currents of death, then blew away.

He sat back in the snow, centered himself, concentrated. The jumble of memories settled. "I can't keep it—twenty-four centuries of people and places. I've got to fight him now before I lose more. It's my only chance."

Both her brows arched. "Confrontation? Is that the only solution? Let us leave this place. Hide. Wait until spring and the world is renewed. We can change everything then."

"We?"

The stone faces stared at him. He hadn't recalled them facing inward.

"Judzyas was right," she said. "We are conspirators. You have shown me how the dry water must be used. No one has to die."

"He will never stop. He's obsessed. He blames himself for the world's sorrows—as if he could change them." Larry examined his hands and found them unfamiliar. How long would he remember how to summon runes and command the dead? How long before he was just Larry Ngitis again? "He thinks I'm the next prophet. But I've seen his divination. He's wrong."

"Reason with him then."

Clouds crossed the moon. They crept over the summit of Mount Taylor, angular vapors, shimmering white, fluttering, and beneath, the prows of ships, tacking against the wind, sails unfurled. There were garbage scows and clippers, galleons and paddle wheels that billowed black smoke from double stacks. A flotilla of the dead.

''Ghost ships,'' Larry whispered. ''Dredged from the Gulf of Mexico and the Caribbean.''

''How do you know?''

''It is where I would have gotten them.''

Cannons fired from the upper deck of the galleon. A trail of smoke arced through the air, thudded into the forest a thousand feet from where they stood. Upon the ship skeletal hands raised their cutlasses in defiance.

''Go,'' Larry told her. ''The end is here.''

Raja hesitated. She leaned close, stopped, then stepped out of the circle of stones, whose faces now peered away from the center. She took refuge under the boughs of a black oak.

Larry tried to keep from shaking with terror. Death surrounded him. It burned through his liver and chest. It lapped at the edges of his life, eroding it. He was dying. On this night death was in every decaying leaf, in every sigh borne by the winds, and in every frozen tear upon the ground.

Images and memories, ghosts and dreams filled the air, saturated the netherealms that overlapped the world. He inhaled, drew them inside, drowned, let them smother his soul, died.

Larry was dead.

Dead as a corpse dangling from a tree.

Dead as a miner in a collapsed shaft, his hands still clutching the matches that wouldn't burn the stale air.

Dead as a child buried by the roadside, wearing bloody pajamas and Keds sneakers, laughing in the wind.

Dead as an outlaw cowboy, angry that he had three rounds in his pistol and fifty dollars, both unspent, when he got shot in bed.

Dead as he had been on the daily commute with the occasional accident, crumpled chrome and body parts strewn upon the asphalt, watched by creeping motorists, then staring at a computer screen the rest of the day, listening to the sixty-cycle hum, losing his bonus to office politics, and wondering which sucker was worse, him or the guy in the wreck.

Dead as the dreams of a man who bought a gas station with his savings, who lost his wife a month after they had eloped, wished for a family that could never be, washed away her memories with a river of Absolut vodka, and ulcerated his liver so he could join her.

Dead as last summer's rose pressed between the pages of T.S.

Eliot's *The Love Song of J. Alfred Prufrock,* brown-edged petals with only the memory of scent.

Dead as Osiris, body flung upon the Nile, eaten by fishes, listening to the cries of his beloved Isis.

Dead as a bottle of poison, glass stained cobalt by decades of sun, full of promises—shattered on the floor.

Dead as winter.

Dead as Judzyas.

He slipped from his body and let it crumple within the circle of stones. He had never abandoned his flesh before. Could he get back in? Would he be swept away? Irrevocable death flowed through him and quenched his panic. Judzyas's power flowed through him. No. Nothing could stop him.

They were nearly equals now. Larry was forgetting at an exponential rate—but he had abilities Judzyas did not. He had seen life through Anne Marie's and Arturo Baldovino's eyes. They gave him perspective, flexibility. Judzyas was paralyzed by twenty-four centuries of ritual and guilt and obsession. Larry was free. He had imagination and vision—skills he had sharpened with his writing. He'd use them in his magic.

Larry rose above the forest. Beneath him, zombies and ghouls poured between the trees, trampling the snow, searching. Raja was gone.

Judzyas had called a navy of ghost ships and a legion of dead.

He'd need an army too. No. Not an army. Cavalry.

Nimbostratus clouds gathered, bunched into fluffy cumulus, stacked and packed into cumulonimbus thunderheads. Dempsey was in the center, subliming vapor from snow, rubbing mist into static and sparks.

Larry dissipated the clouds with a wave of his hand. Droplets crystallized. Snow fell back to the ground. Dempsey fled. The sky had to be clear tonight. Larry needed to see the stars and far to the horizon.

There. North and west of Chaco Canyon, he spotted what he wanted, the Bisti Badlands: eroded sandstone and shale, cliffs the color of bone and blood.

He submerged into the netherealms, shifted deeper through time and death and reality, past the first atomic bomb blast at Trinity site—a second sun that rose in the south, a gale of wind that blew the souls of those who had watched and died of cancer a decade later, past wagon trains lost and dying of thirst, past wandering Indian spirits, marching on the Trail of Tears, past seasons and cycles and ages, he sank.

Only the shadows of shadows remained. He concentrated and resolved images from the layers of death so firmly compressed. They were outlines, traces of ash and coal. The smells came first: humus, decay, algae, and dung. Ferns and palms appeared with a crisscross of streams between them. Fog clung to the ground. Three-foot-long salamanders splashed and slithered away from giant crocodiles.

Herds of triceratops, an ambling forest of curved horns, grazed and eyed him. They were as large as buses, pungent with musk. A dozen iguanodons moved past Larry, rising on their hind legs, running and glancing over their shoulders.

Circling the edge of the herds were Larry's cavalry: eight reptiles with huge heads full of dagger teeth, tiny two-fingered forelimbs, and massive legs that looked like they could run faster than Spencer's truck. They sniffed the air, uncertain what they smelled.

Carnivores. Opportunists. Just what Larry needed.

He took a half step into the present and let the odor of Judzyas's dead waft across.

The dinosaurs snorted and cocked their heads, ambled forward, then trotted, then ran.

Larry hadn't realized how large they were. Thirty feet from nose to tail. Tons of flesh. And hungry.

They thundered across the bridge from the past and screamed when they landed on the snow. They clawed at the cold ground, nipped one another in frustration, then hesitated. Eight pairs of yellow eyes tracked a regiment of Spanish Conquistador ghosts on patrol.

The reptiles sprinted, tore the ground with their claws, grabbed the spirits, and shook them, cracking their ghostly spines. Screams and musket fire. A handful of Spaniards fled. The monsters gorged on the rest. Soldiers writhed in agony, squirmed in their jaws, and wriggled down their throats. The beasts stalked into the forest after fresh prey.

That should keep Judzyas busy, and give Larry a chance to think.

The necromancer enslaved ghosts: to fuel his divinations, to call lightning, to spy, and to possess the living. He depended on them. These undead in the forests were only meant to distract Larry. Judzyas would have something larger in reserve.

Gunshot. A bullet whizzed past Larry's head. He spun, held the utter blackness of an *Eclipse* rune in his left hand. Froze. It was Matt.

" 'Bout time ya showed yer hide 'round here." Matt held his Colt in his right hand; his left hand gripped the barrel, shaking and forcing the muzzle so it was pointed slightly away from Larry. He spit. With both hands still on the pistol, still trembling, he holstered it. ''Lower whatcha got in yer hand,'' he said. ''If I'd wanted to drill ya, I woulda.''

Larry dropped his hand—but kept the rune alive. If his dinosaur ghosts could devour spirits, then Matt's pistol could kill. ''Why shoot at all then?''

''That other fella's got my bullet. He told me to find ya, and shoot ya. Gotta follow them orders.'' He tugged at the end of his mustache. ''Ain't my fault I missed.''

Larry let the rune dissolve. ''Where is he?''

''Holed up in that room of broken glass. Got yer old girlfriend, the witch, and a posse of mean ol' ghosts. I'd be headin' fer San Francisco if I were ya.''

Two days ago Judzyas had divined Larry and Raja would be in that atrium. Larry fit the image, bloody and tattered . . . but he didn't intend to surrender.

''Come on, Matt. Let's get my body. Then we're going back.''

Matt adjusted the brim of his Stetson and stared at Larry. ''Yer different,'' he said. ''Yer colors are darker like the other feller's, but still got them yellows and green and red stars in 'em. Ya look ready to whip yer own weight in wildcats.'' He took his Colt Peacemaker and handed it butt end to Larry. ''You'll be needin' a pistol. Take mine.''

Larry reached for it. Stopped. ''No.''

''Take it, ya damn fool. A man needs a gun.''

It would have been easy to take it. Judzyas had used guns, rifles, artillery, dropped bombs, and thrown grenades, but not Larry. The only people he had killed were by the guardhouse with the Glock. That was enough.

There was a growing distance between Larry and Judzyas. Judzyas survived millennia, but had lived only one life. He was frozen in a single perspective. Larry had his own ideas about how to solve this mess.

''Don't tell me yer gonna jaw with that soul-driver? He's tougher than Gila monster hide. You'll end up chawed.''

''No.'' Larry drew fairy runes and spirals in the air. A plane of gray flames materialized, and he drew his Blade of Veracity—mirror wisp of razor. ''I'm going back there to fight, and to win. Then I'll talk.''

They marched toward the hill and the circle of stones where his body lay. The ground was melting. The forest was gone. Reality and the netherealms overlapped.

He blinked and saw gravestones, orderly rows that extended to the horizon, pure alabaster markers camouflaged by the snow. Tiny American flags fluttered on some, plastic flowers in cups set in others. Wooden crosses grew, black stone Celtic markers, cairns of stone, and a sinkhole opened in the earth, full of naked staring bodies.

"Is this Hell?" Matt whispered.

"Not yet."

The stones in Raja's circle were tilted at a precarious angle and fractured. Larry's body was safe in the center.

What had happened to Raja? Had she gone to Judzyas? And if so, then why leave Larry's body? Had she been captured?

He stepped into his flesh; sensation flooded into his limbs; he inhaled and filled his lungs with crisp, cold air. Dragon roars and gunfire crackled near the mansion. Dinosaurs, ghosts, and ghouls. That's where he had to go.

Overhead the stars were unchanged. Orion's belt twinkled. Larry imagined he was underwater, and the stars were motes of light upon the surface. He imagined Orion's belt was the Hunter's Canoe. The Star Maiden appeared in the sky, dazzled him with a smile, and unveiled her labyrinth.

Larry knew the way through the puzzle.

With saber in hand, he stepped into the maze, past an image of the Silver Bullet's kitchen, gleaming copper pots, and cast-iron stove, past the Three of Diamonds Bookstore, closed and full of whispering books, past Lost Silver Canyon washed white with moonlight, and found the atrium.

Larry stood on the threshold in between. At his back was the circle of stones, and a frigid blast of air. Ahead was Raja's mansion—but like the land, it had been overtaken by the swelling netherealms. Colored glass littered the floor, reds and navy blues and golden topaz. Dark basalt replaced terra cotta and adobe walls. Gargantuan pillars held the roof aloft. The pastel, *Woman Drying Her Neck,* was twisted, her arms contorted and smeared, looking more Dali than Degas. The grandfather clock was still.

Overhead the moon eclipsed.

Darkness swelled . . . slithered, and stretched into every corner of the atrium. Judzyas stood in the shadows by the basement stairs. He burned the blackness with ultraviolet flames. He was an outline swathed with power, a blast furnace of sorcery, both fists clenched.

It was the image Judzyas divined two days ago. Raja was behind him, bound in the same tangle of runes Larry had woven.

Judzyas held lines diaphanous as spidersilk, full of refracted life images like those in the Dai Esthai, only pale, warped, somehow not right.

Shadows fluttered in the corners of Larry's vision, demanding his attention. He ignored them, gazed deeper, and perceived hundreds of lines piercing Judzyas's body like an acupuncture chart. From every nerve, a tendril sprang and waved in the unseen currents of death that swirled through the room.

Larry reviewed the enchantment he had learned as Judzyas—a simple ritual to bind spirits. He had cast it a thousand times . . . yet the memory was evasive. He gambled he could predict the necromancer. If he was wrong, this would be a short battle. Larry would be destroyed.

''If it looks like I'm winning,'' he whispered to Matt, ''then follow me in. If not . . .''

Matt nodded.

A step. Larry appeared.

Judzyas spotted him. He opened his hands and released the filaments; they grew, translucent colors and shape—phantoms boiled and flowed toward Larry: skeletal pirates from a sunken galleon brandished knives, leered at Raja, and shrieked their bloodlust; gunslingers strode forward, hands over their holstered pistols, the nooses they had been lynched with trailing behind; Malchom B. Weavelson, seller of poison, stumbled forth with glass-shard teeth, his eyes vacant behind cracked octagonal spectacles; three dozen townsfolk from Serendipity chased him, smelling of hot metal and garlic, and leaking fluids from dissolved entrails; a flurry of wind devils crackled with static and waved their pitchforks; Raja's lawyer bolted for Larry, still smoking from a shotgun blast; a gangrenous fellow slinked forward, dropping fingers and flakes of skin, clumps of hair, and bits of necrotic flesh; a smoker appeared in a cloud, belching toxic gases, and drifting closer, with blue lips, and three lit cigarettes in either hand; a starved man with hollow eyes, and caved-in abdomen, held his hands outstretched; a sea of spirits—afterimages, blurs, and sighs surged, a rush of stares and claws and gnashing teeth; they all came for Larry.

They were close enough for him to smell the dust from their graves, choke on the vapors of their rotting bodies, and see their empty eyes. Larry shouted: "Come spirits all. The world of your birth calls to you."

They slowed, glanced at Judzyas, then to Larry.

Larry cried, "I summon you and make my will into law that you manifest. Come!"

Judzyas pursed his lips and glared at Larry. He understood.

And together they chanted: "I shackle thee cruelest spirits with knots knotting knots: entwine thine eyes, thy mouths, thy tongues, thy throats, and thy venomous bowels. I repeat the magic, and wildly, with frenzied lips, I chant a conjuration to compel."

Half the captured spirits turned to Larry. Their phantom soul threads ran through his body. They were his to command. The others belonged to Judzyas.

The rotting fellow grabbed Raja's attorney, whose skin turned red and peeled off. The attorney took out a pen and stabbed the leper in the eye, wrestled him to the ground, stomped on him, splintered limbs, broke his body into pieces.

Wind devils laughed and stirred the air and poked whomever they could. The smoker blew fumes at them. A dozen coughed, gagged, and fell to the ground; the rest escaped out broken windows.

The starved man clutched at Larry's thigh, and opened his salivating mouth.

Larry impaled him with the Blade of Veracity. Upon the metal was the man's grave. "You are dead," Larry told him. "A long time ago. Rest and hunger no more."

The starved man slid off his saber, curled into a fetal position, and dissolved.

A group of poisoned Serendipity folk found the noose attached to an outlaw and strung him up. He dangled, one hand around the rope, the other hand trying to unholster his gun.

Matt stepped through, aimed, and fired. The rope snapped. "Hate to see a hangin'," he muttered.

The other gunfighter drew and sprayed bullets into the mob.

Across the room, Judzyas held a rune of *Disunion,* jagged lines that circled an invisible point, magic that perpetually fell apart, perpetually spiraled in, and kept the horde of spirits at bay.

The doors to the garden crashed open. Three dinosaurs poked their heads in, sniffed the air, and pushed through. They tore into the knot of ghosts, biting and snapping necks. They feasted on the dead.

One turned and eyed Larry.

He brandished his saber. ''Look,'' he shouted. ''You are coal and oil. Dust and stone. Begone!''

The dinosaur wasn't looking at his blade. It stared at him and charged.

Larry held his sword before him. He smelled steam from the creature's nostrils, tasted its rotten breath.

Matt fired, fanning the hammer of his Colt.

The beast's eyes exploded in blood and tears. It screamed but didn't stop.

Larry thrust the Blade of Veracity up and through its chin. The saber slid through unhindered. He ripped it free from the specter, and split the head. The dinosaur fell on him, knocked him down, smothered him with a ton of flesh, then vanished.

Larry stood.

Across the atrium, Judzyas stood at the same time.

The ghosts were gone, either scattered by the dinosaurs or dispelled or dragged back to hell where they belonged, save two. Matt stood behind Larry, and Dempsey stood behind Judzyas.

Judzyas stared at Matt. ''Shoot him,'' he said.

Matt turned on Larry, and pointed the barrel of his Peacemaker at him. ''I gotta. He's got my soul snapped up tighter than a bear trap.''

Larry paused a heartbeat, then said, ''You used ten rounds at the shoot-out yesterday, once when you missed me in the forest, and two more here. That's thirteen. That's how many bullets were pumped into you. That's all you get. Your Colt is empty.''

Matt eyed the cylinder of his pistol. He spun it, aimed, fired. Nothing.

Larry turned to Judzyas. ''Stalemate.'' Larry was exhausted. Another battle, and the necromancer would win. ''Let's talk.''

Dempsey drew charge from the wall sockets. Electric arcs jumped and haloed about him. He reached forward.

''Listen to him,'' Raja said, and struggled in the mesh of magic that held her. She had her head and one hand free. ''He's not the prophet. He doesn't want to change the world.''

Judzyas held out his arm and stopped Dempsey. ''Let us hear what you would say, prophet.'' He wiped blood from his forehead.

Maybe Judzyas needed to rest as well. Maybe he was listening to him so he could gather his strength for a final attack. Larry had to make his point quickly. "You have it wrong," he said. "I'm not the man in your divination."

"You are," Judzyas declared. "Every aspect points to you."

"There's another prophet." He held his Blade of Veracity so the flat faced Judzyas. "Look."

Within the mirrored metal, a man appeared.

Judzyas closed one eye, squinted. "Yes. This is my divination. But clearer."

"There's a reason for that too. Watch and you'll understand."

Upon the reflective metal the man kissed a woman farewell; he left her crying. Beyond was the ocean, where the surf pounded cliffs topped by white stucco houses. There were olive trees and herds of sheep, and upon the water the sun rose, scattering the summer stars with its brilliance.

"The sun is rising," Larry said. "It's not me. In Oakland the sun sets on the water. It's Crete. The woman is Raja."

Judzyas glanced back at Raja—who had both her arms free.

"It is," she whispered. "Remember?"

He looked back to the blade. "But the other signs . . . I have seen your van with spots of rust, then primered gray, your metaphorical horse."

Father Woberty's Appaloosa, Dorinda, materialized upon the sword, then the city limits sign for Dry Water appeared. "He will come to Dry Water," Larry said, "which you did."

"Coincidence."

In the divination, silver mist obscured the man's face. "You gaze at yourself. That is why the portent was never clear. Personal fortunes are the hardest to read, ever-shifting and nebulous."

The mist dissolved from the prophet's face, the magic faded, and Judzyas found himself staring into the flat of the blade—at a face he had not seen in millennia—Judzyas the potter. "Impossible," he whispered.

Larry knew Judzyas. He had for more than two thousand years tracked the prophets and stopped them. Now he was the object of his own guilt and vengeance. What would he do? Kill himself? Then who would stop the next prophet? He was trapped.

Larry lowered his saber.

"It is a trick," Judzyas hissed and brought up his hands. The *Disunion* rune flared orange and spun faster.

"No trick. You know the truth when you hear it; that is why you were Socrates's favorite student. You feel the rightness of this. *You* are the prophet.''

''No! Prophets bring change. Change brings ruin. That is not my destiny.''

''You want to see change?'' Larry held the Blade of Veracity aloft. ''See then the world without you!''

Larry didn't know if this was possible. The divinations he had performed were simple, events he had already seen, and familiar people and places. Even Judzyas's divinations had never been so ambitious.

How was he to see the world undone by two millennia of changes? If all the prophets and their ideas and technologies and philosophies had lived?

The Dai Esthai split into a thousand million branches in the future, each a path of possibility. What happened to the branches not taken? He saw the river in his blade, where the first change occurred, the death of Arion. A split, and the path not taken was dry and cracked, a wash of gravel. ''What if . . .'' Larry commanded, and he flooded the arroyo in his imagination, let it course as rivulets of probabilities.

Larry strained to recall Christ and Nostradamus, Galileo and Ovid, General MacArthur and Lincoln. He diverted this river of invention, irrigated the dry streambeds of what could have been, soaked the parched earth of what was never to be—and flowed to the present.

A ghost river ran parallel to the Dai Esthai. The world that Judzyas had murdered.

The Blade of Veracity changed. Gold filigree scrolled across the silver, and jewels winked open upon the metal—white-hot diamonds and languid emeralds, scintillating sapphires as large as his thumb. Gleaming in every facet was another world: primeval forests covered the land, herds of buffalo made a black carpet upon the plains, and passenger pigeons filled the skies; the oceans glowed with schools of bioluminescent krill chased by whales; people appeared and vanished into thin air, and children played hide-and-seek in the dimensions; there were crystal cathedrals, ivory towers in the clouds, and a city upon the moon.

''Man needs change,'' Larry said. ''Man adapts to technology and new philosophies. We need it to thrive. By stopping change, you brought stagnation and suffering to the world. *You* were the first prophet. Maybe the only one.''

Judzyas dropped his hands. The rune shattered, and its jagged lines wriggled on the floor. ''I have spent centuries learning the signs of the prophets,'' he whispered. ''How could I have missed myself? How could I be so blind?''

''There is a solution,'' Larry said. He reached into his back pocket for the silver flask.

He hesitated. He knew what had to be done. It meant giving up Paloma. ''Here.''

Raja slipped free of the runes. She took a step toward Judzyas, opened her mouth as if to speak, then bit her lip, and stayed where she was.

Judzyas reached for the flask. ''Poison? Do you suggest I end my life?''

''Remember the divination: the prophet seeks a water that cannot be drunk. This is it.''

Judzyas opened the flask and looked inside. He sloshed it. ''It has no weight.''

''It is a solvent that seeps through cracks in reality and time.''

Judzyas raised an eyebrow.

Larry continued, ''You have forgotten what it is like to struggle and fail, to be human. You have forgotten that every step mankind takes forward is paid for with blood and pain. That every life is precious.''

''You were me,'' Judzyas whispered. ''My conscience. The feeling of being watched.''

''I've always been with you.''

''Drinking this will not change that I am the prophet.''

''Nothing can. But it will give you the wisdom and insight to accept it. And if not, then you will be no worse off than you are now.''

Judzyas glanced back at Raja. She was gone. He turned to Larry and gazed inside him. Larry let him; he let him see his struggles to cope with his vision, his leaving Linda, his arrival in Dry Water, his love and grief for Paloma, his friendships with Niyol, Spencer, and Matt. He let him see into his soul.

''It is the truth,'' Judzyas whispered. He pondered this a moment, then, ''I shall not come for you again, Mister Ngitis. And as for Raja, when you see her next, tell her I am sorry. Tell her I shall meet her on Crete. Someday.''

Judzyas tilted the silver flask. He drank the last of the water, drank Larry's only route to Paloma, drank, and crumpled to the floor.

Dempsey knelt by his master. He looked to the stars and, with a crack of thunder, vanished.

Larry examined the body Judzyas had worn and found Matt's bullet in his mouth. There was no heartbeat, only an empty husk. Had he drowned in the Dai Esthai? Or become looped as Niyol had? Or found peace? Would Larry ever know?

"Raja?" he called.

Silence. The grandfather clock began to tick. Dawn turned the edge of the sky purple.

"What now, Chinaman?" Matt asked.

"Now? It's over. We find Linda and Spencer. We go home."

SECTION FOUR

spring

Epilogue

JUDZYAS WALKED ALONG A MILE-WIDE RIVER. HE REMOVED HIS BOOTS AND let mud ooze through his toes. The water that was a metaphor for time lapped at his feet. He was unaccustomed to magic so free of death. It was refreshing.

The Dai Esthai reflected his first face, Judzyas the potter, student of Socrates. He toyed with the notion of returning to that time. So much could be set right. Changed? Was that not what prophets did? Perhaps to live another's life would be sufficient . . . perhaps he was the only thing that needed to be changed.

Within the waters men sailed clippers on Chesapeake Bay, climbed Mount Everest, sat in dark cubicles and stared at glowing computer screens, walked through aspen forests, were born, and died. There was much to learn.

He inhaled deeply, exhaled explosively. He felt hope. Something he had forgotten.

But where to go? And when?

He wandered upstream, careful not to retrace his steps and be snared in a tangle of temporal logic.

Larry was there, or rather the shadow he had cast in time; he watched Judzyas's life, then retraced it to the beginning. Raja was there too. She watched another Larry watch her, and slid into the fifteenth century. Another echo of Larry followed her, and undid what she had done.

Others had been here, marked in time, leaving footprints in history. An aboriginal shaman slipped into Harry S. Truman; Dolinski walked upon the water, became a Buddhist monk and Bluebeard the pirate; a girl limped along with a splinted leg, lived as Charlemagne and Odysseus and Joan of Arc.

There was another child, but he did not concern himself with the water. He sat on his haunches, his full attention on the riverbank mud.

The boy looked up at Judzyas. He brushed black hair from his face, then returned his gaze to the earth. "Don't get too close," he said. "You'll mess it up, and I'm almost done."

It was the shaman who had protected Larry. His colors were different, smaller, yet flickering with the vibrancy of youth. This was a true boy, not the image the other shaman had borrowed. Judzyas squinted and saw shadows of the boy: walking the bank of the river, swimming across, turning around, crawling out exhausted—stepping into his own footprints. Caught in a circle of time.

Four heaps of sand were arranged before him: white, blue, yellow, and black. A circle of sand was neatly traced, outlined with white, and filled with figures of snakes and spirals, jagged lines and stick-figure icons.

The boy took a pinch of the dark sand and sprinkled it, filled the body of a dancing man. "That's you," he said to Judzyas. "My dad said all this would happen. He said the Big Spirits would come and fight."

Dad? Was this child the shaman's son? The man whose spirit he had consigned to oblivion? Judzyas shifted uneasily, crouched closer, and said, "If I am the black man, then who is this?" He pointed to the figure on a white square. River mud had soaked through in patches, gray spots upon the white.

"That's Larry and his van. He's been here. He's not very smart."

Judzyas admired the sand painting. Tiny crows rode a thermal current rising off the desert floor. There were clouds, darker thunderheads, and filigreed lightning strikes. In the center clustered miniature buildings, a road map of Dry Water, dark Mount Taylor, silver canyons, a coyote that spoke to the Moon, hummingbirds and Aurora Borealis, a rising sun, and a field of stars.

The boy touched a blue figure, a woman with a triangle head. She sat in a forest, by a pool of water, one hand touching the earth, the other holding a gust of wind. ''That's the witch. She's that color 'cause she's from where it's so cold even the ice turns blue. At least, that's what my dad told me.''

''The last figure,'' Judzyas asked. ''The yellow one. Who is that?''

''I don't know. I think it's me. I hope it is.''

''Why?''

The boy looked at Judzyas. ''If it's me, then I think it means I'll get to go home and see my dad again.''

Judzyas pretended to scrutinize the painting. The boy was without guidance. Trapped. For how long? Even the spirits Judzyas had seen, insane and wandering the netherealms, eventually dissolved into the void. ''When Larry came, whose life did he live?''

The boy bit his upper lip, concentrating, filling in the last bit of the black pictograph. ''He was Anne Marie. I know where she is. If I show you, will you help me out? You look like a good swimmer.''

''This river is more than water,'' Judzyas said. ''It will require more than swimming to cross.''

Niyol knelt closer to his picture. He whispered to it—Navajo words with the cadence of a prayer or an incantation. He then took an eagle feather from his back pocket and swept the grains aside.

''Why do you destroy your work?'' Judzyas asked.

''Magic's done. Can't leave it around for anybody to mess with.''

The boy who was more than a child. He reminded Judzyas of Arion. He knew magic. And he knew how to use it responsibly.

''Show me Anne Marie,'' Judzyas said, and held out his hand.

Niyol hesitated, then took it. ''Come on.'' He pulled Judzyas upstream. ''You'll like her. She's a good place to start.''

Five white oaks surrounded Raja. The winter frosts were gone; fresh greenery made a web over her head. The scent of humus filled the air. Through layers of dead leaves new ferns pushed up, uncurled, and glistened with dew.

She had instructed her staff to tell any who inquired that she was traveling abroad. It was both a lie and the truth. A lie for she sat by her sacred pool. The truth because she would soon not be in their world.

Judzyas had not returned. It was possible that he had perished upon the Dai Esthai . . . though unlikely. He could be anywhere, anyone. The thought of him close made her both pleased and apprehensive.

Her fingers rippled the surface. It had taken a week to coax the earth to open wider, to purge Judzyas's poison from the water. It overflowed her sacred pool and made the trickle that meandered into her meadow a steady stream.

Larry had not found her. He had stumbled upon Dolinski's world, however. He might stumble upon her as well in the future. There was still the matter of Paloma to be resolved. She was certain he had not forgiven her that incident.

Perhaps an intermediary could be employed? Melissa from the bookstore? Larry could be either offended by her presence, or charmed. Raja would think carefully upon the matter. She had time.

Within the pool she mixed the last of her dry water. Rather than alter history, she would change the present. An act neither Larry nor Judzyas could undo. The waters mingled properties—part magic and part fluid—spilled forth, and changed the land.

It became a piece of the Dai Esthai diverted.

Fish swam in the pool, flashes of mirror blue, zebra stripes and leopard spots underwater. They bolted to the surface, splashed, then dove to the bottom.

Raja left her circle of white oaks, brushed aside the curtain of ferns, and strolled along the edge of her stream. The water was silver, ice-cold, aglow with magic. The meadow on her right was a spectrum of flowers, arrived early to please her: lupine and sunflower, basil and mandrake, foxglove and peppermint. The thick grasses rippled in the breeze and lapped the edges of the stream.

Three steppingstones bridged the water, smooth black granite with veins of quartz and gold. She crossed.

The meadow on this side had rings of toadstools, orchids, tiny flowers that chimed like bells in the wind, and fields of saffron.

Twin moons sailed overhead, pale in the early-morning light. Lilac clouds gathered at the horizon. Fairies fluttered by on butterfly wings of gold swirls and emerald spots, hovered a moment, bowed, and said in chorus, ''Good morrow, Mistress.'' A flash of color and they vanished.

The forest on this side was oak and redwood, yew and feather trees so tall clouds clung to their tops. Past the woods stood distant mountains, slate blue capped brilliant white, and a city of glass glittering atop the highest peak. They were her Himalayas. This was her world.

With every trip she would bring part of the old earth into this new one, and when she returned, a piece of this realm would mingle with the old . . . mixing as the dry water and the spring water had. She would change the world bit by bit, trade the mundane and the fantastic. The imagined and real.

She would wait a decade or two, a century perhaps, be forgotten, and spread her roots.

Raja soaked her feet in the water, lay upon a carpet of velvet moss, and drank in the warm spring sun.

Larry chopped. The weight of his arms and the ax did the work, splitting the wood with a single stroke. It was green pine, and he didn't need it. There was a cord piled alongside the cabin, but the rhythmic motion kept his mind clear.

The sky was turquoise. No clouds near Ferrocarril Mountain. It would drop below freezing tonight up here. Any thinking he'd do would be in front of a fire. He loaded up his arms with wood, stacked it, then went inside.

Larry had mixed feelings about this cabin. He had scrubbed Judzyas's runes from the hardwood floor, and expunged every trace of Raja from the place. He hoped Paloma might linger as well, but no matter how hard he concentrated, neither her ghost, nor any remnant of their breakfasts together materialized to haunt him.

The letter from Linda was still on the kitchen counter. She still didn't remember much, only that Raja had called her, and that she had come to New Mexico because Larry needed a familiar face. She stayed for Spencer's funeral, and tried to comfort Larry. She didn't know how.

They parted not enemies, but not quite friends.

Spencer visited him after he had died. He showed Larry all the places he thought his lost Spanish silver might be. Said someone had to find it, and it might as well be him.

They went back to the shaman's cavern. There was no dry water left. Larry would check in a few months to see if more oozed through the cracks in reality.

Spencer had drunk himself to death. The Lobos sin Orejas found him in the hideout, bullet in his shoulder, two empty liter bottles of Absolut vodka, and tears dried in the creases of his face. He must have seen Larry get shot and dragged to Raja's mansion. When Larry tried to talk about it, Spencer changed the subject.

Larry was too much Anne Marie not to see the fatherly love in his eyes.

He'd miss the old man.

He poured himself a cup of coffee and removed Killer of Crickets from the pile of manuscript pages that had been neatly stacked when he went outside. He squared the pages—saw laser flashes and felt the thunder of ion engines within, the crackle of static, and the cheers of a hero's welcome—then tucked them in a box for safekeeping.

The cat cocked his ears and narrowed his eyes at the paper as if there were creatures within to pounce upon and rend.

Last night Larry had printed the final copy of his Captain Kelvin space opera. It wasn't the same novel he started to write a year ago, nor was it like the previous three. It had a theme about life and death and morality. His characters had changed, become less heroes and more human. It probably wasn't what the marketing department at Perspective Publishing wanted, but it satisfied him.

Kindling, newsprint, Linda's letter, and a split log went into the fireplace, and became a blaze.

Larry lay on the couch, arranged a pot of coffee and a box of Oreos, then spread an afghan over his feet. He perused a stack of out-of-print Dolinski novels recently purchased from the Three of Diamonds Bookstore. He intended to read all night.

Outside a flock of crows rode the thermals over Lost Silver Canyon, hundreds of specks that spiraled and soared. Raja's crows.

But there was no trace of Raja, not since the winter solstice. He had gone to her estate and been told she was out of the country. He did some snooping around. Her garden had magic: flowers already in bloom, fruit on the trees, and sprites and water nymphs and dryads chased each other. She had to be there . . . somewhere.

She was dangerous. Was she waiting until the summer solstice? He had no foreboding images. He saw no shadows of her in the future.

Killer of Crickets jumped onto the couch, circled twice, and settled on Larry's feet.

Larry picked up *To Sail an Amethyst Sea.* He had read it twice yesterday, and planned to read it twice more tonight. Things changed in the novel: the characters said different lines; they explored new lands; and they suffered unique perils every time. The woman-pirate on the cover looked more like Paloma.

Matt appeared. ''Mind if I read over yer shoulder? That Dolinski feller knows how to spin a good yarn.''

"Try not to move your lips while you're reading this time. It's distracting."

"That varmint gotta stay? It belongs outside."

Killer glared at him then licked a paw.

Larry scratched behind the cat's ear, made him purr and roll on his back, stretching.

All Larry had to do to be with Paloma was read. Niyol had taught him that magic was subjective. If he concentrated hard enough, illusion became fact. Fantasy was real.

"You ready?" he asked Matt.

"Ready fer anything, pardner."

Larry opened the novel to page one, and they began a new adventure.